THE SORCERER

METAMORPHOSIS

Forge Books by Jack Whyte

THE CAMULOD CHRONICLES

The Skystone
The Singing Sword
The Eagles' Brood
The Saxon Shore
The Fort at River's Bend
The Sorcerer: Metamorphosis

THE SORCERER

METAMORPHOSIS

THE CAMULOD CHRONICLES

JACK WHYTE

A TOM DOHERTY ASSOCIATES BOOK

NEW YORK

THE SORCERER: METAMORPHOSIS

This book is printed on acid-free paper.

A Forge Book
Published by Tom Doherty Associates, Inc.
175 Fifth Avenue
New York, NY 10010

Forge® is a registered trademark of Tom Doherty Associates, Inc.

Library of Congress Cataloging-in-Publication Data

Whyte, Jack.
    The sorcerer : metamorphosis / Jack Whyte. — 1st ed.
        p.   cm. — (The Camulod chronicles ; [6])
    "A Tom Doherty Associates book."
    Originally published in 2 v.: Toronto ; New York : Viking,
1997. bk. 1: The fort at River's Bend; bk. 2: Metamorphosis.
    ISBN 0-312-86598-8 (alk. paper)
    1. Merlin (Legendary character) Fiction. 2. Britons—Kings and
rulers Fiction. 3. Arthurian romances Adaptations. 4. Arthur, King
Fiction. 5. Wizards Fiction. I. Title. II. Title: Metamorphosis.
III. Series: Whyte, Jack. Camulod chronicles ; 6.
PR9199.3.W4589S67   1999
813'.54—dc21   99-24569
                                                        CIP

First Edition: June 1999

Printed in the United States of America

0   9   8   7   6   5   4   3   2   1

To my wife, Beverley

and to my grandson, David Michael Johns, who finally got old
enough to read his Grandpa's books

north

ORCENAY
(ORKNEY ISLANDS)

CALEDONIA

KING ATHOL'S NEW TERRITORIES

Hadrian's Wall

VORTIGERN'S NORTHUMBRIA

HIBERNIA (EIRE)

1 2 3 5
4
6
7
8

CAMBRIA
22
20 19 21
18 17 16 12
15 13
14
11
10

Merlyn's Britain

SAXON TERRITORIES

MAP LEGEND

1. Glannaventa (Ravenglass)
2. Mediobogdum (The Fort)
3. Galava (Ambleside)
4. Manx (Isle of Man)
5. Brocavum (Brougham)
6. Mamucium (Manchester)
7. Deva (Chester)
8. Lindum (Lincoln)
9. Londinium (London)
10. Verulamium (St. Albans)
11. Corinium (Cirencester)
12. Glevum (Gloucester)
13. Aquae Sulis (Bath)
14. Lindinis (Ilchester)
15. Camulod (Camelot)
16. Venta Silurum (Caerwent)
17. Isca Silurum (Caerleon)
18. (Cardiff)
19. Nidum (Neath)
20. Moridunum (Carmarthen)
21. Cicutio (Y Gaer)
22. (Castel Collen)

Key: Roman place names
(English/Welsh in brackets)

THE LEGEND OF THE SKYSTONE

Out of the night sky there will fall a stone
That hides a maiden born of murky deeps,
A maid whose fire-fed, female mysteries
Shall give life to a lambent, gleaming blade,
A blazing, shining sword whose potency
Breeds warriors. More than that,
This weapon will contain a woman's wiles
And draw dire deeds of men: shall name an age;
Shall crown a king, called of a mountain clan
Who dream of being drawn from dragon's seed;
Fell, forceful men, heroic, proud and strong,
With greatness in their souls.
This king, this monarch, mighty beyond ken,
Fashioned of glory, singing a song of swords,
Misting with magic madness mortal men,
Shall sire a legend, yet leave none to lead
His host to triumph after he be lost.
But death shall ne'er demean his destiny who,
Dying not, shall ever live and wait to be
        recalled.

Threats against the life of the young Arthur Pendragon have forced Caius Merlyn Britannicus to take the boy away from Camulod. With a small group of followers he travels to the port town of Ravenglass, in far north-western Britain, looking for sanctuary.

In exchange for the promise of military support, King Derek of Raven-glass agrees to let Merlyn and his followers make their new home in a long-abandoned Roman fort high on a mountain plateau, an isolated place known as Mediobogdum, meaning "in the bend of the river." In order to deflect attention, Merlyn then surrenders his identity as the party's leader and, to the outside world, he and Arthur become known as the farmer "Master Cay" and his young ward. With the help of his closest friends and companions, Merlyn teaches Arthur about justice, honour, his Christian faith and the responsibilities of leadership.

Arthur begins to show the wisdom, common sense and regard for justice that will one day make him a legendary king, and Merlyn sees the day fast approaching when the boy will need to wield the king's sword, Excalibur. Arthur is taught the techniques that will enable him to fight with the new sword, while the smiths in Camulod, in utmost secrecy, fashion two new practice swords from the last of the skystone metal, weapons that will be identical to Excalibur in everything but its glorious appearance.

Merlyn enjoys many peaceful years in Mediobogdum, luxuriating in the new love he has found with Tressa and watching Arthur, along with his constant companions Gwin, Ghilleadh and Bedwyr, grow towards manhood. Connor Mac Athol, whose fleet has been transporting King Athol's Scots to their new lands in Alba, comes often to Ravenglass and keeps him up to date on affairs in Eire, while Merlyn's brother Ambrose visits when he can bringing cheering news of life back in the growing community of Camulod. The only matter that troubles Merlyn is the mark on his chest that he fears might be leprosy, until the physician Lucanus consults his medical author-ities and declares it benign, putting Merlyn's mind at rest.

But beyond their peaceful isolation, violent forces are rising to threaten the tenuous peace of Camulod. Ambrose sends word one day of trouble in Northumbria, the land of King Vortigern. Vortigern's Danish ally Hengist is dead, and the fragile peace that existed there is now threatened by the advances of Hengist's hot-headed son Horsa and his landless, discontented warriors. More urgently, the powerful forces of Merlyn's old enemy Peter Ironhair are gathering strength in Cornwall, while in Cambria, Dergyll ap Griffyd, who rose to lead the Pendragon people after the death of Uther, has been killed by Ironhair's ally, the monstrous Carthac, who has a claim to the Cambrian kingship. Merlyn further learns that a former comrade, Owain *of the Caves, might have been acting as a spy for Ironhair in Camulod. Does Ironhair know where Arthur is hiding, and will he seek to have the boy killed, seeing Arthur's claim to Cambria as a formidable threat to his ambitions?*

Fearing for Arthur's safety, and concerned that the future king's education can go no further in their remote home in Mediobogdum, Merlyn makes the decision to return with his party to Camulod in the spring and prepare to meet Ironhair in battle.

PART ONE
CAMULOD

I

THERE IS NO more important day in a man's life than the day he formally takes up a sword for the first time. At that fateful and long-anticipated moment when a youth extends his hand for the first time, witnessed formally by both his elders and his peers, to grip the hilt of the sword that will be his own, his life and his world are changed forever. In the eyes of men, he has become a man, and his boyhood is irrevocably and publicly discarded for all time, much like the shed skin of a serpent. Far more important and traumatic than his first knowledge of a woman, the commitment of taking up the sword is the last and greatest rite of the passage across the gulf between boyhood and manhood.

Arthur Pendragon's transition, and the ritual entailed in it, was a source, for me at least, of joy, wonder, great satisfaction and an immense, deep-glowing pride. It has been extremely difficult to condense into mere words. A score of times I have set out to write of it and ended up with inkstained fingers, a blotted, much-scratched sheet of papyrus and a quill destroyed because its feathered end is chewed, matted and soggy with my own sucking. Only recently, after many attempts, have I been able to assemble a coherent account of the occasion, and of the events leading up to it, from countless scraps and annotations. Even so, I fear it resembles less a chronology than an anthology of incidents and impressions. Each of those incidents, however, had a direct bearing upon the way in which Arthur came to that threshold of manhood.

Did ever a more alienating gulf exist than that which stretches between boy and man? Few things can be more difficult or vexing than the task a grown man will face in the attempt to recall how it felt, or what it meant, to be a boy. The very coin of life in which the two must deal is different. Boys in their prime, between the ages of eight years and twelve, are yet unburdened by sexuality; they are consumed by other, no less insistent forms of curiosity, and are intent upon learning and discovering everything there is to know about being male and potent, powerful and victorious. Men, on the other hand, may still be curious in their prime, but all their curiosity is tainted by their sexuality: for the ruck of men, all that they do is dominated by the urge for gratification of their sexual needs.

Because of my unique relationship with Arthur Pendragon throughout his life, I was able to observe him closely as he made the transition from one state to the other, but analyse it as I will, I can recall no catalytic moment that marked the transition from boyhood to manhood in the youth whom I had come to regard as my own son. The outward, public moment is a matter of history, but I cannot tell, to this day, when the boy became the man within himself. I know only that I was, and I remain, grateful that all I had loved most in the boy remained present and vibrant in the man. His adult sexuality, all-consuming though it frequently appeared to be, never quite broke free of the restraints imposed by his gentle nature and his fierce, boyhood sense of justice and the fitness of things.

In the years that elapsed between the destruction of the enemy Erse fleet at Ravenglass in the great storm and the day when Arthur Pendragon took up his sword, many of the goals I set out for myself were accomplished, and many of my schemes were set in motion; conversely, many planned events did not transpire. I never got the chance to leave Mediobogdum and travel with Arthur as I intended to. Fear for his safety, and a threat to the safety of our Colony on two fronts, in Cambria and in Vortigern's lands to the north-east, eventually dictated our return to Camulod that spring. And so our final winter in Mediobogdum came and passed with a swiftness I would not have believed possible.

Connor arrived in February, a full month and more sooner than any of us could have thought to look for him. Though an unseasonably early snow had spoiled much of our harvest and threatened a harsh winter, the ensuing season, in fact, had been so mild as to have been no winter at all. In Mediobogdum, the dark, intervening months between the snowfall and the first promise of spring brought almost incessant rain and heavy cloud cover that seldom broke. Only the high peaks of the Fells above our heads showed their normal whiteness. The fierce winter storms that normally ravaged the coastal waters did not occur that year. All of Britain, it seemed, enjoyed the unprecedented warmth and calm.

Connor, never one to linger safe at home when there were things he might be doing, had taken full advantage of the mild weather, keeping much of his fleet afloat year-round for the first time in the memory of his people. Normally, his vessels would have been beached all winter long, for the annual cleaning of their hulls, but, defying all the gods of sea and storm, Connor had kept them in the water, plying up and down the hundreds of miles of coastline of his father's new northern holdings and dispatching galleys individually, in rotation, to have their hulls cleaned and stripped whenever he or his captains came upon a suitable expanse of beach.

He arrived in Ravenglass without warning, and then appeared at our gates the following day, accompanied by a smiling Derek and riding in his flamboyant personal chariot at the head of a cavalcade. And of course, as it always did, his advent brought joyful chaos for the length of time it took everyone to grow used to his mercurial presence and the excitement caused by the appearance and behaviour of his colourful companions.

He came, as usual, burdened with gifts—for me, a clasp knife, made of bronze and iron, its handle clad in plates of polished ram's horn mounted in silver. He tossed it to me as soon as I arrived to welcome him, almost running in my haste to greet him before anyone else could. He had not yet climbed down from his chariot and he paused half-way, with his false leg suspended before him, before lobbing his gift to me. For an instant, before he began to move, I saw an unknown, yet strangely familiar face beyond his shoulder. I had only a momentary glimpse of it, however, before I had to concentrate on catching the magnificent knife, and for the next few moments I was caught up in admiring it, depressing the bronze dorsal spine with my thumb to release the iron blade from its clasp, then flicking my wrist, allowing the blade to spring open. Connor came striding over immediately in his swinging, wooden-legged gait and paused in front of me while I examined it, then stepped forward with a great grin to throw his arms about me when I looked up to thank him. As I embraced him, I looked again for the face I had seen behind him, and saw the stranger being embraced by Donuil. The family resemblance was unmistakable.

"Welcome, old friend," I said into Connor's ear, hugging him hard. "I see you've brought another brother with you this time. Which one is this?"

"That's Brander." He released me and turned to where Donuil and Brander were talking together, looking each other over in the way people do when they meet after having been apart for many years. "Brander! Come you here and meet the man you should have met long years ere now."

Brander and Donuil approached us, their heads close together as Donuil finished saying something to his eldest brother. Brander laughed, and then looked directly into my eyes as he stretched out his hands to me.

"Merlyn Britannicus, finally. I feel as though we have been friends for years."

I clasped hands with him, liking the man immediately. "Brander Mac Athol, Admiral of the Northern Seas. You are welcome here in Mediobogdum, as you will be in Camulod should you ever come that way. Your brothers, and indeed your father, when I met him, have had nothing but good to say of you, and your deeds on behalf of your people ensure you of a place of honour in our homes."

Brander inclined his head and smiled. "They were right, my brethren. They told me you had a golden tongue and more charm than you need to hide the iron in you. I thank you for your courtesy." He paused, his head tilted slightly to one side. "You look . . . perplexed. Is something wrong?"

"No, not at all! Forgive me, it is more curiosity than concern you saw." I glanced from him to Connor, and then back to Brander, shrugging my shoulders. "I simply never thought to see both of King Athol's admirals together in one place without their fleets. Who have you left in charge, up in the north?"

Both men laughed together, but for a fleeting moment I thought I detected a hint, the most fleeting suggestion, of something unspoken, some minor tension, passing between them.

"Oh, the fleet is in good hands," Brander answered me. "I've always thought the best thing that the Romans left for men like me and my brother, here, was a single word: *delegation*. Authority passed downward from the commander, is that not what it means?"

"Aye, it is, from the Legate." I had to fight to suppress the smile tugging at my lips. "I'll admit to you, though, Admiral, I have not heard the word itself in many years, and never thought to hear it used by an Erseman."

"I'm not an Erseman, Merlyn Britannicus, I'm a Gael." He pronounced it "Gaul" as in the name of the country across the Southern Sea, but there was no rebuke in his words. "All of us came from Gaul once, long ago. Didn't you know that? Julius Caesar did! So we have taken once again to calling ourselves by the ancient name, in order to distinguish ourselves and our blood lines from the likes of the Sons of Condran and the Children of Gar, who are barely human, and who remain, you will note, in Eire while we seek sustenance in a new land. So we will be Gaels, henceforth."

"Why not Scots?"

He gazed at me with narrowed eyes, apparently considering my words, then nodded. "It's a Roman name, but it sits well on the tongue." I waited, but it was plain he had finished.

"So," I looked again from the one seaman to the other. "What is it that brings you here?"

"Lust," said Connor, laughing explosively, so that heads turned our way. "Brander has finally fallen to the common fate of men. He has married."

"It's true," Brander admitted. "I have never had a wife till now. Never had time to see to it. But now the wars have slacked a bit. The Sons of Condran and the others from Eire have not dared to show their faces in our north these past three years, and will not do so again, I judge. So I have had time to spend ashore, and there I met—" He broke off, turning to look about him, and his brother cut in.

"The fair Salina! Merlyn, I watched the dissolution of this man, this dauntless warrior, from the moment he first set eyes on the woman who is now his wife."

"Salina? That is a Roman name. Is she—?"

"No, she's a Pict, from the mainland of your Caledonia," Connor answered.

"In truth, she's not." Brander had been gazing around, clearly looking for his new wife, but he now turned back to me. "She is of the Painted People, as they call them, but not from the mainland. She comes from the farthest islands to the north, beyond the mainland, a place called Orcenay. Ah, there she is, among the other women. I'll bring her over."

When he returned, he was accompanied by two women, the younger tall and radiantly beautiful even from afar, and the other older, richly dressed, walking slightly behind them, head downcast as she looked at something she held in her hands.

"She's glorious," Donuil breathed. "And so young."

Connor snorted. "Young? That's her niece, Morag. Think you your brother's an old goat? Salina walks behind her."

As they drew closer to us, the woman Salina raised her head and quickened her step to walk beside her husband, and I watched the way Brander took her hand and brought her forward, slightly ahead of him, to present her to us. Perhaps because of the youthfulness of her companion, some part of me was surprised that this new wife should be so mature, "old" being a word that no man with blood in his veins would ever have thought of applying to a woman such as her. She was a woman in her prime, beautiful, with high cheekbones and a full, sensuous mouth beneath deep-set eyes of blue so bright that even the whites surrounding them looked blue. She wore a hood of some kind, covering her hair, and she moved with great self-assurance and dignity. I watched her closely and with intense curiosity as she greeted her good-brother Donuil, taking his hands in both of hers and smiling radiantly into his eyes. It was clear she had heard much about Donuil, and equally clear, from the flush that suffused his cheeks, that Donuil was abashed by the unexpected warmth of her greeting, so that he sounded flustered making excuses for the absence of his wife, who had ridden off into the hills just after dawn to commune with her own gods on the anniversary of her birth.

Then the younger woman, Morag, moved forward and was presented to Donuil, and I lost awareness of her aunt. I felt Salina's eyes fasten on me, but I was too smitten by the beauty of her niece to look back at her. I was amazed at how Morag had changed in the two score paces she had taken since I saw her first. In that first glimpse, she had appeared a glorious young woman of eighteen years; now she was a beautiful child, tall and slim and delightfully formed with high, proud breasts. But breasts and face were startlingly at variance, for while the former denoted a woman grown, the latter shone with the utter innocence of youth. It was a truly lovely face, with wide, grey eyes and a laughing mouth set between silken, dimpled cheeks. I gauged her age now, on seeing her this close, as being less than Arthur's; newly thirteen, I thought.

And then it was my turn to meet Salina, but as I turned to greet her I saw Tress approaching, tucking her hair hurriedly into place and looking flustered. Her first thought on hearing we had guests had been that our guest quarters were all unprepared, and she had rushed off to rectify that. I smiled towards Salina, holding up one hand in a mute plea for her indulgence while I turned very slightly away, extending my other hand to take Tress's as she arrived.

"Lady," I said then, returning my full attention to my new guests and bowing slightly from the waist before looking fully into Salina's eyes for the first time. "You and yours are welcome here in Mediobogdum. Our home is yours, and everything we possess, crude though it is, is yours to command. Your arrival fills me with pleasure, the more intense for its gladdening suddenness. I have heard many wondrous things about your husband, but none of them mentioned his eye for beauty." I looked from her to Brander. "I wish you well in your new marriage and will pray for many years of happiness ahead for both of you." I urged Tress forward, holding her tense fingers tightly in my own. "May I present my own lady, my Tress? We are to be wed soon, too." I smiled now at Tress, who was wide-eyed with trepidation. "Tress, you've heard much about the celebrated Brander, Admiral of the Northern Seas and brother to Donuil and Connor. This is he, and his new wife, the Lady Salina."

As Tress exchanged greetings with the newcomers, I glanced across at young Morag, with the intention of including her in my welcome, but she was standing, wide-eyed and oblivious, staring at something behind me. Curious, I turned my head and saw Arthur, gazing back at her transfixed.

I might have said something to Arthur at that moment, had I the time, although I doubt if anything could have influenced the outcome of what had already happened there. I know I thought of introducing him to young Morag, but even as I raised my arm to sign to him, I saw the thunderstruck expression in his eyes and knew I might as well be miles away. At precisely the same instant, I saw swift movement from the corner of my eye as Connor surged forward to sweep Tressa off her feet in a great hug, and then the civilized pause we had enjoyed gave way to a swirl of movement and the noisy exchange of greetings among friends.

Connor had more gifts to present, including a supple and intricately worked, fleece-lined leather coat of ring-mail for Arthur and an array of weapons, equipment and clothing for the other boys. Tress was dumbfounded by the gift he gave to her, and it was plain to me he could not possibly have pleased her better. It was a carved, wooden chest of ancient, blackened oak, filled to the lid with hundreds of brightly coloured balls of yarn and thread—yellows and reds and blues and greens and blacks and white and greys—all dyed, Connor maintained, in the mountainous northern mainland close by the islands where he and his father's people now lived. Unable to respond adequately with words, Tress merely smiled at him through tears and then caressed his cheek before removing her treasure, with the willing assistance of several hands, to a private place where she could pore over it in solitude.

As we ushered Connor, Brander and their immediate party through the throng to the quarters they would occupy for the duration of their stay, I learned that Brander's visit was, on the surface at least, simply a temporary and belated visit to his brother Donuil, predicated upon opportunity. Without a war to demand all of his time, Brander had found himself uniquely able to spend time with his new wife, and as a wedding gift to her, he had decided to accompany her southward to visit her sister, who was wife to the Pictish king of the peninsula called Gallowa in Caledonia, a mere two days' sailing time to the north of Ravenglass. Morag's mother had been unable to attend her sister's nuptials, so Morag had attended in her place, and the bridal couple was now escorting the bridesmaid home to Gallowa. Naturally, since chance would bring Brander thus close to Donuil, whom he had not seen in twenty years, he had decided to combine one pleasure with another and to meet, at last, not only Donuil and his wife, but also Merlyn Britannicus, whom he had missed by mere hours years earlier, at the outbreak of the Eirish war, arriving from the northern isles with his father's fleet just after we had left to sail eastward to return to Camulod. It struck me immediately that the political ramifications of a visit from the admiral of the upstart Island Scots to a Pictish mainland king, when both of them had wives who were sisters, were too obvious to be remarked upon then, during a casual stroll. I resolved to find out more about it later, when the timing would be more appropriate.

The quarters assigned to Brander and his people were the best we had at our disposal. As we reached the doors and entered, a group of cleaners rushed to remove themselves, flowing around us on either side to reach the doors, their hurried work completed. The beds, I could see, all had fresh, dry coverings, the concrete floors had all been swept and covered with fresh rushes, and fires had been lit in the braziers on the flagstone squares in each room. I thanked Ascoridorus, the one in charge and the last to leave. He smiled at me and nodded, glancing only briefly at my companions and dipping his head in silent greeting to Connor, the only one he recognized, before he left.

I closed the door behind him and looked again around the room we had entered. The shutters had been opened and bright oblongs of light painted the rush-strewn floor. "Good," I said. "Brander, this entire block of quarters is yours. Distribute your own people where you will, but you might wish to save this space here, on the end of the block, for yourself and your wife, since it is the largest. Connor's accustomed spot lies at the other end, and it is the same size. There are eight living units between the two, and each of those can accommodate as many as four people easily, and six if need be."

Brander had crossed to the brazier and was warming his hands at the new fire, smiling as he looked at his wife. Salina was obviously pleased with the spacious brightness of the room, and Donuil was lounging by the window, leaning against the open shutters.

Beside me, Connor shrugged his heavy travelling cloak free of his shoulders and folded it over his arm. "Well," he grunted, "I don't know about anyone else, but I'm looking forward to undoing this damned harness on my leg and lying back at ease in your hot pool, my friend. I've had a long winter of cold water, and the thought of your bathhouse has sustained me since we set sail almost a week ago."

I grinned and bowed again to Salina. "We'll leave you now to gather yourselves after your journey, and I will have hot water brought to you immediately." I saw her eyes brighten at the thought. "You will be comfortable here, I think. These quarters are reserved for the use of King Athol himself, should he ever come to visit." I glanced at Brander. "How is the King, by the way? I trust he is in good health?"

As I asked the question, everyone went still, and my heart jumped. I saw the way Brander looked immediately to Connor, whose eyes then shifted towards Donuil. He, in turn, stiffened, as alarmed as I had been by the sudden change in the mood. Connor and Brander both looked back at me.

"Of course," Connor said, "I knew that would be one of your first questions, but we had hoped to put it off for at least a little while longer." He turned to Donuil. "Our father is dead, Donuil. He died last summer, while I was at sea to the south, on my last call to your good-father Liam, in south Cambria. By the time I arrived back here, on my way home, he was already dead and in the ground. I found out when I arrived back at his hall."

Donuil's face had drained of all colour. He drew himself up to his full height, sucking in a great, deep breath, then moved away from the window to where he could lean one hip against a high table for support. My eyes were flicking swiftly among all three of them, looking for—what? I could not have answered that question had my life depended on it. Nonetheless, I looked, and carefully. For long moments none among us moved, and I felt Tress's fingers digging deep into my arm. Finally Donuil spoke, his voice tight.

"What—" He coughed, clearing his throat. "What happened? How did he die?"

Connor looked at Brander, inviting him to speak, and the eldest brother cleared his throat.

"He fell, Donuil, boarding my galley. It happened suddenly, as he was stepping from the gangplank to the deck—a fit of dizziness, a sudden nausea, none of us know what caused it, but he threw up his hands to his head, reeled and suddenly staggered backwards. I was right there, and I lunged to help him, but his foot slipped from the gangplank and he fell back, against the wharf. He broke his back." The silence stretched until Brander spoke again. "We pulled him unconscious from the water, thinking him dead, and carried him home. But he revived."

"His back was *broken*?"

"Aye. He lay paralysed thereafter, completely unable to move from his shoulders down, although he could use his arms and hands for several days. On the fifth day, he died. We did all we could for him, but there was no way we could ease his pain."

"Did he . . . was he able to speak at all?"

"Aye, he could speak. Much of the time he was out of his senses with the pain, but there were intervals when he would talk, mainly to me, sometimes to others. Salina was there throughout. I sat with him for hours at a time, and my wrists were blue from the grip of his hands as he fought the pains that racked him. By the time he died, I was thankful to the gods for releasing him, for I had begun to think of killing him myself, so great and ceaseless was his agony. *I* could not bear it, simply watching him."

Donuil turned away and stood staring out the window, his massive shoulders slumped and his hands dangling by his sides.

"He spoke much of you," Brander told him, "for among us all I believe you were his greatest pride. And he passed on to me much that he wanted you to know. You will not want to hear it now, but I'll be here when you are ready to listen."

Donuil turned back to face into the room. His face was lifeless, his eyes seeking out Salina. "What were you doing there, in my father's hall?"

"She was there to discuss an alliance," Brander answered, but Donuil cut him short.

"Let her tell me," he said in a dull tone.

Salina glanced from him to her husband. "I was there to discuss the terms of treaty with your father," she began.

"Treaty? A woman, discussing terms of *treaty*? Women have no business with such things."

"In Eire they may not, but in my land they do. Among our folk, in the far north-east, the women fight beside the men, and often against them. I am Chief among my people, and I am a warrior, as much the king in my home as your father was in his. You call us Picts, a Roman word drawn from our tradition of going into battle painted in the colours of our ancient gods. Your father sought secure holdings in Tod of Gallowa's northern lands, in return for which he was prepared to offer certain accommodations. Tod saw advantages in such an association, but he could not treat openly with Athol for various reasons—among them the fact that his neighbours on all sides would have come together against him, had they suspected he was making alliance with an Outlander king. I could treat with Athol openly, however, as Tod's envoy, since his southern people think, like you, that women have no business with such things and hence they would never consider that a man like Tod would use a woman for such purposes. So I went. While I was there, King Athol had his fall."

"And had you made this treaty, when he fell?" Donuil sounded utterly uncaring.

"No."

"So there is no treaty."

"No, the treaty is in place."

Now Donuil frowned, clearly perplexed. "Made by whom?"

"The King of Scots."

"But—"

Connor cut him off. "Donuil, Brander is king now."

I felt my heartbeat begin to pound in my ears as I turned now to gaze at Brander, seeing him suddenly in an altogether different light.

"King? King Brander?" Donuil seemed bemused, then he gazed at the floor in front of his feet. "Of course," he said quietly. "With Father dead, that's as it should be." He looked up again at Brander and then nodded, once, in acknowledgement, before turning and making for the door. No one sought to hinder him as he made his way outside, but Salina spoke up as soon as he had gone.

"My love, perhaps you should go with him. This has hit him hard."

Brander nodded and followed his younger brother, and when he had gone I heard Connor expel his breath in an explosive rush. When I looked at him he was shaking his head.

"I know how hard it hit me, when I found out," he said. "But Donuil loved the old man even more than we did. I've been dreading this." He paused. "My father Athol is sorely missed, but even so, things have proceeded swiftly. You and I have to talk, Merlyn. I know you'll have a hundred things to ask of me, and I have half a score of things to talk with you about, but—" He stopped, and turned to face the women apologetically. "But it must be alone. I ask for your understanding in the face of what may seem surliness, Salina, and Tress, but what I have to say is truly for Merlyn's ears alone at this time. What he may choose to do with the information afterwards is his affair, but I must deliver it in confidence. Will you pardon us? Merlyn?" He turned to me again. "Take me to my quarters, if you will."

It was some time before Connor and I were truly alone. When we arrived at his quarters, four of his men were moving his gear from where it had been piled in the road outside, stowing the chests and boxes neatly against the wall that faced the door. While we waited for them to finish and leave us, Connor hung his cloak on a peg by the door, placed his helmet on the table by the window and began undoing his armour. I helped him with the buckles that were most difficult to reach, then moved two chairs close to the brazier, which had now been alight for long enough to throw out solid heat. A jug of Shelagh's mead had been placed on the table where Connor's helmet lay, and I poured us each a small measure. The news of Athol's death had shaken me and I wanted to drink deep, but I restrained myself, aware that this was one time when I needed to be clear-headed, for I suspected much that I was about to hear would be surprising; I could only hope it would not be unpleasant, too.

Connor's men left as I moved to sit down, holding the two cups, and he held the door open for them, thanking them for their services. When they were gone, he closed the door and clumped across to where I sat, scratching his armpit and evidently deep in thought. He took the mead I offered him, then stretched his legs towards the brazier, and sat staring into the flames for a spell, sipping occasionally at the cup.

"Well," he grunted finally, turning his head to look at me, "I imagine your head's in a turmoil. Ask me anything you want."

"No, better for me to listen at this stage, I think. You're the one with all the information. I have matters of my own to discuss with you, but even those may be affected by what you tell me now. What is so urgent that we have to speak of it alone?" I waited, saying nothing, giving him room to think.

"Change . . . Or changes . . ." He was thinking aloud, rather than speaking to me, but his voice, and his focus, hardened rapidly, and he launched into a flood of words the like of which I had never heard from him before. "It has been, what, ten years since we first met? Probably more although it seems like less. In that time I've seen more changes than I could ever have thought possible. We've left Eire behind, abandoning our holdings there, and moved our entire people to the north, successfully. So successfully, in fact, that those who choose to stay there now are calling themselves Islesmen, and with pride . . ." He lapsed into silence for a while, then grunted in disgust.

"I wish I could spend all my life at sea, Merlyn, because I'm not suited to deal with stubborn, stupid, discontented people and their changing wishes all the time, and since my father died it seems that's all I've done. Sometimes I wish I had been born a kern with nothing more to worry over than my next good meal or my next bloody fight or even my next belly bump with some wet, willing woman . . ." He stopped, staring into the fire and picking idly at the hairs of his moustache. "But I was born my father's son, as we all are, and that means I must shoulder my father's burdens . . .

"Think of what was involved in moving all our folk from Eire, Merlyn! It was a fearsome task, demanding years, a whole lifetime, of effort, and it was my father's life that went into the doing of it. Oh, we all took part, but his was the vision. He was the one who had to face his people and convince them that the land could no longer support them and their neighbours and that wars and famine were unavoidable unless they, his people, did something they had never done before. Then, on top of that, he had to make them believe they could live better lives elsewhere, beyond the home their fathers had created from the forests, beyond their family fields, beyond Eire itself, in a distant land that none of them had ever seen. I tell you, my friend, I could never have done that, had the task been mine. But Athol Mac Iain did it, and then, having lit the flame of hope within their breasts, he brought them there in safety, despite a raging war against far greater numbers than he himself commanded.

"And what then? After it all was done and they were safely moved, many of the ingrates, hundreds strong, looked about them at the islands of their new home and decided he was *wrong* to have moved them! They could not stay there, they cried. They wanted to return, knowing well that the old place was lost to them and that no life there would be possible. Faugh!"

"They still wish to return, today?"

"No, they've already gone, long since . . . late last year, five hundred of them, not counting children."

"But how? Were they simply landed there and left to die in their old home?"

He looked at me quickly, frowning. "No, what do you take us for? They landed on the northern coast. They'll build a new home there."

"But what about Condran and his people? That's their territory, is it not?"

"It was." His voice was absolutely flat, and the way he said the two words, and then paused, raised the small hairs on the nape of my neck. Fortunately, his pause was brief, because when he spoke again I discovered I had been holding my breath.

"The Sons of Condran have seen change, as well. Brander's last voyage brought an end to them as any kind of force. He sailed right into their harbour and caught them unprepared, in high summer. He took a great risk in doing it, hazarding everything upon surprising them, but it succeeded. He planned his campaign carefully—drew off their main fleet in pursuit of part of his, and as soon as they had cleared the horizon, he struck at their home base, which lay upriver from the sea, much like our own old base to the south. Condran himself was killed in the early fighting, along with three of his blood sons. That kicked the resistance out of the remaining defenders.

"Brander then destroyed their shipyards systematically, managing to capture half a score of unmanned galleys in the process. He made sure that all their master shipbuilders had been either killed or captured—he knew all their names and paid willing turncoats in the town to betray their whereabouts, and he took pains to identify the corpse of each one who died in the fighting. He wanted to leave no possibility of new war galleys being built there in the time to come. Then he set fire to everything that could be burned, the entire town. When that had been achieved, he left some of our men to occupy the lookout posts in the approaches to the river mouth, to give no hint to the returning enemy galleys of anything being wrong, and he withdrew further down the coast to await the return of the enemy fleet. He attacked it in the river mouth and destroyed it by setting fire to all the galleys he had captured earlier and then driving them into the fleet. It was a crushing victory, final and complete. The Sons of Condran will not emerge from their holes again."

"What happened to the smaller part of Brander's fleet, the ships their main fleet chased?"

"Nothing. Brander had sent them out to sea, to pass by Condran's base unseen, on a southward course. Once there, they turned about and waited, concealed in a cove, for a foggy dawn. The remainder of Brander's fleet lay to the north. When the fog came down, the smaller group rowed northward as though they were returning from raiding to the south and were lost in the fog banks, so that they had blundered and been seen. They fled, and Condran's folk gave chase. Our galleys were double-crewed and kept ahead of them, close enough to be pursued, but always too far off, thanks to their extra oarsmen, to be brought to fight. They kept the main fleet occupied for several days, so that the fires on shore had time to burn and die. When Condran's fleet gave up and returned home, they burned, too."

"My God," I whispered. "It sounds final enough almost to be a Roman vengeance."

"Aye, well it was the vengeance of the Gael," he said. "That was last year. Since then, we have re-seeded the north coast with some of our folk, as I told you. They have their own galleys and can guard themselves, and we are close by, should they need us."

"Changes indeed. Tell me about the mainland, this treaty of Brander's."

"A different kind of change." Connor sipped again at his mead. "The treaty was necessary, and I hope it's merely the first. It will be, I know. My brother Brander may have the makings of an even greater king than Athol Mac Iain was."

"How is it different?"

"Well, for one thing, we have become, over the last ten years, a race of fishermen. Now *that* is a change that alters every aspect of our lives. We've always fished, of course, because we lived beside the sea, but now we live *among* the seas, so now most of our food comes from the water. We eat fish, and shellfish, and seal meat, and sometimes whale meat. We eat birds that taste of fish. Most of our lands are rocky and inhospitable to crops. The bigger islands have good soil, but they're all forested, and until we clear them we can't farm them. We grow a little grain, and we have a green crop, kale, that grows well in shallow soil, even through a mild winter. It's not the most pleasant stuff to eat, but it's nourishing and wholesome enough.

"We have hundreds of islands on which we can live, although many more are too small for human habitation. Our people have spread out among them in the past few years, though, and will survive. But we need land that we can farm, and that means we need a foothold, at least, on the mainland, and not simply on the rocky shoreline. Soon after we arrived and had begun to spread our folk about, that need became too urgent for my father and his counsellors to ignore. Our fishing boats were few, back then, too few. So we sent out . . . scouts? What's the word you'd use? Peaceful messengers, looking for opportunities to deal with other kings . . ."

"Emissaries."

He looked at me, quizzically. "If you say so. Emissaries. Sounds impressive. Well then, we sent out emissaries to the kings up and down the mainland coast. They went unarmed, and bearing gifts, and some returned alive. One of the first such groups made contact with a king in the region called Gallowa, to the north of here, a man called Tod, who showed an interest in an alliance. He was willing to exchange land in his northern holdings in return for the protection of our galleys along his southern shores. Turns out that the Sons of Condran had been harrying him for years. He has large armies, but they're almost useless against a fleet, unless they happen to know in advance where the fleet will strike."

I nodded. "I know. The Romans had the same difficulty." I had a sudden thought. "Do you know a king called Crandal?"

"No. Should I?"

"Hmm. He's a Pict. I thought you might have heard of him, at least. I hear he has raised an army and is marching southward into Britain, over in the north-east."

Connor shook his head. "We have made no great attempt to penetrate that far inland. The whole mainland is a morass of different tribes, all at war with each other and all divided by mountain chains. Any attempt to travel is madness, even for the Picts themselves. It means fighting new enemies every step of the way. Worse than it was in Eire. We've heard of one great valley that divides the whole land from sea to sea, with mountains to the north and south of it, but we hear it's thickly peopled and the folk are warlike."

"Then if that is the case—" I stopped, perplexed. "If things are as chaotic as you say, with constant warfare—"

"Raiding," Connor interrupted me. "It's more raiding than warfare. No large armies, no long campaigns, merely one raid after another, unendingly."

"If that is the case, then, how did Salina and her sister come to be involved with your King Tod? You said she comes from Orcenay—was that the name?—in the far north-east."

"Aye, but she's like us, an islander. Her people have boats, galleys of a kind, and travel by water."

"Tell me about these people. What do you know of them?"

He shrugged. "Not much, but I know they are not the same people as the mainlanders. They're very different. Not greatly numerous, from what Salina has told me, but fierce and warlike." He anticipated my next question. "And Salina *is* a chief. She rules one of the two groups of islands they control. Her brother Lot is king over all, in name, but Salina's is the power that counts in her domain."

"*Lot*? Did you say Lot? I hope he's no relation to your former good-brother of Cornwall?"

Connor barked a laugh. "You know, I had almost forgotten that! No, he's no relation. His name's not even Lot. That's just a name they use in dealing with strangers. His real name's unpronounceable, one of those grunting, cough-like sounds no normal human tongue can grapple with. Every time I hear someone say it, it sounds like he's retching and I pull my cloak around me to avoid being splattered. Salina's is the same. She chose the Roman name herself, for her dealings with people *she* calls Outlanders, like us.

"Anyway, Salina's sister married Tod of Gallowa some years ago, and there's some trade between the two kingdoms. Mostly sheep's wool coming down. I don't know what the Gallowans send back. When our emissaries arrived in Tod's kingdom that first time, Salina had just arrived with four of her ships. She took part in the talks, and when it became clear Tod would have problems with some of his chiefs, who knew nothing of us and hence did not trust us, she offered to sail to us and to deal with my father on her good-brother's behalf. That first visit led to Father's crossing to the mainland later that year to meet with Tod and his chiefs and counsellors. The meetings were successful, but it took two more years before a treaty was forged." He paused, remembering.

"It was completed last spring, when Condran's fleet carried out some heavy raids the length of Tod's coastline. Suddenly it became an excellent idea, they realized, to conclude the matter. No sooner were the final agreements reached than Brander sailed off to deal finally with Condran. Of course, we have made no mention to this time of the true extent of the destruction of Condran's sea power. It would be foolish to announce the removal of the prime need for the treaty. And besides, Condran's destruction really makes no difference to the substance of the contract, which promises the protection of our fleet in return for the right to farm the lands in the far north of Tod's holdings, which were lying empty and unused."

I had but one more question for him. "You said you expect more treaties of this type?"

"Aye. We require more mainland territory. Brander is dealing now with four more kings, further to the north, although they call themselves chiefs. He'll be successful, too. He has great strength in that kind of dealing. Then, once we have established footholds for our folk on fertile land, we can leave their prosperity to time and human nature. And we can hope for success now. With the extermination of Condran, we are at peace for the first time in many years. That's why Brander decided to get married, and then to make this journey with Salina and the girl. When we leave here, they'll sail to visit Tod."

"And where will you go?"

"On patrol. Now that Brander is king, he will be bound ashore. I am sole admiral."

I told him then about my decision to return south to Camulod within the month, abandoning our temporary home here in Mediobogdum, and I asked him if he would ferry my main party southward, one last time. He listened quietly, making no attempt to interrupt, but when I had finished he grimaced.

"Normally, I would say yes, but you've reminded me of what I set out to tell you before you distracted me with all this talk of treaties. Do you recall the big ship you encountered, in that coastal town, that first time you met Feargus?"

"Of course, the Roman bireme that the Berbers brought to strip the marble from the buildings of Glevum. What about it?"

"Liam Twistback arrived in the islands just before we left to come here. He undertook the journey in the winter, with only three companions, preferring to run the risk of storms and shipwreck rather than remain where he was, on the coast between Camulod and Cambria. He says the invaders from Cornwall have two of those things, aiding their troop movements. Massive vessels, Liam says they are, with multiple banks of oars and enormous sails. He says they have wooden decked towers, fore and aft, for soldiers and bowmen to fight from, and one of them even has siege engines mounted on the stern platform . . . catapults, can you credit that? And they have long, metal-clad rams projecting from their bows, below the water-line, for sinking enemy ships. They make our biggest galleys look like coracles, Liam says."

"Ironhair *possesses* these things?"

"No, I did not say that. Twistback knows nothing of this Ironhair. He merely said that the forces invading Cambria have two of these wondrous vessels assisting them."

"Aye, then they're Ironhair's." I heard the deadness in my own voice. His words had stunned me, but hard on the shock had come an immediate though unwilling recognition of the truth of what he had told me. Ironhair had proved already in the past that he was no fool and that, like his predecessor, Lot of Cornwall, he knew the value of money shrewdly placed and lavishly provided. The fact that he had followed Lot's example and procured an army of mercenaries with promises of plunder bore that out, but now it was evident that he had carried the procurement of alliances even further and ensured his maritime superiority with these great ships. I looked at Connor more carefully.

"You're sailing south, aren't you?"

"I had considered it." His tone said *Yes, I am.*

"Then you'll take us with you?"

"No. I won't. It's too dangerous. You have women and boys in your party, one of them my own nephew, Arthur. His presence alone would make this voyage far too dangerous."

"But—"

He cut me short with a slash of his open palm. "Sit down, Merlyn, and *think* of what's involved here!"

I was furious, insulted by his outright dismissal of my request. Harsh, angry words sprang to my lips, demanding to be spat out. Yet I knew I was wrong. Finally, I mastered myself and sat down, aware that Connor had much more to say, and that he, not I, commanded on the sea. He watched me with narrowed eyes, and when I sat down, moving slowly, he continued, speaking clearly and calmly.

"Merlyn, I have no idea what we'll encounter when we arrive down there, but the very last thing I might need is passengers aboard my vessels, women and children. I might round some headland there and find myself committed to a fight. We're sailing south, right into the middle of a war, and I tell you frankly, I have no plan, no stratagem for dealing with these . . . things, these biremes. I might have to turn tail and flee before them. I might not find them at all. Then again, I might not even have the opportunity to approach the coast, let alone find a suitable place and sufficient time to land you and your party. Then where would you be? You'd be stuck there, aboard my vessel headed north-west, with no safe way of getting back to Camulod. Better you return by road, with your own garrison. That way your party will be safe and well protected, and you'll experience the land you haven't seen yet." His mouth twisted into a small, ironic smile. "You'll probably arrive in Camulod long before we could deliver you there, given the probable congestion on the waterways."

I sat gazing at him in bafflement, unsettlingly aware that I was missing something here. Finally I grunted in belated realization of another point. If these biremes had seemed threatening enough to Liam Twistback to encourage him to face the perils of a sea voyage in winter in a tiny boat, they also represented a threat to Camulod, which lay within a two-day march of Liam's farm.

"Did Liam say if he had managed to warn Camulod about these vessels?" I asked.

"He didn't have to. Some of your people were there with Liam, on their regular patrol, when the things last approached the shore. They wanted Liam to return with them when they rode back to warn the Colony, but for some reason he chose to sail north and take his chances with the winter gales. Anyway, they know in Camulod. I imagine all their defensive preparations are in place by now."

All at once I knew what it was about Connor's words that had been unsettling me. "Liam was the last of your people down there, wasn't he?" He nodded. "So why are you going there at all? You have no interests to be served down there now."

His mouth twisted again in a wintry smile. "What about gratitude to you and yours and to the Cambrians who let us use their land?"

"Admirable, but unnecessary. What would your people have to gain from such a course? God knows, you've much to lose, going against such ships."

"I want one of them."

He spoke so softly that I barely heard his words, and then I doubted my own hearing.

"You what?"

"You heard me clearly, I want one of them—at least one. Both, if I can have them."

"Are you mad? You've never seen these things. I have. The two of them together could probably defeat your entire fleet, just by their combined weight and strength. Your galleys would be wrecked and ruined before you ever could approach them. Those catapults you mentioned are used to hurl burning pots of oil into an enemy's rigging and sails. You know what fire does to ships, Connor—it was you who described it to me, on the walls of Ravenglass—and you've just been telling me about Brander's destruction of Condran's fleet with fireships. And even without the fire, their prow rams would smash even your biggest galley beneath the water-line. Then the weight of the forepart of the ship, propelled by hundreds of great sweeps, would thunder down and crush your vessel like an egg. Their archers would slaughter those of your men who didn't drown immediately. No, Connor, if you have any mind for the welfare of your ships and men, empty your mind of any thought of fighting these machines. They're Roman-built, my friend, and Roman-designed to be invincible in their own element."

"Aye, Liam said something of the same, although he didn't know the workings of the things as you do. Where did you learn all this?"

"From books. I read it all. The Roman navy ruled the seas for hundreds of years, and their genius lay in taking infantry to sea. Their warships were built as floating platforms for their soldiery—"

He held up his hand to prevent me from saying any more. "I'm as sane as you are, good-brother. I've no intention of sailing to my death and hearing the noise of my own galleys being destroyed."

"Then what?"

"I shall wait. They must put into land at some time or another, these mighty beasts. They sail like other vessels, and they're being used to supply the armies on the mainland. The Pendragon Cambrians have no naval force, so these great ships can have no opposition. They'll be like shepherds to the smaller galleys in their fleet, plying between whatever southern port they use and their base in Cambria, and when they arrive, they'll put into shore, to be unloaded. That's when I'll take them."

I laughed aloud in simple disbelief. "You intend to walk on board and take over a ship like that? Don't you think they'll be guarded?"

"Of course they'll be guarded, dear good-brother, but how well? Think about that. These things are without equal on the sea, requiring special skills and seamanship to operate them properly, and when they come to shore, they'll be among their own. They will be guarded, certainly, but who among their crews would dream that anyone would ever be mad enough to think to steal one from its base ashore?"

"How will you get close to them?"

"Mercenaries, Merlyn. We'll be among their own, in their own camp. Why should they suspect us of anything? We're not their enemies. In fact, they won't know who we are or whence we came. We'll be but mercenaries like the rest of them."

"By the sweet Christus! What happens then if you succeed and get aboard, past the guards? How will you get the thing away?"

"We'll row it out of there! If we can be mercenaries on the land, why shouldn't some of us be afloat, too?" I realized only then that Connor was extemporizing, improvising even as he spoke. "Who will know we are not theirs? They have no enemies afloat, they think—or I believe they think that." His brow was creased now with the speed and concentration of his thoughts. "A small number of galleys, extracrewed, their arrival timed to coincide with our attack . . . But returning galleys . . . galleys that left the same harbour the day before . . . no one will think to question their arrival, if they think it's their return. And when the moment's right, we strike. We take the ship and board a crew from the galleys, on the water side. It will work, Merlyn, it will work!" He slapped his hands on his knees and stood up, suddenly alight with resolve.

"When will you leave?" I half expected him to rush off then and there.

"A week or so, no more." He clumped his way across to the window, his false leg sweeping aside the rushes on the floor with each step, and opened wide the shutters, twisting his neck to lean out and look up at the sky. I was surprised to the see the sun was still shining brightly. I felt as though we had been cloistered here for hours.

"Have you any food around here?" he asked. "I'm famished."

I had to smile. "We'll find something cold in the kitchens, but there won't be anything hot until the evening meal."

"Then cold it is, so long as it be soon."

As we walked towards the kitchens in the refectory block, my head was spinning with all we had discussed, and I had the feeling that much of the ensuing week would be dedicated to the Admiral's new-developed stratagem for enlarging his fleet.

II

By the end of that week, the days had warmed up almost to summertime heat and the skies remained cloudless. New grass shot up everywhere and the first mountain flowers, which would not normally have begun to grow for at least another month, matured swiftly and broke into bloom, so that the hillsides outside our walls were soon dotted with tiny clusters of brilliant yellows, blues and whites. By the roadside, beneath the trees along the forest fringes, thick clusters of dark-green growth sprang up and blanketed the ground, promising that within the next few weeks the entire hillside, seen from the fort beneath, would be misted with a purplish haze of bluebells to perfume the air.

In the fort itself, life progressed with a high-spirited urgency made the greater by the beauty of the weather. Connor's estimated week before departure lengthened to two as he enlarged and refined his plans to voyage south. He spent most of that time working closely with Feargus and big Logan, his most trusted captains, their counsel strengthened and abetted by contributions from Brander, whose enthusiasm for the task ahead was greater, if anything, than Connor's own. Brander might be King of Scots today, tied to the land henceforth, but he was still very much Brander the Admiral, and his eyes glistened at the thought of having a Roman bireme, or perhaps even two of them, added to his fleet.

I sat among them frequently, listening to their conversations, and often I had to force myself to keep silent, stifling my criticism by reminding myself that they knew exactly how dependent this entire venture would be upon the disposition of the enemy ships when Connor arrived in the waters off Cambria. They accepted the hazards, the high degree of random chance they faced and the seeming impossibility of outmanoeuvring the gods of war and fate; and in that acceptance, they attempted to foresee all the variations of opportunity that might present themselves and bent their combined abilities to create the simplest, most intrinsically flexible strategic outline they could devise.

I had my own tasks to perform while the mariners were planning their great quest. We had committed ourselves to return to Camulod in the spring, and that withdrawal could no longer be deferred. Spring was here now, and early, and despite long months of systematic preparation, we were not yet ready to leave. I worked all day, most days, and long into the nights, bullying everyone time and again into checking and reviewing all the thousand and one things that had already been reviewed and checked, packed and loaded and made ready for transportation.

In all of this, Rufio was one of my greatest strengths. He worked even harder than me. His recovery from the awful wounds the bear had inflicted on him had been more complete and more rapid than any of us would have dared to hope. But Rufio would never fight again. The deep gouges on his shoulder and upper arm from the beast's claws had turned toxic, and while our brillant surgeon and physician Lucanus had been successful, prior to his own death, in keeping the killing poisons in the wounds from spreading, the damage to the muscles of Rufio's left arm had been irreversible, so that the limb now resembled a withered stick rather than a human appendage. His spirit, though, remained indomitable, and within two months his legs were sound enough that he could walk almost without a limp.

Rufio's first request was to be given a task that he could organize alone, without assistance. That was when I came up with the idea of wiping out all visible traces of our occupation of the fort. Mediobogdum had sat unoccupied for two hundred years, we believed. Were we to leave it looking as though it had not been occupied since then, that might encourage others to avoid it. If we were successful in that, and if we then decided to return at some future date, we could simply move in again without obstruction.

Rufio thought this was an excellent idea, and he took the task I had set him very seriously. At one time or another over the ensuing weeks and months, everyone in the fort worked to his orders, stripping the place of every sign we could find of human habitation. We shut the bathhouse down, for instance, and boarded up the doors as we had found them, then blocked the entry to the furnaces with care, protecting them from damage and decay as best we could.

Then came the day I knew we were ready, and we could appoint a day for our departure. Our guests were still hip-deep in their planning sessions, however, and that presented me with a dilemma: should I or should I not inform them that we were now fully prepared to leave Mediobogdum and ought to leave immediately? The laws of hospitality demanded that I give no sign that they might interpret as an invitation to be gone, and yet I was acutely aware of the urgencies in Camulod, where Ambrose was awaiting our arrival. Fortunately, neither Connor nor his brother was as blind to what was happening as I had begun to fear. That same afternoon, when I joined them both in Brander's quarters, they were ready for me, and they informed me that they would leave for Ravenglass the moment I decided on the day of our own departure. I told them we would leave in three days' time, thereby giving them another full day to conclude their own affairs in Mediobogdum.

Later that afternoon, while I sat alone in my quarters conducting one more check of all that had been done, working with the long lists complied by Hector and his clerks, I called Donuil in and asked him if he would find Arthur and send him to me. He left at once and I went back to work, losing myself in my lists again and making notations, until I realized that the room had grown quite dark and Arthur had not arrived. It had been late afternoon when I sent Donuil to find him, the light from my window still bright enough to read by, and now it was dusk. Frowning, I left my table and made my way outside in time to meet Donuil coming back. He had searched the entire fort without finding Arthur, he informed me, so he had sent Gwin, Bedwyr and Ghilly outside to look for him and to send him here immediately. Better that they, who knew all the boy's favourite haunts, should look for him directly, he had reasoned. But that had been an hour earlier. He had heard nothing since then.

That he should have had to send the boys was, in itself, a worrisome revelation, and it set me fretting. For years, all four boys had been insep-arable. Where one was found, the others were close by, and that had always been a simple fact of life. Until today. What, in the name of the sweet Christus, I wondered now, could Arthur be about? Where would he have gone, without his friends? And then my mind leaped to consider unpleasant possibilities. Had he been harmed? Was he perhaps in danger, lost or injured somewhere out in the rough country beyond the walls? A sudden vision of Rufio, lying bleeding after his encounter with the bear in the forest, chilled me to the bone. But even as these thoughts teemed in my head, I saw Arthur running towards me, rounding the corner from the central road that divided the fort. He was red-faced and out of breath, and I merely stood and looked at him, disapprovingly, as he came to a halt before us, panting as though he had run for miles.

"I'm sorry, Cay," he gasped. "I would not have kept you waiting had I known. I came as soon as Bedwyr found me." I said nothing, and his face grew redder. "I was out on the hillside, beneath the walls. I had no thought you might have need of me."

"You had no thought at all, that's plain." I was aware how very un-usual such behaviour was for him, and yet I could not let the occasion pass without a reprimand. "You know better, Arthur, than to disappear without informing someone of your whereabouts. Have you forgotten Ru-fio's misfortune so soon, and the upheaval it provoked?" He hung his head now, shamefaced and making no attempt to defend himself. "Have you nothing more to say, then?"

He sucked in a deep breath, then shook his head, his eyes still cast down. "No, nothing more, except to say I'm sorry."

There was little more for me to say. The lad had committed no crime. He had not even misbehaved, other than to slip away on his own. No point, then, in punishing him further, for I was under no illusions; his red

face and his general air of guilt declared that he considered this ques-
tioning a form of punishment. I thanked Donuil, who had been standing
beside me, and allowed him to leave before I led the boy into my quarters.
He stood meekly in the middle of the floor until I waved him to a chair
and seated myself across from him.

"I know I seldom send for you at this time of the day, so there's no
reason why you should have kept yourself available to me, none at all. I
was concerned when I discovered that you had gone off alone and could
not be found immediately, that is all. If you think about it, you'll agree
that that is most unusual, as well as simply dangerous and foolish, when
the woods and hills about us are full of savage animals who see us as the
interlopers on *their* mountains. What *were* you doing?" I waved him to
silence as soon as I had asked the question, seeing the alarm that flared
in his wide, gold-flecked eyes. "You needn't answer that. It's really none
of my concern, mere curiosity."

He answered anyway. "I was close by, Cay, close beneath the walls. I
was merely . . . in an unusual place, that is all. Bed found me, by accident,
on his way to rejoin Gwin and Ghilly. As soon as he told me you were
looking for me, I ran all the way here. But I was never in any danger and
never beyond shouting distance of the guards on the wall."

"Hmm," I grunted. "Well, that's some relief, at any rate. Now listen,
I have decided that we'll leave in three days' time to return to Camulod.
We'll travel by road, with the returning garrison, because Connor has
other affairs to be about and he believes the sea route may be much too
perilous to risk at this time, with Ironhair's armies invading Cambria by
sea and therefore plying to and fro across our only path." I paused, to see
that I had his full attention. His eyes were fixed on my lips, waiting for
me to speak again. "So," I continued, "everything is ready now, at last,
although I had begun to doubt it ever would be! I want you to ride to Ravenglass, to take that word from me to Derek. You will leave in the morning, as
soon as you have broken your night fast. You may take the others with you
if you wish, but there will be no time for play along the way. I need you to
go there, as quickly as you may, to find Derek, and give him word from
me in confidence, for his ears alone. Is that clear?"

"Aye. What must I tell him?"

"Straightforward tidings, for the most part. You will inform him that
Connor and his party will leave here tomorrow, later in the day, to return
to Ravenglass. We ourselves will leave Mediobogdum to return to Camulod on the second day after that—What's wrong with you? Are you
not well?"

His face suddenly looked ashen, but when I questioned him he sat
up straight and shook his head, the muscles of his jaw outlined, so tightly
were they clenched.

"No! I'm . . ." He blinked then, widening his eyes and fluttering his eyelids and shaking his head like someone waking from a dream. "I'll be fine, Cay." His voice, very slightly slurred, made him sound dazed. I stood up, alarmed, but he stopped me with an upraised hand, shaking his head. "It was . . . a sudden vertigo, that's all." He shuddered and then sat straight, evidently attempting to pull himself together. "Perhaps from running," he continued in a more normal tone.

I watched him silently for several moments more, then thought to offer him something to drink. He cut my offer short, however, albeit not rudely, and his voice sounded normal again. I was thankful to see, too, that the colour was beginning to return to his cheeks. "No, Cay. I thank you, but I'm well enough now. It was a momentary thing and now it's gone. You were telling me about the message to Derek. Please go on. Why must it be so secret? Nothing you have said indicates a need for that."

Reassured by the calmness of his tone, I nodded. "That's correct, on the surface, but I believe there is a need at least for circumspection. When I first spoke to Derek of our decision to leave here and return home, he spoke of coming with us and leaving his kingdom to his eldest son, Owen. He was adamant about it at the time, but he has not mentioned it since. I don't know whether he has changed his mind and decided to stay here in Ravenglass, or whether he is simply waiting for the word from me to join us. You will carry that word to him tomorrow, simple and unadorned, but you must deliver it to him alone, in private, for whether he still intends to come with us or not, he is king of Ravenglass. The announcement of his departure must be his to make. Similarly, if he has changed his mind, he might not wish it to be known, for reasons of policy, that he had considered leaving. Do you understand?" The boy nodded. "Good. How are you feeling now?"

He nodded again, frowning slightly. "I'm perfect. Nothing wrong with me at all. May I go now?"

"Aye, of course. You'll leave in the morning, as soon as the sun is up, and I'll expect you back before nightfall." He stood up and started to leave, but I stopped him as he reached the door. "Will you take Bedwyr and the others with you?"

"I don't know." He hesitated, his hand on the latch. "Could I remain in Ravenglass tomorrow night, and come home the following morning?"

"No, Arthur, not this time. That's the day before we leave. You'll be needed here. Everyone will be needed that day, every pair of hands will work at packing and lading. We must be away from here and across the pass long before noon on the morning after that, and beyond Galava, on the Great Mere, before nightfall."

His frown grew more pronounced, suggesting a hint of defiance, which

perplexed me. It was unmistakable in his next words. "But what about
King Derek? If he is to come with us, he'll come the following day. Could
I not ride back here with him?"

I turned slowly to look directly at him, feeling, for the first time ever
with the boy, a real need to assert discipline. "What?" I said, keeping my
tone cool and level yet with a hint of asperity. "And leave your work here
to be done by others who will have their own hands full while you amuse
yourself in Ravenglass? I'm surprised you would even think to ask such a
thing. No, you will return tomorrow afternoon, obeying my instructions
and arriving before nightfall. Is that clear enough?" He nodded, but his
face was set in lines of displeasure, almost a scowl, and I hardened my
voice. "Good, then we understand each other perfectly. Besides, you will
find that if King Derek had decided to come with us, he will be ready
and will doubtless ride back with you tomorrow. He has known for months
that we are leaving as soon as we may. If he has decided to remain, on
the other hand, he will come back with you tomorrow anyway, to say
goodbye. So the true answer to your ill-considered question is both no
and yes. No, you may not stay in Ravenglass, and yes, you may ride back
with Derek. Clear? Good. That's all, young man. You may go now."

He stood there in the doorway, clearly angry and struggling for words,
but then he lowered his head, biting at his lip. Finally he nodded, his
head still downcast, and went out without looking at me again, closing
the door gently behind him. I had the distinct impression that he wanted
to slam it shut, however, and I opened it slightly again to watch him walk
stiffly away into the gathering dusk with his fists clenched and his entire
bearing radiating anger and frustration. Then I heard Tressa's voice calling
his name from the street on my right and I pulled the door to as he
turned around to look for her.

Moments later, she opened the door and came in, unwinding the long
stola she had wrapped around her shoulders.

"Cay, what on earth did you say to Arthur? I've never seen him so
upset. He could barely stand to talk to me and I swear he was on the
point of tears. Did you two quarrel?"

"No, my love," I said with a sigh, "we did not." I went to her and
threw my arms about her, holding her close and kissing her deeply before
moving away again to the high-backed chair at my table, where I seated
myself and told her everything that had passed between the boy and me,
making no attempt to disguise my bafflement at his strange behaviour.

When I had finished, throwing up my arms and declaring my exas-
peration, she simply smiled and shook her head. "Rebellious, was that the
word you stopped yourself from saying a moment ago?" She did not wait
for me to respond; she had heard me correctly. "Arthur is not rebellious,
Cay, you know that. He's the best-natured boy in the world, and what
you've said here confirms that. But the first words that come to you when

now he shows a spark of his own feelings are 'surly' and 'selfish.' You really have no idea what's wrong with him, do you?"

I placed both hands flat on the table top and looked at her, raising my eyebrows, aware I was about to learn. "Haven't I made myself clear on that, woman? If I understood any of it, I would not be so frustrated, would I?"

"The boy's in love, you great, clumsy, dim-witted male!" Her perplexed but understanding smile robbed her words of any sting, and in the tone of them I heard her ask, wordlessly, *What am I going to do with you, when you are so thick-skulled?* "Have you no sense at all, no eyes, no empathy in you? He's changed, Cay, forever. Gone, vanished. What was that great long word you told to Derek, about butterflies? Meta . . ."

"Metamorphosis."

"Aye, that's it. Well, that's what's happened to the boy. He's metamorphosized."

I had to smile, she looked so earnest and concerned. "*Metamorphosed,* we say."

"Pah! You say it—it's too big for me, twisting in my mouth like something alive. But changed completely, that's what it means, howe'er you say it. The Arthur that you've always known is lost, Cay. Lost in love, for the first time in his life, and all he knows is that it's about to end and he is powerless to stop it. For you've just told him that you're ending it, tomorrow, come sunrise, tearing him and his love apart, sending her home and carrying him away to Camulod."

"*Love?*" I sat staring at her, attempting to grapple with what she had told me. "Arthur's in love? That's nonsense. With whom?" But even as I spoke the words, I saw it, my mind showing me images that I had seen in open view these past two weeks and chosen to ignore: Arthur, cow-eyed and spellbound as he sat at dinner, gazing wordlessly at the beautiful young woman who sat demurely with her aunt and uncle, turning her head from time to time to smile in his direction; Bedwyr, grinning and slyly nudging Gwin as they watched Arthur watching her; the two young girls from Ravenglass, Stella and Rena, their faces the very picture of dislike and open hostility as they glared at the sight of Arthur in the street, standing alone with Morag between the buttresses of the central granaries, in a flood of bright sunlight that painted the entire west wall; and last, but most telling, the memory of that first moment when I had seen the two of them staring raptly at each other on the day she first arrived, each of them utterly, compellingly, immediately absorbed in the blinding totality of the other.

Thunderbolted. The term sprang into my mind, jarring me with bittersweet recollections forgotten thirty years before; the word we had used, as boys, to indicate the crippling swiftness with which love could strike. I had been thunderbolted once, and lost my love, a bright-faced girl of twelve whose father had been banished for some crime against the Colony, and now the sharp, aching strangeness of the feelings that had filled my breast returned—the incredulous joy and wonder of sharing the world with her—and unreal though it was, the merest, fleeting shadow of a memory, the painful sweetness of it yet reminded me of what it had been like to *live* with such a love possessing me: terror and awe, offset by wild, thrilling joy and disbelief that I could be so blessed; capering, carefree madness spurred by an excitement beyond bearing; soaring elation blended with an incendiary purity of thought and purpose and the grand resolve to lay the whole world at my true love's feet. Her name had been Lueth, and now I wondered, for a flickering moment during which her face burned in my mind, how life had dealt with her. I thought, too, of Publius Varrus and how he, in his day, had been thunderbolted by a girl in blue, a girl whose real name might or might not have been the one she had given him on the sole summer afternoon they spent together. He had lost her in finding her, that single afternoon, and had spent years searching for her face throughout the Empire.

Tress moved now to sit on the floor by my feet, and she leaned against my knee, her bent arm on my thigh, supporting her face in her hand as she gazed up at me.

"What is it, Cay? What are you thinking?"

I reached down to stroke her hair, then looked at her, feeling suddenly very old. "About first love, and what it does to us. It shatters us, that first time when we see that there's another species in our world of men, a species concerning whose existence we had been in utter ignorance—the goddess species. First love, the thunderbolt, is the loss of innocence." I stopped, feeling a swelling in my throat the like of which I had not felt in years. And then, because Tressa was so wide-eyed and intent, staring up at me, I rubbed my thumb against the smoothness of her cheek and spoke what lay within my mind.

"I simply never thought of that before, and even so, had I ever thought of such a thing, I would never have imagined that I might . . . that I might be the one to cause such direct pain to any boy, far less a boy who means as much to me as Arthur does. And yet there's nothing I can do to change it, to change anything. We *have* to leave this place now, and so does young Morag. It's time for us to go, and the world of men and women cannot wait upon the love of almost-children."

The melancholy that I felt at that moment was almost insupportable, but Tress saved me from the depths of it. "You can do much to help him," she said, in a tone that pronounced my anguish to be baseless. Ignoring my philosophical maunderings, she had fastened on the crux of the matter. "You can support him through this pain. You can give him hope."

"How?" I was looking at her keenly now. "Forgive me, Tress, I don't know what you mean. Hope of what? Meeting another such goddess? He never will. Never again another first love."

"No, not another! Hope of seeing Morag again, you silly man. Her father is a king, is he not? Well, so was Arthur's. King's sons wed the daughters of other kings, is that not so? Her uncle, married to her beloved Aunt Salina, is Arthur's uncle, too, and he's another king, in his own right, the king of the Scots. Have you no plans to welcome him to Camulod some day? Well, when he comes, if you invite the lass and play the game with anything approaching wisdom, might not King Brander and his wife bring the fair Morag to visit with them, serving her aunt, as the queen's own attendant? You talk of politics, among your friends—is that not politics, to talk of binding kingdoms and close friendships? Talk about that, then, to Arthur, and see how he responds. But do it now, before he has to leave in the morning with his whole world tumbling about his ears."

I found Arthur in the dining hall, where the tables had already been prepared for supper. He was moping alone in a corner with a mug that I suspected, from the way he straightened up on seeing me and pushed it furtively aside, might be full of ale, or of forbidden, full-strength wine. I did not approach him but merely beckoned, crooking my finger at him, and then turned to walk out without waiting to see what he would do. Now that I understood his pain, I also understood his anger and I had no wish to provoke a possible confrontation in such a public place.

I walked slowly and quietly on the cobbled roadway, placing my iron-studded boots with care to reduce the noise they made, while I listened for the sounds of him following me. He was there, behind me, and I slowed even more, waiting for him to catch up to me. And then I heard Connor calling my name and I cursed quietly, even as I turned to wave and greet him. He and Brander and some others would be gathering after the evening meal, he told me, to say their mutual farewells over a jug of ale or a beaker of mead, and he hoped that I would join them. As Arthur came up beside me I reached out and gripped him gently by the back of the neck, and I told Connor that I would be glad to join them and that Arthur, too, might come along with me. We were going to talk now, I said, about an errand he must do for me the following day, but we would meet everyone at dinner and proceed from there.

Tressa was absent when we reached my quarters, but she had lit a fire in the brazier before leaving and it was evident that she had left only moments earlier. I waved Arthur to a seat and crossed directly to the carved chest that contained my mead.

"Will you drink some mead with me?"

He stared at me as if he thought I had lost my wits. He might have tasted mead before this night, but never in my company. The rule we had was simple and absolute: mead was for adults, as was wine. Boys might drink ale—one cup, no more—with dinner. Otherwise they drank water, infrequently mixed with a modicum of wine, for flavour, and occasionally they drank milk and the juice of crushed fruit when it was in season. Now I was offering him mead, in my own quarters, and I was sure the significance of that would not escape him for long.

Finally he nodded, very slowly and judiciously, evidently fearing to appear to be too eager. I poured him the same measure that I poured for myself and carried it to where he sat. He took it and watched me warily as I sat down across from him and raised my cup, saluting Bacchus in the ancient way. He pursed his lips and savoured the liquor cautiously, as though afraid of what it might do to him. Perhaps I had been wrong, I thought. Perhaps this too, like Morag, was a first.

"Well, what do you think? Your Aunt Shelagh made it." He had not said a single word since I found him, and I would have been prepared to wager that he had not, in fact, spoken since he left Tressa, in the street, an hour and more before. Now he nodded again, sucking at his cheeks.

"It's very sweet," he said, his voice pitched low. "But fiery. It catches at the throat. Makes you want to cough."

"Aye, but if you sip it, you'll find you can handle it and the urge to cough will pass." I looked into my cup. "Drink it too fast, or drink too much of it, you'll feel the urge to vomit, and *that* one is irresistible. Then, after that, depending on how much you've had, you'll think you're going to die, and if you've had *too* much, you'll sometimes wish you *could* die." I spoke slowly, overemphasizing certain words, hoping the humour of it might encourage him to smile, but he was too far gone in his self-absorbed tragedy. I decided to be direct.

"Tell me about Morag."

He flinched as though I had hit him. "What? Who?"

I sighed elaborately, gesturing with my cup. "Arthur, that is mead. It is the drink of men. I gave it to you freely, as a man. Now, I believe, we need to talk as men, about the girl Morag and the parting I have thrust on you today. I know that you and she are in love—"

"How can you know that?" His challenge was sharp-edged and defensive.

I raised my eyebrows. "Tress told me."

"And how could *she* know such a thing?"

"Because, my bold young cousin, she's a woman. Women *do* know such things. No man can hope to fool them, not for long, at least."

I stopped short. His eyes were frantic, filled with panic and with shame, fixed on some point beyond my shoulder, and his entire body was straining as though he meant to leap to his feet and run out into the night again. My heart went out to him in his needless agony.

"Arthur," I said, keeping my voice pitched low. "Look at me. Look me in the eye, Arthur." My words sank home to him and he looked at me directly, his face pale, the knuckles of his hand bone-white with the pressure he was exerting on the cup he clutched. I nodded towards that. "That cup is hard-fired clay, but you're about to break it." His face flickered with doubt, and he looked down at his hand, and then, after the space of three heartbeats, the hand relaxed and he began to stoop, to place the beaker on the floor.

"No, don't do that," I said. "Take another sip."

He did, and I watched his eyes, locked on my own, above the rim of the cup. He lowered the cup and swallowed, convulsively, fighting the urge to cough, but the panic was gone now from his eyes.

"Good. Now what is so dreadful about Tressa knowing how you feel for Morag?"

He shuddered, perhaps from the mead. "I . . . I didn't think it was so obvious. Didn't know everyone knew."

"Everyone *didn't* know. I certainly did not, for if I had I would have made allowances and warned you what must happen, given you the chance to prepare yourself for this parting in advance, you and the girl. I hope you can see that? I had no idea you felt so strongly about Morag until Tress belaboured me for my blindness. Yet I watch you all the time. So if I didn't know, then no one else knew either, among the men. If they had, they surely would have let me know, probably in jest. The women knew, but women never jest about such things as sweet young girls and brave young men in love . . . unless they're jealous, and then that's merely spite. So be at peace . . ." I allowed that to sink into his mind before I continued. "Besides, why should you feel shame? A man's love is the dearest thing in his heart, whether it be given to a woman, or to a shining cause, or to a strongly held ideal—and the love of a good woman is all three of those. Where is the shame in that, in knowing such a love, in being thus fulfilled? Love that's shared and returned is a cause for pride, Arthur. It makes towering giants out of ordinary men and gentle gods out of towering giants. Have you heard one word of what I've said?"

He sat nodding now, his face transformed, and this time when he looked at me he smiled, although fleetingly, and then his mouth drooped down again, as though afraid to lose the bitter taste of sorrow.

"What's wrong now? Come on, take another drink and spit out what you think. There are only we two here."

He gulped at the mead this time and I braced myself, prepared to leap up and pound him on the back, but the fiery drink went down without producing anything more than a brief shudder. Then he sniffed and looked me in the eye. "I'm sick in my soul, Cay, terrified to lose her. I'll never see her again once she goes home and we ride south to Camulod. She lives in Gallava . . . in *Caledonia!*"

"A different land, aye. But you're wrong, lad. You'll see her again, and soon, and I'm going to tell you how and why. But first I have some things to clarify, for myself, and for you. They are important to me—to both of us in truth—so let me deal with those, ere we move on to talk of Morag. Will you listen?"

He nodded, sipping at his drink again, more temperately this time, and I wondered how long it would take for the potent brew to work its will on him. I had, in truth, poured but a small amount for both of us, but he was unused to its effects.

"Good. Here's the crux of it, so listen closely." I stood up and moved away from him, speaking directly towards him as I moved about the room. "The main thing I want you to know is that, had I been aware of how you feel about Morag, I would not have thrust the matter upon you so suddenly and so thoughtlessly today. I would, however, have given you the same instructions, and the same restrictions would have governed your obedience to them. You must go to Derek tomorrow morning, and you must return without fail tomorrow evening. None of the imperatives governing our behaviour have changed since first I spoke to you. You have duties to perform here and, in justice, you must be seen to perform them. If you are to lead men of your own in the time ahead, you must be seen to be above claiming privileges unavailable to those you lead. A really great leader is the one who shares the burdens of his men in the small trials. They cannot take his place when great events occur, but he will share their tribulations, and then he will assume his own burden, unaided, when the crisis is at hand. At that point they will follow him and fight for his cause, and die for his objectives and his will, for love of him and what he represents: their best interests. That is true leadership, Arthur, and it is almost impossible to achieve, though thousands attempt it. And one of the most chronic difficulties in achieving it lies in the kind of thing you faced today—the temptation to advance your own desires, your own well-being, at the cost of those who depend on you and trust you to be true to them. Give in to that temptation once, and you'll do it again, and as surely as running water erodes rock, you'll destroy your own leadership."

I stopped pacing and faced him across the back of my chair, leaning my hands on the topmost rung. "That's really all I wanted to tell you. Does it make sense?"

"Aye," he said, his voice a husky growl. "It makes perfect sense."

"Good, I'm happy you see it. Now, what I said, among all that, was that you'll leave tomorrow and return tomorrow, doubtless passing Morag and the returning party on the way. But several matters have come up since first we talked of this, and I have something now to offer you." I stepped around my chair and took hold of his hand, tipping his cup towards me. There was still some mead in the bottom of it. "Do you want to finish that?"

"No, not really."

I took it from his hand and poured the remainder into my own cup.

"You heard what Connor said as we were coming here. The men will gather after dinner, to drink mead and make their farewells. It will be a celebration, probably long and noisy. The women will attend as well, of course, but there will be much drinking, and no doubt songs and music. I invited you to come with me—I mean as a man—and Connor made no objection." I sipped. "It occurs to me, however, that you might not wish to come with me. Tress, I know, has talked of returning here tonight, after dinner, to show her finest needlework to young Morag. If such things interest you, I'm sure Tress would be proud and pleased to show you her work, too. What say you?" The joy on his face was all the reward I had hoped for. "Very well, then, I'll make excuses for you to the other gathering, since you must be astir and away to Ravenglass early in the morning. Now, there's one thing more: the future. Morag is a king's daughter, and you are a king's son . . ."

I went on then to describe to him at length, using Tress's logic and words, how he would, in fact, see young Morag in years to come, providing he and I emerged victorious from our wars. By the time I had finished, he was a warrior indeed, sparks flashing from his eager eyes, and I knew he would ride into Ravenglass the next day with his soul ablaze with hopes and dreams.

I placed our empty cups on the table top and we walked together to the dining hall, my arm about his shoulders and my chest swollen with the satisfaction of hearing him talking normally again, his excitement and exuberance spilling out into my ears. He did not mention Morag once by name, but all his fire, his passion and enthusiasm, was for her and for the hope that lay ahead of them.

III

 IN MY TRAVELS the length and breadth of Britain, I have always found time and provocation to wonder at the influence of the Romans—an influence they have continued to exert long decades after their withdrawal. Perhaps one should expect no less; after all, Britain was a Roman province for nigh on five centuries and thus almost purely Roman in all its civilized ways. But the ubiquitous Romans were predominantly urbanites in Britain, seldom venturing outside the vicinity of the towns they built around their forts, which nurtured them and their civilization. Beyond the towns, the land itself knew another life, supporting other peoples who had lived according to their own ancient ways since long before Julius Caesar first turned his acquisitive eyes towards these shores. These were the true *Britanni*, the real people of Britain, and they were a tribal race, perhaps a mix of races commingled in the lost and ancient past. The Romans, with their passion for organization, named these clans according to their tribal territories, Romanizing the alien sounds of what the federations living there called themselves and labelling them *Trinovantes*, *Belgae*, *Iceni*, *Dobunni* and similar names, most of which have been long since unused.

The entire north-western area, through which we travelled first that spring, was the traditional territory of the Brigantes, the clan from which Derek and his folk had sprung, and it stretched clear across Britain to the Eastern Sea, into the area Vortigern had claimed, within living memory, as his Northumbria. We had left Ravenglass and travelled inland, north by east along the Roman road, the Tenth Iter, to a place that had been known as Brocavum and that now lay empty and abandoned, too close to the Pictish lands above the Wall to be safe for habitation. From there, we turned south, following the high road to yet another empty, ruined fort, this one much smaller and so long forgotten that its name had been lost, despite the fact that it stood at a crossroads. We spent a pleasant afternoon and night in the shelter of its crumbling walls, then swung west on the right arm of the crossroad for a few miles, before turning southward again at an unnamed bridge over the river there. After travelling some fifty miles, we gained the westward fork that would bring us to Deva, the great fortress town of the Twentieth Valeria Victrix Legion.

There, even decades after it had been abandoned by its renowned garrison, we found that little had changed. The great fortress that had stood invulnerable and inviolable for so many scores of decades had not yet begun to bow its mighty head to decay, and it hosted a strong and self-sufficient populace who had no patience with visiting soldiery, even those who came in peace. These people, presumably descendants of the *Cornovii* whose ancient territory this was, called their fortress home Chester, a corruption of the Latin word *castra*, meaning the fort or camp. Although the people there showed us no overt belligerence, they locked and barred their massive gates against us and disdained to recognize our overtures of peace and friendship. Regretfully, we left them to their self-willed isolation and continued southward, embarking now upon a journey of more than two hundred miles, on roads that stretched through otherwise impenetrable forest, towards the town the Romans had called Corinium, which had been, for untold centuries, the main territorial town of the Dobunni. From Corinium it would be a mere fifty miles to Aquae Sulis, and from there another overnight camp would bring us within reach of Camulod.

Only near the fort towns where the Roman garrisons and their suppliers once lived had we seen signs of organized, if limited, agriculture: cleared lands, regular fields and marked divisions and boundaries. Now, however, as we approached Corinium, the forests fell away and disappeared and we found ourselves moving through what had evidently once been an arable, treeless landscape with extensive meadows and even cultivated fields, some of which, despite having lain fallow for decades, still showed clear lines of boundaries distinguishing each from its neighbours. We saw no signs of recent agriculture in the first few miles of this terrain; what had once been fertile fields were grossly overgrown with weeds and thistles, rioting shrubs and acres of thriving saplings. Eventually, however, we reached an area where small plots of land had recently been ploughed and planted. These were few and far between, at first, but as we neared the district surrounding Corinium, the cultivated plots grew larger and more numerous. Less than one quarter of the land available had been ploughed or planted, but every field, including those that lay fallow and overgrown, showed the evidence that proclaimed its origins in Roman organization.

"They grow bigger and more numerous as we approach the town, but you'll see no sign of the farmers." The words, spoken close to my ear, startled me out of my musings and I turned towards Philip, the commander of the Camulodian cavalry column, who had been riding by my side in silence for more than a mile. He must have been watching me eyeing the fields and had read my mind. As I thought about what he had said, I thought, too, fleetingly and irrelevantly, about this mind reading ability among close comrades. Philip and I had been through much together, as close friends and comrades-in-arms. We had soldiered together as trainee troopers and junior officers and he had been one of the faithful companions who rode with me into Eire to reclaim the infant Arthur from the Scots who held him hostage against the safe return of their prince, Donuil Mac Athol. Small wonder then, I thought, that he should read my thoughts so clearly. Philip, who had been riding by my side in silence for more than a mile, must have been watching me eyeing the fields and had read my mind. I shifted my sore buttocks, grimacing and grunting involuntarily as I silently cursed the unyielding hardness of the saddle that had made them so painful.

"I had noticed that they seem shy," I growled. "But why won't I see any sign of them?"

Philip grinned before he answered, his eyes flicking downward to my seat. "Because they've learned to stay well away from targets. Growing things—fresh foodstuffs—attract two-legged predators. They fade into the greenwood the moment any unknown faces appear in the region. Farmers nowadays are a strange breed. They've grown afraid of strangers since the armies left, and who can blame them?" Seized by a sudden cramp I shifted again, bracing myself in the stirrups and vainly trying to show no reaction as the movement sent a fresh spasm of pain through my buttocks. His grin widened at the sight of my obvious discomfort. "You've been spending too much time afoot, these past years, Commander Merlyn."

"Aye," I agreed wryly, "but we've been in the saddle now for fourteen straight days. My seat should be toughened again by this time."

Philip laughed and shook his head. "This has been a long day. My own backside is sore enough that I can think of nothing else but climbing down. We camped close by here on the way up—an old legionary marching camp on the right of the road, about two miles further on, close by a clear stream. There's little left of it by this time—you can barely see where the old dirt walls used to be—but it's a good spot and still defensible, should the need arise."

"Excellent. Then we'll use it, soon, I hope." I reached down and dug my fingertips tentatively into my right buttock, then winced from the pain of it. "Tell me more about the local farmers. Ambrose told me some time ago that they had started gathering close by the old Roman towns again but were not living in them. Where do they live, then?"

Philip shrugged, lifting himself up in his stirrups to look over his shoulder, checking on the group that stretched out behind us. Satisfied that all was as it should be, he settled into the saddle again and eased the weight of his helmet from his forehead, loosening the catch beneath his chin and pushing the brim of the heavy headpiece upward with his thumb.

"Anywhere they can find a place that offers them some safety. And you're right, they avoid the towns." He hawked and spat, leaning forward and away from me. "That seems strange, I know," he continued, straightening again and curbing his horse, which had shied at the sound of his spitting close by its ear. "But it's as it should be. The towns attract unwelcome attention from visitors, and the walls around them too often represent more of a prison than a defence. They also tend to avoid living together in groups of families, and that's something new to me, although I can see a certain sense to it. There was a time when strength in numbers meant safety, but that's no longer the case when the threat to your safety comes from greater numbers who are better armed and trained to fight in concert. Under those conditions, the surest safety lies in flight, and the advantage of flight lies in being alone, or at least fleeing in the smallest possible group.

"The farmers nowadays tend to isolate themselves in small, tight family units. Each family takes care of its own fields from a distance, travelling to and from them every day. It makes sense, considering the risks involved in growing crops. If a family decides to tackle it at all—and they really have no choice—they'll farm at least two fields, but more often three or more, and they take care that each is as distant from the others as possible. Once the crops are ready to be harvested in safety, then they'll bring them in as quietly as possible, one field at a time. If a crop is lost for any reason—if one, let's say, is harvested by bandits forcing locals to do the work for them—why then the family simply hopes that their remaining fields will rest untouched, and they'll be able to live off those crops. In the meantime, they live in a hut or a lean-to somewhere close to the woods. If they're threatened, they flee into the forest, and if their hovel is burned or torn down, they can build another just like it within a day or so."

As I listened to Philip, the realization came to me, tinged with a sense of shame, that I had never thought, analytically, about the lives of ordinary people, out here in the open countryside, without the benefit of a colony or a fortified town to protect them. While I had dreamed of the future of Britain in the safety of my secluded fort, with the strength of Camulod's troops and all the trappings of Roman civilization at my disposal, these people—the very people who would live out that dream and bring it to fruition—were leading lives that were brutal, bloody and fearful. I found myself staring at Philip, appalled both by the implications of his words, and by the casual way he uttered them. I had to fight down an unjust urge to turn the rough edge of my tongue on him. Instead, I forced myself to sit quietly and look about me until I had regained control of my suddenly turbulent emotions.

"So," I said eventually. "I have not heard you say so, but you give me the impression you believe these people deserve their lot in life?"

Philip looked at me now as if I were the one saying appalling things, and then his eyes narrowed and he nodded, a tiny gesture of acknowledgement. "They live the only kind of life they know, Commander, and it *is* their lot, beyond our power to change or influence." I noted his use of my formal title, rather than the name he was entitled to use as an old friend. "All we can do is thank God our lives are as they are, and not like theirs. Short of establishing a garrison in Corinium, which would be impossible, I can't think of a thing we could do to improve their lot."

I grunted, and spurred my horse to a trot, leaving Philip behind. He made no effort to catch up to me, and for the next half hour I rode alone, mulling over what he had told me.

I was still thinking on it when we reached the appointed campground and our people began setting up our tents and horse-lines for the night. I maintained my distance from everyone, even at supper, carrying my meal away and sitting alone with my thoughts. Tress obviously knew that I had some concern or other nagging at me. She was clever enough and considerate enough to keep her distance and allow me to stew in my own juices for as long as necessary, knowing that I would come to her soon. I was grateful to her for that, and aware that she would also keep others away from me.

Philip and the others might think of these farm folk as a breed apart, but I knew that opinion to be a vessel that would not hold water. Most of the soldiers of Camulod, and the majority of our most worthy Colonists, had been drawn from this region and from the ranks of these same people. We had been forced to close our gates against the others, immuring ourselves for our own protection and welfare in the face of the impossibility of feeding and protecting everyone in Britain. This was something I had always known and accepted, from my earliest boyhood. Why then, I asked myself, should I be feeling guilt and anger at myself now?

I was still thinking the same discomforting thoughts as I made my way to my tent, but there was to be little sleep for me that night. I had barely begun to unbuckle my armour when I heard a minor commotion outside. I refastened my harness and made my way back out into the firelight, wondering what was happening. At first I could see nothing, although the rising sounds of voices and approaching feet told me that I would, soon. I started towards the centre of the encampment and saw the crowd come into view: at least half a score of men carrying spears and looking purposeful. Philip had emerged from the headquarters tent and was moving towards them, but as I approached the central fire I heard my name being called quietly and saw Dedalus coming towards me. He held up his hand to silence me before I could speak, and, taking me by the elbow, he steered me away from the fire again.

"We have a prisoner."

"A prisoner? Ded, we're not at war."

"Well then, we have an unwilling guest."

"Who is he?"

"I don't know. A local, I suppose. Falvo's people picked him up, on the far leg of their patrol. He was alone, and armed. He tried to run and they surrounded him. Didn't know what to do with him, so they brought him back."

"Very well, then, what was it about this man that made Falvo decide to bring him in? I'm presuming the man's no ordinary farmer, otherwise, knowing Falvo, he'd have knocked him on the head and left him there asleep, where they found him. And yet you said the fellow's local."

"Well, that's my guess, but he's no local Celt. I'm sure of that. He's Roman or I'm a barbarian. And judging from his clothing and weapons, he's wealthy."

"What d'you mean, *Roman?*"

The answer was preceded by a snort of impatience. "What should I mean? He's short, squat, arrogant, black-eyed, clean-shaven, and he's got a beak like an eagle. He's as Roman as I am."

I sighed. "Hmm. Roman, well dressed, well armed and wealthy. Well, we haven't seen much evidence of his like around here. So let's go and meet him." I paused, looking across the fire to Falvo's patrol. "Before we do that, though, perhaps you should tell me exactly what happened."

The knot of men surrounding the newcomer was no more than ten long paces from where Ded and I stood watching, and I could see the glint of firelight reflecting from their spearheads. Philip, who was Officer of the Watch, was huddled there with Falvo, slightly apart from the group, his head down as he listened. I looked beyond them, hoping to find a glimpse of the stranger, but I could see only my own men. Dedalus, in the meantime, had launched into his account.

"Falvo and his troop were at the far end of their sweep, about ten miles from here—"

"Ten miles? What in Hades was he doing that far away?"

Dedalus shrugged. "What he was supposed to be doing, scouting. He had good reason to be there, too. Falvo will tell you all of it himself, in his patrol report, but I think you should hear the gist of it now, before you speak to our pris—, to our guest. They were about five miles out, on a normal, uneventful sweep, when one of Falvo's men remarked that the fields they were riding through were very different to those they'd passed earlier. They were bigger, and more of them were under cultivation. Falvo realized the man was right and that the further they went, the more fields they saw, but they'd seen no farms, no houses, no people. He was curious, and so he decided to keep riding. Within a few more miles, they were riding through the richest farmland Falvo has ever seen. He says it looks as though someone has organized land holdings out there at least as big as ours in the Colony.

"They were riding in an arc, veering eastward and following a river valley, looking for any signs of life they could find, and they saw none. It was about mid-afternoon, and Falvo told me he was starting to grow itchy—not because he was afraid, but because he knew he was well beyond where he ought to be, out of touch with us. Anyone he met out there would be hostile—because they'd think he and his men were up to no good. And he was beginning to realize, too, that trouble could come in large numbers. Hundreds of fields, hundreds of angry people.

"Falvo decided to finish his sweep then and there by swinging east. There's a road there, which leads directly south again to join this one just outside Corinium. Then he discovered that there's a mile-thick belt of forest between the fields and the road—obviously a screen to discourage visitors. As they approached the edge of the trees, riding in skirmish line abreast, one of his men, Samuel Cato, flushed our visitor, by sheer accident. The fellow's a fighter, that much is obvious. He attacked Cato on foot immediately he was discovered. Charged right at him with only a shortsword. He should have died right then and there, but he succeeded in frightening Cato's horse and unseating him. He ran then, making no attempt to injure Cato once he was unhorsed, but before he could get away the troopers on either side caught up to him and one of them, seeing what the fellow was wearing, tripped him by thrusting a spear between his feet. Knocked the wind out of him, apparently, and by the time he recovered they had him in custody."

"What was he wearing?"

"Armour—Roman armour."

"Hmm. Quick thinking on the part of the trooper who tripped him. He should be commended. Was Cato badly hurt?"

"Only in his dignity. He'll be more careful in future. Anyway, as soon as Falvo saw what this fellow looked like, he thought you might like to talk to him, so he brought him in under guard, although he did permit the man to keep his weapons. Fellow was on foot, and only had a short-sword and a dagger, but he seemed honourable. That was Falvo's word. It impressed me, coming from him. Anyway, Falvo spoke to the fellow in Latin, told him he wasn't really a prisoner but that he'd have to come along, and asked him for his parole not to attempt escape, in return for being able to ride behind one of the men. I met up with them a couple of miles from here, down where the road forks, and the rest you know. And now, if you're going to ask me what I think you should do, I've no idea."

I smiled. "We have absolutely no idea who he is?"

"No, nor where he comes from. Only thing we know is that he was either there alone or he has very pusillanimous friends."

"Hmm," I grunted again, my thoughts racing. "Well, let's find out."

As we approached the group on the other side of the fire, I saw the stranger notice me and fasten his attention on me. The others fell back on either side, and Dedalus stopped a few paces to my rear. Soon I stood facing the newcomer, taking his measure as he was taking mine.

Dedalus was right. This man was a fighter—it was stamped into his bearing. And there was no mistaking his Roman heritage, even had he not been wearing the telltale armour; his Romanness leaped from his face and form as though written there in letters of light. His stance and bearing showed that he was accustomed to deference and to obedience—more than a mere fighter, this was a leader of men, and the fact that I towered over him by a full head and more made absolutely no difference in my assessment of him. Publius Varrus, years earlier, had described the Emperor Honorius's regent, Flavius Stilicho, as a Vandal hawk; the man who faced me now was the same type, radiating menace, self-confidence and absolute competence. He was young, on the lighter side of thirty, his well-formed muscles full of the vigour of prime manhood. High, sharp cheekbones defined a lean face with a wide mouth, narrow lips and deep, dark, sunken eyes on either side of a dominating, sharp-ridged, aquiline nose. The breadth of his high forehead was emphasized by the sharp widow's peak of hair that bisected it, reminding me fleetingly of Lucanus and drawing my attention to the raptor-like quality of the face beneath. He was clean-shaven, and his hair was close-shorn in the Roman fashion.

From his broad, strong shoulders, a dark-red cloak hung, fastened in the Roman manner through the breast-rosettes of the metal cuirass he wore. He wore a quilted, knee-length tunic of thick, white wool, and an officer's kirtle of heavy, armoured straps was belted about his waist. The red cloak showed clear signs of having been carefully repaired in several places, and the relief work and decorative rosettes on his metal breastplate were worn almost smooth from years of polishing. The same polished lustre of loving care betrayed itself on the worn scrollwork of the bronze-sheathed sword and dagger at his waist.

I returned my gaze to his eyes, which, as he stared back at me, betrayed nothing of his thoughts. I nodded, keeping my own expression benign, if noncommittal.

"Welcome," I said quietly, "although you may doubt my sincerity at this point. May we know your name?"

He sucked in one cheek, biting it as he gazed at me, narrow-eyed, and considered his response. "Call me *Abductus*," he said eventually, his voice betraying no emotion.

I nodded, twisting my own mouth to hide an admiring smile. "Hardly accurate," I responded mildly. "You were not really abducted, nor were you taken prisoner. You were merely invited—"

"Forcibly . . ."

I nodded. "Forcibly, and I suspect tacitly, but nonetheless invited, to attend us here for purposes of mutual examination. You still wear your weapons, no? Prisoners and abductees are seldom permitted that."

The black eyes were flat and unreadable. "Who are you, and what do you want of me?"

"We'll come to that, but first I have to ask you why you were spying on my men."

"What?" He spat the word in disbelief, then struggled with his anger before he could school his face once more to show nothing. When he resumed, his tone was flat again. "Your men were on my land, among my crops, trespassing close to my home."

"I see. You live alone, farming so many fields?"

I saw him frown, but my eyes had returned to the worn short-sword by his side. I knew that I was being foolish, allowing it to distract me, no matter what I thought I saw in it.

"Does it surprise you that I should farm my own fields?"

A clever answer to an unexpected question, but I pressed on. "Dressed as you are, yes, it does. You are no farmer. Your armour makes a liar out of you."

He looked down at himself, then back at me. "I wear this seldom, nowadays. I am a farmer, first and foremost, as were the soldiers of Rome in ancient times. I take up the sword only when I need to. The presence of your people gave me cause. And as a soldier, I have given you all the information you will receive from me."

"Very well." I could feel the others all looking hard at me. "I shall respect your wish to remain silent. But would you mind showing me your sword? I'm sure you realize," I added, seeing the sudden suspicion in his eyes, "that had we wished to harm you, you would now be dead. May I?"

I held out my hand, and he hesitated for only a moment before un-hooking the short-sword and passing it over to me. I held it up close and examined the scabbard, then eased the sword itself partly from its sheath. Sure enough, as I had expected, there was a tiny "V" stamped into the top of the blade, just below the hilt.

"How did you come by this?"

He frowned again, clearly wondering how such a thing could have any importance, and then he blinked and shrugged his shoulders.

"It was my father's. And before that, it was his father's."

"So it belonged to your grandfather. Where did he obtain it, do you know?"

He had decided to humour me, it seemed, yet when he spoke his voice betrayed contempt. "How could I know that? He was an old man when I was born. Grandfathers are, you know."

"Yes, I know." I ignored his truculence completely. "But I had good reason for asking the question. My great-uncle made this sword. His name was Varrus. He was a sword-maker, but some of his weapons, a very few—his special, finest works—he stamped with his personal mark, V for Varrus. He gave those only to his friends. This is one of them, so your grandfather and my great-uncle must have known each other. Look for yourself."

I tossed the sword back to him and he caught it deftly, pulling the blade partway out and peering at the mark, twisting it to catch the fire's light. He stood gazing at it for a space of heartbeats, then straightened up, sheathed the blade completely and clipped the scabbard back onto his belt before looking back at me.

"I don't know what you are about," he said. "But I don't believe you. I don't believe in coincidences—not like that. You looked first, and then made up the rest."

I was ready for him, however, and had already unclipped my own sheathed dagger. "There's no coincidence. I simply recognized my uncle's handiwork. Look at the scrollwork on that sheath, then look at the V." I tossed the dagger to him as I spoke.

He looked at it as I had told him to, then handed it back. He cleared his throat, his expression, for the first time, suggesting uncertainty.

"My name is Caius Britannicus, and I have some excellent mead in the headquarters tent. May I offer you some? I think we two have much to talk about. Thank you, gentlemen," I added, looking around at my men. "You may leave us now."

I turned on my heel and walked directly to the single large tent in the middle of our encampment, knowing without looking that our visitor was walking behind me, and trying to imagine what he must be thinking.

The tent was brightly lit and empty for the moment, although I did not expect that to last for long. Philip, as Officer of the Watch, would be returning shortly and would have need of the table and the lights. I poured a cup of the amber liquid for myself and my "guest" from the flask of mead kept in a chest by the Officer of the Watch for special occasions. He took the cup I offered him and sat in the chair I indicated, moving slowly, his eyes on mine. Then he sighed quietly and sipped at the drink. Only after he had savoured it, rolling it around on his tongue, did he allow himself to relax slightly and lean back. I sat opposite him and waited.

"So," he said, eventually. "You are Caius Britannicus. I am Appius Niger." He raised his cup in a small, ironic salute. "My thanks for the welcome. What do we do now?"

I smiled. "We talk."

"To what end?"

"To an end of hostility, I should think. We have much in common."

He pursed his lips and his eyes flicked from me to the appointments of the tent in which we sat. It was high and roomy and four-cornered, six paces long on each side with a twin-peaked roof supported by poles and guy-ropes, and it was made from score upon score of uniform panels of soft leather, assiduously stitched together with strong, waxed twine so as to be both waterproof and windproof. It could hold a score of people in comfort and was military in every respect, clearly a command point for a mobile expedition. To his credit, my guest made no comment on any of that, unwilling, I assumed, to volunteer any information even by comparing what we had to what he might not have. Instead, he confined himself to responding to what I had already said.

"Our names are both Roman, but the Romans are long departed. Beyond that, I can find little in common between us.

"Well then," I offered, "let me make a suggestion. We are both of Roman descent, as you say, and we live here in Britain. That means we both have learned to live in amity with the Celts here. And that sets us both squarely against the newcomers who have been swarming over Britain since the armies left."

He sat without moving for several moments more, then sniffed. "The newcomers. You mean the *Picti*, the Painted People from beyond the Wall in the north?"

"Aye, in part, although I doubt they come this far south in any organized manner. But I also mean the Danes and the Saxons."

"We have had no trouble from either of those. We have heard of them, of course, the Saxons at least, but they are only names, nightmare names with which to frighten children."

I shrugged. "Nightmare names, perhaps, but you have been singularly fortunate if you have lived this long without ever meeting any of them. Only a few years ago, not far south of here, in Glevum, we encountered Berbers from the Central Sea. Corsairs, raiding here in a massive Roman bireme. They were stripping the marble from the public buildings in the town there, presumably to sell it beyond the seas, and they'll be back. When they've stripped everything of value from the towns close by the coast, they'll venture further inland. The Saxons and the Danes, for the time being, are content to remain in the eastern parts of the country, but they won't stay there forever, not when there is rich land to be had here in the west. You gull yourself if you believe you'll never meet them."

Appius Niger sipped again at his mead, giving every indication of appreciating its excellence, then looked me in the eye and nodded slightly. "I've no doubt you're right. But our main difficulty until now has lain in dealing with wanderers, people from other parts of the country who range abroad looking to relieve people like me of crops and livestock." He paused, then added, "People like you."

"No." My denial was instantaneous but not defensive. "You've had, and you will have, no difficulty with us." I kept right on, ignoring his attempt to interrupt with some caustic comment about having been abducted. I did not raise my voice but merely kept speaking over his objections. "We have no interest in your lands or in your crops, other than to take note of their existence, since we had not expected to find their like near here. Our scouting party was withdrawing when it encountered you, and having seen you and the style of your armour, the commander decided to bring you back with him, to me."

"And you are Caius Britannicus. Should I be impressed?"

His effrontery amused me. I found myself liking him, despite his attitude. "No," I replied. "But I'm also known as Merlyn, of Camulod."

The change that came into his face was immediate, but I could not define it. He sat up straighter, however, and I sensed a sharp, sudden tension in him. My immediate thought was that he had reacted like a woodland stag, alert by nature and suddenly attuned to danger. Yet when he spoke, there was nothing of this in his words.

"Now there's a name I've heard," he drawled, his voice and face devoid of all expression.

"Well, now you have a face to put with it. What have you heard of me?"

"That you serve excellent mead." He emptied his cup and held it out to me. "More, if I may."

When I had finished pouring and replaced the flask a second time, I stood by the table that held the chest and looked down at him. "What else?"

He tilted his head, appearing more at ease by the moment. "That you have a fabulous kingdom, far to the south, with an invincible army, supplied by the Empire." That made me laugh. "Don't tell me you're denying it!" he continued. "You and your men are wearing the evidence that proves it."

That sobered me, and I placed my cup quickly on the table before stepping closer to him.

"I can't believe you might be stupid enough to believe such twaddle, Niger. The Romans have been gone for generations now, and they will not be coming back."

He blinked at me, keeping his face expressionless, but made no effort to reply. For long moments I hovered there, standing over him, before I stepped away, took up my drink again and lowered myself into a chair. Then I told him about Camulod. I told him we wore the Roman armour because of its superiority and because the legacy of our founding craftsmen, Publius Varrus first among them, enabled us to make it still. I went on to tell him of my grandfather, Caius Britannicus, and his dream of founding a defensible community that could survive the departure of the legions, and finally I outlined the role played by my father, Picus, in building our near-invincible cavalry.

"You've seen my men, and their horses," I concluded. "We are no more than a small patrol, an exploratory force. I promise you the world has seen nothing like the cavalry of Camulod since the days of Alexander of Macedon, the man they called Alexander the Great because he used cavalry to conquer the world."

Appius was listening intently, his face rapt, and I drove onward.

"Now I command the army of Camulod jointly with my brother, Ambrose. The cavalry is mine, by and large. The infantry is his, equally so. The Colony, however, is governed by a Council of Elders. It is a fine place to live. We have no slaves, no poverty and no deprivation. We are self-sufficient in food and in other resources, and we are strong enough to withstand danger from outside—at least, we have been until now." I paused, for a space of three heartbeats, then continued. "Now, what have you to tell me of yourself?"

Once again, my question was met with blank-faced silence, but my patience was at an end.

"Appius Niger, think of what I have said. If my people and I were hungry for conquest, we should already be making plans to conquer you and lay your possessions waste. You were the one who spoke of our 'Roman' army. Believe me when I say it is substantial. Nothing would be easier for us than to return to Camulod—which, incidentally, is a mere four-day journey from here—and then ride back at the head of a force that would obliterate whatever you might rally to meet us. We would find you—you cannot hide a settlement any more than you can hide fields. So be sensible. Believe me when I tell you that we have no plans to conquer or enslave you or to steal from you. Then be even more sensible and ask me what I have in mind for you."

He started to drink again, but his hand stopped before it reached his mouth, and then he slowly reached down and placed the cup on the floor by his feet, looking carefully to see that he did not spill it. Finally he looked back at me, and again, knowing how his thoughts must have been racing throughout all this, I had to admire his self-possession.

"Very well, then, what *do* you have in mind for me?"

"I know you have a community, simply because of the number and richness of your fields, and I know, by the same logic, that it must be a strong one . . . reasonably so, at any rate. I think I might be able to advise you on how to strengthen it further. I'm no magician, but logic, applied judiciously, can perform seemingly magical things, and I pride myself on being logical."

"Hmm." He sat staring at the wall opposite him for a count of ten, then pursed his lips and sucked air through them sharply. His decision was made.

"My family calls me Nero," he said. "Don't ask me why, because the reason is long lost, but that's my name." He leaned down to recover his cup of mead and sipped at it reflectively, clearly ordering his thoughts. Then, when he had satisfied himself that what he had to say was right, he began to speak, and I listened for the next quarter of an hour.

The story he told was much akin to ours in Camulod, but with several large and significant differences.

He came of wealthy Roman–British family, the Appius clan, collectively called Niger for the blackness of their hair and eyes and the swarthiness of their skin. He was the first-born of the fifth generation bred in Britain. Despite his youth, he was currently the *paterfamilias*, the senior surviving Appius following his father's recent death. His grandfather, he told me, had been dead these twenty years.

The Appius clan had settled enormous holdings more than a century earlier, in this fertile region to the north and east of Corinium. Their family lands, which had no name of their own, had lain close enough to Corinium for the town to be both the source of their supplies and the destination for their saleable crops, but they were, at the same time, far enough removed from the town that this business required a well-regulated schedule of excursions. They were also far enough removed from the town, he added with some pride, to allow the Nigers to maintain a community that was uninfluenced by the urbanites of Corinium.

Then, with the departure of the legions four decades and more earlier, enormous changes had taken place. Their markets had disappeared within three years, because the fleets of seagoing vessels that had shipped their corn and oats no longer plied the dangerous waters off Britain, afraid of the pirates that had begun swarming everywhere even before the Navy had departed. The port towns themselves had quickly been deserted by the suddenly defenceless people who had lived in them for so long, secure in the Roman presence. Commerce vanished overnight. Money became worthless. Hunger soon became commonplace among those people who had neither the skills nor the wherewithal to produce their own food, and plunder and pillage became widespread in a region that had known only peaceful trade and amicable living for centuries.

The Niger community had had no long-sighted Caius Britannicus to prepare it in advance for such catastrophe, and no Publius Varrus to supply its people with the tools they would require in order to survive in harsher times. In spite of that, however, they had managed to adapt very quickly to their new circumstances. Soldiers and tacticians they had aplenty, for the Niger family had served the Empire well for centuries. Nero's grandfather, accurately gauging the extent and ramifications of the earliest changes—a drastic decrease in the quantity of crops being planted and raised and an equally radical increase in the amount of work necessary to protect those crops against depredation—had quickly directed his now-idle farmers to the reclamation and refurbishment of an ancient Roman encampment near the home farm. The camp, a long-disused marching camp, was situated more than a mile from the nearest road and had lain abandoned for more than a hundred years and probably closer to two hundred, but its outlines were classical and clearly marked, and in its day it had offered ample, if Spartan, accommodations for a transient cohort of five hundred men. The Appius farmers, glad of a purpose and a clear

objective once again, had had the place rebuilt and strongly fortified
within the year.

Then, realizing the strength and safety offered by the refurbished fort,
they had moved their families and dependants within their newly raised
walls and redefined their arable holdings, arranging them so that every
field they farmed was defensible and within easy reach. That meant abandoning many outlying fields, as we had done in Camulod at first, and
clearing new lands from the forest around their new fort, so that their
collective farms came to form a broad, irregular circle, the extent of which
was determined by the distance a column of men could march to its
defense within half a day. That, too, stirred memories in me, for until the
development of our cavalry strength, we in Camulod had been bound by
the same constraints.

Since then, their entire community had adapted constantly, making
adjustments and accommodations for a host of circumstances and events.
Where every man had initially been a farmer, all were now soldiers or, at
the very least, fighters, able to defend themselves individually and capable
of joining together to form a united front should the need arise. They did
not all drill regularly, every day, in the way of traditional soldiers, Nero
said, but they learned the techniques and disciplines appropriate to the
weapons they had, sufficient to enable them to fight together as a group.

I interrupted to ask how many men they had currently under arms.
His response was that they had a central core of a round hundred men,
and they went to great lengths to keep that number whole. This central
cadre was tightly disciplined and close to professional in its capabilities,
according to the senior soldier in their ranks, a grizzled veteran of seventy
years who had seen service with the legions. Nero's father had commanded
the cadre before his death. Now it was Nero's charge.

In addition to that hundred, he told me, they had a fluctuating
strength of perhaps sixty more, who trained irregularly and individually,
and who were nominally kept in reserve, their primary duty being to the
fields of grain, rather than the field of war. I could see from his tiny smile
that Nero was quite pleased with his analogy.

I nodded, waiting for him to continue, but he had evidently said all
he intended to say.

"So how often are you called upon to fight?"

"Not often, thank God. We discovered long ago that a good show of
force is often a sufficient deterrent. That's why we keep our hundred on
their toes and disciplined. Ten ten-man squads look impressive, when they
form up quickly and appear to know what they're about. Nine times out
of ten the opposition simply drifts away, in search of easier conquest."

"Then I must ask you this: how came you to be alone when our men
found you?"

Nero shrugged. "Mere accident. I was hunting, and when first I saw your men, I hid, more out of curiosity than fear. Uniformed horsemen was a phenomenon I'd never seen before."

"Are you saying that you hunt in armour? What in God's name were you hunting?"

This time he laughed aloud. "No, no! Truth told, I had words with my wife this morning and stormed out in a rage, with no thought of where I was going. I was wearing my armour at the time, because I had been drilling with my men, and I took my bow and arrows with me merely because I had been carrying them when I went home. Denalda was out of sorts and angry at me for something I had not done—are you married?"

I shook my head. "Not yet."

"Don't do it, ever. Anyway, I was fuming—wives have more power to reduce a man to gibbering than any enemy—and I walked heedlessly for miles, until the weight of my armour told me I was tiring and had been stupid. I sat down under a tree—this must have been shortly after noon—and while I was sitting there, I saw a stag entering the woods in the distance. I shrugged out of my armour, gratefully enough, took up my bow and arrows, and went hunting.

"About an hour later, perhaps more, I saw the first of your men riding through our fields. As I said, I grew curious, and so I watched them for a while, trying to discover whether or not they might be hostile. My intelligence told me they must be, but their demeanour—simply the way they were riding—indicated otherwise. After a time, I crept away to where I had left my armour and put it on again, thinking to return home and alert my people. Only moments after that, your men changed direction and came straight towards where I was sitting. I tried to hide. The rest you know."

"Hmm. So you have, what? Five hundred people, more or less, living in your fort?"

"More than that. We're nigh unto a thousand nowadays, counting women and children. We outgrew the fort itself more than ten years ago, and there's a thriving community now, outside the walls. It was inevitable. There simply wasn't room for all the workshops we required—the pottery and the barrel-maker's shop, the cobbler's workshop and the tiler's yard, the alehouse and the bakery, not to mention the cattle pens and stock yards. Surely you must have those in Camulod?"

"Aye, we do, but our fort stands on a hilltop. Have you enlarged your walls to protect your vicus?"

"No. We've been discussing it for years, and everyone agrees that something ought to be done. It's our greatest and most dangerous weakness. We know our situation is perilous, the way things stand today. Some day, someone is going to come marching—or riding—against us, and if we are as unprepared then as we are today, we will all suffer for it. The truth, though, incredible as it may seem when discussing it like this, is that when it comes to committing the real, sustained effort for what will be a long and difficult task, there always seems to be a more pressing need at hand, and the building is deferred yet again." He paused, considering, then added, "People are lazy when they don't feel threatened . . . or when they lack a decisive leader who will simply demand obedience."

"Are you indecisive?"

He looked at me, that wry half-smile still in place. "No, but I'm young and too recently come to power. Too many interests, longer set than mine, take precedence."

"Then you must change that."

"I know that. What I don't know is how."

I grinned at him. "Would you like to hear my idea now? It's still a bit thin, but we might be able to expand it, working together."

"I think I might, now," he said, nodding his head. "Because I've just had an idea of my own."

"Good. No more mead, for now. Come, walk with me and meet some of my men while I show you how a cavalry encampment operates."

IV

Our ideas melded together very quickly, and Nero Niger threw himself wholeheartedly into the easy relationship that I had sensed might be possible between us. We had both had the same idea: that our presence in his territory, properly used, might convince his people of the need to improve their defences immediately. But our discussions went much further than that, towards an idea that made the lesson we would deliver to his people seem almost inconsequential by comparison.

As is so often the case with matters of real significance, the constituent parts came together very gradually at first, but then they fused together at the end in a crescendo of insights and explosive recognition. I can clearly recall being genuinely surprised to discover, towards the end of our deliberations, that my problem with respect to the people in the lands beyond Camulod concerned nothing less than the goals of the original Colony founded by Caius Britannicus and Publius Varrus—adaptation and survival in the face of the unthinkable. My unexpected and intense involvement with Nero Niger and his Appius clan over the course of the ensuing few weeks provided the different perspective that stripped the shutters from my mind and allowed me to see the path I had been unaware of for so long.

I have resisted the temptation to describe what happened in those weeks as a beginning, because that would be inaccurate—the true beginnings had come decades earlier. Publius Varrus had witnessed the beginning of our Colony on his wedding night, before the birth of my own mother, and had described it as a birthing, the emergence of potential independence and self-sufficiency in Britain. The Roman evacuations at the start of the new century had been another beginning: the beginning of vulnerability and uncertainty in what had been, for hundreds of years, a strong and vibrant outpost of the Empire; the beginning of the invasions that now threatened the very existence of the people who for centuries had called this country home. What happened during those few weeks with Nero Niger was more akin to the start of a new phase of progress.

The end of the first phase, I came to realize long afterward, had been initiated when the first, hundred-plus-strong detachment of Camulodian cavalry had been dispatched in support of Dergyll ap Griffyd's war in

Cambria, years earlier. That force had remained in the field for nigh on two years, engaging in very little warfare and living in encampments the entire time. Because their movements had been constant and ranged the length and breadth of southern Cambria, it would never have occurred to anyone concerned to think of those troopers as garrison troops, but that is precisely what they were, although their role had been ambassadorial rather than purely military: a mobile, reinforcing presence, the potential force of which had kept the enemy from descending from the hills before Dergyll could crush them. That expedition, marking the first time a self-sufficient corps of our troopers had sustained itself away from home, operating independently of Camulod, was a test of our Colony's ability to shape the events governing other, friendly groups.

Similarly, the establishment of a garrison in Mediobogdum, regularly supplied with reinforcements, replacement personnel, weapons, and horses from Camulod, had demonstrated that the Colony was now strong enough to be able to maintain its own forces plus another army, small as it might be, hundreds of miles distant, without major inconvenience. That we were on our way home, having abandoned our briefly held outpost in the far north-west, was no reflection on the success of the garrison. What was important, what really mattered most, was that we had lived there for more than half a decade, and that the garrison we had installed there during that time had functioned with complete success, integrating itself seamlessly with the local inhabitants, coexisting with them in harmony and to mutual benefit. Logic dictated, therefore, that a Camulodian garrison could conceivably flourish anywhere in Britain.

It was the seed of that realization that prompted me to consider the dilemma of the Appius clan and their small army and too-small walls. And out of my solution to that dilemma, simple as it was, came progress.

We had decided, by the end of that first night, that Nero would return home the following day and say nothing of his encounter with us. The day after that, we would stage a mock attack on his holdings, with the object of frightening his people badly enough to make them see that, next time, such an attack might be real, and they had better be prepared. The plan, simple enough on the surface, required a full strategy session, attended by every officer we had, followed by a briefing of our entire complement. The last thing any of us wanted was for a single drop of blood to be spilled in the course of this demonstration. On the following morning, therefore, I convened the officers' session, and then followed it up with a briefing to our troopers, outlining the objectives of the exercise, from their viewpoint, and introducing them in the process to Nero Niger.

Nero left to return home as soon as the assembly had been dismissed, and Dedalus and I accompanied him to the outskirts of our camp. On the way back, Dedalus was unusually quiet, and I asked him what was on his mind. He walked on for a few paces without answering, then looked up at me from beneath lowered brows.

"You want this make-believe raid to work, don't you? I can see that, but I don't like it. It's as dangerous as a sharp-toothed whore. Why run the risk of having any of these know-nothings panic and let fly with a lucky arrow or two and do us damage before we can reveal that it's all just mummery, an exercise in preparedness? One of our men dead would be too high a price to pay, it seems to me, for whatever might be achieved here. What does it matter if they're prepared or unprepared? There's not enough of them to make a difference either way. A hundred men they have? That's not a garrison, it's a holding force, and a skeletal one at that."

I made no effort to respond until we had regained the centre of the camp, then I nodded towards the headquarters tent and suggested we talk in there. He followed me wordlessly and settled into the only comfortable chair, at the table assigned to the Officer of the Watch. He sat back and folded his arms across his chest, hooking his fingers into the armholes of his cuirass, clearly waiting for me to speak. Dedalus possessed the sharpest tongue, and perhaps the sharpest wits, of all of us. He had impressed me so many times in the past with his insight and his ability to cut right to the heart of troublesome things that I had come to expect nothing less of him. I perched on the edge of the table in front of him.

"You're right, Ded," I conceded. "It is dangerous. But I've considered the risk, and I think it will be worthwhile. If we can convince these people to build stronger defences, then we'll have created an island of strength in this region. I agree that a hundred men is not a garrison, but it could be the start of one. Camulod once had no more than a hundred trained men under arms, and look at our strength today."

"Aye, but we've had how long? Sixty-five years? Sixty-five years to build our strength up to this point. These people don't have anything like that. And why would you want to create an island out here? What difference could it make to anything? These people could be wiped out tomorrow or next week."

"True, but perhaps not if they had help."

He stiffened very slightly and his eyes widened almost imperceptibly. "Help from where, from Camulod?"

"Why not?"

He looked away, as I had expected him to, his face going sombre as he chased and enumerated the thoughts going through his head. Finally he looked back into my eyes.

"Are you considering keeping our lads here, to help these people?"

"No, not at all."

"Well, thank the Christ for that! Our troopers are looking forward to going home, and they've earned that right."

"They have, indeed. But I would like to dispatch another force, once we are home, to serve the same purpose. Perhaps a hundred men."

"Merlyn, we won't have a hundred men for that kind of luxury. We're going to be at war, at least in Cambria, and possibly against the Danes from Northumbria as well."

"It's not a luxury, Ded, it's a necessity. We're going to need the strength of people like the Appius clan some day. And there must scores, perhaps hundreds, of similar settlements all over this territory. Even a score of them, fielding a hundred men apiece, would give us a force of two thousand men."

"No, Merlyn, use your head! Where's your logic? *Half* a score of similar settlements would leave us *short* a thousand men, spread out in ten separate, piddly little garrisons."

My shoulders slumped as I digested the incontrovertible truth of what he had said, and yet . . .

"Damnation, Ded, I know I'm right. You read Ambrose's last letter, where he talked about the problems facing them in Camulod. Even with much of our force quartered now in Ilchester, and the fields we've added to our granaries there, we have almost too many mouths to feed, and too few roofs to cover all their heads. Here could be a way to relieve the congestion, temporarily at least, and to feed everyone better!

"Look at the fertile fields here, going to waste, lying unused, and tell my why that must be so! There is a wealth of manpower lying idle around here, and I'm not just speaking of fighting men. I'm thinking about the farmers—the homeless people living on the edges of the forest, the people living in temporary huts on the outskirts of the ruined towns, the people, helpless thousands of them, who subsist alone, because they're all afraid to gather into numbers worth slaughtering. If there are enough of them out there, and if they can be rallied and joined together for their own good, their own protection and welfare—if they can be taught, somehow, to believe in the mere *possibility* of that—then they would be invincible in their number.

"But I know you're right, as well. The logistics would be next to impossible, and there's no getting around that. We can't establish garrison in every place that begs for help. We lack the strength in men, strong as we are. It was wishful thinking on my part, that's all. Forgive me for tugging at your ears."

Dedalus sat silent for a while longer, plucking at his lip and surprising me by not bounding to his feet and congratulating me on my openness to argument. "Well," he drawled, his tone speculative, "having heard what you've just said, if I look at this thing from a slightly different line of sight, I don't know how far off balance your thinking is. You do have a point worth making. There's a lot of sound sense in the idea. Hmm . . ."

I waited as his voice tailed into a long silence. Finally he grunted again. "Y'know, I really think the only thing that's wrong with it is the scope."

"What d'you mean by that?"

He snorted, and it was almost a laugh. "You're half Roman. Do it by half Roman way, but make your half-measures full steps."

I blinked at him. "I have no idea what you are talking about."

"Yes you do, if you'll but think about it. How did the Romans build their holdings, first the Republic, then the Empire?"

I gazed back at him, conscious of a tiny flicker of excitement in my chest. "By converting those they conquered into allies, making them auxilliaries and teaching them the Roman way of fighting."

"That's right. Camulod has no need to *conquer* these folk you're considering, so there's no bloodshed involved at that stage. All you have to do is convince them they need help and that you're willing to provide it. That shouldn't be difficult. You need to give 'em back the hope they've lost. Nothing's easier than that.

"Send out patrols, routinely, each one consisting of one cohort of our troops. Order each cohort to spend two days in each place they visit. They'll construct a fortified camp while they are there, then leave it intact for the use of the locals. No shortage of trees, anywhere, for palisades. Log walls and earthen breastworks. That offers safety in a very real sense. Once the camps are built, the local people can build their own buildings inside the walls and be their own garrisons, and Camulod can supply the basic military training they'll require. That won't require a permanent base of a thousand men, but it will ease congestion in our own home jurisdiction, keeping a thousand men gainfully occupied and out of Camulod full-time, if you dedicate four separate cohorts to the job and keep them busy, alternating two and two on continuous patrols. And the beauty of it is, they'll all be within easy recall, should any trouble threaten us at home. Twenty men to each camp, at first, one squad each of infantry and cavalry, should achieve the effect you want. Enlist the support of the local leaders, chiefs and elders, and their enthusiasm will stir the flames in others. Once the people see they can defend themselves, our job will be almost done. All it will require on top of that will be the regular patrols, passing by on schedule and offering the hope of assistance if invasion or attack happens. Nothing to it. Then, if war comes into this region, we'll have a home-grown force to fight it with." He paused, giving me time to digest what he had said before he added, "It'll work, Merlyn. Your idea was right, merely askew in its conception. Don't thank me for my insight. It is damn tedious to have to listen to outpourings of gratitude all the time . . ."

I sat stunned, seeing the possibilities of what he had described. And Dedalus, once he had seen that he had given me enough to think about, yawned and stretched and then stood up and muttered something about taking a nap, since he had been on duty all night long. I barely noticed him leave.

And so, thus simply and apparently by chance began the process that would transform the land of Britain and alter Arthur's destiny from that of Legate Commander of the Forces of Camulod to *Riothamus*, the High King of Western Britain. That the process occurred at all was astounding; that it occurred as quickly as it did was akin to miraculous; but the time and the conditions were appropriate to the needs, and the leaven that inspired the change was hope.

Our "attack" on Nero's holdings was a complete success. Despite the terror it produced in the inhabitants, the relief it occasioned afterwards, once the realization dawned that it was but a ruse arranged by their leader, was sufficient to overcome any resentment that might have been harboured by some of Nero's elders. No one was injured in the foray, and that in itself was an indication of the success of the attack and of the level of unpreparedness we found on our arrival. In the aftermath, once Nero had explained to a general assembly of his people all that we intended to achieve—an alliance between them and Camulod that would be heavily weighted in their favour in the early stages—the decision was quickly made to begin the work of refortification immediately. That led to the recognition of the real, underlying reason why nothing had been done before this time: there was no lack of willing hands to undertake the labour, but no one among Nero's folk had any knowledge of the architectural skills required to build the needed walls. Even their senior soldier, an ancient veteran of the legions, had never been required to take part in the building of a fortified camp. Plainly he had never served with Caius Britannicus and Publius Varrus.

As we stood listening to the rising consternation among Nero's people, I glanced at Dedalus, who looked at Benedict and Philip and then huddled with them, speaking quietly. Mere moments later, he turned and nodded to me.

"Two days," he said. "In that time we can lay out the design, show them which trees to cut and how to stake them, and help them to make a start on the digging." He stopped, looking at me straight in the eye. "You wouldn't want our men to do the digging for them, would you?"

I smiled at him. "How could you even ask such a question?"

We resumed our homeward journey on the third day after that, leaving Nero's people in a sweat of industrious cooperation. I had promised to send another expedition to check on their progress as soon as we had arrived home and explained our newly formed alliance to the Council of Camulod. Should the Council approve, I promised that the returning expedition would bring with them additional supplies and support in the

form of weapons and armour, and training personnel whose task would
be to work with the Appius garrison, instructing new, local levies in weaponry techniques and simple tactics. These troops would work simultaneously with Nero and his senior people to develop strategies to govern the
defensive structure of their community from that time on. Our taciturn
Benedict had already volunteered to lead the returning expedition, and
that in itself augured well for the campaign's success.

During much of the five-year period that was to follow, Camulod itself
went to war without committing any of its new allies, and it did so on
two widely separated fronts, which is considered by military strategists to
be suicidal. And yet the process of radical change described above continued without impediment, fostered to a very large extent by Camulod's
constant efforts and encouragement.

At any other time and in any other place, what our armies achieved
in those five years would have been deemed impossible. That one community—for that is all we were, a community, not a state or even a city—
should commit itself and all its resources to two different, simultaneous
wars would defy credence in the eyes of sane and civilized men. Yet that
is precisely what we did, and the reason we were able to do it seems purely
arrogant when stated baldly: it was our time.

Camulod, the young, lusty Colony that embodied the dream of its
two founders, was coming to its prime. More than sixty years had passed
since its formation, and those years had been dedicated diligently and
incessantly to preparation for the confrontation of catastrophe, and survival in its aftermath. We had a tightly disciplined army of nine thousand,
more than half of them intensively trained, heavy cavalry, and all of them
commanded by an officer corps that was superb, its codes and ethics
modelled upon the ancient ideals of Republican Rome. We had formed
three small but hard-hitting armies from our complement, each of them
half the size of a traditional Roman legion, comprising fifteen hundred
infantry and the same amount of cavalry, and although but half the size
of a legion, each was more than twice as powerful as any legion had ever
been. That power, and the crushing force of it, was the result of the
mobility and versatility offered by our cavalry: a full thousand heavy troopers plus five hundred of our lighter, faster force—an innovation developed
and launched on my brother's initiative, during the five years I had spent
in Ravenglass—in each of our three armies. The combination of superior
weaponry, entrenched discipline and inspired leadership brought Camulod
to pre-eminence in Britain, and each of those three elements depended
absolutely upon each of the others.

V

ALTHOUGH I WAS born and raised in Camulod, and had served as its Legate Commander since before the death of my father, I found myself taken aback and almost moved to tears by what I found on my return. I had left a thriving Colony that was, in spite of its military strength, in essence an overgrown farming community dominated by a hilltop fortress. What I found on my return was so different that I could scarcely grasp the change.

It began with our arrival at the point where the side road to Camulod joined the main route south to Isca. This side road had always been well enough used, but it was a mere track nonetheless, two broad, parallel wheel ruts divided by a humped mound of grassy earth the width of a wagon axle. Now the track was a road, twice as broad as it had been before and uniformly flat, with no sign of grass or wheel ruts on its crushed-flint surface. Instead of running straight to form a T with the road, however, this new road curved right at the junction, to blend into the great Roman road, heading south—towards Ilchester and the new garrison, I realized belatedly.

Some fifty paces in from the main road, a new stone guardhouse had been built, roofed in thick tiles and big enough, I guessed, to house some twenty men, with stables for ten horses. The guards came spilling out to form up almost as soon as Dedalus, Philip and I, riding ahead of our group, arrived at the junction. Everything was militarily crisp, the discipline of the guard detail exemplary. The Commander of the Guard, a decurion unknown to me, stepped forward to welcome Philip and Dedalus formally home to Camulod, then allowed us to pass on our way immediately. He had looked at me and through me without recognition, and the shock of being unrecognized in my own home reminded me that I had made extensive changes to my appearance since my departure six years earlier, altering everything as radically as possible, from the colour of my hair to the style of my dress and bearing. I had set out to be, and had become, plain Master Cay, a farmer as different from the former Merlyn of Camulod as I could make him. The Commander of the Guard had looked at me and seen only a mounted farmer, plainly dressed, riding alongside the leaders of a returning military expedition.

My shock gave way quickly, however, and turned to ironic self-mockery. I remained behind, waiting by the guardhouse while my military companions rode on, allowing the formations I had previously led to pass by until the wagons reached me. Shelagh and Donuil and their entire household filled up the first of them, and then Tressa came, sitting high on the driver's bench of our own wagon beside Derek, who was driving. His horse, one of ours and a gift from me, walked placidly behind, tethered to the back. I nodded to them as they passed, then swung my leg over and stepped directly from my stirrup into the back of the wagon, tying my own mount's reins beside Derek's before making my way carefully along the wagon bed to the front, sidling around and sometimes clambering over the crates and cases. I positioned myself behind the two of them, kneeling on a sack and thrusting my head between them after kissing Tress on the cheek.

Derek turned his head to look at me over his shoulder. "Why are we thus honoured? We're naught but visitors. This is your homecoming—you should be out there at the head of your men."

I laughed, wryly enough to make him twist around further to look at me, and then I told them what I had just discovered about my own appearance. After a while Tress asked, "Were you really that different, back then?"

Of course, Tress had never seen me as my true self, the man Connor called Yellow Head. I had been Cay of the brown hair and plain clothing since before she ever met me. No sooner had I begun to laugh again than the reality sobered me, so that my laugh died on my lips.

"Well," Derek growled, "Merlyn of Camulod does not exist outside his armour. Is that important at this moment? I don't think so, since the armour can't do anything without the man inside it. This lack of recognition means no more than that no one will see you've come home until you choose to show them, and that means you're free, for now, to sit up here with us and explain all the sights we'll see along the road."

I slipped my right arm about Tress's soft and supple waist and laid my left hand on Derek's shoulder. "I may not even be able to do that, my friend, for I'm already perplexed. That guardhouse wasn't there when I left, and this road we're travelling on was an old, grassy track. Those are the only two things I've seen so far that should be familiar, and they're both changed beyond recognition. But I'll explain what I can, so move over, both of you. Tress, you move towards the middle and I'll perch beside you, on the outside."

From that point onward, all along the road to Camulod itself, I saw differences everywhere and did my best, for a time at least, to point all of them out. Many of the great trees on both sides of the road, once so thick they had almost formed a wall, had been cut down and uprooted, their wood, I later learned, used to build houses and furniture, and new barracks blocks and stables down in Ilchester. As a result of the tree-clearing, there were more fields in evidence now, too, on either side of the road. And everywhere I looked, there were houses, all of them wooden, some more strongly built than others. Multitudes of people were going about the business of their daily lives where once there had been nothing but rabbits, squirrels, deer and bears moving silently through dense thickets. All around me, as I rode, I saw the differences, and eventually my mind grew numb with the scope of them. I rode in silence then, trying *not* to see so many changes, and my companions left me to my thoughts.

As we neared the end of the road, concealed from the sight of Camulod's hill fort by no more than a few hundred paces of fringing trees, the sound of children's voices, growing steadily louder, forced itself into my awareness. We came to a place where no more than a few giant trees remained on the right of the road. Arthur, Bedwyr, Gwin and Ghilly sat on their horses by the roadside, staring silently down into the open meadow beyond them. Now as we slowly approached, Arthur turned to look at me, his eyebrows raised high in a wordless question. The children's voices, raised in noisy, boisterous play, were loud enough here to cover the creaking of the wagons' axles and the crunching of the flint roadbed beneath our metal-tyred wheels.

There appeared to be hundreds of children in the meadow, close to the road, ranging in age from five or six to some as old as ten or even twelve. They were surging everywhere, in front of and around a long, low building built of logs and roofed with thatch, the upper parts of its walls open to the weather, although I could see where shutters would be hung on less pleasant days. I wanted to stop and look, but I could not have reasonably done so without interrupting the entire train that followed us, and so I contented myself with craning my neck to see all that I could see in passing. Arthur pulled his horse around and brought it to the side of the wagon, where he could look up at me, but it was Derek who spoke first.

"What's going on there, then? I've never seen so many brats assembled in one place. Is it a camp? A camp for children?"

I shook my head, glancing at Arthur, who, I knew, was listening closely. "No, I don't think so. Not a camp. But a school, I think."

Derek's face was blank. "A what? What's one of them?"

"It's a place where children go to learn their lessons—how to read and write. The way Arthur and the boys did in Mediobogdum. We had a school there, too, though there were only a few children involved. This one looks far more organized." I looked down at Arthur. "What are you looking so glum about?"

He kneed his horse slightly away from the wagon, to where he would not have to peer up at me so sharply. "Will I have to go to school there?" He did not appear to relish the prospect.

I grinned at him. "I doubt it. Your next classroom will be the campaign trail, if I'm any judge. Besides, the oldest child I saw back there might have been twelve. You *are* beyond that, aren't you?"

He frowned slightly, until he saw that I was tweaking him, and then he smiled and pulled back on his reins, allowing us to pass by him as he swung about to rejoin his friends. The first brazen peal of a trumpet soon sounded ahead of us, to be echoed and answered by others in the distance as the word was passed from point to point that newcomers were arriving.

Moments later we rounded the last bend, and there sat Camulod, upon its hilltop. Tress caught her breath audibly, and Derek whistled softly through his teeth.

"So that's Camulod," he murmured, more to himself than to anyone.

"Aye, that is Camulod. We're home. Tress? What think you?"

"It's . . . it's very grand," she whispered, and I laughed again, feeling the pride swell in me.

"No more than you are, lass, and it's yours—all of it."

She turned sideways to look at me, thinking I was teasing her. "Why would you say that, Cay?"

"Say what, that it's yours? It is! At least, as much of it as is mine is yours—in other words, all of it, and none of it. My family, Britannicus and Varrus mixed, created and built this place, Tress, and we have guarded it and governed it ever since. It stands on Britannicus land, but we have never sought to own it. The Britannici are the custodians of this place, holding it in trust but holding it nonetheless. And as my wife, you will be the castellan."

"And what about Ludmilla?"

The unexpected chill in her tone disconcerted me. "What about her? You and she—"

"Ludmilla is the mistress here in Camulod, Cay—the castellan, as you call it—and she has been since you left, perhaps since even before you left. She is your brother's wife and he has been in sole command here for the past six, almost seven, years, which means that she has, too, within her own domain. Do you expect to walk in there today and oust her, replacing her with me?"

"No, but—"

"No, but what? Think you Ludmilla will be grateful to simply back away and give up whatever systems she has put in place to run this . . ." She fumbled, searching for a word to complete her thought. ". . . this *town*? Do you believe she will be thankful to me, a simple servant girl from Ravenglass, for stepping into her world and dispossessing her?"

"*Tressa!*"

"Don't 'Tressa' me, Cay. I'm very serious." Though she spoke in a moderate tone, her disapproval *seemed* progressively louder to me as she continued. "Have you thought *at all* about my situation here? I am not your wife, not yet. I have no rights here in this place, and I won't permit you to act or speak as though I have, or should have, or might wish to have. I am your . . . companion, nothing more, your consort—though most folk here will simply say your mistress, which is true enough. But I won't be thought of as an upstart or a troublemaker, and I won't be made to look like one against my will. Do you hear me?"

"Yes, Tress, I hear you very well. So does Shelagh, in the wagon up ahead, I'm sure." I was amazed at what I had provoked with what I had taken to be a simple, truthful observation.

My quiet statement checked her, and she glanced quickly around her. "Was I being loud? I wasn't being loud."

"Well, not loud, perhaps, but vehement."

Her voice returned to its normal pitch. "Vehement? Does that mean firm? If it does then that's the way I feel. I don't want to be . . . that word . . . castellan, here. The thought of it is frightening, Cay. I know nothing about how to do such things."

I slipped my arm about her shoulders. "I know that, Tress, I know. But you can learn, and you will, at your own pace. Ludmilla will teach you, you'll see. No need to take the task upon yourself today or even tomorrow or next week, my love. No one would ask that of you. You'll live with me, in my own house, and we'll be wed. And as my wife, you'll learn the running of the place in due time, with ease and with Ludmilla's willing help. You'll see. Now hush you, here comes someone to meet us."

Ahead, in the distance, I had seen bright colours and movement on the road from the main gates of the fort as a welcoming party headed down to greet us. Tressa looked and then stood up and climbed gracefully over the bench, disappearing into the body of the wagon beneath the leather canopy. She had time, I knew, to do what she needed to do, which was to make herself presentable according to her own criteria. The welcoming party would not reach us for some time yet.

I shifted into a more comfortable position on the bench beside Derek, who was gazing off to my right, towards the broad drilling plain, where several formations of cavalry had been wheeling and cantering as we emerged from the forest road. Now they were all motionless, their eyes on our approach. As I noticed their stillness, a distant voice rang out, loud and peremptory, and they surged into motion again, resuming their interrupted patterns.

"That's the campus. Derek, the drilling ground. It's been there since first we started building the fort above. No weed, no flower, no blade of grass ever had time to root itself here before some horse's hoof either trampled it flat or dug it up. In high summer, the dust of it never has a chance to settle. The fort is the centre of Camulod's defences, but the campus is the heart of its strength."

Derek did not address that directly. He simply muttered, "This is a *big* place."

"Aye, it is. Much bigger than it was when I set out for Ravenglass, six years ago. That's Ambrose, at the head of the group, there. There's no mistaking him, is there?"

The welcoming party had reached the head of our procession, and were exchanging greetings with Philip, Falvo and Dominic, who rode at the point. I could see my brother pull his horse around in a rearing turn as he searched for me back among the wagons, and then he was cantering towards us, calling the occasional greeting to familiar faces as he passed. When he reached the first wagon, with Donuil and Shelagh on the driver's bench, he reined in his horse to exchange a few words with them.

As they spoke, Arthur came thundering up with his trio of friends, and then stopped, suddenly shy, waiting for his Uncle Ambrose to acknowledge him. Ambrose welcomed all four boys expansively, and then leaned forward in his saddle. He whispered something into Arthur's ear and then slapped the boy's mount on the rump, sending all four of the lads galloping off towards the distant fort. He watched them ride off, said something further to Donuil or Shelagh, then swung down to the ground and strode back to where we waited, his whole face alight in a great, beaming smile. I leaped down to meet him and we threw our arms about each other.

He pushed me back from him eventually, his hands grasping the points of my shoulders firmly, and looked into my eyes. "Welcome home, Brother," he said softly. "Your place awaits you, and everything is ready for your arrival." His smile broadened to a grin. "Your clothes, your *proper* clothes, are cleaned and dried and all laid out for you, and your armour is polished brighter than it has ever been. Time to wash out the drab brown from your hair and take your place in Camulod again. The farmer Cay has no place here. This is Merlyn's home." He glanced up at the wagon. "Where is Tressa?" But then his eyes widened in surprise. "Derek of Ravenglass! Welcome to Camulod."

Tress now emerged from the rear of the wagon and stood, holding the edge of the bench and smiling down at Ambrose, her eyes wide and timid-looking. He stepped forward and placed his foot on the hub of the lead wheel, then swung himself up to take her hand and kiss her cheek. "And you, too, Lady Tressa. We've looked for you this past week and more. Welcome. Ludmilla has been fretting, thinking that some ill might have befallen you along the way, but had we known King Derek himself rode with you, her mind would have been eased." Derek flushed and smiled at the words.

Ambrose perched on the end of the bench and spoke down to me, still holding Tressa's hand. "You've seen some changes here, eh, Brother? I promise you, there are more yet. But we'll talk of all that later. For now, we have to take you home and feed you. You must all be hungry and ready for a good, hot bath and a deep massage. After that, we will relax, drink a little mead, perhaps, and exchange idle talk in warmth and comfort. Tomorrow tonight, we'll feast and celebrate your coming, since everyone wants to join the celebration. The only place big enough to accommodate that gathering is the campus itself, and that will take the entire day to organize."

He turned to Tress again, raising her hand. "We regret the delay of an entire day when we should celebrate tonight, dear Tressa, but we have no other option. The campus is in daily use, since it's our only training ground. Tomorrow, therefore, will be a day of rest and preparation for the coming night. There are tents to put up, seats and tables to be put in place, fires to be built and cooking to be done. We have plenty of food, though. Hunting and fishing parties have been going out every day for the past week and more, so no one will go hungry. We have mountain-stream salmon and river trout and saltwater fish to offer you, and we have venison, wild boar and fattened swine, goat flesh for those who like it—I do not—and an entire fat ox, well fed on grain and groomed for just this feast. What have I missed? Ah yes, the birds of the air! We have geese, swans and ducks, partridge and grouse and many smaller fowl. And in addition to all of that we have music, mummers, acrobats and wrestlers, and prodigious horsemanship, which we are ever eager to display. So, this afternoon, when you have bathed and rested for a while, we will show you our Colony, or as much as we may without tiring you. After that, your man and I must talk, at great and serious length, of many things, so I must ask you to be patient with my demands on him."

Tressa lowered her head in a gracious nod. "My man, sir, as you call him, came back to pursue his obligation to serve this Colony, not to please me. I am quite happy to be here with him and I've no doubt I shall find much to occupy me while he spends time with you."

I was smiling, proud of Tressa's self-possession and amused and pleased by Ambrose's courteous reception. "Have we then so many things to talk about, Ambrose?"

"Oh, aye, Brother, I fear we have, and few of them are pleasant. But none of them are dire enough they cannot wait until tonight. You have been gone nigh on seven years while they were all agrowing, so a few more hours will make no massy difference to them. So come, let's move on, up to the fort. Merlyn, you take my horse and tell the other wagon drivers to follow us, while I stay here and talk with this beautiful woman and enjoy being conducted by a king. Derek, if you would, pull to the side of the road here on the right, and take us past this blockage. We'll lead the wagons separately up to the gates. The troopers will disperse down here when they're dismissed and we've no need to wait for them."

Derek swung the lead horse out to pull the wagon forward as I began to pull myself up into the saddle of my brother's horse, thinking that I would find time in the course of the afternoon to ask at least a few of the questions he had postponed so lightly. I heard Ambrose calling to Donuil in the cart ahead, telling him to fall in behind our wagon. And now as I rode back and forth, marshalling the wagons of our train, I saw recognition in the faces of the people of Camulod as they saw me, mounted upon my brother's splendid horse, which alone informed them who I was.

The time that followed was hectic. Our return, as I should have anticipated, was seen as a cause for great rejoicing in a time when there was little else to celebrate. During the course of that day and the one that followed, I met and greeted everyone I knew in Camulod, together with a large number of people whom I did not know at all. Many of the latter were new officers, selected from the ranks of the new intakes assembled since my departure, and most of them seemed ludicrously young to me.

I spent the very first hour after my return, along with several of my travelling companions, exulting in the delights of Camulod's bathhouse and masseurs. Then, dressed in rich clothing for the first time in years and feeling like a new man, I was able to enjoy a light meal before being introduced to each of the new officers individually, with great solemnity, in a ceremony organized in advance by my brother and staged in the Officers' Tribunal. The Tribunal itself was an innovation, a new building erected against the postern wall of the fort for the dual purpose of serving regulatory tribunal requirements whenever necessary and housing the garrison officers in their off-duty hours.

Accepting a suggestion from Ambrose, I contrived, throughout the course of that ceremony, to maintain an air of august gravity. As my brother had so wisely observed, although the men I was to meet were all unknown to me, I was known, by repute, to all of them. I soon discovered that my reputation had evidently grown to be far greater than I had thought it could be, and I had great difficulty, at first, in adjusting to that, once I had learned to recognize—and finally to accept—the look of awe they had, one and all, on meeting me.

I say I learned to accept it, because my first reaction to this uniform, awe-stricken expression was to assume immediately that it sprang from the legendary exaggerations soldiers thrive upon, particularly when they want to impress recruits and newcomers with stories of their own veteran status. So my first urge was to challenge the look and dispel it, forcefully. Such unearned deference—for so I saw it—embarrassed me.

They came into my presence in unsmiling, sharply regimented groups, marching in perfect step under the watchful, disapproving eye of Tertius Lucca, our *primus pilus*, or Senior Soldier, and segregated into their groups by their cohortal designations: First Cavalry, First Scouting, First Infantry and so on, all the way through to Third Infantry. I realized only belatedly, after being introduced individually to the first group of nine of these earnest and deeply dutiful young men, that Ambrose had been prescient. I had been away from Camulod for a long time, and in my desire to be accepted again, I might easily have been over-eager to ingratiate myself with these new, young and impressionable men. As it was, I maintained my dignity and my distance as a commander, speaking briefly but pleasantly with each new face and inquiring solicitously about the rank and station each one held, so that as the last group of them strode away after delivering a crisp salute in unison, Ambrose smiled at me.

"Now *that* was a tribunal reception worthy of an Imperial Legate. Well done, Brother. That leaves you to face only the new Councillors, for we have a few of those whom you have never met, and a few of the more prominently successful new Colonists—very few of those. It's difficult to be new, prominent *and* successful in our egalitarian Colony. That won't be until tomorrow, at the feast. Tonight, we dine in private, more or less informally, with our close friends and family. Ludmilla and I decided some time ago, presupposing your agreement, that we should hold that particular gathering down in the Villa Britannicus. The facilities there are much more suited to our needs for tonight, the kitchens are larger and more spacious. Besides, the old place doesn't get enough use nowadays. I mean, it's often used, but only as ancillary premises, if you see what I mean. It's finally complete again, you know, totally refurbished after the damage done to it in Lot's attack eleven years ago. It's exactly as it was before the family moved up here to live in the fort. Ludmilla would move back down again in an instant, but I believe my place is up here, in the centre of things." He paused, looking sideways at me. "You know, it has just occurred to me that you and Tress might enjoy living there, for a while, at least. What think you?"

Ambrose's suggestion intrigued me. Although I had been born in the Villa Britannicus, and had always loved the grand old house, I had never lived there. My grandfather had died there, brutally murdered, as had my mother, but that knowledge had never deterred me in my love for the place that had been our family home for generations. It was less than a mile from the fort, no great distance, and now, remembering Tressa's remarks from earlier that day, it occurred to me that it might be a perfect place for her to begin learning how to run a large household, free of the fear of countering Ludmilla's will.

"You know, that might be a splendid idea, Ambrose, and it would never have occurred to me. But it would have to be Tressa's decision. The sheer size of it might frighten her. She has never seen such a house, let alone lived in one. Derek's house is the finest in Ravenglass, and it's a hovel compared to the Villa. Anyway, let me mention it to her, after she's seen the place tonight and had a look at the way it is run. When are we to go down?"

"We have several hours to pass until dinner, but that will give us time

to walk around the place and admire it. Our carpenters have done magnificent work on the interior, and so have some of our masons, on the
inside as well as the outside walls. They've even restored some of the old
mosaics that were damaged. You'll be impressed, I promise you. Let's go
and find Derek and Donuil and the women, and we can all ride down
together in one of the big wagons."

On the few occasions I was alone with Ambrose that day I tried to
question him about conditions in Cambria and Northumbria, but he
would have none of it. I made one more attempt to question him then
as we set out, but he stopped me with a raised palm before I could really
begin and pointed out to me that we did not have the time, right then,
to discuss fully the matters that would have to be resolved. People were
coming and going all around us, and we would be interrupted constantly,
unless we made ourselves grossly discourteous to our Colony's new guests
while we indulged ourselves in matters that could very easily wait until
that night. He was right, of course, so I buried my impatience and resigned
myself to making the best of the postponement.

Ambrose dispatched a soldier to the stables to arrange for one of the
big, seat-filled wagons to be prepared and placed at our disposal, and then
we made our way directly to the former Varrus household, where we found
our friends returning from a walk in the late-afternoon sunlight. Seeing
them approach from the far side of the central courtyard, I stopped by
the three large slabs of slate stone sunk in the centre of the yard and
waited for them to reach us. To Tress and Derek, I pointed out the graves
of Caius Britannicus, Publius and Luceiia Varrus, and my own father,
Picus Britannicus. These, I explained, had been the founders of Camulod,
the progenitors of everything that flourished in the Colony today. I could
think of no more to say, but I trusted that they would understand the
import of these people in my life, and to what I saw as our shared future.
Derek merely nodded and remained silent for a few moments, gazing
down at the three stones, and then he straightened up and nodded again.
I turned and led the group towards the stables and the waiting wagon.

Only nine of us rode down the hillside road to the Villa Britannicus
on that first journey—the sightseers. I sat on the bench beside the driver
while the others, Tressa and Derek, Donuil and Shelagh, Rufio and Turga,
and Ambrose and Ludmilla as our host and hostess, ranged themselves
on the seats at our backs.

Ambrose explained that they had begun the refurbishing four years
earlier, initially as a summer project aimed at instilling discipline in those
young people of the Colony not yet old enough to take part in adult
activities. That first summer had been dedicated to cleaning up the
grounds and removing the rubble that remained from the damage caused
in the raid years earlier, when Lot's soldiers had almost overrun the Villa
in the first treacherous attack, the night my father was murdered in his

bed. Many of the outbuildings, which had borne the burnt of the damage, had been refurbished after the war, but since the war itself had shifted most of the Colony's activities to the fort on the hilltop, the priorities governing the reclamation had been less urgent, and the task had not been carried out as thoroughly as it might have been. Walls and sometimes entire buildings had been reconstructed, for example, but the debris of the old walls had been left heaped in great piles of broken masonry scattered haphazardly about the perimeter. Organized groups of children, working under adult supervision, made short work of carting away the rubble and burying it beyond the grounds.

As the Colony had continue to grow, however, and the tempo of that growth increased, it had become inevitable that more and more effort should be poured into "the Villa Task," as it soon became known, in the years that followed. Camulod was almost visibly beginning to bulge at its seams, and no one had yet thought to establish a second, ancillary garrison. From a mere beautification effort, the Villa Task quickly grew in importance to become a first-priority endeavour; every possible resource at the Colony's disposal was being exploited to its maximum, and the Villa was one of the richest. Other villas existed within the colonial holdings—fourteen of them, in fact—and all of them were already being used to capacity. The Villa Britannicus, closest of all to the fort and the original home farm of the Colony, had become an anomaly, a spacious and gracious house lying, for all intents and purposes, untenanted.

Within two more years, the Villa had been refitted and restored to much of its former beauty, and for a time it was used to house the garrison officers and their wives, and its walls had resounded for a time with the sounds of life. That same year, however, the garrison in Ilchester had been established, and the resultant exodus of more than a thousand souls and mouths from Camulod had eased tensions all around, permitting breathing space again, and time for reflection. At that juncture, Ambrose and Ludmilla had approached the Council to enlist its help in completing the Villa Task properly. The Council had concurred, and the fine finishing work had begun; the Villa Britannicus, already restored to soundness, was now returned, as Ambrose put it, to its former greatness.

Ambrose had not exaggerated. The Villa Britannicus looked better than I had ever seen it look before, and I took great pride in showing it to my guests. I was reminded of the description in my Uncle Varrus's writings of how he had first seen the place, and so I endeavoured to show it to them just as his future wife, Luceiia Britannicus, had shown it to Publius Varrus.

The entire house was laid out in the form of an enormous H built on an east-west axis, with the family living quarters closing off the open, western end to form an enclosed quadrangle. All four sides of the building facing into the courtyard of this quadrangle, I pointed out, were domestic buildings, originally built to house the serving staff and the domestic facilities, such as baths, laundry, kitchens, bakery, butchery, wine storage and the like. The main cross-bar of the H was pierced by an ornate, pillared portico that led onto a second, outer courtyard at the eastern end. The north and south wings held stables, livestock barns, cool rooms for long-term food storage, a spacious carpentry shop with a cooperage attached, a pottery, a tannery, a roomy smithy with several forges and a large granary.

The entire Villa was two-storeyed, and I pointed out that the ground-floor walls surrounding the inner courtyard, the oldest part of the house, were enormously thick and built of huge, solid granite pebbles, smoothed and rounded on the outer surfaces, shaped around the edges to fit together and bonded with strong concrete. Above, on the upper level, the construction was similar, but the walls were less thick, the granite pebbles smaller, and the walls themselves were pierced by the shuttered, evenly spaced windows of the family's sleeping chambers, an innovation peculiar to this house and one which I had never seen repeated elsewhere. Beyond the portico, on the other hand, the extended walls flanking the outer courtyard were of timber framing and plaster mixed with broken flint.

I took delight in pointing out that all the buildings flanking the inner courtyard were entered from the courtyard, but all of those surrounding the outer one opened out into the fields surrounding the villa. Only four small doors permitted pedestrian access from these buildings into the outer yard. This was an innovation designed by Luceiia Britannicus herself when she had decided, long before she met Publius Varrus, to make the approach to the house more beautiful. She had closed up all of the entrances to the buildings around the outer yard and cut new ones in the former rear walls, and had then built a great, sweeping, semicircular road to the main portico, weaving her roadway in places to go around and among the twelve great trees that stood there: four oaks, three elms and five great, copper beech trees. She had then seeded the entire yard with grass and lavished attention on it, and when it had grown rich, she had planted formal gardens of flowers—roses, violets, pansies and poppies—among the trees.

Awe gave place immediately to open-mouthed wonder from the moment I led my guests inside the house itself. I must admit that even I was stunned by the opulence that awaited us. When I was a boy, it was simply my grandfather's home, the house where I had been born and where no one really lived any longer. Today, I was seeing it through the eyes of others and comparing it with all the other houses I had ever seen. It was matchless.

The ground floor of the family quarters, where we began, had been accurately described by Uncle Varrus as palatial. Every room was differently floored. Those in the main rooms were mosaic, in a multitude of

colours, depicting scenes from Greek myth and legend: Europa and the
Bull, Theseus and the Minotaur of Crete, and Leda and the Swan. The
lesser rooms on that floor were merely tessellated, the marble stones of
their floors laid out in geometric shapes and patterns that dazzled the
eyes with their brightness and colours. The triclinium, the great dining
room where we would eat that night, was floored in large, lustrous squares
of dark-green marble alternating with flawless white, on which was an
open-sided arrangement of matched oaken dining tables that would seat
upwards of sixty guests in comfort. The walls were panelled in sheets of
pale-green and yellow marble so highly polished that the occupants of the
room were reflected in them. Against the walls, ranked side by side, were
deep-shelved cabinets, some of them open-fronted and others with doors,
that held the family's wealth of plate and dinnerware. There were platters
and bowls and serving dishes and utensils of gold and silver and copper
and tin and bronze; exquisite and ancient Samian pottery, richly glazed
and decorated; cups and beakers and vases of polished glass; and two
enormous drinking cups of aurochs horn, polished and worn, glossy with
age and ornamented with mounts of finely crafted gold.

Ludmilla had evidently decided to return these items to their proper
place as part of the general refurbishment. I immediately wondered then
if she would resent our presence in the house because of that. Had she
intended to move her household here? And if so, would she then wish to
reclaim the various pieces of plate and ornamentation?

Thinking that thought, and looking at my dear Tress gaping wide-
eyed at these treasures, a vision of my beloved Cassandra flashed into my
mind, and I felt a momentary stirring of some ancient guilt. What would
she think of this, I wondered, if she were looking down on me right now,
and how would she feel about this young woman sharing my life and my
possessions? And then the answer came to me as clearly as if Cassandra
herself had spoken the words in my ear. Like Ludmilla, Cassandra would
be glad for me, happy that I had found a woman to brighten my life as
this one did. Left to my care alone, this villa would have continued to
degenerate as it had for the past forty years and more. The scars it bore
would have grown darker; the dust would have grown thick in its corners.
Now, with Tressa, my life had changed, just as Ludmilla had brought life
back to the Villa Britannicus itself.

I led the group up the double flight of wide, marble stairs to the
family sleeping chambers on the upper floor. The entire upper storey was
floored with thick, interlocking planks of solid pine, glazed with the patina
of more than a hundred years of care. Each of the ten sleeping chambers
there had its own window and was filled with spring sunlight at this hour
of the afternoon. The windows were small, and covered with wooden shutters inside and out, the inner set fitted with adjustable slats that could
be closed completely, or angled to permit light and air to enter. The air

circulating throughout the villa, I pointed out for the sole benefit of Tress, was uniformly warm, thanks to the heated air carried throughout by the hypocausts, hot-air ducts fed by the furnace that burned constantly beneath the bathhouse and was refuelled twice each day. And the house had two sets of baths, one for the family and another for the household staff, each of them walled entirely with tiny, white, glazed tiles imported from beyond the seas when first the house was built.

We completed our tour with a visit to the facilities surrounding the interior courtyard, although the bustle of activity of the staff in the kitchens and bakery discouraged us from interrupting. Marco, the chief cook of Camulod's kitchens, whom I had known since he first apprenticed to my old friend Ludo thirty years before, greeted me warmly and was happy to make Tressa's acquaintance. Marco, as his mentor Ludo had been before him, was openly and unabashedly homosexual. He was gifted in the preparation of food of any kind, although his greatest talents were reserved for the preparation of pies and pastries. He paid Tress the signal honour of allowing her to taste and test one of his sauces, and rolled his eyes in delight when she moaned with the pleasure of it. Then, graciously, he eased us out of his kitchen again, recommending the beauty of the inner courtyard and the afternoon.

The courtyard contained a garden—more of an orchard, really, with apple, pear, cherry and plum trees as well as vegetables and herbs. The earth in some of the beds was freshly turned, and the debris of winter had been swept up into neat piles in the corners of the two sections where the soil lay undisturbed.

When we had seen all there was to see there, I led the entire group, largely silent now and much subdued, back into the family living room. Ambrose's earlier suggestion of a cup of mead and a comfortable sprawl around a brazier now seemed like an excellent idea, and we passed the interval before dinner in pleasant, general conversation, most of it dedicated to admiration of the villa and the reclamation work done under the supervision of my brother and his wife.

I was happy to see that Tressa seemed at ease with Ambrose and Ludmilla. She sat listening closely, and on one occasion Ludmilla asked her something about the fabrics on the walls and chairs. Tressa brightened and launched immediately into a response that interested me not a whit and quickly lost me in a sea of feminine intricacies. Watching the two of them talking easily, however, I was relieved to know I had been right. These two would become close friends.

As the dinner hour approached, the others who would join us began to arrive from the fort, some of them in wagons and others, notably the officers of the former Mediobogdum garrison, on horseback. We had decided that, on this first evening of homecoming celebration, the boys and other children should be accommodated elsewhere, to allow their parents the unaccustomed luxury of being themselves for once, without fear of being overheard or interrupted at their meal. All the children, therefore, including the four boys who would have been mortified at that description, were being cared for by the household staff up on the hill. As each group arrived, Ambrose and Ludmilla welcomed them and Plato plied them all with wine, ale or mead, and they were soon absorbed into the ongoing conversations.

At one point, Shelagh approached and took me by the arm, smiling at Benedict, with whom I had been discussing something trivial, and leading me away to stand against a corner wall where she could talk with me alone. I was curious to know what had prompted this move, but for some time she spoke only of the afternoon's activities and the changes Ambrose and Ludmilla had effected in the old house. Finally, prompted by her evident unwillingness to say what was really on her mind, I asked her outright why she had taken me aside. She stilled, and then she smiled.

"Why should you even have to ask? Don't you think it possible I might have wished for a few moments alone with you, to thank you personally for this afternoon? You taught me more than I have ever known about this place."

I grinned right back at her. "Aye, of course, darling Shelagh, that's it. After all the years we've known each other with our gentle lusts and unfulfilled attraction, you've chosen today to declare your love, in full view of Tress, your husband, and our assembled friends. What's wrong, really? Something's troubling you."

"No, it's not troubling. Merely that . . . I had a dream last night, one of those strange ones, the first I've had in years."

I felt my heartbeat surge immediately and my breath grew tight in my chest. "What? What was it?"

She shook her head. "I saw you and Ambrose, side by side, in a strange place filled with swirling smoke. He stood above you, bare-headed, the light from . . . from something . . . reflected in his hair. You sat huddled at his feet, your hair dull brown as now, your shoulders hunched. But then you sprang erect and into him, and the two of you became one, brilliant with light and surrounded by swirling smoke . . ."

"What? I sprang into him, you said. I knocked him down?"

"No, you sprang into him . . . inside him. You lost yourself in him, and he in you. You became one."

"Oh . . . What happened then?"

She shook her head. "Nothing. I woke up. That is all there was."

I turned to look to where my brother stood laughing with Tress and Mark, our carpenter, and then I looked back at Shelagh, who stood watching me with no expression that I could define.

"Shelagh, that makes no sense to me at all. Does it to you?"

She shrugged. "No, but when did these dreams ever make sense? I know only that when they occur, I recognize them for what they are, and they always have meaning of some kind. But the thing I noticed most in there was the colour of your hair. Will you change it back to yellow, now that we've come home?"

"I expect so. I'll simply stop using the berry juice that stains it brown. You think that has import, my hair colour?"

"How would I know? It changes the look of you, but I've grown accustomed to it for years now. Anyway, you would look good even if you were bald."

"Oh, would he, indeed? Should I be feeling jealousy here, you two?" Donuil had approached silently while we were talking, holding a drink he had brought for Shelagh.

I turned to him, laughing, and told him we had been discussing the colour of my hair and what I should do to it now that I was home. He eyed my head and nodded sagely, then advised me to take his wife's advice and shave it all off.

We moved to join the others after that, and I forgot about Shelagh's dream for the time being, caught up in the general conversations that were swirling everywhere. On several occasions, some of the other men, most notably among our military contingent, attempted to bring up the subject of political affairs beyond our lands, but Ambrose would have none of that and made it abundantly clear that all information would be shared equally among everyone *after* he and I, as joint Commanders, had had the opportunity to meet and discuss it. None sought to argue against that, and the talk returned each time to more innocuous subjects.

By the time Plato summoned us to dinner in the triclinium, there were thirty of us present: all of the original party who had left Camulod six years before, save one, and twelve new immigrants from Ravenglass, plus Ambrose and Ludmilla. And when we were assembled around the open-sided square of tables Plato had arranged for us, before the first course was served, we drank together to the memory of our sole absentee, our dear friend Lucanus, whose recent death, so unanticipated despite his age, had left each and every one of us feeling personally deprived.

VI

 "So, HERE WE are, alone at last." Ambrose lowered himself into an armchair, smiling, and pressed his hands into his face, squeezing his eyes and then drawing his fingers down to his chin, leaving white pressure marks that faded quickly. He opened his eyes wide and yawned. "Do you feel up to this? I don't, really. Dinner was too good, and I may have had too much wine. I'm stuffed like one of Marco's roasted fowl." He stretched mightily. "I had hoped to reach this point an hour and more ago. We have much to discuss."

"Aye, so you said this afternoon, when we arrived." I settled myself comfortably into my own chair, close by the brazier. "I don't know whether I'm any more fit than you are to talk long into the night. It seems like days since I last slept, and it's been weeks since I last slept in a bed. That's seductive. But I think we'd better make the most of this time, tonight. We may not have a better chance than this to say all that needs to be said."

Ambrose glanced at me quizzically. "You have things you wish to tell me, too?"

"I do, and perhaps we should deal with that first. My information is less urgent than yours, I suspect, but I think it is important. I'll keep it brief." I then launched into the tale of my interference in the affairs of Nero Niger and his Appius clan, and detailed my thoughts on how we might be able to develop a network of useful alliances with the common people around places like Corinium.

Ambrose listened carefully, and when I had finished speaking he nodded, his expression thoughtful. He then began firing rapid questions at me, all of them concerned with the implementation of my less than lucid plan and the methods I had conceived for making it a reality. I had the answers, incomplete and tentative as they were, at my fingertips, and he weighed each of them judiciously, sometimes reshaping or realigning the thrust of them but not once dismissing anything out of hand.

Within a remarkably short while, working in easy, intuitive harmony, we had transformed my original, optimistic suggestions into a concrete and feasible campaign plan. We would put the proposal to the Council at the next meeting, and put the campaign into effect as soon as possible thereafter.

"Good," Ambrose said then, after we had both sat for a while in silence, pleased with what we had achieved. "Anything else?"

I shook my head. "No, that was all I had. Now what's going on in Cambria, and have you had any word of Vortigern?"

"No, no word of Vortigern, and too much word of Cambria. We're ready to go, you know. As soon as you're prepared. Within the week, if possible."

"To Cambria? In what kind of force?"

"One third. The First Legion—sounds grand, doesn't it? But what else could we call our groups? They're half the size of a legion—"

"I know, but probably three times as powerful. I've heard all about them from Benedict and the others. Tell me about this new Scouting Force you've organized."

For some time, Ambrose had been concerned about an inefficiency in the use of Camulod's fighting resources. Our entire way of life in Camulod was built around the breeding of horses for our cavalry, and our heavy cavalry mounts were our greatest pride. But not all of the enormous number of horses that we bred were large enough to meet our criteria for service. Camulodian cavalry was heavy cavalry, the only force of its kind in Britain, perhaps in the world, and only the largest animals could be strong enough to bear the weight of our heavily armoured troopers. That requirement had left us, over the years, with a large reserve of smaller but otherwise magnificent animals for which we had no purpose, apart from putting them to work in the fields, and the finest of those creatures, my brother had long thought, were going to waste.

Ambrose was aware of our peculiar disdain in Camulod for the light, skirmishing cavalry the Romans had used throughout their history. Primarily mounted archers with short, puny bows, Roman cavalry, in our eyes, had been useless except in the role for which it had been developed: providing a mobile defensive screen for the cumbersome legions while they were forming up in their battle order. But Ambrose had not been born and raised in Camulod, so he did not share that disdain. He was perceptive enough to realize that under certain conditions, such as heavy rain and muddy terrain, lighter—and therefore speedier—cavalry might be extremely effective. He put his findings into effect and created a new branch of Camulodian cavalry—on smaller mounts, with stirrupped saddles and with lighter armour and weapons—and called it a Scouting Force, thereby avoiding the pejorative "light cavalry."

"They're brilliant troops, Cay—hard-hitting and unbelievably mobile. But most of all they're fast, and they can go to places where the heavy cavalry can't go. The heavy troopers require space and dry, level land to do their best fighting. When they have all of those, as you know, they are invincible and terrifying. Unfortunately, we seldom find all three together. The Scouts, though, can go anywhere. They can fight on level ground and they can charge uphill and down because their horses are lighter in every respect. They travel farther and faster, too, and yet tactically, fighting in formation, they're almost as awe-inspiring as the heavy cavalry."

"Sounds excellent. You have them organized in the same way as the regular troopers, I presume."

"Of course. Anything else would be madness. The only difference is in the weight of the horses, and the proportional weight and weaponry of the armed riders. Their primary weapon is the light spear we designed after the one your Erse friend sent from Athol's kingdom."

Years earlier, while visiting Athol Mac Iain in Eire, I had worked with a smith called Maddan on a design for a new cavalry spear, loosely based on the long spears used by the Scots for hunting boars. Much later, when he felt he had perfected it, Maddan sent it to Camulod aboard one of Connor's ships, as a gift, and Ambrose had appropriated it in my absence. It was far lighter and less cumbersome than its size and shape suggested it would be, owing to the construction of the shaft. It had a slender, lethal head welded to a thin iron rod that stretched the entire length of the weapon. The shaft was built around the rod, a laminated cladding of tough, dried, feather-light wattle—the same reeds used in house-building in Eire, and in shield-making by the Saxons—fastened securely along its length with tightly wound bindings of soaked, stretched deerhide that dried out iron hard. The result was a spear that was light, almost flexible and incredibly strong—a perfect weapon for a mounted man.

I was reminded then that I had not yet told Ambrose the sad news that Connor had brought. I watched his expression carefully as I spoke. "You do know that Athol is dead, don't you? Brander is the new king." Clearly he had not heard.

"Strange," he muttered. "You would think the news would have reached us before now, if he died that long ago. The death of a king is noteworthy, cause for much talk."

"Aye, but Athol's new holdings are far north of here, and newly won. And they are islands. The people have been winterbound. No means existed for the tidings to travel to Mediobogdum, or even to Ravenglass."

I went on to ask him about the biremes supposedly being used by Ironhair's armies. Ambrose nodded, looking grim. "Aye, he has them, two of the whoresons. I haven't seen them, but I've heard all about them. They're the biggest ships ever seen in these seas, I'm told, and they carry enormous numbers of men and great quantities of stores. Roman navy biremes, here in Britain, fighting for Ironhair! They have an army of oarsmen, but each of them also carries its own army of warriors! And then, in addition to all that, they ferry levies for Ironhair in the bellies of the things. Apparently they have huge cargo holds, built right into the bodies of the ships themselves, and they carry their own cranes to load them and unload them."

"Aye, well that's nothing new—the cranes, I mean. Connor's galleys have the same device, although probably much smaller. Where did they come from, these ships?"

Ambrose shrugged his shoulders. "I have no idea. The vessel you told me about, the one you saw on your way to Eire, is the only thing of *that* type I've ever heard of, and I've never been able to imagine what that looked like. The thought of two of them, and the possibility that there might be even more, confounds me. God knows where Ironhair found the things."

"Well, Brother, wherever he found them, they were for sale or for hire, and now they're here, ferrying his vermin into Cambria. What about Carthac, is he still alive?"

That brought a grunt of disgust. "Aye, he is, still alive and still demented. He'll always be demented, but I'm beginning to fear he'll always be alive, too. He seems to be unkillable. God knows many have tried. I've heard two different reports of close-shot Pendragon arrows being deflected from his armour."

"I don't believe it. Who told you that?"

He shrugged. "Two people. Two separate reports, two separate incidents."

"How close were the shots? Did you speak to either bowman?"

"No, I merely heard the reports."

"Rumours, then. Soldiers' stories. Those bows are accurate from a quarter-mile away. A close shot from a Pendragon longbow will pierce any armour ever made, if it hits clean. Someone ought to have killed him by now with one of those things. I'll grant he may be formidable, fighting hand to hand—from all reports he's big enough to be indomitable—but he's not immortal. And you say there's no word at all of Vortigern?"

"Not a breath. Utter silence out of the north-east."

"But Hengist is dead, you are sure of that?" He nodded. "Well, you and I agreed years ago that when Hengist died, Vortigern would have trouble with Horsa. For all we know, Vortigern might be at war right now, or he might be dead, long since. If he's at war, he might appreciate some token of support, to keep Horsa off balance. If he is dead, on the other hand, then Horsa is at large, and in power. I think we ought to try and find out what the situation is up there, don't you agree?"

Ambrose thought about that as he leaned forward to stir the fire with an iron rod that lay before the brazier. "Aye, I do," he murmured eventually. "But how? It's a long way from here to there, and logic dictates that we would only be inviting grief by going looking for trouble that might otherwise pass us by."

"Horse turds, Ambrose! You don't believe that any more than I do. Logic dictates that whatever can go wrong will go wrong if you choose to leave your fate in any way in the hands of a mad young bull like Horsa.

You once told me Vortigern thought of himself as High King of all Britain, remember? Well, he has never ruled down here, so his fancies were no more than that. But what if he discussed those fancies with others? All it would take for Horsa would be the suggestion that there might be more settled areas of Britain ripe for conquest, and he'd be here, at the head of his hordes. I don't think we can afford to wait for that to happen, and I don't think we can afford to take the risk that it won't. I think we have to go and see what's going on, up there in Northumbria, and I believe we should go up along the Saxon Shore, now, immediately."

"What? You mean an expedition in force? But that would mean—"

"Aye, I know it would. It would mean splitting our forces when we have a war to deal with here already. I know it's not feasible to do the thing now as it ought to be done, but I still think it's foolish not to slip up there and take a look, at least. The thought of an army of Horsa's Danes falling about our necks while we're involved with Ironhair is not a pleasant notion."

"No, I've known that for months, but I've been hesitant to commit any kind of force to the task while you were away in the north. I've had enough trouble with the thought of leaving this place in other hands while I ride off to Cambria." He pulled himself out of his chair and went to stand over the fire, rubbing his hands together in the heat rising from the coals. "That sounded different from what I had been thinking, when I said it aloud, so I don't want you to misunderstand me. We have good men here. Any one of our senior people is more than capable of looking after things in my absence, commanding the garrison and tending to daily affairs. Tactically speaking, they're all superb. But in terms of strategic ability, I don't know, Cay. There's not a single man I can think of whom I'd care—perhaps even dare—to trust with the responsibility of reacting instantaneously and decisively should the drastic need arise." He held up a hand to forestall my objections, but I had none because I knew exactly what was in his mind. Seeing that, he continued.

"I know I should be able to delegate absolute authority in my absence. That's not my concern. My problem is, quite simply, that none of our second-level commanders has ever had that kind of requirement thrust upon him. Any one of them would accept my dictates, and assume the command and the responsibility, I've no doubt of that. But could any one of them act decisively, should the need arise? Would he commit every resource he had at his disposal to all-out war on a new front—here, at home—on his own authority, or would he hesitate and wait for some kind of endorsement from me? I simply don't know, Cay, and I haven't dared risk the uncertainty. Lip service and willingness are not enough, not with so much at stake, and until I've seen with my own eyes that whoever I choose is capable of taking absolute control—and that's impossible, since

I would have to be here when he needed to and that would negate the need—Ach! I can't even make sense to me!"

I cleared my throat and sat forward in my seat. "I know you expected me to interrupt you, but you are right. The problem is real and worrisome, and it has occurred to me long before now. I suppose it means, in the absolute, that armies require wars—not merely defensive disciplines—to evoke their true strength, and that's a sobering thought."

"You've thought of this before? How? When?"

"Oh, a few years ago, before I left for Ravenglass. I meant to talk with you about it at the time, but the opportunity never arose. It came to me one night, when I was thinking about ambition and what that entails. It began with Peter Ironhair. I realized that none of our senior officers seem to possess his ruthless ambition, the kind that's necessary to achieve true greatness as commanders. They're good and able men, one and all, but they're all followers. And so I began to wonder why that should be so."

"And? Did you discover any reasons?"

"Of course I did, the best of reasons: there's nowhere for them to go."

"I don't follow you."

"You will, if you think about it. We have the only army of its kind in Britain, as far as I'm aware. No?" He nodded slowly, looking bemused. "Well then, what can they aspire to, in terms of supreme command? You're here, and so am I, and we're both young enough yet to have decades ahead of us, barring sickness and accident. We have no wars—or we had none at that time—so the risk of either one of us meeting death in battle has been negligible. So the only route to supremacy for any of them must lie in fomenting mutiny here in Camulod—and who would follow them, were they to try? Where would any malcontent find cause for general mutiny? When did we last execute a soldier? Our greatest penalty is banishment, and the fear of that alone is sufficient to maintain order in our ranks, because banishment from Camulod means perdition: where is a banished man to go? Will he wait around our borders, living on what he can hunt and trap, in the hope of being joined by others, then raiding us? I think not.

"And so our soldiers recognize the benefits they enjoy here, and so do our senior officers. The highest rank they can attain, they hold already, and they seem content with that. We alone, Brother, you and I, must face and live with the disadvantages in such a system, which arise only at times like this. When a man—any man—has reached the limits of his progress, he tends to accept those limits and grow comfortable. There is your dilemma."

"Hmm . . ." Ambrose had been pacing as he listened, and now he sat down across from me again. "You're absolutely right. And now that we are faced with war again, those expectations will all change. The dilemma will resolve itself as individual field commanders rise to the challenges they meet."

"Aye, or fail to rise, in which case they will be replaced. Either way, we'll soon have no lack of qualified field commanders. But let's get back to the original point, which was the threat from the north-east, Horsa's Danes. Your hands have been tied in that by your not knowing whom to leave in charge, given the risk of attack from that direction. Now they're untied. I'm here, and so is Dedalus, and Ded, next to you and me, is the best man we have, in terms of possessing the will and the flair for absolute command. You were going to leave two legions here, taking the First with you to Cambria. Why? Why wouldn't you take two into Cambria?"

He held up his hands. "Because of the danger from the north-east— precisely what you were talking about earlier. I had decided that with you away in the north-east, should everything go wrong while I was in Cambria, and Camulod's defenders were essentially left lacking decisive strategic leadership, they ought at least to have sufficient defensive strength to survive until we could provide that leadership. That meant two legions, sufficient to hold and patrol our borders."

"Good enough. But that's all changed now. I think you have to take two legions into Cambria, less one tenth."

"*I* have to take them? So you've decided not to come. What do you intend to do with the tenth I leave behind, as if I did not already know?"

I nodded. "An expedition in force, into Northumbria. You'll have six thousand men, less my six hundred. That will allow you to win in Cambria, smashing Ironhair, and it will allow me to penetrate to Northumbria in relative safety. I'll have two hundred heavy cavalry, a hundred of your Scouts, and three hundred infantry. That will discourage unwelcome attention."

"Aye, it should, but you'll have two hundred and more miles to travel, each way, and much of it across rough country. To take the roads would not be worth the risk—people tend to congregate along the open routes."

"No, you're wrong there, Ambrose. The roads offer the greatest advantage for speedy progress, there and back. There might be people lining the routes on either side, all the way, but we'll be travelling quickly, at the forced march."

"You'll be tied to the speed of your infantry. The roads are speediest for heavy cavalry and infantry. But the roads also offer endless opportunities for entrapment. The news of your coming will precede you at the speed a man can run to pass on word to another runner. On any of them, your progress and your arrival at any given point will be predictable. You could lose your entire party over the course of a hundred miles, one arrow at a time."

"True enough, I suppose, if you look only at the bleakest picture."

"I do, and so do you. That's our responsibility. That's command."

"Accepted. So are you telling me I should remain here and wait to see what might come down against us from the north?"

"No, not at all. I'm thinking about Cambria, *my* battleground. Most of it is mountainous, except for the coastal areas, which means that most of it is bad cavalry country. I've been aware of that all along, and I have what I think will be a successful strategy for using our infantry in the hills, supported by our cavalry working from base camps in the valleys beneath. I intend to flush Ironhair's levies the way boys flush out wild game for hunters to kill. One hill, one hill range at a time, I intend to push them back and off the summits, thrusting them down into the valleys beyond and into our cavalry. We can count on the Pendragon warriors and bowmen to join us, and we've trained enough of them in our own ways for us to hope, at the very least, that they'll be able to work with us in concert. Our discipline will win the battles and the war for us. In addition to that, the Scouts should be able to work well in all but the most inaccessible mountain terrain, although not in massive numbers, and that has an effect on you."

"Very well, now it's my turn to be lost."

He smiled. "Test this then, for logic. I need every infantry soldier we possess. I also need every individual unit of heavy cavalry. I intend to divide my force, initially, and to interdict Ironhair's fleet from using the harbours they now hold. To do that, I need cavalry and infantry both, to seal each harbour from the land side and then drive the defenders into the sea. One legion should suffice for that, at the beginning, and I'll be able to reduce that number later, once we hold the harbours.

"In the meantime, I won't need the full complement of Scouts, while you, on the other hand, can use them. I'm suggesting you exchange your force of six hundred mixed troops for five hundred Scouts. That will allow you to move more quickly than otherwise possible, and to pick your own route at every stage of your journey. I'd suggest you'll be invulnerable, too, until you decide if and when to stand and fight. No one who doesn't have an army of his own would ever dream of attacking five hundred armed and disciplined mounted men. There's never been a force like that seen outside the bounds of Camulod, Cay."

My heart had begun to pound as he spoke, and now my excitement was unbearable, so that I rose to my feet and began pacing the room. From the corner of my eye, I saw one of the lamps gutter and go out, and so I knew that time had passed quickly. Ambrose was watching, making no attempt to hurry me. I forced myself to stop pacing and faced him.

"No fault in your logic, Brother, none at all. But are you sure you won't have need of the Scouts?"

"Of course I will, but we have a thousand, and I'll need no more than half of them. I'll have two thousand heavy troopers and three thousand infantry to back them up, remember. You won't, but you'll be carrying surprise with you all the way. No one will oppose you on the road to Northumbria."

"What about spare horses? Do we have enough?"

Ambrose laughed aloud. "Enough? There are more horses in this colony than there are people, Caius. How many will you require?"

"A spare for every man. That should do it."

"Good, then take half as many again, as a reserve. You can't replace a cavalry mount in the field unless you have one with you."

I had a sudden image of my expedition travelling overland: more than twelve hundred horses! "My God," I said. "The logistics of that are frightening!"

"Then delegate, Brother. We've no lack of logistics personnel. You'll need either wagons or pack animals to carry grain and other supplies. Wagons would be better, but they'll tie you to the roads again. Your spare animals can carry packs and your Scouts will all care for their own animals, so you won't need an army of camp-followers to tend your needs."

"We'll be moving slowly, then."

He looked at me from beneath raised eyebrows. "What does that mean? Your 'slowly' will yet be faster than heavy troopers or infantry could move. You won't be galloping all the way, but you'll move easily enough. So, are we agreed on this? Me for Cambria with the two legions and you for the far north-east with five hundred Scouts?"

I nodded my head. "We are. When do we begin?"

"We've begun, Brother. Now all we have to do is put our agreement into effect. Within the week, we'll both be gone from here, and Camulod will be safe in the able hands of Dedalus. Have you given any thought to your route? And how long would you expect to be away?"

"Two questions, one affecting the other." I paused considering both of them. "I think my best route would be the one you and I took last time. At least I'm familiar with it. We'll head east from here until we reach the Saxon-occupied territories, and then abandon the roads and strike out northward, overland, probably sooner than we did before, since the occupied area has probably grown bigger. What are you smiling at?"

His smile grew broader. "Remembering our magic feat, the day we made ourselves identical and terrified those raiders by shooting at them alternately from places we could not possibly have been as one man alone, and yet all they could see was one man. What was that big Anglian's name, the farmer whose life we saved, do you recall?"

I thought for a moment, remembering the occasion from eight, could it have been nine years earlier? "Something ungodly, almost unpronounceable. Guth? Guth-something-or-other."

"Guthilrod, wasn't it? There was a strange 'thlr' not a Celtic one—in there somewhere."

"Gethelrud! That was it, Gethelrud."

"Will you visit him, think you?"

"Visit him? D'you think me mad, with five hundred men and three times that many horses? I can imagine his face, seeing me there in his yard! We couldn't even speak to each other last time, when I was alone."

My brother was still smiling. "He may have learned our tongue since then."

"Latin? Oh yes, I'm sure he must have, almost certainly. He probably writes regularly to the Emperor nowadays, in Constantinople. No, Brother, I'll be doing no visiting. I'll be moving as quickly as I can. As for how long it may take me to come back, how long do you expect to be in Cambria? I'll come back when I can, but not before I've done what must be done. Three months would be the shortest time, I'd guess."

"Aye, that's what I thought. You might then have to come and rescue me from Cambria."

I smiled at that. "I will, if I have to, and I'll bring the Third Legion with me, since the threat from the north-east will be resolved by then." I looked at my brother, taking great strength from his confidence and his ardour for the crucial task at hand. "Have I ever told you how glad I am you're here?" He looked at me in surprise and I grinned at him. "No, I mean it. I shudder to think of what my life would be, had you and I not met. I would have missed the better half of myself and would have had to live with half a brain. I thank God, frequently, for your existence, for the fact that we are kin, and for the miracle of meeting you."

"Kin? Man, we are practically twins."

"I know, and that calls for a drink." I glanced around me. "I suppose everyone else is long abed. We've been talking here for long enough to outlive the lamps, and the fire's almost dead."

Ambrose sat up straight and grunted. "Aye, well I'll replenish the fire and see to some of the lamps, if you'll find us some mead. There should be some left on the shelves in the triclinium."

By the time I returned, clutching a flask and two stemmed glass cups, he had remade the fire and was pouring oil carefully into one of the failing lamps. I sat down and poured mead for both of us, then waited until he returned to his seat and picked up his cup.

"You know, while I was looking for the mead, one thing occurred to me—a flaw. It's the only one I can see in what we've planned, but it's enormous."

He sipped at his drink, and I watched the expressions flow across his face as he tried to guess what I was talking about. "Very well, you must be more perceptive than I am, because I can't see it. What is it?"

"The whole thing is backwards."

He frowned, trying to make sense of that. "I don't follow you. What's backwards?"

"Our plan. *I* should be the one going to Cambria and *you* the one headed for Northumbria, because I don't speak the languages they use up there and you do."

Now he scowled. "That's nonsense, on three counts. First, Vortigern speaks Latin—"

"Granted, but Vortigern and all his people might be dead, and you speak the tongue of the Outlanders, the Danes."

"Aye, but only poorly, and I've no knowledge of the other tongues at all—Anglian, and the gibbering of the Jutes."

"But it's Horsa's Danes who worry us. Theirs is the tongue we need, even for listening. It doesn't matter if we ever talk to them, as long as we can listen to them speak among themselves, hear them and know what they are saying. I'm useless there. You should be the one to go."

"No, I disagree. And here's my second objection. If I go there and find Vortigern alive, I might have difficulty leaving again."

That caught me unprepared. "What d'you mean? You would prefer to *stay* there?"

"Of course not! It's simply that . . ." He hesitated, seeking the right words. "If Vortigern's alive, and I turn up there in his lands with half a thousand horsemen, he might be inclined to . . . seek to restrain me from leaving again. My force would give him an enormous advantage."

"You think he might use force?"

"No, not at all. Discourage me from leaving would be more accurate. Don't forget, I was once among his senior and most trusted captains. Until I met you and decided to come south to meet my own people, he had all my loyalty. In any event, he would try to find some way to persuade me to use my troops in his support."

"It would be no different if I were leading them."

"Ah, but it would. You would leave when the time came, and he would be quite powerless to stop you, whereas he might convince himself that I yet owe him loyalty. He might make it very . . . difficult for me. I would defy him, if I had to, but I would not enjoy that, and the thought of having to lead my men against his—against him—makes me cold with loathing."

That made me pause. I had almost forgotten the extent of Ambrose's former ties to Vortigern. But then, evaluating what he had said, I accepted it and moved on. "You said my suggestion made no sense on three counts. You've given me two—what is the other?"

"Ah! You're not familiar with my campaign plan for Cambria, or with the strategy I've devised."

"We can change that in a matter of days. How well do you know Cambria?"

"I don't, not well at all."

"And do you speak the tongue fluently? Or that of Cornwall?"

He shook his head.

"And I do. I speak the tongues, and I know the land and the terrain. You explain your strategy to me, and I'll carry it out. On the matter of Vortigern's being tempted to coerce you into staying, I doubt that's likely. I don't think Vortigern would dare to make an enemy of you and your force. He has too many real enemies already. So I'll act as you intended to, and you will act as I would have, had I gone to Northumbria. Remember, we are almost identical, so no one seeing either of us from afar will be able to tell which of us he is seeing anyway. It only makes sense, then, that each of us should do what he does best. Don't you agree?"

"Partially." He was still far from convinced. "I'm an infantry commander, Cay, not a cavalryman."

"Horse turds. The Scouts are yours. You created them. They'd follow you into Hades." I stopped, then spoke more quietly. "Look, Ambrose, it's too important to decide right now, tonight, in haste. Why don't you think about it overnight. Then, in the morning, if you're still reluctant, we'll proceed as planned. Either one of us can go to either place. It simply seems more sensible to me that we should make the most of what we have, and that means using your skills in the north-east and mine in the west, where we are both familiar with the surroundings. Will you think about it?"

He smiled. "No need to think on it. You are obviously right, and what you have said makes sense in every detail. We'll do as you suggest. But there's a price to pay, for convincing me so easily to accept your plan over my own."

"And what is that?"

"I want to take young Arthur with me, make the next stage of his training my responsibility. You've had the shaping of him exclusively for six years and more. I think it might be good for him to have a change of teacher, at this stage, and it might be safer for him, too. You will be riding into certain war in Cambria, with all its risks. I might encounter no hostility at all in the north-east. What say you?"

I did not even have to hesitate. I would, indeed, be riding into certain war, with all its risks, in Cambria, and the greatest risk of all was that I might miss my chance at Ironhair were I to adopt my brother's plan and let him go there in my stead. Now, visualizing Ironhair's corpse sprawled at my feet, I nodded briskly, eager to proceed and have this matter disposed of.

"I think young Arthur will be delighted, and you're right about the risk. Good. I'll pay your price, and I'll take on young Bedwyr. But you've reminded me of another thing I wanted to ask you about. I saw a school on the plain, today, did I not? Is it a school?"

"Yes, it is. One of Ludmilla's female Councillors suggested it, about four years ago, and it started the year before last, in the late summer. What about it?"

"Tell me about the priests I saw there."

He looked surprised. "What do you want to know?"

"Who are they and where did they come from? Were they invited here, and if so, why? They looked to me to be monastics."

The corner of my brother's mouth flickered upwards, but he did not quite smile. "Monastics? There are few monastics in Britain, Cay, to the best of my knowledge." He paused. "That is a fashion of worship and a way of life that has not yet come to our shores. The men you ask about live in seclusion, communally, cut off from the world . . . but they are not monastics in the sense I believe you mean, the monastics from beyond the seas."

"Brother, you are making no sense at all."

He sipped at his mead and swilled it around in his mouth before swallowing. "I am making perfect sense, Cay, and you'll agree, once you understand what I'm talking about. The men you saw today, although they are not priests, are from the ancient Christian community at Glastonbury, not twenty miles from here. They are followers of your good friend Germanus, who, as you may recall, decreed at Verulamium that schools should be set up to teach the ways and the word of God to the youth of this country."

That gave me pause. Glastonbury was the oldest seat of Christianity in Britain, and there had been a community of anchorites in residence there almost since the days of the Christ himself. Some said, indeed, that the Christ himself had visited the place. I had heard the tale told several times, but I gave it no credence. The thought of the carpenter of Galilee travelling to the wilds of western Britain had always struck me, as it had most people, as being ludicrous. Nevertheless, there had always been a religious community in residence there, living in a collection of stone-walled hovels high on the shelving beach above the surrounding marshes, huddled at the base of the high tor that gave the place its name, and barely subsisting on the charity of local residents. I saw immediately what Ambrose had meant by calling them monastics. The new fashion among the religious overseas was to gather in closed communities, living in filth and poverty and in contemplation of God's works, eschewing the temptations of Devil, World and Flesh. The anchorites of Glastonbury had been living that way for hundred of years, quietly and without notice.

"I've never been there," I said. "I've heard tell of it, but never in any way that might have attracted me. How did the priests come here?"

Ambrose smiled. "I invited them. I have been there, you see."

I looked at him in amazement. "You have? Why would you go there? There's nothing there but the tor."

"And the community. We had a visitor, in the summer, four years ago, a churchman named Ludovic who had come from Gaul, from Germanus, and was on his way to Glastonbury. His ship had been blown off course and wrecked on the north Cornish coast, and he had been washed ashore, clinging to a piece of wreckage. From there he'd made his way towards us on foot. Our guards found him on our perimeter and brought him here to me. He spent a week with us, and then I escorted him to Glastonbury. That's where I met my namesake, Ambrose, who is the leader of the congregation there. Ludovic had brought Ambrose word from Germanus, bidding him send his people out to set up schools. That was coincidence, because we had just heard from our Women's Council that they wished us to establish a school of some description here in Camulod. There was a fatefulness to it that I could not ignore, and so Ambrose's people came down here the following year, once we had built our school, and began teaching."

"Teaching what?"

"Christianity, mainly, its principles and tenets. Not all of them are literate themselves—very few are, in fact. Ambrose teaches writing and reading, and so does Thomas. Baloric, the eldest of them, knows computation and Euclid's geometry, so he teaches those subjects to a small number of our brightest. These men refer to themselves as the Fraternity of Joseph, and their lives consist of work and prayer. They spend the autumn and winter months with us, once the harvest is gathered in, but they return to their community in spring and remain there through the summer, while our children are working with their parents in the fields."

"Hmm. And you are satisfied their presence here is a benefit to the Colony?"

"Completely satisfied."

"Good, then I'll say no more about them. Just don't expect me to ride to Glastonbury with them, though. My Christianity does not extend that far."

"We demonstrate our own beliefs in our own ways." He smiled again.

"What does that mean?"

"Whatever you wish it to mean. Some of us live our beliefs in our hearts, others show them more openly. That's all."

"Aye, well . . ." I looked at the fire, and it had burned low again, mere embers glowing in the bottom of the iron basket. "It's late, but we still have to talk about young Arthur."

"Arthur's grown tall. No doubting he is one of us. And he's filling out hugely."

"Aye, and he's fallen in love, too."

I told him briefly about Arthur's thunderbolting, and we laughed gently together before Ambrose asked, "You think it's time he learned to go to war?"

"I do, and I've promised him he can ride out with us, he and his friends, Bedwyr, Gwin and Ghilly. They're of the age for it. But we'll have to separate them. They'll learn best in isolation from each other. You will take Arthur with you into the north-east, on this first foray. When you return, we two will be his teachers. He knows he must start out as a mere slave, a servant and a messenger. He'll tend our weapons, polish our armour, bed down our animals, run errands for us and learn to stand on his own feet and trust his own judgment. Meanwhile, I'll take young Bedwyr with me into Cambria, and perhaps Ghilly, too, though he's a year younger. He might serve well with Philip, on campaign, for I know he was impressed with Philip when he commanded our garrison."

"I see no objection to that. What about the other lad, Gwin?"

"I'll leave him here in Camulod, as servant to Dedalus. He won't like that, at first. He'll be bitterly disappointed at not riding out with the others, but he couldn't have a better mentor than Ded will be. Then, when we return, the boys will all change masters, and Gwin will have his turn on the campaign trail. You think that will work?"

"I think there are only three things more certain, at this point."

"And what are those?"

"It's very late, my mead is gone, and I am going to bed. Sleep well, Brother, because tomorrow will be a long day. It may all be celebrations of one kind or another, but by the end of it you'll be whimpering for sleep. Blow out the lamps when you leave, and don't be mean enough to waken Tress when you slip into bed."

I yawned and followed him out towards the stairway to the upper floor, blowing out the last two lamps as I went.

The day that followed was as long as Ambrose had predicted, but paradoxically it flew by, from the early-morning trumpet calls that turned out the garrison to prepare the campus for the coming celebrations, to the late-night gatherings around bonfires where the sounds of singing and stringed instruments spread outward from the various assemblies and mingled at times into a cacophonous welter in the ears of the people moving from group to group.

I have only two lasting impressions of that day. One was the realization, shortly after daybreak, that we did, in fact, have thousands of soldiers in Camulod. The day had been decreed a festival and the entire garrison excused from formal duty, save only for a skeletal force selected by lot to form the guard for the day. The troopers still had lesser responsibilities governing them; however, the task of setting up the venue for the afternoon's gathering was theirs, and their freedom to make merry afterwards was strictly curtailed by a ban on drinking during daylight hours.

I watched them from above, from a bend in the hill road, as they swarmed upon the broad campus below, transforming it in a few short hours from a dirt-grey, barren space to a sprawling tent town dotted with massive, unlit fires in shallow depressions around which heavy, wooden tables with attached benches, all made from raw lumber, had been arranged in concentric rings. In the centre of all, they left a rectangular space, some sixty paces long by forty wide, which would accommodate the major spectacles later in the day. Some of them had dug pits for the cooking fires the night before, off to the side of the main campus, close to the fringe of trees on the south side.

The spit-roast cooking of the largest animals had begun long before dawn, under the watchful eyes of Marco and his staff of cooks. That entire southern area, on the grassy, lightly treed meadows flanking the great drilling ground, had been fenced off, and guards had been posted there to keep the curious outside and away from the preparation of the food. Within the fence was a bustling chaos of activity. My primary impression, however, was that the number of men working on the drilling ground itself seemed beyond credence. I had never seen so many soldiers in one place before.

My second memory is of the exhibition of horsemanship and weapons skills that took place in the afternoon. Then, for the first time, I witnessed what a body of mounted men—our new Scouts—could do with the new, light spears. Group after group swept forward, covered from head to foot in toughened leather armour, galloping at full speed and leaning far out from their saddles, braced only by reins and stirrups, to pluck brightly beribboned coloured targets from the ground on the points of their spears. Later, others advanced in lines at the full charge against a row of propped-up shields, to pull their horses up into rearing turns, moving as one, while the riders braced themselves and threw their spears above the edges of the shields to where they would have skewered the men who held them. As they rode away from the "encounter," swerving easily between the riders now approaching in the following lines, each rider held a new spear, drawn from its carrying place behind his saddle. I knew, watching these manoeuvres, that I was witnessing a new form of tactical warfare.

Dedalus had been standing beside me throughout all this, as had Rufio, and now, as the last of the demonstration teams rode off the field to enormous applause, Rufio spoke up. "See what our fellows have learned while we've been gone? Makes you feel inadequate, doesn't it?"

Ded glanced sideways at him, smiling. "Rufe, if you hadn't met that demon-cursed bear, we could have given them a display of swordsmanship, with our game of two-stick, that would have made them all feel sick."

As Rufio nodded and spat disconsolately, Ded turned back to me. "The boys still could, you know. Not two-stick, they don't have the skill for that, but they're good enough with one oak staff each to raise these people's eyebrows. What think you, Cay?"

The thought had already occured to me, but I had dismissed the notion. "No, Ded, I don't think that would be a good idea. In the first place, it might not look right—might give the impression we're feeling as inadequate as we are, and trying to compensate by showing off. And in the second place, I don't think it would be good for the boys to be singled out like that. Let's not do anything to call unnecessary attention to Arthur."

Ded shrugged and nodded. "You're the Commander, so be it." He raised his head and sniffed. "God, that meat smells good. I'm starved. Let's go see if they're ready to start serving."

We strolled together towards the cooking area, and that, as it happens, constitutes my last distinct memory of that day. I know that Tress had a wonderful time, for I recall her flushed and laughing, bright-eyed and slightly out of breath from dancing with one of the young men; and I know that the food was varied and excellent, for I remember Marco being carried shoulder-high by a boisterous crew of troopers and cooks; and I know I met many more new faces throughout the day—but I remember none of that in detail nor do I remember going to bed that night.

The day that followed was dedicated to cleaning up, and once again the troopers overran the great campus. By the end of the day, in the brief spring twilight, there was no sign that the tent had ever been there; even the blackened rings of the fire-scorched earth had been raked over with harrows, their depressions filled and the ashes buried or scattered.

By the time the sun rose the morning after that, the enormous campus was transformed yet again, its entire surface covered by precisely aligned formations of motionless men: the rearmost half was made up of squadrons of heavy cavalry, the flanking troops were composed of smaller bodies of the Scouting Force, and the front central ranks and files were composed entirely of foot soldiers. Riding through the front gates, on my way down with Ambrose to inspect them, I pulled my horse to a stop. Ambrose reined in, too, looking at me.

"What?"

"Brown," I replied. "They're all brown."

He turned away for a moment, looking down on the army assembled below us, trying to decipher my meaning, and then he looked back at me. "The armour, you mean?"

"Yes. Seeing them all together like that, as an entity, it suddenly struck me. There's not much metal."

"No, we don't have much metal, not enough to armour thousands. But we don't really need metal armour. The Romans conquered the world in leather armour, didn't you know that?" He grinned. "Triple layers of toughened oxhide with metal studs will turn most weapons. Besides, our weapons are all iron, and they are the best in Britain, made in our own smithies. And if you look closely, you'll see that our officers are all armoured in metal. They're the ones who need it most, since they're the ones who stand most exposed to the enemy. Shall we go on?"

"In a moment, wait!" He had begun to urge his horse forward, but now he stopped again. "Where are we obtaining our iron nowadays?"

"Where we always have—anywhere we can find it. Carol has contacts scouring the countryside all the time. The ore beds are mostly in south Cambria to the north of Glevum, and along the south-east shore. But few people are mining them now and, of course, the south-eastern shores are Saxon-occupied. So most of our raw iron still comes from Pendragon country . . ." He fell silent, thinking, then sniffed. "Publius Varrus said in his writings that iron would one day have more worth than gold. I wish he had been wrong." So did I, but the accuracy of my great-uncle's vision had been a reality for many years now. Carol was Camulod's senior armourer, one of the three middle-aged sons of Equus, Publius Varrus's long-time friend and business partner, and I knew how much of his time went into the increasingly fruitless hunt for raw-smelted iron, and even raw ore.

"Publius Varrus was seldom wrong, in matters of metal. But speaking of Carol reminds me that I have something for you, in my quarters. It's not a gift, since it's as much yours as mine, but it will please you. As soon as we are finished down below, if you'll ride back with me, I'll give it to you. In the meantime, our troops look magnificent, as they ought to . . . Let's ride on down. We have kept them waiting long enough."

We made our way down onto the plain, and as we approached the dense mass of our army, coming close enough finally to be able to discern the unsmiling, individual features beneath the rows and rows of identical war helmets, it struck me forcibly that I would be seeing very few soft, feminine faces in the days and months that stretched ahead.

It took more than two hours to inspect our troopers, but it was a pleasant and rewarding task in the warm springtime sunlight. Our men were ready, primed for war, and there was a sense of bubbling anticipation among them, though they stood silent and arrow straight as we walked among them, peering critically at their weapons and armour, their animals and saddlery.

The veterans of Lot's War, years earlier, stood out unmistakably among the assembly, distinguished by the decorations they had won in the conflict. They alone had the right to wear a stiff, whitish crest of boar bristle on their parade helmets in commemoration of the fact that they had fought and defeated Gulrhys Lot, whose emblem had been the Boar of Cornwall. All other Camulodian troopers wore crests made of brown horsehair.

In addition to the crests, many of our veterans also wore combat rings, directly adapted by my grandfather Caius from the ritualized reward system employed by the Romans, where meritorious service in varying degrees won individual soldiers the right to carry rings of differing sizes and metals—gold, silver, bronze and iron—mounted on their cuirasses. Some of these rings were ornate, others were plain, and each of them had its own significance. The largest, the size of a man's palm, symbolized the crowns that could be won by heroic soldiers in ancient times for outstanding deeds of valour, such as capturing an enemy stronghold.

Tertius Lucca, our *primus pilus*, wore three rows of three such rings on his breastplate, covering his whole chest. Two were of plain gold, indicating instances of unparalleled personal valour and achievement, while two more were of silver carved to look like rope, announcing to the world his leadership of victorious companies in two distinct campaigns; two more were plain silver, and the three on the bottom row were bronze, each denoting a companion's life saved single-handedly in battle. He wore shoulder flashes, too, of polished iron, covering the seams of his front and rear armour, and these were crusted thick with twelve smaller honour rings, welded atop each other in layers. Atop his helmet, which was equipped with full face flaps that protected everything except his gleaming eyes, he wore a huge, spectacular crest of stiffened white horsehair, sweeping from shoulder to shoulder in the centurion's manner.

Tertius Lucca, in the prime of his manhood, made an impressive sight in his parade armour, and at the conclusion of our formal inspection of his troops we thanked him ceremonially and returned the control of the assembly into his hands after our final salute to the podium, where the massed standards of our formations were ranked together. As we rode away then, the two Commanders side by side, followed by our corps of staff officers, we heard Lucca's voice, as loud as Stentor's, marshalling the throngs one last time, bidding them prepare to be dismissed in good order.

Back at the fort, I thanked the other officers and dismissed them, before leading Ambrose into the room in my quarters into which I had piled all the crates and cases I had not yet unpacked. I quickly identified the one I sought and prised the lid off it to reveal Excalibur's case, carefully packed in wood shavings, and the two replicas made from the last of the skystone metal. I hoisted one out and tossed it to Ambrose. He caught it by the sheathed blade and held it up to the light, staring at it.

"I thought of this the other night, when you reminded me about making ourselves identical that day in Saxon country. Remember how you worried because our bows were different, as if the people we attacked could notice such a thing from a hundred paces distant?" He smiled and brought the hilt closer to his eyes. "Well, our swords will be identical from now on, at least." I held out the other of the pair, so that he could see that they were, in every respect, identical from pommel to sheath tip.

"Who made the scabbards?"

I held mine out and withdrew the blade. "Joseph made them, using the same techniques Uncle Varrus used. They're sheepskin, as you can see, folded and sewn, with the fleece inside and shaved away to a mere nap that polishes and cleans the blade each time you draw it out or slip it in. The upper part is reinforced with a metal sleeve, to keep it stiff and snug around the top of the blade, and to support that long, straight hook on the back of the scabbard. We needed something to enable us to carry these things, and this hook is what Joseph came up with.

"The blade's too long to permit a straight-arm draw, either over your shoulder or from your side, and it's far too long even to let you walk, if you are carrying the sword hanging by your side. The only alternative you have is to carry the thing in your hand all the time, and that is obviously ridiculous. So, the long-tongued hook on the back of the sheath slips into the harness ring between your shoulders, and the sheathed blade hangs down your back, the hilt above your shoulder. Nothing new there. The new part comes when you need the sword. See?" I had been demonstrating as I spoke. "You take hold of the hilt, reach behind you with your free hand, low, push the scabbard up until the hook clears the ring at your back, then flip the blade forward, over your shoulder, to where you can catch it again in your free hand. Draw the sword, like that, and slip the sheath hook into your belt, so you don't lose it. The sheath dangles, flexible and harmless, and you have a naked, dangerous weapon in your hand. You approve?"

"Hmm, I do. Very ingenious. Joseph came up with this?" Ambrose was fumbling behind him, attempting to insert the long, straight hook of the scabbard into the ring at his back where his long-bladed cavalry *spatha* normally hung, its blade through the ring.

"He did. You'll grow used to that manoeuvre. I had difficulty with it myself, for the first few days, but it's usage, like anything else—balance and feel. I slip the hook in there nowadays without even thinking about it, and I can have the sword drawn and bare in my hand before a man can count to three."

He slid the scabbard into place eventually and then went through the motions of drawing the weapon, his movements slow and clumsy. I repeated them, my own movements smooth and liquid, bouncing the sheathed blade against my right shoulder for impetus, then twisting my wrist inward on the down pull, bringing the blade across my chest to where my left hand could grasp the scabbard just below the hilt; a straight pull in opposite directions with either hand, and I had my bared sword ready to strike. The scabbard flopped empty in my left hand as I slipped the retaining hook into my belt.

"As I said, you'll soon capture the trick of it, and the marvellous thing is that it works even better on horseback than it does on foot."

Ambrose was examining the blade of his sword, holding it close to his face and angling it so that the light reflected along the length of it. "Aye," he said, absently. "I'm sure it does. You know, this thing even *looks* better—I mean up close like this, close to the eye—than any other sword I've ever seen. It has a wavy pattern in the iron, much more than in any other sword. I know it's from the way the smiths fold and twist the metal bars that make up the blade, when they heat them and then hammer them flat, but it looks different, somehow."

"It is different. The metal's different. It's skystone metal, not mere iron."

He glanced at me and straightened his shoulders before sliding the blade of his new sword carefully back into its leather sheath. "Where is Excalibur now?"

I nodded towards the open crate. "In there."

"May I look at it?"

I retrieved the polished wooden case from the packing crate, blowing away a few tiny curls of wood shavings that clung to its gloss, and then I opened it and produced Excalibur, grasping it through the silken cloth that covered the blade and offering it hilt first to my brother. Ambrose gazed at it in silent wonder, making no move to reach for it, and then he quickly stripped the scabbard again from the sword he held, dropping the empty sheath on a table top and transferring the sword hilt to his left hand before reaching for Excalibur with his right. He stood with both arms stretched ahead of him, comparing the two swords side by side.

"It's so much more . . . elaborate," he whispered.

"Aye, it is. It's as much for display as for use—a king's weapon. The other, by comparison, is a working sword, a fighting man's weapon."

He jerked his head to look at me, his mouth quirking into a half-grin. "May not a king, then, be a fighting man?"

"You know better than that, Brother. But many's the fine fighting man could never be a king."

"No, nor would want to be." He had turned back to his comparison. "See how shiny the blade is! There has never been anything like it."

"No, you are wrong, Ambrose. There are two others like it, and you are holding one of them in your other hand. Their blades seem duller, that is all, but that is simply because Excalibur is burnished. They are exact replicas, merely plain and unadorned, while their companion piece is gaudier."

"Gaudier . . . that's an ugly word, Clay. It smacks of falseness. This is Excalibur! There's nothing false about it. Has Arthur seen it yet?"

"No, not yet. He's still too young to take it. Soon, now, it will be his, but I will have to be convinced that he is old enough to understand why I have kept it from him until then."

Ambrose looked at me from beneath a raised eyebrow, then smiled sardonically, changing his grip on Excalibur to grasp it by the cross-guard and extending the hilt to me. "Now, that," he drawled, "was a convoluted statement, but I think I understood it."

"Excellent. Let's hear you repeat it, then."

"The boy's too young and won't be old enough to know until he's old enough to know that he's too young. Is that not what you said?"

I laughed and closed the lid on the polished case, returning the glorious sword to its storage space. "Exactly, Brother! That is precisely what I said."

PART TWO

CAMBRIA

VII

"BEDWYR, MERLYN." Donuil's words brought me back from my thoughts and I turned my head to look where he was pointing. I saw young Bedwyr immediately as he brought his horse at full gallop down the smoothly sloping hillside across from where we sat, guiding it easily between the rock outcrops that littered the short-grassed ground, picking the shortest, easiest route to the knoll from which we watched his progress.

"He rides like a centaur, doesn't he?"

"Aye, he does," I answered. "But what we need are warriors who can fly like eagles."

I twisted around in my saddle to look behind me, down to where my forces were spread out for more than a mile along the broad belt of land by the water's edge. Beyond them, the late-morning sunlight reflected dazzlingly from the waves that still churned the surface of the sea, restive, despite the now cloudless skies, from the fury of the violent summer storm that had swept over this area the previous night. The coastal plain was wide here, along the westernmost edge of south Cambria, and I had no fears of being entrapped, despite the apparent unpreparedness of my army, spread out as it was, its soldiers sprawling at leisure on the ground. Now I heard Rufio's rough voice, growling in response to my comment.

"I doubt that, Merlyn. We're in Cambria, remember? Even a soaring eagle can be felled up here by a well-flighted Pendragon arrow."

Smiling, I turned to face him. Beside him, standing with one hand on the neck of Rufio's horse, his friend Huw Strongarm, the leader of our Pendragon contingent, stood looking at me and shaking his head tolerantly at Rufe's bluntness. His great longbow was slung over his shoulder and the flights of a full quiver of arrows rose behind his head. I winked at him and answered Rufio's remark.

"True, Rufe, but all the Pendragon longbows are with us, so your point is weakened."

"Hmm'phmm!" The sound was loaded with disgust. "Most of them are, Commander, most of them. But there are too many turncoat whoresons out there with Ironhair for my taste."

He was referring, I knew, to Owain of the Caves. I nodded, then spoke to Benedict, whose mount was so close to me on my left side that my knee touched his. "Well, we'll know now what Philip has found inland. Judging by the speed young Bedwyr's making, it must be significant."

Benedict grinned. "Aye. Unless, of course, he's trying to kill his horse simply because he sees us watching him."

Behind me, I heard Derek bark a gruff laugh at Benedict's quip. The king of Ravenglass sat astride a horse that was as big as my Germanicus. Derek had changed greatly since reaching Camulod. His resolve to fight no more had given way beneath an increasing belief that Ironhair and his demented ally Carthac should be put down once and for all. A king himself, Derek of Ravenglass had a sense of natural justice that offered no quarter to usurpers. He now wore a uniform that would have marked him as a Roman tribune in earlier times, complete with scarlet cloak, plumed helmet and richly figured, polished leather cuirasses front and back.

I looked from Derek to Benedict and shook my head in mock regret. "Cynics! I am surrounded by cynics and pessimists. No wonder we are faring less than well here in Cambria."

I kneed my horse gently forward, moving beyond the others of my command group to where I could see Bedwyr clearly and he could see me awaiting him. I remained motionless as he put his mount to the slope in front of me, and in a short time he had reached the summit, blowing almost as hard as his horse. He had grown taller and filled out impressively in the months we had spent together in Cambria, and I found myself wondering if Arthur had made such evident progress, wherever he was in the north-east.

Bedwyr brought his horse to a halt and jumped down. He approached me and then drew himself to attention with a stiff salute, bringing his right fist to smack against his left breast and gazing up wide-eyed to where I sat looking down at him.

"Legate Commander Merlyn!"

I nodded to him, repressing an urge to smile at his frowning earnestness. "Stand easy, Trooper, and make your report."

He sucked in a deep breath and stood even straighter, his elbows slightly bent and braced to hold his body motionless, his clenched fists resting slightly forward of his hipbones. Then, in a clipped and formal voice very different from his normal tone, he rattled off his message.

"Legate Commander, the Legate Philip wishes to report that he has been unable to make significant contact with the enemy forces opposing him. He has penetrated the territories assigned to his attention on this sweep during the past six days, as planned and according to his instructions, and has encountered no resistance. He wishes to report that the territories and all the hills between his present position, fifteen miles directly north from here, and your present position, including all the coastal region, are free of enemy infestation. His foot cohorts have swept the crests and upper slopes without incident, and his cavalry forces, split between the command of squadron tribunes Falvo and Tessius, have completed their patrols of the lower slopes and valleys on both sides of the range of hills being invested. They joined ranks two days ago, having encountered nothing to impede their progress towards the meeting point.

"The Legate's objectives have been achieved, and he now holds the ground as commanded. He awaits additional instructions, but respectfully informs you that his northernmost observers yesterday reported a passing fleet, holding far out to sea but heading swiftly southward, with the potential of changing course towards your present position. The storm last night, the Legate suggests, might have scattered or destroyed them, but he dispatched me at the utmost speed at first light to bring the tidings. The fleet consists of one large bireme, accompanied by an unconfirmed number of galleys, too far offshore to be counted accurately but estimated to be no less than fifteen craft. Legate Commander!"

The final salutation was accompanied by another crashing salute, indicating that the report was complete. I expelled air sibilantly between compressed lips and then nodded to him. "Thank you, Trooper. An excellent, succinct report. No questions. Report now to Tertius Lucca, if you will, and have him assign you to a place where you can eat and sleep, once you have cared for your mount. When you are rested, you may come back to me for further instructions."

Bedwyr saluted me again, then turned and left. I watched him mount and ride away, then turned to my companions.

"Same story, but this time there's a fleet out there. They'll probably sail by, but we had better be prepared, just in case Ironhair has decided to annoy us." I looked up at the sky, still clear and cloudless. "Gather the troop commanders, if you please. We'll meet by the command tent in half an hour. Thank you."

As they began to disperse, Donuil caught my eye and pointed to his chest, one eyebrow raised, asking me mutely if I wished him to remain. I shook my head and waved him away. Moments later I was alone.

I looked about me, to be sure that no one was paying me attention, then kneed Germanicus slightly downhill on the landward side of the summit, towards a narrow, three-sided niche in the cliff overlooking the valley Bedwyr had crossed a short time earlier. I had found and used the spot the day before, when I had been equally in need of solitude. Once in there, I knew I was concealed from all eyes.

I dismounted and removed my heavy helmet, wiping my brow and the inside rim of the headpiece with one of the soft, daintily bordered kerchiefs Tress had made for me for just that purpose. Then I stretched hugely, rising to my tiptoes, and yawned, kneading the soreness from my buttocks. I rummaged in my saddle-bag for the whetstone I carried there, unhooked and unsheathed my sword, then made myself comfortable on a rock outcrop that formed a natural chair against the sloping cliff face.

I began to sharpen my weapon then, allowing my thoughts to come and go with the rhythmic, abrasive sweep of the stone's surface against the keen edge of my blade. Bedwyr maintained my weapons perfectly, as part of his training discipline, but the habits of a lifetime remained intact, and I found security in sharpening my own blades at least once each day. Then, as my mind was lulled by the sameness of the mechanical actions I was performing, my thoughts began to flow more smoothly.

Four months had passed since I last spoke with Ambrose, and more than three since I had arrived in Cambria at the head of Camulod's two legions. Since then we had been waging a make-believe war, marching and countermarching the length and breadth of Cambria, it seemed, attempting to come to grips with an enemy as ethereal and insubstantial as the clouds and mists that shrouded the mountains in the early mornings. And yet the enemy was very real and numerous. We saw them frequently, in the distances ahead of us, but they remained frustratingly beyond our grasp, for the most part, melting away into nothingness as we approached.

From time to time in the earlier days of the campaign, a foolhardy group of them, as frustrated as we were by this inactivity, would try to turn our flank, hiding in the bracken as we passed by and then springing from concealment to attack us from the rear. Our strategy had been designed to encourage that, however, and to punish such incursions swiftly and mercilessly, enfolding the interlopers and destroying them. The time soon came when no one tried it again.

In the first days of the campaign, in truth, we had been too successful. Our arrival had attracted great attention, and a large army of the enemy, numbering several thousand, had assembled to await us and drive us back out of Cambria. Unaware of the impending confrontation, I had split my forces a few days earlier, sending half of my troops, most of them infantry, accompanied by our five hundred Scouts, southward and west along the coastal plain under the command of Tertius Lucca, to capture the harbours of Caerdyff and Caerwent, driving the occupying Cornishmen out and denying access to their supply vessels. In consequence, the force I commanded when we came to face Ironhair's host was largely made up of cavalry. Less than one thousand of my three thousand infantry remained to me, along with two thousand heavy horse.

Warned only slightly in advance that an army had materialized under cover of the night and awaited us a mere three miles distant, in an open, rising valley where they held the high ground, I had been forced to make my dispositions in some haste, and to assume a greater risk than I might otherwise have chosen to consider. I was bolstered, however, by my firm belief that the odds would be in my favour if our most fundamental assumption was correct: that our heavy cavalry would be an unknown factor in the eyes of Ironhair's mercenaries. Allowing myself no time to waver, since I truly had none, I split the infantry into two five-hundred-man cohorts and sent them forward in formation, marching ten abreast, each division forming a block fifty ranks deep, with the cohortal standard bearers marching between the two. Ahead of these and behind them, vanguard and rearguard, I sent two heavy formations, each of two hundred cavalry, again riding ten abreast by twenty deep, the entire progression flanked by one mobile unit of fifty troopers on each side, deployed as a defensive screen. The result was a long, vulnerable-looking, greatly extended line that I hoped would invite instant attack from both sides.

My remaining force of cavalry, fifteen hundred strong, I split into three equal groups. Two were sent off on either side of the route the main force would take, instructed to find the quickest, easiest way to circumvent the enemy while remaining undetected, and then to hold themselves prepared to attack from either flank upon my signal. I held the third group close to me, hanging well back behind the main advance and moving forward slowly in an extended line abreast, five ranks deep.

As I have said, my plan, extemporaneous as it was, worked all too well. The host we faced was almost leaderless, with no general, no strategist ruling the various contingents to give direction to their strength. Ironhair was far distant, we discovered later, and Carthac with him. The army that we faced was an amalgam of what remained in south Cambria, assembled on a whim of opportunity and composed of differing levies of mercenaries. Lesser leaders were there in plenty, even in profusion, but none who was there possessed the power to lead any group other than his own, and not one of them brought to send out scouts to verify our strength. Because of that, my two converging units of troopers, sent out to slip around the enemy's flanks, were able to occupy the prime high ground at the head of the valley unnoticed and unopposed, after the enemy threw away their one advantage by instantly quitting the high ground they held to charge downhill, with howls of glee, against the long, thin line they saw approaching them along the valley floor. As the howling masses charged, the cavalry contingent facing them, at the head of the column, appeared to wilt and flee, falling back and away to either side, withdrawing at full speed and leaving the long files of infantry exposed to the oncoming horde.

None of the attackers had ever dealt with Roman tactics, it was plain. None of them noticed that the fleeing cavalry regrouped immediately, on either side of the phalanx of the rearguard, which had stopped at the first sign of attack, and then stood firm. None saw—or if they did, they were too far committed to regroup—that the exposed infantry was regrouping rapidly as well, deploying outwards upon itself to form two hollow squares, each three men deep, each forming an unbreakable, four-sided defensive wall before the nearest enemy could close to within throwing distance.

As the first waves of attackers began to throw themselves uselessly and suicidally against the standing squares, I arrived in the valley at the head of my five hundred and aligned my troops to the right of the rear-guard. No one sought to interfere with any of us. The fighting was contained about the squares of infantry, who were having no difficulty standing off the enemy. I looked up to the head of the valley, where my other thousand cavalry sat waiting, less than a mile away, commanded by Tessius. I realized then that I had one more order to deliver before signalling them down. I called young Bedwyr to me and sent him galloping, escorted by six troopers, to tell Tessius to lead his charge westward, downhill along the line of the squares to my left. He was to charge immediately upon receiving my order, and I would move when he did, leading my forces upward to the east, on the right of the squares. On either side, we would trample the enemy beneath our hooves, while remaining far enough away from the squares themselves to present no threat to our own infantry. I watched Bedwyr and his escort gallop away and settled back to wait for him to make the transit of the field. Nothing is as difficult for a leader as having to wait, while in front of him his men are being killed.

Even in the short time it took for Bedwyr to ride up the valley floor, however, it was becoming evident that we had won a victory. The enemy were bloodthirsty and fierce, ferocious and undisciplined, but they were not stupid. They had already recognized the folly of throwing themselves against the unwavering rows of our shields and spears, and now many of them hung back, their weapons dangling from their hands, looking about them to the east and west, peering towards where our cavalry sat motionless and filled with menace. I saw several men running this way and that, exhorting others, tugging at arms and clothing, and then a barely discernible progress began away from the fight as groups and bands began to disengage and move away.

Next came the brazen peal of Tessius's trumpets, and his long line of men surged into motion. My own trumpets sounded immediately, and I stripped the sheath from my sword and sank my spurs into Germanicus, sending him forward.

It was slaughter—nothing less. One pass we made, from west to east, and scarce a living man was left to face us. They had outnumbered us, it seemed, by almost a full thousand, but we had lost less than a score of our infantry and captured half a hundred of theirs. The others, nigh on four full thousand of them, lay dead. Several score escaped the field and we made no attempt to hinder them. We left the dead to rot where they had fallen, since we had neither the time nor the means to bury them, and left that dismal place to be whispered of by our enemies, and to be cleansed in time by birds, animals, insects and the purifying actions of the weather.

From that day forward, no enemy had stood against us. The report I had received today from Philip had become routine. We had no belligerent opposition in Cambria, despite the fact that the Pendragon lands still swarmed with Ironhair's mercenaries and the war of invasion was being fought daily. The enemy was near, but always out of our reach. Yet we had tried, and had come close to winning. Twice now we had been successful in driving the enemy ahead of us like partridges, pushing them towards the coast, but on each occasion, thanks to some form of signalling or communication that might tempt a man to believe in magic, a fleet of galleys had been waiting just offshore to spirit them away to safety before we could close with them. Something new was called for, but to this point I had been unable to find any alternative strategy that might offer hope for more success.

Our campaign along the southern coast, on the other hand, where our objectives were fixed towns and harbours, had been hearteningly successful and our victory complete. There was no place now in all of the southern half of Cambria where Ironhair could land his vessels without fear of being attacked and losing his cargo. Nowadays, his fleets plied north and south, maintaining a safe distance from the shore, and the few new levies that his vessels ferried must land in the far north, then make their way southwards through inhospitable terrain that was filled with dour and bitter enemies.

My thoughts were interrupted by the clatter of a rolling stone, and then came Donuil's voice from above and behind me, calling to me that my officers were assembled and waiting. I sighed and rose to my feet, then put away my stone and sheathed my sword before replacing my helmet and climbing up onto Germanicus, who made his way without urging towards the sound of Donuil's voice. The big Celt sat waiting for me, his face expressionless, and when I drew level with him he reined his own horse about and rode knee to knee with me.

"Look yonder," he said. I turned and gazed along the coastline to my right, shielding my eyes against the water-reflected brightness of the sun.

"What? I can't see anything."

Donuil was squinting, too. "Neither can I, now," he murmured. "But the big bireme's out there, just a dot on the skyline. Derek saw it first and gave voice."

I stared hard now, squinting almost directly into the brightness, but it was hopeless; there was nothing to see except scintillating sheets of blinding brilliance. "What about the other ships accompanying it? How many?"

We were headed steeply downhill now, towards the command tent on the level turf above the sloping beach. "Too far away to see, let alone count," Donuil said. "But you'll see better, once we get down there. The angle's better, and there's less reflection."

Sure enough, when we reached the level land above the beach the coruscating brilliance of the sun on the waves was greatly diminished and I could see the huge shape of the bireme, clearly accompanied now by a host of lesser ships. I reached the command tent to find everyone staring off to sea, talking among themselves and unaware of my approach.

I dismounted and walked towards the table set up on the rostrum outside the tent. "Well, gentlemen," I called. "Does anyone have any advice to offer on the disposition of this fleet? Will it come down on us, think you? Or is it merely passing us by to relieve some harbour to the east of us?"

Huw Strongarm swung around to face me and approached. "They won't come near us here."

"Why not, Huw?"

"There's no place for them to land, for one thing, other than this beach behind us, and it slopes too much to let them close to us. By the time they disembarked and charged this far, through water up to their waists, they'd all be dead and we'd be out of arrows."

I nodded. "Right. So they won't be coming here. But they'll see us clearly enough. Is there a disadvantage to us in that?"

The other officers, some forty of them, had surrounded us by now, and stood listening to what we were saying. The big Pendragon captain shrugged, clearly having nothing more to add, and I changed topic.

"How long would it take you to arrange for me to meet with Uderic, Huw?" I ignored the sudden buzz that greeted my mention of the name of the mercurial man who had sprung up to replace the fallen Dergyll ap Griffyd as leader of the Pendragon Celts. I held up my hand to still the noise as Huw considered my surprising question.

"Uderic?" He shook his grizzled head. "Who knows? It might take me a month to find out where he is. He has no trust in me, nor I in him. Once I find him, though, if I can hold him down for long enough to listen to what I have to say, it should be an easy matter to arrange a meeting between you. Why would you want to speak with Uderic?"

"Because I should have spoken with him months ago. He refused to meet me then, for reasons of his own. But we have amassed victories lately, and those have worked to his advantage. He and I have need of each other, despite his reluctance to share anything with me. He is the closest thing Pendragon has right now to a king and supreme leader. He also seems to be the only man in Cambria who can move swiftly and decisively to counteract Ironhair's manoeuvres and convince others to move with him." I saw the protest forming in Huw's eyes and spoke quickly to forestall him. "I know that is not strictly true, and there are others who have arguably stronger rights to the kingship. I also know that some of those are able leaders, too. But there's no denying that Uderic is the most dynamic leader among them, or that he has the loyalty of his own men, and of some of those who follow others, too. He's the only one of the Pendragon chiefs I have not yet met, and I think the time to rectify that is now. Will you find him for me?"

"Aye, but he mislikes you even more than he mistrusts me." Huw looked uncomfortable, speaking the words.

"No, Huw, he *thinks* he mislikes me, but he has never met me. He may mislike the *thought* of me, and he may *mistrust* me—that I can understand, since I believe he sees in me some threat to his ambitions. He is insecure in his new kingship, having seized it by conquest, and he knows me as kin to Uther. But I hope that he will be clever enough see the advantages of having me—having all of us here—as allies. Uderic has a war to fight and win, and so have we, for reasons of our own. Acting together we could win it quickly, saving thousands of lives."

"The big one is heading this way!" This shout from the beach caused a general turning towards the sea. I eased my way among my men to where I could see what was happening, Derek and Donuil flanking me on either side. Sure enough, the massive bireme had come much closer to us and would soon draw level with our position, perhaps less than half a mile out to sea. Its lesser, consort galleys, of which I counted ten at first glance, were sweeping closer to shore, spying on us, yet keeping just beyond Pendragon bow range.

"They won't come closer, but they're curious." I turned to Donuil. "Show them our standards, Donuil. Have our trumpeters sound out a challenge for them. And post a squad of bowmen on the rocks above, in hopes that some of them may row too close." As he left to carry out my orders, I turned back to Huw, who had come to stand behind me. "So, Huw, how many men will you take with you and how long will you require to make ready? I'd like to see you on your way today."

"Then you will. I'll take my own half-hundred with me. I'll feel safe with my own Pendragon bowmen against any number of heathen Outlanders. With the goodwill of the gods, I'll find Uderic within the week, unless he's dead and in the ground, and I'll be back within three days of that. Where should I arrange for you to meet with him?"

"I've no idea," I told him honestly. "You pick the place, as close as possible to half-way between where we are now and where you find Uderic. But be sure to leave yourself sufficient time to get back here and lead me to the meeting place before the appointed time."

He nodded, grinning. "Should I go now? I'm ready."

"Then do so, and accept my thanks."

He spun on his heel and walked away, and as I watched him go I heard another shout from the beach. "Tell Commander Merlyn one of them's coming in!" I was moving again before the word was relayed. As I stepped clear of the throng, on to the bare strand above the beach, I saw Donuil come galloping towards me along the hard sand at the water's edge.

"That's Feargus, Merlyn!" he shouted.

Sure enough, I recognized the racing galley instantly by the red of its

sail. My jaw dropped as I looked again to where the massive bireme
ploughed ahead of its escorts.

"Connor Mac Athol!" I roared into the sudden stillness. "You crazed,
intemperate, one-legged madman!"

Feargus's galley heeled hard over and came scything towards the
beach, its oars scattering water and flashing wet in the sunlight. I made
my way straight down the sand to the water's edge, holding my arms
widespread in welcome and restraining myself with difficulty from breaking into a headlong run. Donuil, I knew, had jumped down from his horse
and was close behind me, as would be the others. The galley sped straight
towards me until, at the last possible moment, the oarsmen shipped their
oars in unison and the long, sleek craft glided forward unaided, its speed
dwindling rapidly, to grate to a halt on the shallow, sandy bottom less
than a score of paces from where I stood. The tiny man who captained
this graceful craft leaped to the prow and hailed me.

"Merlyn of Camulod! The Admiral of King Brander's seas sends greetings! Would you care to step aboard his bireme?"

"Gladly," I roared. "But I cannot walk on water, nor can I swim in
armour." Even as I shouted, however, I saw the tiny boat being pushed
away to fetch me and I turned to Donuil. "Your brother never fails to
amaze me. The last time we spoke, he told me he intended to steal one
of Ironhair's biremes. I should have been expecting this! Come with me."
I looked beyond his shoulder to where Derek, Benedict and Rufio stood
grinning. "We'll be gone but a short time. My apologies to the others for
the interrupted meeting, but this development may change everything.
Connor Mac Athol may have won our war for us!"

Connor made us royally welcome aboard his magnificent new ship, and
as soon as the amenities of greetings and exchange of family trivia had
been concluded, he told us the tale of how he had procured it, slipping
unnoticed with more than a hundred men into the armed camp that
served as its major harbour on the northern coast of Cornwall.

His plan had succeeded without a setback. He and his men and ships
were welcomed by the Cornishmen, accepted unquestioningly as mercenaries no different from the hundreds of others who came and went constantly, and Connor had bided his time, establishing himself and his
followers, over the course of six days, as belonging. Then, on the seventh
day, the bireme had arrived and the booty captured in the previous
month's raids in Cambria had been unloaded and dispatched in wagons
to wherever Ironhair stored such things. Connor had discovered that new
levies would be boarded the following day for transportation into Cambria,
and thus had been presented with two alternative courses: loading his
own men aboard the following day, then capturing the vessel once at sea,
or taking the initiative immediately and capturing the ship that very night.

He had chosen the latter, because the cargo holds his men would occupy in travelling were deep, and they might not be able to leave them before the end of the voyage. He had heard tales aplenty of mercenaries confined in the holds beneath locked hatches throughout entire voyages, especially in foul weather. Furthermore, at sea the ship would have its own armed defenders.

Connor had issued his commands, and his men had boarded the bireme in the dead of night, easily overcoming the few guards posted in the ship's home port. Once aboard, the remainder had been simple, and the bireme had quietly slipped from its moorings, under new command, with no one noticing.

Two things, however, had appalled him and his men: the rank stench of the ship, emanating from the decks where the rowers were chained to their sweeps; and the unsuspected fact that such ships were powered by slaves. Connor had been completely unprepared for that. When he had discovered it, he had been forced to consider abandoning his attempt to steal it, knowing that the vessel's oarsmen would be confined there, and aware of what was afoot. The size of the ship, however, the overwhelming bulk of it and the power it offered, had convinced him that he could not simply do nothing merely because he feared the possible reaction of a crew of slaves. Certainly, he reasoned, they might rebel and raise the alarm when they discovered the theft, in which case Connor and his men would be in dire straits; or they might even refuse to row the vessel, which would be scarcely better. Connor, however, had elected to believe they might choose freedom, and so he offered it, overcoming language difficulties by the simple expedient of choking a hulking overseer with his own whip, striking the chains off the leading slaves and setting some of his own men to toil beside them in starting the ship away from the dock. His message of hope spread quickly, and the galley slaves worked harder, without goading, than they had probably ever worked before. By dawn, the bireme was safe in deep, blue water, surrounded by Connor's own galleys and unthreatened by pursuit.

I interrupted him at that point to ask him what he had done with the slaves, and he smiled at me.

"Almost half of them are here aboard, those who were fit enough to want to fight."

"And what about the others?"

"They're in the north, among our Isles. Some died, but very few. The others are . . . mending."

"How long ago did all this occur?"

His smile grew wider. "What was it, three months ago? No, it was four. I sailed directly south on leaving you, and we took the ship a short time after that . . . perhaps two weeks. My plan was right, you see. No point in putting off what could be done right then and there."

"And then you sailed home again, all the way north, directly?"

He laughed. "We had to, man! We couldn't stay down here. You've never smelled a stink the like of what we found aboard. Those rowers were chained to their oars, never released for any purpose, so they lived in their own filth. My men were vomiting all the time from the stench of it. You couldn't eat your food and hold it down! We had to clean the whole ship, stern to stern. We beached it, north of here, as soon as we were free of interference, and swilled it out, but the stink was settled deep in the wood and would not be swiftly moved."

I nodded. "It still smells ripe," I said, but Connor waved my comment away disdainfully.

"Ah, it's almost nothing now, and growing fainter all the time. I tell you, at the start, it was unbearable. When we won home, to the Isles, we didn't dare take the thing near any of our people, so we beached it again on a sand bar and then spent two months scraping the hull and scrubbing the wood inside it with lye soap to root out the stink. Even then, it was hard to bear. We floated it again and built slow fires of peat along the decks, in braziers, letting the sweet smell of the smoke hang tight inside the walls for two full weeks, and that made things a little better. After that, we filled the space between the decks with fresh-mown hay. Soon we'll fumigate the place again with sweet peat smoke, and that should finish it. Now no man shits or pisses between decks, on pain of flogging.

"But what a ship, eh, Merlyn? What a ship! Nigh on five hundred men I have in her right now. Five hundred men! It's cramped—there's no denying that—but five hundred on one ship!" He stopped, then shook his head. "Mind you, that's a lot of men to drown if she ever sank under us." He stood up and strode across his cabin, and the deck above his head was high enough to permit him to do so without stooping. He thumped the sloping wall. "Little chance of that, though. Solid, this is, and iron hard, though I've not the least idea what kind of wood it is."

"What of the other one?"

"The other one like this? I've no idea, nor have I ever seen it. If it's still in these waters, I'll find it one day."

"And then? What will you do?"

"I'll burn it, or I'll capture it."

"You mean you'll fight it, ship to ship?"

His grin was ferocious. "Why not? All the advantages would lie with me. Their ship is crewed by slaves, mine by free men. We'll out-row them, out-sail them and out-fight them."

I glanced at Donuil, to see how he was taking this, and found him grinning at his brother. "So be it," I said. "Where are you headed now, and how did you happen to come by here?"

Connor shrugged his broad shoulders. "I knew you were in Cambria, but I didn't know where. We rode out last night's storm in a small bay two hours' sailing time from here, and now I'm on my way to join forces with Logan. I'll sweep along the coast here, till I reach the river mouth, then turn south and sail back westward along the northern coast of Cornwall. Logan will sail east, from the end of the Cornish horn, to join me in visiting Ironhair's harbour there, the one where we found this beauty. It's defended by a fort, built into the cliff, but like all forts, it's built facing the land, so it offers us no great threat. That's why we were able to sail out so easily. This time we'll sail in, but of course they'll know us as enemies, even before we attack. They'll know this beauty immediately. Her sister may even be there when we arrive, in which case we'll take her if we can, or destroy her if we must. In either event, I intend to make life unpleasant for the troops along that coast, outside the fort and close to the town." He paused. "You've a look in your eye, Merlyn Britannicus, a look I knew well when you were yellow-headed the first time. What have you in your mind?"

I shook my head. "Nothing, really. What's this fort called? Is it Tintagel, by any chance?"

Connor nodded. "Aye, that's the name. You know it?"

"I know of it. Lot of Cornwall's father started building it, and Lot carried on with the work. Is it made of stone?"

"Some of it. Some parts of it. They've had masons working on it for years, but it's nowhere near complete. Mainly it's built of wood—log palisades. Would you like to come with me and see it?"

I answered his grin with my own. "I would dearly love to, but my troops might grow confused, seeing me sail off like that. I think I'd better stay right here, in case fighting breaks out."

"Well, then, let me show you my ship, before I have to go. Logan has less than ten craft with him, in the south, so I've no wish to keep him waiting for my arrival. Come."

I was stunned by the spaciousness of his new craft. From the exterior view it looked enormous, but walking between the multiple decks, its real dimensions became awesomely apparent. It stretched fully eighty paces long, from stem to stern as Connor said, while the width of the main deck was twenty-five paces. The hatches to the cargo holds ran in a line along the middle of the craft, giving access to the holds themselves, three full decks beneath. The great double banks of oars were handled from a stepped deck in the very centre of the craft, where the rowers of alternate sweeps worked above and below each other, half the height of a tall man separating them. The signs of recent slavery were still apparent there: iron rings set into the floor and smooth-worn channels in the wooden deck showed where the chains that bound the rowers had run. At the rear end of the rowing deck, directly at the foot of the companionway leading up to the steering deck, a massive kettledrum sat mounted on a tripod. This, Connor explained, was the post of the oarmaster, the man who dictated the rhythm of the huge sweeps that propelled the ship. From his position just below the shipmaster on the stern steering deck, the oarmaster could clearly hear the commands passed down to him, and the rhythmic pounding of his drum hammers decreed the pace of the rowers' efforts.

Below the rowing deck was a deck for cargo storage, while another above provided accommodation for the ship's warriors. The original biremes of Rome had been no more than floating platforms from which land-trained troops fought land-based wars, and that priority had altered little over the centuries. Front and rear, great towers soared above the main deck, giving the vessel an ungainly appearance when seen from either side; these provided viciously effective advantages as platforms for the ship's catapults and other artillery, and also housed the ship's officers and troop commanders. At either end of the deck drawbridges reared high. Lowered by pulleys, they were used to attach the ship to land when the vessel was in port, but they were equally capable of locking it similarly to another ship's side in battle, allowing soldiers to pour across on to the enemy's decks.

Connor, I knew, had good reason to be proud of owning this floating fortification, but his greatest source of pride was the enormous, copperclad battering ram of solid wood, wider than my outspread arms where it formed the prow of the ship. This stretched out a full six long-legged strides from the bireme's bows and tapered to a wicked point below the water-line. Heaven help any other vessel that found itself facing this, I thought when he pointed it out to us.

Connor shipped us ashore again, promising to return by the shortest route to visit us after he had sacked Ironhair's harbour in Cornwall. He estimated that it would take him less than a week to go there, do what he must do, and return. I promised him we would still be there when he did return, providing his estimate was accurate, since I was committed to await Huw Strongarm's return, and that would take no less than a week. After that, though, I would be leaving as soon as I had to, in order to meet with Uderic Pendragon.

He walked with Donuil and me to the side of his ship and then braced himself with his wooden leg against the rail before leaning outward, clinging to a rope, to watch with a wide grin of delight as we made our way nervously down a narrow wooden ladder lashed to the side of the great ship. We were suddenly terrifyingly aware of how simple it had been to board this monster from the tiny boat that now bobbed sickeningly on the leaping waves, slightly beyond our reach.

Clinging there above the lurch of the slapping waves, we gauged our time and distance and leaped to where willing hands waited to grasp us and save us from overturning the boat. We both made the transit safely, albeit with a decided lack of dignity. My stomach was still swooping distressingly when the hull of the boat grated on the sand and I leaped out, wading through ankle-deep water to the satisfying solidness of the dry beach, carefully avoiding the eyes of any of the watchers who stood there.

For the remainder of that day I had but one pressing priority. I reconvened the officers and apologized for the interruption of our session, after which I set them to drawing up rosters of activities that would keep our troops occupied and usefully employed during the time we must wait for Huw's return. That done, I handed command over to Donuil, as adjutant, and withdrew to my own tent to bring my diurnal log up to date.

The wording of the first two sentences I wrote that day has remained bright in my memory, because they fell so far short of the truth that, when I read them again later, I laughed aloud at the power we have to surprise ourselves with our own ineptitude. "Connor has returned unexpectedly," I wrote, "in possession of one of Ironhair's biremes. Now, after months of inaction, it appears that things might start to change." Well, change they did.

It began the following day, just before noon, when a squadron of cavalry arrived from Camulod. I had been expecting no word from home and I strode out to meet them, my insides knotted with apprehension, since here, I suspected, could be no good tidings. My apprehension flared into fear when I recognized the officer in charge as one of the junior tribunes I had last seen leaving Camulod with Ambrose, headed north.

"You should be with my brother," I snapped at the man, as he stood rigidly to attention in front of me. "Why are you here, and where is he?"

"The Legate Commander Ambrose is safe and well in Northumbria with King Vortigern, Commander Merlyn. He dispatched me immediately upon our arrival there to put your mind at rest as to his welfare, since he now believes he might be detained in Northumbria for slightly longer than he originally thought. I came with all speed, stopping but briefly in Camulod to gain fresh horses. I bear dispatches, sir, for your attention. This from the Legate Commander, and the smaller is from the Legate Dedalus, in Camulod."

I took the two carrying cases young Sulla held out to me and thanked him kindly for his trouble, feeling somewhat guilty now for the coldness of my initial greeting. I sent him off with Donuil, accompanied by his men, then dismissed everyone else and withdrew to my tent.

Once confident that I would remain undisturbed, I found myself postponing the moment when I would open up the thick leather wallet that contained Ambrose's dispatches. I poured myself a cup of ale and made myself comfortable in my folding chair, tilting it back onto its hind legs as I sat with my feet up on the old, scarred campaign desk that had been my father's and his father's before that, rubbing the thick leather of the

wallet with my thumb. At length, however, I had to admit to myself that
I was merely putting off the inevitable, and I untied the thongs that
bound the wallet tight.

There were two scrolls in the receptacle, one of them much heavier
than the other, and I saw at first glance that they were not both from
Ambrose. His letter bore his seal, a floral emblem petalled like a daisy,
with his personal crest of an eagle's head embossed in the centre. The
other bore a common seal of wax, pressed flat with the point of a knife.
I smiled as I broke it and unrolled the single sheet of papyrus covered
with small, tightly compressed letters. It was from Arthur, the first letter
I had ever received from him, and it showed evidence of torturous effort
in its composition, with many words written and then struck out afterwards.

The Legate Commander Caius Merlyn Britannicus
Greetings, Cousin:

I write this on the instructions of the Legate Commander
Ambrose, who has decided that I must learn the power of words
on papyrus. As part of my assigned duties each day, I now must
keep a daily log, presenting it to him for his inspection and approval each morning. ~~I find the writing difficult.~~ The writing of
the log is not, in itself, difficult, but the selection of the proper
words, to describe events ~~without being too~~ precisely, without
wasting time or space, consumes much time.

We have come safely to Lindum, where Vortigern the King
now keeps his strength, after moving south from his former
stronghold in Eboracum three years ago. We are quartered in the
ancient Roman fort of Lindum itself, which is being fortified
anew, with stone walls being erected atop the old, earthen walls.
We had no trouble on the road, except for one incident which I
unfortunately missed, when a small party of our advance scouts
was waylaid by a band of wandering brigands who outnumbered
them by five to one. The brigands had never fought armed
horsemen before, and they fared ill. I wish I had been there.

Our troopers have struck wonder into all the people here in
Lindum. Nothing like them has ever been seen in these lands.
King Vortigern would be well pleased were we to stay here, but
Ambrose has told him that we must return. Ambrose, I felt, was
as unhappy to say so as the King was to hear it. He has much
loyalty to Vortigern, from former times, I think. We are to make
one great, rapid sweep around the King's main holdings here, in
company with Vortigern, before we leave. Ambrose plans to penetrate the great forests to the south and east, to show our strength
to the Danes and Saxons living there. ~~I am really looking~~ Sadly,

Ambrose says we will not fight, but that we will appear prepared to fight. King Vortigern has never ridden in a saddle with stirrups, and he says that he is now too old to learn, so he will ride bareback as he always has.

Ambrose says that when we have completed that long sweep, we will leave for home immediately, but I hope that he will bring us directly to Cambria and that the war will still be in progress.

I look forward to seeing you again. Greet Bedwyr for me. I wonder if he has blooded his sword yet.

Arthur

I read the epistle three times, smiling more broadly each time as I imagined the effort the boy had put into its composition. I sympathized utterly with him, recalling clearly my own laborious attempts at writing down my thoughts when I was even older than he now was. The stricken-out words and the few blots that marred the sheet delighted me particularly, since they showed that Arthur had not yet progressed sufficiently along the path to have realized that a letter could be drafted first, painfully and messily, then rewritten completely. Well, I thought, he would soon learn all of that, just as surely as he would learn not to yearn for the death and violence of war. That thought, with all its implications, robbed me of any further desire to smile, and I turned to Ambrose's letter.

Lindum

Ambrose Britannicus to Caius Merlyn Britannicus;

Hail, Brother!

I wonder which of these two missives you will open first? My intuition tells me that, despite your need to learn the status quo here in the north-east from me, your natural decision will be to read what Arthur has to say first. I must remember to ask you, when next we meet.

Vortigern is well and, to my delight, living in Lindum, which has permitted me to spend some time with my adoptive parents, Jacob and Gwilla. You have never met Gwilla, my mother's sister, but she has asked me to convey her best wishes to you, and so has Jacob who remembers you well from your first and last encounter in Verulamium, when he rode with Vortigern to attend the Great Debate where you and I first met, so many years ago.

The King is as healthy and as ambitious as he ever was, and the knowledge came as a pleasant surprise. I truly had expected that he would be dead, and that his territories would be torn by civil war, but that is not the case. He has great problems, nevertheless, all of them emanating from Hengist's brat Horsa, but it has not come to open war between them, to this point. I have little faith it will remain that way, however. Horsa, from all I hear, has been preparing for war in earnest now for several years and has amassed a mighty army—five to ten thousand warriors, depending upon the source one listens to—which, to this time, he has kept firmly based far south and east of here, among the great marshes of the coastal fens. From there, they have historically raided south, against the Saxon newcomers established there, and that honours the bargain made initially with Vortigern—to help him keep his kingdom free of Saxon invaders—and has led to the precarious, hostile peace that has prevailed up here for years now.

As I say, I expect that to change very soon. My own analysis leads me to suspect that, in terms of his rumoured strength, the ten thousand estimate might be more accurate, and even short of the mark. I base that upon my own evaluation of his immediate fighting requirements, taking into account the vastness of the territory he has to contain: the area we call the Saxon Shore, directly southward of his base. Recent, reliable reports gathered by Vortigern indicate that the Saxons in the south grow stronger and more numerous every year. The fleets arriving annually are growing larger, bringing hordes of land-hungry Outlanders to swell the numbers already here, and new fleets are coming, too, from new directions, as the word of land for the taking spreads among the tribes of the Germanic territories that the Romans held underfoot for so long. There is nothing to hold them now, with the Roman restraint abolished, and they are sweeping into Britain in multiplying thousands each year, claiming and clearing land and spreading outwards all the time from the boundaries they held the previous year.

Much of that outward spread nowadays is focused northward, in order to keep the sea within their reach, for these are all seafaring tribes; that means Horsa has his hands full, at present, in beating back these incursions, and he has neither the time nor the resources to cast his eyes backward at Vortigern's kingdom. But the enemy is being constantly renewed and re-supplied, and I believe that Horsa must soon fall back into Vortigern's domain, in order to establish a new line that he can hold against the incursions from the south. At that point, the northward surge may flag and stop, but the expansion will then seek other outlets, and in the meantime, Horsa's army will be cheek by jowl with Vortigern's.

I greatly fear we may have grown complacent in our western Colony, assuming a safety that is spurious, simply because we are removed from sight and sound of these upheavals. Numbers of such vastness as those reportedly pouring into the eastern lands will not be long contained, because, extensive as the Saxon Shore may seem to us in Camulod, it cannot long sustain the kind of crowding that is occurring now, and the time must soon come when the exploding growth must spill out into other regions of Britain. It follows logically that any such spillage must be to the west, toward us.

How goes the Cambrian campaign, I wonder. It is much in my thoughts, because I now fear that the war against Ironhair and Carthac is by far the lesser of the problems facing us; a local squabble when compared to the threat stirring here on the other side of Britain. Because of the seriousness of my concern over matters here, I have decided to look into things myself, and that will mean extending my stay here by not less than a month, in order to undertake a wide-ranging and fast-moving sweep of the southern territories. I do not intend to linger anywhere during that manoeuvre, nor will I seek conflict. I simply intend to demonstrate our presence and potential force, as allies of Vortigern, and to gain a clearer understanding at first hand of the forces that may be ranged against us in the future. In the meantime, I am sending this dispatch in the hands of Paul Sulla, to forewarn you.

Vortigern, as we surmised he might, wants me to remain here in the north for an extended time, but I have already convinced him that I must return to Camulod as soon as possible. I have, however, promised to return next year, in even greater strength. I am convinced that this is the proper and appropriate course to adopt, and I am equally convinced you will agree, once you come to understand the gravity of what I have discovered.

Two alternative courses lie open to us next year, as I see it: if the Cambrian war is concluded, you and I will ride up here together; if it still drags on, however, then I will conduct it while you come north to form your own opinion of matters here. I consider that need—for you to come here personally—to be imperative. I see enormous danger here, the potential for great and dire conflict, and that has forced me to reconsider most of the beliefs I once questioned in you, when I thought you guilty of unwarranted xenophobia. Ironhair and Carthac and their like may be contentious and intractable, but I now see that they are Celts like us, our own people in the final analysis. The threats we face from the seething hordes now investing this north-eastern land, on the other hand, might well culminate in the annihilation of our people and our very way of life in Britain, should we not take timely steps to counteract them.

I shall return to Camulod as soon as I am able. If you are
then still in Cambria, I shall join you there. In either eventuality,
I will have far more information by that time than I possess now.

Farewell, and may the gods of war smile upon your army.

                                                        Ambrose

I sat motionless after the first reading of that long, astonishing missive, allowing its tone and tidings to settle themselves within my mind at
their own speed and making no attempt to analyse what Ambrose had
actually said therein. I knew that anything else, any reaction I permitted
myself at that time, would be ill considered. I wished to reread the letter
several times and then think the entire situation through in detail before
I spoke of it to anyone else. And then, knowing how my own mind works,
I turned to Dedalus's dispatch, trusting myself to work on Ambrose's information while I digested Ded's.

I opened the cylinder and broke the plain seal on the document. As
I might have expected, Ded wasted no time on salutations or frippery but
came straight to the point.

Cay:

Young Paul Sulla arrived today, on his way to find you and
deliver dispatches from Ambrose, so I am sending this with him.
He is preparing to leave now, so I have little time. I have no idea
what Ambrose might have said to you in his dispatches, but from
the few hints I have squeezed out of young Sulla, I gather he will
not be back as soon as he had thought, and also that there is
more going on up in Northumbria than we might have suspected.
At least Vortigern is still alive, and Sulla said nothing of war.

This now in relation to your arrangements for the build-up
of new, allied forces outside Camulod: the expedition we had
planned, one hundred strong, went out to Nero Niger Appius and
Corinium within the first week after you left, and it has met with
great success. Corinium is now alive again, with people living behind its walls and the beginnings of a garrison undergoing training
with our men. Early reports seem confident, although I continue
to have doubts about making soldiers out of farmers and peasants.
Those doubts are my own, however, and I am prepared to be
convinced of my error.

Two similar expeditions have gone out since then, one of
them to the next town north of Corinium. It had no name, or if
it ever did it has been long forgotten. Our people are now calling
it Secunda. The third expedition went to Tertia—as you might
expect—another nameless old marching-camp fortification to the

south of us, some twenty miles west of Lindinis. That was un-expected, but a delegation arrived here one day, prompted by the success of the Corinium plan. Someone from the Tertia region had been up there and spoken with Nero Niger, and had returned home filled with enthusiasm. Apparently Tertia is good farm country and well populated. I took the matter to Council, and they approved, so Tertia was launched, and I am told that in the space of less than two months they have progressed as far as the Corinium people have in four.

Now there are two more expeditions being prepared, both of them bound for similar places with no name, but with the rem-nants of old Roman walls in place and fertile fields nearby.

Your plan for this region is working, my friend, no matter what frustrations you are facing where you are. I thought you might be glad to know that.

Everything here is as it should be, though I do not enjoy working with the Council—too much discussion, too little deci-sion. The garrison matters proceed smoothly, nonetheless, and that I do enjoy. I see your Lady Tressa frequently, usually with your brother's wife Ludmilla. It is clear they have become good friends, so disabuse yourself of any thought that she is languishing without you. In truth, she seems so much at home here now in Camulod, no one would ever think she is but a new arrival. I know that, too, will please you. I would have asked her if she had words for me to send to you with this, had that been possible, but Sulla is anxious to be on his way and is fretting as he waits even for this from me.

Get rid of Ironhair and Carthac quickly, but do it thoroughly.
Decapitation is thorough.

Dedalus

Decapitation! I grinned to myself, shaking my head as I released Ded's letter and allowed it to roll up on itself.

The news was good concerning the outlying settlements, and I was grateful, and a little surprised, that he had thought to send it. His reser-vations on the quality of the garrisons we were building in those new settlements were no surprise to me, though. Ded was a professional sol-dier, and he simply could not believe that any other kind of man could be successful in soldiery. The best tidings, however, were those concerning Tress and Ludmilla. The mere mention of Tressa's name had filled me with warmth and homesickness, and now I allowed myself to think of her for long moments, recalling the smell and the taste of her, the laughter in her eyes and the sound of her voice, admitting to myself that I missed her sorely. Then, aware that I was being self-indulgent, I replaced Ded's letter in its cylinder and took up Ambrose's lengthy dispatch again.

I had barely finished reading it for the second time when I heard Donuil's voice speaking my name. He pulled back the flap of my tent and entered, followed closely by Derek. Donuil had a strange look on his face, and I was suddenly aware of a hubbub of raised voices outside.

"What's wrong?"

Donuil shook his head in a tiny gesture of perplexity. "I'm not sure. Connor sailed east—d'you expect him to come back that way?"

"Aye, or directly from the south. What are you talking about?"

"Well, either he's coming back from the west, or there's another big bireme coming to visit us."

"Coming from the west? Show me."

I forced myself to move slowly and deliberately, rolling my brother's letter up carefully and slipping it back into its wallet. That done, I moved to the entrance, holding the flap open for Donuil to pass in front of me. There was no need to go any further; the great, dark, solitary shape approaching rapidly in the offshore waters was unmistakable.

"Well, that's not Connor," I said softly, after my first glance. "So whoever it might be, he's from Ironhair, and he's not passing by. I doubt he'd be foolhardy enough to attempt an attack of any kind from there, and he has no other vessels with him, so we must presume we have a visitor wishing to speak with us."

Donuil stood close by, watching me as I spoke, and I was conscious that his were not the only eyes on me.

"Let's show them some discipline, Donuil. Assemble our people on the beach in full battle order. I'd estimate we may have half an hour before they reach us—that is, if they don't sheer off and resume their journey. Pass word to the senior commanders to change to full parade armour immediately, if you please, and send my orderly here at once, to help me with my own preparations. We have no time to waste."

VIII

 DONUIL RETURNED TO my tent just as I was removing my heavy war cape, having decided that it was too hot and that I had put it on too soon. He, too, had changed into parade gear and carried his ornately crested helmet in the crook of his left arm, and I looked him up and down approvingly.

"They're here, Merlyn," he announced quietly. "Lying in deep water, no more than fifty or sixty paces from the beach. But they've made no move to hail us. How do you want to proceed?"

"Have they given any sign of their intent?"

"No, but it's not hostile. They drifted into place, barely moving through the water, and there's no sign of bared weapons anywhere that I could see."

"They haven't lowered a boat?"

"No, nothing. They've done nothing. There's a group of what must be officers—"

"Armies have officers, Donuil, and a formal structure. These men may be leaders, but they are not officers."

"Aye, well, there's a group of them at the bow of the ship, just staring down at us."

"And are we staring back?"

He blinked at me. "I suppose so. We're facing them. There's nothing else to look at."

"You're wrong there, Donuil. There are a hundred other things out there, all of them better to look at than these people."

I opened the flap of my tent and looked outside to where several of my own officers stood waiting. "Gentlemen, will you come here?" When they were crowded into my tent, I looked at Donuil. "Donuil here tells me that the enemy are looking—staring—at us, and that we may be staring back. I want that stopped now. You will move among our units, please, and instruct all of them to ignore these people. They are to stand at attention with their eyes on the horizon straight ahead. They may look at the sea, the waves, the clouds in the sky, or at the back of the head of the man in front of them. But they are not to look at the enemy ship, or at any of its crew, is that clear?" I looked at each man individually and they all nodded.

"Good. Thank you all. In a moment I shall require you to go and spread that word among our people, beginning with those units closest to the enemy ship. Before you do, however, I want to tell you how we will behave, and continue to behave, in this encounter. These people appear to believe they are on an embassy of some kind, bringing word to me from Ironhair, one equal to another. That implication of equality is offensive, completely unacceptable, and I want that clearly understood. I will not truck with Ironhair, or with any of his minions, on anything that seems to approach equal terms. I have no wish to give *anyone* the slightest false impression that I might be even slightly concerned to hear whatever it is they may have to say." Again I looked from face to face and each man nodded gravely in return. "Good. Donuil, here, will therefore be the only one to deal with them or speak to them. I'll ask you one more time: do you all understand what I am saying?" They all nodded, with a chorus of "Aye, Commander," and I dismissed them to spread the word. When they had gone, I turned to Donuil.

"These people will undoubtedly have the effrontery to expect me to go to meet them. I will not. Ironhair is not on that ship. He wouldn't endanger himself so foolishly. Whoever leads this expedition, therefore, is a deputy, and he will deal with you, *my* deputy. They may be mute for now, but sooner or later they will have to speak, or shout, then come to us. No one from our army will go to them, under any circumstances. If they wish to speak to us, they must come ashore, and when they do, they must speak to you and to you alone. When you have listened, if you think I should hear what they have to say, you will bring them to me, and then they may wait until I have time for them. You will bring no more than three or four of them, fewer if possible, and you will bring them under guard—an armed escort. There will be *nothing* to suggest that it might be honorary—no ceremony, no deference, no courtesy other than the barest necessary to avoid violence. They are to be treated as invading brigands under a temporary and unwelcome truce. Brigands, Donuil, not warriors, not men of honour."

Donuil was gazing at me steadily, absorbing every word, and now he nodded. "I will make sure there is no doubt of the regard in which we hold them."

"Good, but understand clearly what I have just said. You alone will judge the import of their words and decide whether or not *I* should talk to them thereafter. Should you decide against that, you will escort them back to the water's edge and see them off." I saw his eyebrow quirk at that. "I mean it, Donuil. This is your confrontation, to conduct how you will. You are my adjutant, and you have full discretion to decide if this matter is worth my time. I won't question your judgment. Now go down there to the water's edge and wait for them to shout to you, but don't encourage them. Don't look curious, and under no circumstances be the first to speak or initiate anything. Just stare at them as though they were some kind of noxious matter floating on the water. When they see you won't be moved, they'll come to you."

He nodded, snapped a smart salute, pressed his helmet onto his head and left me alone to wait.

I paced my tent for a time, straining to hear what was going on outside, but the silence was astonishing. From time to time I would hear a quiet-spoken sentence, or an order from one of the officers, and the occasional crunch of pebbly sand as someone's horse shifted and sidled, but little else. I wanted to step outside, or at least part the tent flaps so that I could see something, but I was unwilling to show the slightest sign of interest.

Eventually, in the distance, I heard a voice raised in a shout, but I could not hear what was said. There was no response, and I began to count, slowly. When I reached fifteen, the shout came again, still too muffled by distance for me to decipher it, and this time Donuil's voice rang out in response.

"If you have words to say to us, come here and say them like a man, instead of bellowing like a bull. No one will harm you."

A long period of silence ensued, and then came the sound of footsteps approaching my tent, and young Bedwyr drew back the flaps.

"Commander Merlyn? I am to inform you that a boat is approaching, with five men on board, apart from four oarsmen."

"Thank you, Bedwyr," I said. "Now remain where you are and look back. Can you see what is happening?"

"Aye, Commander. The boat is approaching the shore."

"Good. Now close the flaps and stand outside. Face the beach and simply report to me what is happening. I can hear you perfectly well without your having to raise your voice."

"Aye, sir." A long silence, then, "They've stopped rowing, Commander. Now the oarsmen are in the water, pulling the boat up onto the beach . . . The others are out, approaching Tribune Donuil. They don't like the bowmen."

"What bowmen?"

"The adjutant has ordered two squadrons of Pendragon longbows to assemble on either side of him with arrows drawn, slanting out towards the water's edge in a funnel shape. The newcomers are walking between those files, approaching the adjutant."

"Good, and what is Donuil doing?"

"Nothing, sir. He stands waiting, facing them, his hands clasped at his back. Now they are talking, but I can't hear them . . . The adjutant is leading them away now, towards the quartermaster's tent . . . He's sitting down at the quartermaster's table, in front of the tent, facing them, saying something . . . I'm sorry, sir, his back is to me. I can't hear what he's saying."

"That's fine, Bedwyr. What's happening elsewhere? What are the other troops doing?"

"Nothing, sir. No one has moved."

"Thank you. Stay there, and warn me the moment anyone starts to move again."

I forced myself to walk to my table and sit down, and then to withdraw Ambrose's dispatch from its holder and read it again. I have no knowledge of how many times I started reading it only to realize that I had lost all sense of what it said, and each time I would return to it, starting again from the salutation.

Eventually, after what seemed like an age, Bedwyr spoke again.

"Tribune Donuil has stood up, sir. He's coming this way."

"Good. Come inside."

"Sir!" He stepped inside and stood at attention just inside the doorway.

Donuil's footsteps approached and his shadow fell across the slight opening in the flaps. By the time he entered I was facing him. He glanced at Bedwyr, then turned to me.

"I think you ought to talk to them, Merlyn."

"About what? What's their purpose?"

"I don't know, but they have one. You'll judge the content better than I could. Their leader is a man called Retorix, a captain of Ironhair's Cornwall levies. He's an arrogant blowhard, full of blustering menace, but he's more articulate than any of the others. He's the one charged by Ironhair to speak with you. He won't tell me what he has to say to you, and I've been tempted to kick him back on board his ship, but something tells me that would not be the right thing to do. I think you have to meet him."

"Very well then, bring him in, but leave the rest of his people standing out there on the sand."

Donuil nodded and began to turn away, but he hesitated, obviously caught short by some impulse. "D'you think that's wise, Merlyn, to leave all four of them out there? I mean, if you have things to say to him, harsh things or otherwise, wouldn't it be better to have witnesses? You speak to him alone, with no one to hear you, then there's no telling what he might report to Ironhair, and no refuting what he says. If others are here, it seems to me, he'll be more tightly bound to tell the truth, or something close to it."

"You're right, my friend. Bring them all here, but stop them short outside. I don't want them inside my tent."

I waited for the sounds of their approach, and then listened with appreciation to the stilted, metallic rattling of arms and armour as the guard who surrounded them responded to the clipped commands of their officer. Moments later, Donuil approached again and informed me that the delegation from Cornwall awaited me.

I sat still, at my desk, and forced myself to read Ambrose's letter, in its entirety, one more time. Then I rose and threw my ceremonial war cloak about my shoulders, adjusting the hang of it until the heavy, silver-wire mass of the great bear embroidered across its back sat snugly, perfectly draped from my shoulders. Beckoning to Bedwyr to accompany me, I picked up my parade helmet and walked outside to where the newcomers stood clustered together under the watchful eyes of a full squadron of the guard who surrounded them on three sides.

Retorix, their leader, was not hard to pick out. He stood half a head taller than his companions, and his clothes were richer and more finely made. He was a well-made man himself, broad in the shoulders, narrow of waist and thick-legged, perhaps thirty-three years of age. He was clean-shaven, with no moustache, and armoured in a vaguely Roman fashion: bronze back- and breastplates and a domed helmet with a skirt that covered his neck but failed to conceal the thick, rank curls of black hair that hung down past his shoulders. From the waist down he wore no armour. A padded tunic came down to his knees and beneath that he wore breeches of heavy, homespun cloth, cross-bound from ankle to knee. The boots he wore were of heavy leather and looked hard and comfortless. A thick, grey cloak of rich wool enhanced the Romanish look of him, hanging from his right shoulder with one end looping up beneath his left arm, where a thick, barbaric ring pin of silver held it in place. I deliberately ignored the other four men and fixed my eyes on Retorix alone.

"Who are you?"

"They call me Retorix."

"Hot wind?" I saw his eyes widen. "That is what 'rhetoric' means in my world—hot wind and bullying argument. Rhetorics would be a plurality—a profusion of hot wind." I could see that my meaning, though not my tone, had blown right over his head, and I chided myself silently for stooping to such a level. "Who are these 'they' that call you Retorix?"

"My people."

"I knew *that*, since I presume only your own people would care to own you. Who are your people? That is what I am asking you."

He drew himself up, his bearing expressing outrage. "The Romans called them the Belgae, the people of Cornwall."

I stared him in the eye. "The Romans are long since gone. Their day is past. We are Britons. Would you like to know what *we* call the people of Cornwall nowadays, the people who would submit to the will of such a thing as Peter Ironhair?" I looked away from him, making no effort to disguise my disgust, and then swung back. "My adjutant tells me you have words for me, but I have little time to listen, so spit out what you have to say and then be gone."

I could see the fellow growing angrier with each word, but he reined himself in and breathed deeply through his nostrils several times before beginning to speak. "You are Merlyn of Camulod, am I right?"

"What of it?"

I saw his eyes move beyond me to where Bedwyr stood at my back, and as I watched his eyes flick up and down, scanning the boy from head to foot, I had a sudden certainty that he thought Bedwyr was Arthur. He had looked at no one else but me since I appeared. He quickly brought his gaze back, however, and try as I might I could discern no sign of interest in the boy in his eyes.

"I bring greetings from my leader, Iron—"

"Then you may take them back with you. I have no wish for them."

Again he stopped, visibly restraining his anger. "I have a charge upon me, *Master* Merlyn! Will you permit me to deliver it without being interrupted at every word?"

I stared at him, feeling a reluctant stir of admiration for his self-command. Donuil had named him an arrogant blowhard, but I had seen nothing so far to suggest that. "Very well, I will. Say what you have to say to me."

"Ironhair sends his greetings as one leader to another. You as Legate Commander of Camulod, himself as Supreme Commander of the Armies of Cornwall. He will not insult you by pretending that friendship could ever exist between you, nor will he claim that you might negotiate together based upon mutual esteem. But he believes you will acknowledge that both of you, and those associated with you, have much to gain from a cessation of this war." He paused, evidently expecting some kind of response, but I continued to stare at him, allowing no expression to show on my face. Eventually he had no choice but to continue.

"Your presence in Cambria is an intrusion, he believes, while his activities here are legitimate. He represents your distant kinsman, Carthac, whose claim to the vacant kingship of Pendragon is the strongest, claimed through the line of direct parentage." He could not resist the temptation to glance again towards young Bedwyr. It was the merest flicker of movement, quickly controlled, but it verified what I had thought before. Unfortunately, his companions were less disciplined than he, because they all looked at the boy, too, so obviously that even Bedwyr noticed their interest. I heard him start to speak and swung abruptly around to cut him short.

"Why are—?"

"Be quiet, boy!" Bedwyr's eyes flew wide with shock at the harshness of my voice. I stood motionless, my back to the others, until I had his eyes on mine, and then I winked at him before continuing in the same, harsh tones. "Are you mad? How dare you raise your voice when I have guaranteed no interruption? Get you into my tent immediately and stay there until I send for you. Move!"

The poor lad took one step backward, his confusion and embarrassment taking him visibly to the edge of tears, and then he drew himself together, squared his shoulders, turned smartly about and marched into my tent, closing the flaps behind him.

I swung back to the others. "You may continue, and *no one* will interrupt you further. You were speaking of Carthac." I moved my eyes slowly around my men, making no attempt to disguise the anger in them. The source of my anger, however, was the intolerable hubris of what I was listening to. When my gaze came back to him, Retorix was watching me closely, his eyes boring into mine, and I wondered if I had managed to disguise my recognition of his interest in Bedwyr—Arthur, as he believed the boy to be.

Finally he nodded, cleared his throat and continued speaking. "Carthac's father was Mor, youngest brother to Uric Pendragon, father of Uther. Carthac has requested, and enlisted, the aid of Peter Ironhair to help him claim his kingship, and so Ironhair is here in Cambria. Your presence, on the other hand, is unsolicited by anyone. Dergyll ap Griffyd, with whom you once had dealings, is dead, his so-called kingship taken by the usurper Uderic, who is no friend of yours. Your army therefore stands as an invading force, a status both amplified and verified by the fact that none but a few of the Pendragon have joined you. They seek no help from you in settling their affairs. In fact, they believe themselves to be quite capable of resolving their differences without your interference." Again he paused, gathering his thoughts before proceeding, and as he did so I tried to empty my mind of his reference to Uderic's being a usurper. Ironhair would say so, of course, but Uderic had won his title in battle, leading his people in their war against Carthac's attempt at usurpation. Retorix spoke again.

"My Commander's proposal, in outline—to be expanded to your mutual satisfaction later—is this: he believes that you perceive his presence here in Cambria to be a threat against your own security and safety in your Colony of Camulod. He suggests that there is no such threat, and that his presence here is temporary, dedicated only to the swift success of the campaign he is waging on behalf of Carthac Pendragon. When that has been concluded, Ironhair will withdraw his forces into Cornwall once more, content that he has a strong ally in Cambria to the north and, conceivably, an ally of convenience in Camulod to the north-east—yourselves.

"You, on the other hand, would benefit greatly by being free of involvement in the affairs of Cambria, since that would enable you to give your full attention to the emerging threat from the Saxon territories to the east and north of you, and even to extend terms of alliance and cooperation to the king, Vortigern, in Northumbria, should you decide it prudent to protect your interests in that way. As for your peace of mind over Cambria, Ironhair suggests that a precedent already exists for taking care of that: a patrolling force of your cavalry, much like the one that formerly assisted Dergyll ap Griffyd, could be established and maintained as a safeguarding buffer between Cambria and Camulod. That force would be recognized and permitted to function without interference."

At several points I had turned away from Retorix, taking great pains to do it casually and feigning interest in the conduct of my motionless troopers, in order to school my features more rigidly. The news that Ironhair was aware of our involvement with Vortigern, and of the threat from the Saxon Shore, came as a revelation, despite the fact that I already knew how wide a net Ironhair was capable of casting. The information about Uderic—that he was no friend of mine—was less surprising, since Uderic made no secret that he was suspicious of my motives in being here. It was his specious championship of Carthac that was hardest for me to bear without protest, however much I tried to tell myself that I was listening to mere words, designed to keep me off balance and distracted from taking another course. That angered me, because the course itself remained unclear to me. The suggestion, even by omission, that Ironhair could see it more clearly than I could, and that he could move against me to block it even before I saw it, was infuriating.

There was also the matter of Arthur. Ironhair knew about Arthur—his blood lines, his paternity, and therefore the primacy of his claim to the Cambrian kingship. Our move to Mediobogdum had been the result of one assassination attempt on the boy, fomented by Ironhair himself. Now that I was back from my long disappearance, it was presumable that I would keep the boy close by me. Retorix and his companions had clearly been warned to keep a lookout for the boy who would accompany me, and their reaction to Bedwyr told me they knew Arthur's age but had no idea what he might look like.

Why then, I wondered, would Ironhair feed me this mess of pottage about Carthac's claim? He must know that I would scorn it, so what did he seek to gain? In what way would I damage my own cause and advance Ironhair's by rejecting his proposal on the grounds of Arthur's claim? That perplexed me greatly, for I knew that Ironhair must know the answer. And then it came to me, in a burst of sudden understanding that almost took my breath away, so quickly did it supplant Ironhair's apparent advantage over me.

To cover my reaction to the awareness that had flared in me, I stepped forward slowly, my eyes downcast, and made a lengthy display of settling myself into the only chair at the table between Retorix and me. I leaned back and crossed my left arm over my chest, resting my right elbow on my fist and plucking at my lower lip with the thumb and forefinger of my right hand. Retorix watched me, narrow-eyed, assuming that I was considering his words. What I was considering, in fact, was what I should do with the knowledge that now throbbed in me, and what I wanted to do most was to stride off into my tent to be alone with my thoughts. I needed to analyse this new awareness immediately and to probe it for weaknesses. But I knew that Bedwyr waited for me in my tent and would distract me from thinking clearly, whereas, if I simply remained where I was, no one would dare to break in on my thoughts.

Ironhair, I was now convinced, was wagering heavily that I would be able to tolerate neither his insolence in making this approach nor the spurious cloak of respectability he was holding up for Carthac. Fully aware of the legitimacy of Arthur's claim as Uther's heir, he was gambling that I would react in outraged fury to his proposal and would—must—expel his hirelings from my presence. His reasoning, and his hopes for success, were now clear in my mind, and he himself had given me the key to resolving the entire matter. By mentioning Uderic, and the dislike he held for me, Ironhair had overplayed his advantage. When I refused his invitation to withdraw based upon his terms, which depended heavily on his definition of my presence in Cambria as an invading force, I would define myself as a third force in this conflict, inimical, by that definition, to both sides. Bolstered by the false legitimacy of his support of Carthac, who was a Pendragon, Ironhair could then approach Uderic and make common cause with him—albeit temporarily—to drive the invading forces of Camulod out of Cambria.

I had no illusions about Uderic. His ambition was as great as Ironhair's, and his eyes were set on the same prize: the gold circlet that sat upon the brows of whoever ruled as king of the Pendragon. The fact that many, perhaps a majority, of his Pendragon people would refuse to accept that Camulod might have designs on Cambria would have little sway over Uderic's designs. He would form an alliance with Ironhair to drive us out of the Pendragon territories. Then, once we were gone, crushed between the armies of both enemies, he would think he could turn his attention to Ironhair and Carthac, dealing with them at leisure. Uderic was a strong war chief and a natural successor to Dergyll, but he lacked Dergyll's brains and the popular support the former king had attracted without effort. I would pick Ironhair, ten times out of ten, to win any contest with Uderic. But none of that had any direct bearing on my immediate concerns, which had to do with Ironhair's beliefs.

When I was a child of ten, perhaps eleven years old, Publius Varrus had said something to me that I had never forgotten. He had caught me lying to him over some minor boyhood scrape, when, seeking to protect Uther from some unspecified punishment, I had claimed ignorance of my cousin's whereabouts. Uncle Varrus had taken me severely to task over the lie, emphasizing and reiterating that lying consistently contains its own punishments, feeding upon itself to the point at which the liar loses all respect and credibility. He had kept coming back to the point for weeks, until I grew heartily sick of it, but then he had concluded the lesson by asking me if I knew what the liar's tragedy was. He insisted that I think about his question and find an answer to it, so I thought, and I thought. Finally, I thought I knew the answer.

"Well?" Uncle Varrus asked me.

"I think . . . once a man has become a really bad liar . . . a habitual liar . . . then his tragedy must be that, no matter what he says, no one will ever be able to believe him."

My uncle nodded. "That is really awful, isn't it? Would you like to be in that situation?"

"No."

"No, nor would I. To go through life knowing that no one will believe you about anything must be truly terrible. But you know, Cay, that is not the liar's tragedy. The liar's tragedy is far, far worse."

I gazed at him, wide-eyed. "How, Uncle? What could be worse than that?"

"This, Cay: the real tragedy of the liar is that he can never believe anyone else."

That befuddled me, for I was yet too young to grasp its full implication, but I never forgot it, and I never stopped thinking about it, and as I grew older I began to see the extent of the tragedy: for if a man knows, deep in his heart, that he is a liar and a fraud and a hypocrite, how can he ever ascribe any honesty, sincerity or integrity to any other?

Ironhair was judging me according to his own criteria, and he was wrong. He was ascribing his own venal ambitions to me, believing that I truly did seek to rule in Cambria and that I lusted to be king in the same way he did, for I had not the slightest belief that Carthac would survive Ironhair's friendship long enough to claim the crown. He would never believe the truth: that my motivation was revenge for the treachery he had brought into Camulod. I sought his death, and Carthac's, simply because I believed the world would be a better place were they both dead, and I could withdraw to Camulod and live there happily until the time arrived when Arthur would step forth to claim his own.

Now I believed I had the measure of him. He was unaware that I had sent Huw Strongarm to meet with Uderic. When Uderic and I met face to face, I would tell him what Ironhair sought to do, and we would thwart him together, with an alliance between our armies. Uderic had many faults, and until I discovered otherwise, I was prepared to accept that he might not be trustworthy, but he was sane, unlike Carthac.

I sucked air with a hiss through my front teeth, then rose to my feet. Retorix and his people stood facing me stalwartly, flanked by my troopers, and I hesitated for a heartbeat, wondering for a strange, brief moment, if I was about to make a serious error. Connor would be active in the waters below Tintagel, even now. He would have scant cause to thank me were I to send these people slinking home to arrive at his back unexpectedly.

I spoke directly to Retorix again, watching his eyes closely. "How long will it take you to bear my message back to Ironhair? I presume he is sitting safely in Tintagel, awaiting your return?"

The eyes widened very slightly, but he answered immediately, his voice calm. "He awaits our coming, but not in Tintagel."

"No, of course not. You came from the west." Then, knowing I was right, I hardened my tone and rattled off what I had to say, speaking harshly and giving him no chance to interject or quibble. "But whichever way you came, from south or west, you came here uninvited, and I have listened to you with patience, despite my own inclinations. Now, having listened, here is my decision . . ." I walked around the table to face them from less than two paces, with nothing between us. "Let me begin from the beginning. I am Legate Commander of Camulod, and you addressed me correctly. Your 'Supreme Commander,' as you call him, is, on the other hand, an upstart and an exile from that Camulod. He is a liar and a murderer of women, and though he may seek to assume it by himself, he is completely unworthy of being accorded any kind of nobility. His friend Carthac, whom he refers to as my distant kinsman, is no kin of mine. He is a demented degenerate and utterly unworthy to be called human. As for his so-called claim to the kingship of Cambria, it is ludicrous to suggest that the Pendragon people would ever willingly place themselves beneath his heel.

"The reason for my presence here in Cambria, uninvited and accompanied by my army, is quickly explained. I have but one purpose: to bring about the death and destruction of Ironhair and everything he represents. Get you then aboard your ship and take that word back to your upstart kingling. And if you should ever be unwise enough to come this way again, you will find yourself treated appropriately, the way we should have treated you today." I turned to the guard commander. "Escort these people back to the water's edge and get them out of my sight." I then spun on my heel and marched back inside my tent.

Bedwyr stood waiting for me there, his eyes serene, his expression resigned, his square-shouldered demeanour reflecting his decision to accept whatever punishment I might assign. I nodded to him.

"Do you understand what happened there, and why I had to turn on you?"

Whatever he had expected to hear, it was not that, and his eyes clouded with perplexity as he wrestled with my meaning. Finally he shook his head. "No, I didn't."

"They thought you were Arthur. That's why they were all staring at you. They had been talking about Carthac's claim to the Pendragon king-ship, but they all knew Arthur's is stronger, and they all knew Arthur is my responsibility. Therefore, they assumed that you were Arthur. I wanted them to continue thinking that, and so when you began to speak, I si-lenced you. I was never angry with you, not for a moment, but I did not want you to say anything that might betray that you are *not* Arthur. Now, be a good lad and go and find Donuil, down on the beach. Ask him to come to me as soon as he is free."

"He's here now, sir." The boy nodded towards the open flaps of my tent and I turned to see Donuil approaching, accompanied by Benedict, Derek and Rufio.

"Good. In that case, I have another task for you now. Go you and see if you can find something to eat, for I have not seen your jaw move in hours, and I find that most unusual and perhaps alarming." He flushed, grinning, because his amazing appetite had made him the butt of jests for months. He made to salute me, but I stopped him. "After that, when you have regained your strength, I want you to select an escort of six good men from among the Scouts, draw rations from the commissary and make your way back to the Legate Philip. You need not kill your horse with speed on the way, but don't waste time, either. Inform the Legate that I have dispatched Huw Strongarm to treat with Uderic, and inform him also of what has passed here today. Tell him I have need of him as quickly as he can bring his forces back. And the same thing applies, there, in the matter of returning. There is no crisis, so please make that clear to Philip. He may come back at route-march speed, there is no need to wear out his men and horses. That's all. But eat first, before you go. That is an order. Go now, and I'll see you in two days or so."

Bedwyr saluted me and spun smartly away, flushed again, but this time with the consciousness of his responsibility. He passed the others in the entranceway and I told them to find someplace to sit as they came in. Donuil dropped into my chair and pulled off his heavy helmet while Benedict settled himself on my wooden map chest. Rufio dragged in the chair I had used earlier from the table outside. Derek remained standing by the entrance of the tent, his hands clasped together over his belt buc-kle, his newly acquired Roman-patterned leather cuirass making him seem even larger than he was.

"Well?" I asked when they were all settled. "Did I choose rightly?"

"I'm prepared to accept that you did." Donuil wiped the brim of his helmet with the hem of his cloak, and then scrubbed at the sweat on his temples before tilting his head back to squint up at me. "But none of us has any idea what your choices were. One thing is certain, you left them in no doubt of your opinions about their masters."

"Good, that's what I intended. Which way did they go, when they left?"

"West, the way they came, and they were moving quickly by the time they had made a score of oar strokes from the beach. By now they should be fairly flying over the wave tops. What do we do now?"

I glanced from him to Benedict and then to Rufio. "We hope Huw Strongarm gets back here quickly, and in the meantime we plan what we intend to do after that. Young Bedwyr is leaving now, at my orders, to recall Philip and his people from their patrol, since there's no one up there to patrol against." I paused. "I realized something out there, while I was listening to that diatribe from Retorix. Ironhair's not as clever as he thinks he is, and he's suffering from a disadvantage he doesn't know about."

Rufio cocked his head. "What disadvantage?"

I told them, briefly, what I had remembered about the liar's tragedy. Then, as I had expected, Donuil and Benedict sat silent and motionless, absorbing what I had said while Rufio shook his head.

"What's wrong, Rufe? You don't like my story?"

"The story's fine, Cay, and I've no fault with it for what it is, but it treats all liars as equal, and Ironhair's not equal to any common liar. Your story tempts you to think he'll be weakened by not being able to believe the truth, that you've no interest in becoming king of Cambria. So what? You might be right, but I'd hate to have to risk my life on that 'might.' "

"You think there's a more likely outcome?"

"Aye, I do. Whether Ironhair believes you or not will make no difference to what he'll do. Ironhair is Ironhair, Cay. He sees things differently from us. Where we see white, he sees black, and a thousand oaths from men who see our way will never convince him that he's seeing wrongly. He believes his own lies because in his twisted mind they are the truth— the only truth he has ever known or will know. He doesn't give a damn about what's true or false to others. His own truth is all that counts. He'll play you false at every turn—you and every other being who steps into his way—and never lose a wink of sleep over any of it, because he believes, deep in the bottom of his own soul, that he sits at the centre of the universe and everything in the world has been created for his use and benefit. He is the Lord of Creation in his own mind, and no one—not you, or me or anyone else—can influence that."

This was perhaps the longest speech I had ever heard from Rufio, and his lack of profanity impressed me and disturbed me even more than his unusual eloquence. It betrayed a far greater respect for Ironhair, backhanded though it might be, than I had ever felt Rufio could possess. I made no effort to debate him.

"As you say, none can influence his mind, but he is less than perfect in his mind, for all that. He does not know, for example, that we've already sent out word to Uderic, asking him to meet with us. Now, when we do meet, which will be sooner than Ironhair could guess, I'll undo all his planning. We will form the alliance with Uderic, and between us we'll drive Ironhair and Carthac into the sea."

"Aye, if Uderic can be trusted."

"Why would you even say that? What we're proposing will be in his own best interests. Of course he will be trustworthy, when he knows he's having his own way to his own ends."

"*If* he believes and trusts *you*. From all accounts I've heard, he doesn't."

I looked at the others, hoping for some support, but they sat silent. Seeing that I had nothing to add for the moment, Rufio spoke up again.

"Look, Caius, I'm not trying to dissuade you from anything here, but it seems to me your logic isn't thorough enough in this case. You're basing everything, it seems to me, on an underestimation of Ironhair's deviousness."

That caught my attention. "What do you mean?"

"I mean that Ironhair is far from being a stupid man, and he has shown us damn few weaknesses in the past. Suppose, just suppose for a moment, that he has already thought this through. Suppose that, having seen the route he ought to take, he had the brains to guess that you might see it, too. Alliance with Uderic. Think of that. So, having thought of it, and being aware that you, too, might have thought of it, what would he do then, think you? Would he approach you with an offer, as he has, knowing that you, seeing the offer for the insult that it was, would refuse it? And would he then run to Uderic, seeking alliance the moment that you *do* refuse it?" Rufio paused, looking me straight in the eye, giving me time to think before he continued.

"Or do you think he might send men to Uderic first, to talk, just as he did with you today, making a proposal to an enemy—a proposal that would sound reasonable and temperate—that they bury their differences for as long as it might take to destroy a common enemy—us, but primarily you, Merlyn of Camulod. Uderic might consider it, don't you think? He already sees you as a threat." He stopped again, still gazing at me steadily.

"Now, if Ironhair's proposal were carefully structured, and included telling Uderic about this visit we were to receive today, Uderic might perceive Ironhair's proposal as holding two advantages for him: it would contain an offer to eliminate the threat you pose, by convincing you to retire peacefully, with no risk to Uderic. Failing that, it offers a way to be rid of you completely, citing your ambition and your arrogant refusal to withdraw from a struggle that is no concern of yours. If you withdraw now, the threat to Uderic is gone and he's lost nothing. If you remain, you'll be declared an enemy and he'll unite with Cornwall to smash you, thinking to go back and deal with Ironhair later."

"Damnation, Rufe, you make me feel stupid!"

"Why? There's no reason to. You and Ironhair are completely different creatures. I'm not so constrained by your ideas of honor and nobility, so I can think like Ironhair. I might also be wrong."

I stared at him, trying to read his mind. "Aye, you might, but you're probably right."

"Perhaps." His face showed no trace of self-satisfaction. "We have no way of knowing one way or the other—"

"But we should plan accordingly . . ."

He nodded. "We need a plan that will work in both eventualities, and be flexible enough to change half-way, if necessary."

"But you are adamant I shouldn't trust Uderic."

Rufio glanced from Donuil to the others, shaking his head, and then turned back to me with a wry look. "You didn't need me to tell you that, my friend. Did you? Would you have trusted him if I had not spoken?"

I shook my head gently. "No, Rufe, I would not, because I never have. I had not seen so far into the folds of policy as you have taken me, but I would not have ridden blindly into Uderic's clutches. But now, let's talk about what's likely to transpire here. I believe that, no matter what happens, and simply because Uderic is so loudly vocal in his distrust of me, he is likely to insist that our meeting be held in some place safe for him, secluded, so that he can control the gathering. He's also almost certain to insist that I bring only a few men with me. He'll allow me an escort, but not a large one. I know—" I held up my hand to forestall his protest. "That opens up the possibility of treachery. I think, nonetheless, that that is the way it will be."

Benedict cleared his throat. "That ship went west, at great speed. I don't know much about these things, but it looked to me as though the rowers couldn't sustain a pace like that for very long, so they might not be going very far."

Rufio was watching him, frowning slightly. "Don't follow you, Ben."

Benedict grinned a small, unamused grin. "Be interesting to see what direction Huw comes in from. Should it be west, I'll be inclined to wear ring mail beneath my armour for the next few weeks."

Donuil spoke for the first time since he had sat down. "We'll need two groups, Cay, one mounted, the other afoot, with bows—Pendragons. You should have no less than ten men in each group, the first to ride openly, the other to follow unseen."

I looked at Benedict. He shrugged and dipped his head, pushing his palms together. "As many men as we can take, in both groups, but no less than ten on horseback. I'm riding with you, and I agree with Rufe. I think we're going to ride into treachery and betrayal, so we had best be prepared for it."

IX

THE HILLSIDE ACROSS from where we stood was a vast expanse of dun-coloured bareness, with a faint wash of green here and there from the moss, lichen and occasional patch of stunted grass that maintained a tenuous hold on the naked rock. Against that background, a single, jagged patch of dark, lush green stood out like a scab, crusting a deep, vertical gash carved by the waters of the stream that fell from the summit to join the narrow river far below. Across the broad stream bed, cut deep into the rock over the course of aeons and sheltered from the prevailing winds that scoured the open hillsides, hardy, indomitable trees had rooted and grown to fill the ravine completely, their ancient trunks and gnarled boughs coated with the thick mosses that made their appearance so startlingly stark. Slightly more than half-way down the stream's chute, the mid-morning sun flashed bright reflections from a cataract that leaped from the trees to fall down a short but sheer cliff face before vanishing again among the trees below.

As I watched, I saw a man come into view, balance briefly on the cataract's edge and lower himself cautiously to arm's length before leaping sideways, into the trees and out of sight again.

"That's fifty, and they're still coming," Huw grunted.

I answered without looking at him. "Fifty-seven." And then, as yet another moved forward to teeter, lower himself and leap, "And he's fifty-eight."

Ten days had passed since Ironhair's deputation had approached us. We stood now on a hilltop close by the west coast of Cambria, screened from detection by a fringe of bushes, watching Rufio's prophesied treachery and betrayal unfolding as the long file of men made their way with extreme caution down the steep hill on the other side of the narrow valley that divided us from them.

One of Huw Strongarm's men had sat among these cautious prowlers the previous night and learned much from them. They were Ironhair's mercenaries, mainly, guided by a few Cambrian locals, and their plan was to scale the hill from the coastal side and make their way unseen down the deep ravine and into the woods along the valley bottom, where they would wait for us to cross the narrow bridge over the swift-flowing river, and then seal it behind us. Huw's man, whose name was Gwynn Blood-

Eye, had slipped away silently and brought the word to us immediately, travelling by moonlight for most of the night and reaching our encampment just at dawn, so that by the time the first of the Cornwall mercenaries breasted the summit across from where we now stood concealed, there was no sign of life on the valley floor below, and I was safely ensconced with my retinue on the hillside facing them.

Below us, in the valley bottom, lay the river, the confined belt of forest that lined it on both sides, and the narrow, stone-arched bridge built by the legions of Paulinus four hundred years before in his campaign to wipe out Cambria's Druids. Beyond the bridge, the ancient legionary road swung north again, following the river's edge until it emerged onto a plain formed by the convergence of three valleys. More than a hundred additional mercenaries lay concealed on the flat-topped hill that divided the two most northern of those valleys. We had discovered their presence the day before, thanks again to Huw's amazing hill scouts.

The design was clear: we were to ride out into the plain following the ancient road, which would lead us beneath the slopes where our murderers lay hidden. When they attacked, we would either fight or flee, and it must have seemed likely to them that we might do both, outnumbered as we would be. Those who remained to fight would die there, and those who fled would die at the hands of the group behind them, waiting at the bridge. The flaw in the design lay in the fact that they expected twenty of us to ride into their ambush, whereas they would, in fact, find fifty of us, backed by fifteen hundred more.

Rufio's suspicions had had a salutary effect on me. Everything we had planned, from the moment he had so eloquently stated his beliefs, had been designed to encompass and eliminate the threats we were all convinced would now materialize. Philip had returned quickly, summoned by Bedwyr, and had agreed immediately with Rufio's interpretation of events. Thereafter, as our plans progressed and we became accustomed to the steps we had decided to take, the scope of our thinking developed and our manipulation of events and probabilities had grown more deft, more sure-handed and more confident.

Connor had returned on the fourth day, flushed with triumph at the success of his raid on Ironhair's home base in Tintagel. He had been virtually unopposed and had achieved complete surprise, capturing two of the six galleys moored below Ironhair's cliff-top fortifications and burning the other four. After that, secure in their possession of the seaward approaches, his men had ranged far inland, seizing great stores of food, drink and booty from the supplies in Cornwall storehouses, all of them destined for Ironhair's armies. Our own army feasted on the beaches on the night of their return, gorging themselves, after four months of campaign rations, on the food, wine, mead and casks of ale Connor's fleet had pillaged.

Connor had listened that night to our suspicions about Ironhair and Uderic, and had agreed with our reasoning and our proposed responses without a blink. His sole amendment was to suggest acting with even greater strength. He believed we should field every unit at our disposal, and he argued that, were we to do what must be done, and do it stealthily and subtly, we could turn all threats to our immense advantage. To illustrate his point, he gave us all a lesson in fleet warfare, scratching a battle plan in the dirt by the fireside and demonstrating how his individual galleys could combine, in line abreast or line astern, to concentrate the heaviest weight on the enemy's weakest point. As he spoke, I looked from face to face among my troop commanders, some score of whom had gathered around our fire to listen. All of them, standing or sitting, were bent forward, narrow-eyed with concentration. When he had finished, Connor looked up at me, and every eye in the assembly turned to see what I would say.

"So you would have me take my entire strength into the hills to this upcoming meeting, and you would prefer it if I could achieve that without their being seen? Do I understand you clearly?"

He looked at Derek, one eyebrow raised high, and then his teeth flashed in a great grin. "Perfectly!"

"Wonderful, Connor. Now would you have any idea how I might do that? I know there are stories among my troops that I was something of a sorcerer in my youth, gifted in the ways of the gods. And I know Derek, there, for one, believes me to have mystical and superhuman attributes. To this time, however, I have never found a way to transport a thousand men and five hundred cavalry invisibly. But that, apparently, is what you'd have me do. How? If either you or Derek, with whom you seem to be sharing something humorous, could suggest some means of achieving that, I would be most grateful."

"Tomorrow," he said, his grin still in place.

"Tomorrow. What about tomorrow?"

"Huw Strongarm might come back."

"Aye, he might, and ... ? Is there significance to that? How will it help me take my army unseen through the mountains?"

"That might depend upon where you wish to go." Connor glanced around the assembly, catching Derek's eye again. When he spoke again to me, no trace of humour was left on his face.

"Look you, Merlyn, you suspect collusion between Ironhair and Uderic, no? Well, in order to collude, they have to take you to some place close by the sea, for Ironhair will not stray far inland from his ships and his escape route, I promise you. There's a terrible attraction in the safety of a heaving deck when your enemies are all behind you, on dry land. Two things occur to me. Either they will combine to wipe you out, expecting you to come as Uderic instructs you to, with but a few strong, trusted men. Or they will ambush you along the route, with Ironhair attacking you before you get to Uderic, thereby leaving Uderic's hands clean. They won't try either method far inland. Deep enough into the central mountains, the glens and hills will work against them as much as for them. So they'll keep you close to the coast, where they can use the terrain to their own advantage.

"As soon as Huw returns we'll know the where and when. Once we do, then I can take your thousand infantry along the coast in my own ships and land them safely and unseen, long before you reach the meeting place. That was Derek's idea, and he would come with us, being more at home on a galley than on a horse. You travel inland with your scouting force, your full five hundred, but you yourself ride out in front with thirty or forty men, leaving the other hundreds to follow behind you, well out of sight of spying eyes. Huw's own Pendragons—how many of those are there?"

"Some two hundred, all told. He took less than a hundred with him, and the rest are here with us now."

"Then Huw's two hundred, native to this land, can throw a broad screen out in front of you, dealing with any prying eyes they find. With them covering every stride of land for two full miles ahead of you and out on both flanks, no one should come near enough to you to see the force that follows you. Remember, they will expect you to have no suspicion in you at all. You are riding to convince a potential ally that you wish him naught but well, so you'll ride openly, secure in the safe conduct you've been offered."

He was right, of course, and we adapted our plans accordingly.

Huw arrived the following day, and I knew from the moment I first saw his face that he was unhappy with the outcome of his mission. I took him aside immediately and asked him to say nothing until I had assembled Connor, Rufio, Benedict, Derek and Donuil.

His report was brief and succinct: he had found Uderic not far distant from our current position, to the west of us, after first having sought him further to the north. Uderic had received him with barely concealed hostility and had listened to my message with disdain, but had then quite patently allowed himself to be convinced that it would be to his advantage to meet with me. He had set a time and a place: seven days from that day, on the site of the abandoned Roman fort of Moridunum. I recognized the name of the place, from my readings in my grandfather's journals. I knew it lay some two miles inland from the sea, on a narrow but navigable river, and it had been the westernmost Roman fortification in south Cambria, one of the few that had remained fully garrisoned until the legions were withdrawn from Britain. I was to come to Uderic there, escorted by no more than thirty men, and he would send out word to permit me safe conduct through "his" territories.

Uderic had appeared ill at ease in committing to this meeting, betraying a shiftiness that was all the more upsetting to Huw simply because of its inscrutable nature. Nothing he had said or done had been identifiably contrived or false, yet Huw had had the distinct impression that nothing truly was as it appeared to be.

As soon as Huw had finished, I told him about Retorix's visit and exactly what we had decided in its aftermath. The big man's concern fell away immediately, replaced by visible relief as he listened to what I had to say, and then he joined the rest of us in reviewing what would happen next. Yes, he told Connor, he had a score of men among his most trusted warriors who were native to the region around the old fort at Moridunum, and he would send them with the fleet, to guide our foot soldiers, and the others, a full complement of two hundred and forty bowmen, would serve as a scouting screen for our cavalry in their westward advance through Cambria.

On the morning following Huw's arrival, I rode at the head of our five hundred Scouts, accompanied by Donuil and by Philip, who would command the main cavalry body advancing some two miles behind us. Huw and his twelve score of bowmen had left at dawn, three hours ahead of us, to give themselves time to separate and form a far-flung, semicircular protective fan about our front. Benedict and Rufio remained behind with all our infantry. They would depart the following morning, aboard Connor's fleet, and would arrive within a few miles of our destination no less than one full day in advance of our arrival.

The last man lowered himself down the edge of the cataract across from us. After he passed from sight, I waited for a count of one hundred before turning my head to where Huw leaned against a tree trunk.

"I think that's all of them. I counted seventy-one."

Huw grunted. "I must have lost count, then, because I only saw sixty-four. Anyway, you're right, they're all gone now. The first of them must be in the trees at the bottom by this time. We won't see them again until they attack."

"Well then, let's give them something to attack. How long will it take you to reach your men down there?" Fully half of Huw's bowmen had crossed the river bridge much earlier and were now securely hidden in the forest to the north of it.

"Less than a half-hour, to get there unseen. There's a ravine on this side, too, just beyond the bow of the hillside there, on the right. It leads almost directly to where I told my men to wait for me. They'll have a rope across the river for me by this time."

I nodded. "Go, then, and make good time. It will take me half an hour to reach my own people, and half an hour longer to lead them back along the river road towards the bridge. Once we're across, they'll move to close the bridge at our backs, and that's when your bowmen can hit them. We'll ride on until we reach you and your forward group, and then we'll lead the enemy right back into your trap." I stopped, seeing the worried look on his face. "What's wrong?"

"What if they're impatient? They outnumber you. What happens if they attack you, instead of merely letting you ride past?"

"Hmm." I shrugged my shoulders. "I doubt they will. They're mercenaries. Some might have bows, but most would have to fight us hand to hand, them on foot, us on horseback and unblooded yet. I don't think that is likely. But, if they do, well then, we'll have to hope your bowmen are as accurate as ever and come to our rescue swiftly." I held up my hand in a farewell salute, then watched him as he nodded and then turned away, making his way along the crest of the hill to where he would enter the ravine for his downhill journey. When he had disappeared, I turned and made my own way to the rear of the crest, where I had left Germanicus haltered safely below the skyline.

The engagement was short and punitive.

I crossed the bridge at the head of my fifty horsemen and no one sought to challenge us. The forest around us, briefly severed by the rushing channel of the narrow, turbulent river, lay silent and seemingly empty of life, though I knew Ironhair's people were there and searched for them diligently as we passed. Nothing stirred in the fastnesses of the woodland beyond the thick fringe of shrubs and saplings lining the narrow road, and I marvelled at the stealth possessed by such men as these surrounding us. Our cavalry were forthright and noisy in their progress, resigned to the impossibility of muffling or disguising the metallic chink of military harness and the creaks and groans of leather saddlery. Ironhair's men and Huw's, on the other hand, moved in stealth, in complete silence. I knew we were being watched by scores of eyes as we passed by, but I took satisfaction in my awareness that the watchers, in turn, were unaware that a full hundred of Huw Strongarm's men lay securely concealed behind them.

Once across the stone arch, moving in columns of four, we pressed straight ahead, riding at an easy lope and following the road as it swept northward to our right, so that we were soon out of sight of anyone on the bridge and riding between the dense banks of close-packed trees that fringed the roadway on both sides. Less than a mile now lay between us and the site of the ambush. As we approached the end of that stretch, I signalled to the men behind me and slowed down to a walk just before we reached the limits of the wood that screened us from the valley ahead. I saw a stirring in the greenery ahead and to my right, and Huw Strongarm stepped forward to the edge of the road. He carried his strung longbow in his left hand, and as I reined in he spoke up.

"No trouble back there?"

"No, not a sign of anything. Are your men ready?"

"Aye, all in place. We'll be in range of you, concealed by just the front bushes. As soon as they attack, have your men fall back this way, along the road. As soon as they've passed by, we'll step out and give your harriers a welcome they'll not be expecting."

"Fine, Huw. There will be an appearance of panic and disarray among us as we break up. Every man knows his own part. We will scatter at first and look disorganized. Some will not come back your way at all, but we'll all stay well clear of your arrows: Warn your men that when they hear my trumpeter they should beware, for we'll be coming back together to finish up the action. My men need some blooding, too. Then, when the opposition has been silenced here, we'll turn around and head back to the bridge. Your other hundred should be in place behind Ironhair's infiltrators by then, to make short work of them." I checked my men, who were sitting quietly, their eyes on me. "Very well, then, let's be about it." I raised my arm in a pumping gesture and led my men forward again.

We advanced in good order, proceeding at the canter as we entered the open, grass-strewn convergence of the valleys ahead of us, giving no indication to watching eyes that we expected trouble. Directly ahead of us, appearing to block our route at this point, was the flat-topped hill described to us by Huw, its upper slopes and featureless top appearing empty and deserted. We bore gradually to our right, heading for the valley to the east. I passed the word back to spread out slightly, allowing our appearance to suggest a casual disregard for danger, and kept pressing steadily forward. I could feel the tension building in my chest as we passed beyond the point of the projecting hill, so that we now had threatening slopes dominating all of our left flank.

Suddenly, the first hostiles appeared on the slopes above and beyond us. They were premature, undone by their own lack of discipline. Their appearance would have given us sufficient advance notice of attack for us to have reformed and escaped the trap, had we, in fact, been unaware of the ambush. As it was, their enthusiasm caused difficulties for me, because I then had to appear to miss my opportunity for flight. I swung my horse around and saw that my men were as aware as I of the enemy's error and were swerving and cavorting madly, giving a convincing show of panic and indecisiveness.

Above us on the hilltop, whoever was in charge could see what had happened, and soon the upper slopes were aswarm with running men, leaping and bounding down towards us, the strident ululations of their battle cries shattering the quiet of the summer afternoon. Paul Scorvo, one of my best independent squadron leaders, now broke away to the rear as planned, trailing a formless squad of eight behind him as he angled his horse slightly uphill, across the front of the attackers, drawing them down and to the right to converge with his escape route. Rufus Metellus, another of the young firebrands Ambrose had promoted to squadron leader, was galloping off now to the north, leading a motley herd of sixteen more troopers down and away from the exposed slopes, to the right of the road, and making sufficient speed already to outdistance any pursuit. I put my spurs to Germanicus and aimed him back along the road we had come by, shouting as I plunged right through the middle of my own troops, who surged together in a rabble at my back and kicked their mounts into a flat-out run following my panicked example. The battle screams above our heads changed now to howls of exultation as our attackers saw us disintegrate and flee, most of us back towards the other trap that now lay set for us.

I stood upright in my stirrups, balancing easily now that Germanicus had found his stride, and turned to look over my shoulder, sweeping my eyes along the crest of the hill. The entire complement of our attackers were now in full pursuit. The bulk of them were rushing in pursuit of my own party, while a small number on either flank went bounding after the two lesser groups led by Scorvo and Metellus. I saw a flicker from the corner of my eye as an arrow skimmed down towards us, and then I saw the bowman, poised on the hillside. The brief glimpse I had was sufficient for me to see that his bow was short, the standard bow in use by all save the Pendragon. And then I heard a crash and a double scream behind me as a horse went down into ruin. I swung Germanicus hard to the left, reining him in brutally as I sought to see what had happened.

One of our troopers lay on the ground, his back arched in pain, his mouth forming a gaping black hole as he screamed. His horse lay nearby, struggling to rise to its feet, the shaft of an arrow protruding from its neck. I kicked my horse forward and leaned from the saddle, my hand outstretched to pull the man erect, but he kept screaming, his staring eyes looking through and beyond me. I could see from the ungodly way his back was twisted that he was beyond my help.

Now I became aware of running footsteps closing rapidly. I reached behind me and unhooked my sword, drawing it quickly and hooking the scabbard to the ring at my belt. The weapon felt strange in my grip, feather-light and almost insubstantial, and I knew that this was because I had never yet swung the sword in earnest against a living enemy. I heard coarse breathing and a muttered curse. I turned to my left to see an enormous man throwing himself towards me, his short sword drawn back for a killing chop. With no time to do anything else, I swung my own sword overhand, chopping it downward towards him and bracing my foot in the stirrup for leverage. The hasty blow missed my assailant's head but came down on his right arm, drawn back for the kill, and severed it so cleanly that I barely felt the impact, even though I had cleft cleanly through bone. He screamed and fell away, clutching at the sudden stump

even before it had time to begin spewing his life blood, and I pulled
Germanicus up into a rearing turn, spurring him to the run as his front
hooves found the earth again. Only one other was close enough to me to
offer danger, and Germanicus hammered him flat to the ground.

As we began to pick up speed, surging steadily forward and slightly
downhill, other shapes came hurtling towards me, none close enough to
make contact. Then a spinning knife clanged frighteningly against the
front of my helmet, snapping my head backwards and filling my mind
with the deafening clangour of the unexpected blow. I reeled and fought
momentarily for balance, struggling against my own reflexive recoil. Then
I was among my own and in control again, overtaking the rearmost of my
troopers, and I dimly saw the moving shapes of Huw's bowmen as they
stepped forward from concealment among the trees on our left to form
massed ranks on the short grass between the road and the forest's edge.
Realizing that I had passed beyond the last of them, I immediately reined
in again and turned to watch.

The charging mercenaries from the hilltop were skidding to a halt,
the nearest of them no more than ten or twenty paces from the formidable
obstacle that had sprung up in front of them. Huw's people were drawn
up in three ranks, each containing perhaps thirty men. Almost before my
mind could grasp what I was seeing, the first rank launched their arrows
and stepped aside, each man to the right. Now the second rank stepped
forward, bows already drawn, and loosed their arrows. They, too, stepped
aside to make way for the fellows at their back and to fill the spaces left
by the men of the first rank, who had already fallen back one pace and
were now fitting arrows to their bows and drawing them, preparing to step
forward into the front rank again. Almost more quickly than I can describe, four lethal flights of arrows sought and found targets among the
stupefied attackers facing them, and the fifth flight was in the air before
the first of the confounded mercenaries rallied enough to try to run for
safety.

They had no place to run, and so they were cut down in moments.
The ground was filled with squirming, writhing men kicking in agony, and
the air was dense with screams and choking gurgles of pain. Every living
man in the main body of the enemy was down, and the fight was over,
except in the distance to my right and left. There, the charade of indecisiveness long since abandoned, the three eight-men squads commanded
by Scorvo and Metellus were delivering an object lesson in military pre-
cision to the hapless survivors who had chosen to pursue them.

My own trumpeter was sitting on my left, awaiting my signal, but I
waved him down. My own group would not be needed. Moments later, I
saw Paul Scorvo wave his men back towards me, and almost before they
had swung into motion, Rufus Metellus and his sixteen men were cantering in my direction, too. Now I turned to Benedict and bade him send

two men to find and comfort the trooper who had gone down behind me. They found him quickly, his throat cut from ear to ear.

Huw Strongarm's men assembled in front of me, their faces strangely blank, showing no pleasure in the slaughter. I was preparing to lead our party back to the bridge when I heard a commotion behind me and turned to see three more of Strongarm's men approaching at the run. The fight there was over, too, with losses of only four of Strongarm's bowmen. None of the interlopers from the ravine had survived. Thereafter, I led our party back into the convergence of the two valleys and settled in to wait for the remainder of our troops.

The cavalry came first, four hundred and sixty troopers, by the route we had followed. Within half an hour of their arrival, the blare of a trumpet to the west announced the arrival of our infantry from the coast, and soon they, too, came into view, marching along the valley bottom in columns of ten, led by Huw Strongarm's scouts. When all had assembled—five hundred cavalry, a thousand foot soldiers and more than two hundred Pendragon bowmen—I climbed to a prominent rock on the hillside and addressed them all briefly, outlining what we must do next. Then I led them north and east at the forced-march pace toward the place where we had been summoned to meet with Uderic Pendragon.

The "king" was not in residence when we reached Moridunum. Word of our surprise must have passed ahead of us. The Roman fort lay still and vacant, although the debris littering the ground and the smoke from numerous smouldering fires made it quite obvious that large numbers of men had waited here but a short time previously. Without dismounting, I dispatched Benedict and our five hundred Scouts in pursuit of whoever they might find, and then I ordered the remainder of our people to set up camp here for the night.

I set out on a short inspection of the old fort itself. It reminded me considerably of our former home in Mediobogdum, save that it was situated in a valley rather than on the heights. Fundamentally, it was exactly the same fort, built to the classical design of a cohortal unit and meant to house as many as six hundred men in comfort. Even the bathhouse, built beyond the walls, was comparable, although it had not been quite as lavishly appointed, and the furnaces were cold and long since dead, their flues blocked by soot and the detritus of decades. Unlike Mediobogdum, however, which had sat high and inaccessible among its mountains, remaining almost inviolate for more than two hundred years, all of the buildings here in Moridunum had been used and abused by careless strangers and were far advanced in ruin, roofless and crumbling after a mere four decades of abandonment.

I finished my tour, accompanied by Rufio, and returned to the fort's ruinous main gate, where Donuil called out to me, inviting me to come and look at something he had discovered. I could see young Bedwyr kneeling on the ground by his feet, his body partly concealed by the stone gatepost. As I stood up in the stirrups to step down from the saddle, I heard an angry, lethal, hissing noise, lightning fast, and saw a flash of movement at the edge of my sight. Then, before I could react, I was hammered by a stunning concussion between my shoulder-blades and flung over my horse's head to crash to the ground, unconscious.

I came to my senses in one of the ruined buildings in the fort, beneath the remnants of a sagging roof that extended for about three paces from the gable end before giving way to open sky. As my eyes opened and my vision swam for a few moments, I saw Donuil and Rufio, Derek of Ravenglass, Benedict, Philip, Paul Scorvo, Rufus Metellus and several others, including Huw Strongarm. They were all looking at someone to my left and their faces wavered in my sight during those first few, blinking moments, dissolving and reshaping themselves as my eyes struggled to adjust to the brightness that filled the room. As I lay there, my head ringing, the memory came back to me—the crashing blow against my back, the clang against my helmet and the swooping vision of my horse's ears looming in my face and then passing beneath me. No one had seen my eyes open, and now I heard the sounds of their voices, unintelligible for a time, then sharpening into a babble of discrete words.

It was Donuil who glanced down and saw me watching him, and his shocked reaction, uttering my name, silenced everyone else and brought them closer. Slowly, fuzzily, I raised my arm and waved them all away and they moved back, tentatively, watchful and wary. A new face now bent close to me, that of Mucius Quinto, our senior surgeon since the death of Lucanus and himself almost as old as Luke had been. He laid his hand on my forehead, pressing me back down onto the pallet, and asked me if I knew him. I was astonished to discover that my voice would not respond when I sought to answer him, but I swallowed, then breathed deeply several times and tried again. This time my tongue worked.

"I'm fine, Quinto," I rasped, in a voice unlike my own. "What happened? Something hit me. Did I fall?"

He nodded, the frown fading from his face as he concluded I was no longer at death's door. "Aye," he answered. "You fell on your head, from your horse. You were shot, with a Pendragon arrow."

"A Pendragon arrow?" I digested that for the space of several heartbeats. "Then I should be dead."

"Aye, you should." This was Derek's voice, and I could see the concern stamped on his ruddy, bearded face. "On two counts, you should be dead, but the arrow hit the blade of the sword across your back, and apparently that's even harder than your head."

Donuil, it transpired, had saved my life by noticing that there was still grease in the pivot-wells of the lintel that held the great gateposts.

He was amazed that the lubricant had remained in place for more than forty years, and that was what he had wanted me to look at. In standing up to go to him, I had moved my neck out of the bowman's sights, replacing it with the cross-slung upper blade of the long sword that hung between my shoulders. Only that sword, made of the skystone's metal, could have deflected the hard-shot Pendragon arrow. A mere cuirass would have been pierced and I would have died instantly. Instead, the arrow struck the blade exactly in the centre and shattered upon impact, the force of it slamming the cross-hilt of the sword against my helm, concussing me and hurling me forward between my horse's ears, so that I fell to the stony ground head first and remained deeply unconscious for more than an hour. The blade of the sword, when I examined it later, showed not even a tiny scratch, although the thin iron cladding of the scabbard that had housed it was mangled and ruined.

I grunted and grimaced, feeling a stabbing pain now at my right shoulder. I tried to sit up but fell backwards again, my head swimming. Quinto leaned over me immediately, his face crumpled in solicitous concern, his hand reaching for my forehead, but I brushed it away. "Don't do that, Quinto, there's nothing wrong with me but vertigo. Help me sit up."

He supported me with his right arm, and I leaned on him. Once I had taken several deep breaths, the room settled down again and I could see clearly. I began to feel better, and my deep breathing soon dispelled the nausea that had threatened to overcome me at first. Finally I felt strong enough to sit fully erect, moving away from the support of Quinto's arm. I drew one more deep breath and then looked around at the small group hovering in front of me, watching me with varying degrees of concern on their faces.

"Very well, then, I'm not dead and I do not intend to die, so will someone tell me who it was that shot me?"

Several heads turned towards Huw Strongarm. He stepped forward, flushing slightly, and threw a Pendragon longbow onto my bed, where it landed across my legs. "Owain," he growled. "The Cave Man."

Owain of the Caves, the traitor who had deserted us to join with Ironhair, the man I had eventually come to suspect of complicity in the attempt on Arthur's life. I looked into Huw's eyes, knowing the answer to my question even as I asked it.

"Where is he now?"

"He's dead. I wish I could say I killed him, but mine was but one of seven arrows in his corpse when I reached him, and Llewellyn had struck off his head even before I arrived." Huw paused, and no one else sought to speak during his hesitation. "He had lain hidden, here, in one of the wall towers. He must have hoped to get a shot at you and thought his life well worth the risk, for he knew he'd never get away alive, once he had shown himself. He hit you from no more than sixty paces. Don't know how he missed you the first time, but the second shot was right on target. He must have died happy, thinking you were dead."

The man had sacrificed his life simply to kill me. Why? And then I recalled what I had seen last, and I knew.

"Where's Bedwyr?"

It was Philip who answered me. "He's outside, trying to mend the covering on the scabbard of your sword. Why, do you want me to send for him?"

I sank back immediately, only then aware of how much I had stiffened in protest at what my mind had told me. "No, leave him." I looked back at Huw. "He wasn't only after me. He wanted the boy, too. They thought he was Arthur."

Huw was the only one there who did not yield in the general buzz of speculation. His eyes narrowed, and then he nodded. "Aye," he growled. "That makes sense. He *didn't* miss you with his first shot, then. From that distance, the Cave Man never would have missed a mark as big and plain as you. His first shot was for the boy. But the lad was on the ground, and kneeling half behind the gatepost, looking down at the shit in the hole there—people moving between him and Owain, too. First shot missed, hitting the gatepost. Second shot for you, knowing that everyone would run to you, leaving the boy as a clear target. Except that Llewellyn just happened to be looking in the right direction at the right time. Suspicious whoreson, Llewellyn One-Eye, trusts no one and likes no strange places. He never lets his guard down, and he sees more than most people do with two good eyes. He saw Owain move to make his first shot, and by the time the second was on its way, Llewellyn had already fired and death was on its way to Owain of the Caves. Good man, Llewellyn, for a suspicious, one-eyed, ugly whoreson."

I smiled at Huw, feeling suddenly very tired. I fought off the weariness and swung my feet over the side of the cot to the floor, bracing myself with my hands on the edge of my bed. The room swayed again, but then held steady, and I forced myself to breathe deeply again.

"Send him to me later, would you? I would like to thank him personally for saving my life."

Huw Strongarm made a dismissive noise with his pursed lips. "Llewellyn? Forget that, Caius Merlyn. He won't thank you for thanks, and he won't thank you for making him feel obligated to you for noticing. He won't thank you for anything, in fact, and the best thanks you can give him is to stay far from him and say nothing."

My smile broadened to a grin and I shook my head. "Can't do that, my friend. Send him. I'll find a way to thank him—a way that he will like." I paused, wondering how I might even begin to make that last statement true. "You like him, this Llewellyn. And he has your especial trust, I suspect."

Big Huw nodded. "Aye. As I said, he doesn't look like much—an ugly, ill-looking whoreson and that's a fact—but one of my sisters married him some years ago, seeing the man beneath the ill-used countenance, and now she thinks she's chosen by the gods and he's the god who chose her. He has been good to her—to her and for her—and to everyone around him, too. Apart from the mess that is his face, there's not a flaw in his make-up. He's the best of the best."

As Huw turned to leave, picking up Owain's bow to take it with him, I stopped him with a gesture of my hand. It was an impulse, and just as capriciously I changed my mind. I shook my head and waved him away again, but still he hesitated.

"What? You wanted to say something?"

"Aye, but it's pointless. Owain's dead. I was merely going to say I wish I could have looked him in the eye one last time before he died."

Huw nodded again, then he grinned a crooked grin. "Aye, well, you might still look him in the eye, but you won't get much out of him in response. I'll send Llewellyn to you later."

I watched him go, wondering what he could have meant, but I soon dismissed it and turned back to the others.

"Donuil, is there any word of Connor?"

"He's patrolling the coastal waters with his fleet, hoping to intercept Ironhair in the other big bireme."

"Philip?"

Philip interrupted his conversation with Benedict to face me, and as he did so I held out my hand to him. He grasped my wrist and I pulled myself to my feet, gripping him strongly and using his solid bulk to anchor myself against the unsteadiness that threatened to dump me unceremoniously back onto the cot. Once I had steadied myself, I loosened my grip on his arm. I stood spread-legged, still unsteady but feeling the strength sweeping back into my legs with every heartbeat. I looked at Benedict now, over Philip's shoulder, remembering that I had sent him away earlier to look for any signs of Uderic's contingent.

"Ben. Did you find anyone out there?"

He grunted a negative, emphasizing it with a shake of his close-cropped head. "We searched for about an hour, but the ground's too hard up here to hold a trail of any kind. Once beyond the end of this valley, there were three separate ways they might have gone without climbing the hills. I suspected they might have split up and gone in all three directions, but I didn't want to split my forces on the strength of suspicion alone, so I brought our people back."

I nodded, accepting his judgment, and spoke to Philip. "Well, what have you to tell me about Connor?"

Philip shook his head slightly. "Nothing, really. I know nothing more concrete than Donuil has already told you. But Connor said to tell you that he'll sweep steadily north, doubling back as necessary from time to time to make sure the waters at his back are, as he put it, kept clear of offal. He'll stay close to the coast, though, and maintain a land watch from every galley. Should you want or need him to touch shore, his people will be watching for three equal fires set burning side by side. That will summon Connor. Four fires will summon all the fleet. When they see either signal, they'll land with the next high tide. His assumption was that you'll keep penetrating northward, hugging the western shore."

"Good, so be it." I took my first hesitant step then, and made my way completely around the cot unaided, watched by all of them. When I had done so, I reversed myself and did it again. "I'm fine," I told them then. "Nothing wrong with me that a short sleep won't cure. Will you leave me now? Wake me if anything happens. If any messengers arrive, I want to hear what they have to say immediately. Thank you, gentlemen."

They left me alone then, all save Quinto, who hovered nearby, watching me anxiously as I lowered myself back to the cot and closed my eyes. I could tell he was loath to leave.

"What is it, Quinto? What do you want?"

He cleared his throat. "I want you to sleep, Caius. Will you drink a potion if I prepare it for you?"

I opened my eyes again and squinted up at him, wondering whether I could trust the soldier in him to prevail over the physician. "Aye," I grunted, "providing you can guarantee your potion will not keep me laid out here for days, unconscious. I need to keep my wits about me, much as I need to sleep. If they have cause to wake me, I want to come awake alert and able to do anything I need to do. Can you ensure that?"

"Yes, I believe I can. A simple sedative, to help you sleep, that's all I'll give you. Three or four hours should see its force dissipate. After that, you ought to be yourself again."

"Ought to be? Not *will* be?"

He dipped his head sideways. "Ought to be. My calling is physician, not magician."

"Hmm. So be it. Go and fetch your foul brew, then."

He left immediately, but by the time he returned I was already deeply asleep, and the potion sat unused on the folding table beside my cot.

X

QUINTO'S SLEEPING DRAUGHT was the first thing I saw when I awoke by myself several hours later, just before sunset, feeling completely normal again.

Someone had set a leather basin in a frame beside my cot, and I rose easily and rinsed my face in the cold water from a leather bucket that hung beside it from a tripod. After that, I went outside to see what was happening.

The fort was bustling, jammed to capacity, bodies moving everywhere. A sprawling community of leather campaign tents had been established in the surrounding meadows. Perhaps because of the brief spell of injury I had endured, my sense of smell seemed unusually acute, and I stood for a while with my head tilted back, singling out the various aromas that filled the late-afternoon air: the smell of horses and dung from the huge area at the rear where the horse-lines had been set up; heavy wood smoke from hundreds of fires; and then the more elusive scents of cooking meats and bread baking among coals. Someone not far from me was frying smoked, salted ham, and from another direction, fleetingly, came the smell of wild onions and garlic. As the mixture of unmistakable savours entered my nostrils, it brought the saliva spurting from beneath my tongue, reminding me that I was ravenously hungry.

I began to look about me, searching for the familiar outline of the large field-cooks' tent that served us as a commissary on campaign. As I did so, I noticed something I had missed before, and my jaw dropped in astonishment as I realized that I must have passed within a few paces of it without seeing it.

The corpse of Owain of the Caves had been decapitated; his head had been stuck on a sharpened stake and set up outside the building in which I had lain unconscious. That was what Huw had been trying to tell me in his cryptic way. Now, as I saw it, with its pallid, waxen, moustached face framed by lank, dull brown hair, all thoughts of hunger fled.

I stepped closer to the atrocious thing, at war within myself. This, I knew, was Pendragon justice, an example set up for others to note and take warning from, and yet a terrible outrage stirred within me, evoked by its mere presence. I wanted to snatch the disgusting thing off its spike and hurl it from me as hard as I could, but I also knew that the last thing on earth I wished to do was touch it. I imagined myself clutching it by the hair and whirling it around my head before I threw it, scattering gouts of congealed blood in a circle, feeling the greasy hair slipping through my fingers. Instead, I merely shuddered in revulsion and forced myself to stand there, close to it, and look at it, remembering the man whose head this once had been.

He had been a ferocious and successful warrior who had served my cousin Uther well and honourably in his time, fighting throughout Lot's War as one of Uther's most trusted captains. Only after Uther's death, for reasons that would now forever be unknown, had Owain turned away from his service, from his own Pendragon loyalties and from Camulod, selling himself to Ironhair and working thereafter to set that upstart in place as ruler of the Cambrian Pendragon. To that end he had conspired to bring death to Uther's own son, and he had finally, willingly, given up his own life in the attempt to achieve that goal. Why? What kind of powers did Ironhair possess that could subvert a man as strong as Owain of the Caves and induce him to turn against his lifelong loyalties? I had asked myself the same question a hundred times before, and I had never come any closer to answering it than I was now. Strangely, as I stood gazing at the lifeless head, wondering vainly what thoughts, desires and drives had filled it during life, I found my horror at its presence leaving me, draining away. I finally nodded to it, gazing into the open, opaque eyes. "Rest then, and settle your own debts with God," I murmured.

As I turned to walk away, one of the men squatting at a nearby cooking fire stood up, watching me. Though my view of him was obscured by thick smoke, I saw enough of him at first glance to be struck by his physical appearance. Whoever he was, I thought, he dressed to be noticed. He was of medium height, and well made, with a narrow waist that tapered from wide, straight shoulders. He wore a short, startlingly beautiful cape of winter ermine furs, one end thrown back over his left shoulder so that the black tips of its outer fringe of tails hung in a brilliant bar across his chest. White and black were his colours, enhanced by siver metalwork and jewellery. I wondered fleetingly who he was, but as soon as the smoke cleared and I saw his narrow, ravaged, hatchet face, I knew he was Llewellyn One-Eye. I stopped short, gazing right back at him and struggling to disguise my reaction to his hideous disfigurement. Then I turned my head slightly to indicate the staring trophy on the stake, pitching my voice so he would hear me clearly.

"This is your work, Llewellyn?"

He came towards me, walking slowly, clutching a cooked leg of some kind of bird in one hand. When he reached my side, he looked at the head on its stake and bit off a mouthful of meat before he made any attempt to answer me. I felt my hunger come back, stronger than ever, as I watched him chewing. He inspected the impaled head as though he had never seen its like before.

"Aye," he said eventually, speaking around the mouthful of meat he had wadded into one cheek. "It's mine. Does it displease you?"

I felt myself start to smile. "No, he's well dead, and your arrow saved my life. I wanted to thank you."

He looked at me sideways, tilting his head strangely to see me with his single eye, the right one. "Horseshit," he said, disparagingly. "Your sword saved your life, and his next arrow would have been for the boy. I thought you were dead before I loosed my shot. Besides, I was shooting for myself. He was a treacherous whoreson, that one, a disgrace to his name and his people."

"How, and why? Because he fought for Ironhair?"

Now Llewellyn turned to look me full in the face. "No, because he sold himself to Outlanders. He was a Pendragon born and bred, a son of these mountains, and he betrayed his birthright and his people. For that he died. It matters not what the Outlander's name was, except that it was other than Pendragon."

"What happened to your eye?" I had been staring at Llewellyn as he spoke, analysing the startling horror of his face, and the question had left my mouth before I was even aware I was going to ask it. He went very still, and then he cocked his head to one side again, peering up at me with his good right eye, thrusting the disfigured side of his face into grim prominence.

"An accident," he said, mildly. "When I was a boy, apprenticed to an ironmaker. I was puddling iron and the metal splashed." I winced at the thought, but he went on as though he had not noticed. "It caught me in the eye and splashed down onto my cheek and nose. The smith pushed my head into a tub of water and expected me to die. I didn't. So when the iron drops had cooled, he plucked them out of me . . . Well, some he had to cut out, I've been told, because the flesh was roasted into them. But I was out of my senses at the time, so I don't remember that. You can see the shapes of them, if you look close."

He suddenly leaned nearer to me, cocking his head in an invitation to examine his disfigurement, and even though I knew he expected me to cringe and pull away, I looked. Sure enough, I saw the evidence clearly. One large, tearshaped drop had settled on the plane of his left cheekbone, its tail stretching upwards and in towards his eye, where its ferocious heat had blinded him on that side, burning away the eye and carving a channel deep into his lower lid. As it healed, the tension of the scar tissue had twisted and pulled the skin and flesh downward, exposing his eye socket horribly and creating a deep fissure down the distorted flesh beneath the eye to join the large teardrop. Three other drops had landed on his face, as well. The smallest of them was in the hollow of his nose, just above the pad of his left nostril, another fell on the outer end of his upper lip, and the third, almost as large as the main splash, had caught him on the outside of his face, beneath the crest of his cheekbone close to the ear, searing a deep hole there before trickling down the line of his jawbone and melting the flesh as it rolled.

Afterwards, as the flesh healed, the shape and depth of the injuries had resulted in the grotesque facial mutilations that now set this man apart. The entire left side of his face was a sight to frighten children, with a leering, empty eye socket set above a ropy network of scars leaving no discernible trace of normal humanity. Above the edge of his mouth, emphasizing the terrifying differentness of this face from all others, a circular hole the size of a fingernail showed his eye tooth and the gum that held it.

He was staring at me intently, waiting for me to say something that would betray my revulsion. But I felt none.

"Yes, you're right. The marks are plain. Four drops—two small, two large, one of them huge. At least you still have your teeth."

He glared at me for a moment, and then his face creased into a huge grin. He finished chewing the food in his mouth and swallowed, before sucking at a tooth on the right side of his mouth and rubbing his lips with the back of his hand.

"Huw told me you wanted to talk to me. What was it about?"

"I told you, I want to offer you my thanks, but Huw warned me you would accept no gratitude. Do you still work with iron, or—"

"Did the experience frighten me away?" He laughed, a single bark. "No, I kept at it and I'm an ironsmith now, save when we're at war. Then I'm a Pendragon, first and foremost, and so I fight."

"An ironsmith."

"Aye, you might say iron's a part of me." He laughed again. "It certainly consumed a part of me, but I'm more careful now, by far. Do you know anything of smithing?"

"But little. When I was a boy, I had a favourite uncle who was a master of the craft. A man called Publius Varrus. He taught me something of forging and shaping iron."

Llewellyn stood slightly straighter. "I know the name. You own his great bow now, do you not?"

"I do. How did you know that?"

"Huw told me about you, and I've seen the badge he wears, the one with the arrow nicks in it."

I nodded, remembering with pleasure the time I had matched shots with Huw. Both of us had landed arrows side by side within the tiny circle of the brooch his wife had given him, filling the space so closely that our arrowheads had left parallel nicks in the upper and lower edges of the silver bauble's inner rim. Huw wore the brooch as proudly as a Roman centurion might have worn the corona on his breastplate. Another thought occurred to me.

"Tell me, how did you know the Cave Man's next arrow would have been for the boy?"

"I didn't, until Huw told me what you said."

I looked straight at Llewellyn now, assessing the man, gauging his mettle. "And have you any idea why he tried to kill the lad, even before me?"

"Aye, he thought him someone else. Young Arthur Pendragon."

"Hmm. And what do you know of Arthur Pendragon?"

Llewellyn twisted his mouth up in what might have been a lopsided smile, except that it exposed the tooth beneath the hole in his cheek. "He's Uther's son, they say. Sired upon Lot of Cornwall's willing wife."

He took another bite from the leg he held in his hand, and I distinctly heard the juicy sound of the meat ripping away from the bone. "Is there any left where that came from?"

"Aye, or there was when I left the fire. Come." He led me back, and as we approached, the two men who sat there yet stood up.

Llewellyn waved his hand from me to them. "Gwynn Blood-Eye and Daffyd, Merlyn of Camulod. Daffyd's our cook, and better than any you have brought with you, I'd wager. Gwynn Blood-Eye's here because he's the only whoreson in this place who's uglier than me! Sit you."

I nodded to the two men and sat down on a rock, gazing at the whole, spitted carcasses of two fowls that still hung above the fire, the grease from them dripping onto the coals beneath and flaring in small, furious bursts of fire. A large pile of bones lay on a square wooden platter close by Daffyd's feet and a half-eaten carcass clung to another spit. As I sat down, the man called Gwynn Blood-Eye, who indeed had one eye that was the deep red of blood, with no discernible iris or pupil, reached down to his side and passed me a wooden board like the one that lay by Daffyd. I thanked him and balanced the thing on my knee as Llewellyn reached across the fire, deftly lifted off another spit and then slid the carcass of the bird free of its spike and onto my platter.

"Eat," he said. "It's duck, basted with pig fat. You'll like it. There's some salt there, in the clay pot." He returned to his own fowl as I began to rip mine apart, heedless of the searing heat of it. I raised a dripping thigh and crunched my teeth into it, burning my lips with hot fat, yet utterly uncaring as the delicious flavour of the hot meat filled my mouth. For a while, there was no more talking around our fire, until I had stripped the bird's bones clean. As I finished it, throwing the last of the remnants into the fire, Llewellyn handed me a cloth to clean my hands.

"You were ready for that."

"Aye, it's the first real food I've eaten in the past two days. I didn't know how hungry I was until I came outside to look around and met you, with that leg in your fist."

"Here." He reached down and handed me a clay pot filled with ale, and I drank deeply. The taste of it was quite unlike anything I had ever tasted before. When I had slaked my thirst, I lowered the pot and looked at him.

"That, I believe, is the finest ale I've ever drunk. Where in the name of God did you get it?"

"You're the stranger here, Merlyn of Camulod. We live here. And that ale was made not five of your Roman miles from where we sit now." As Llewellyn spoke, Gwynn Blood-Eye and Daffyd both rose to their feet, nodded to me and left the fire, heading in different directions, Daffyd carrying the last remaining spitted bird.

I looked inquiringly at my host. "Where have they gone?"

"Who knows? They have things to do and they know we have matters to discuss. You were asking me about the boy, Arthur, before your hunger got the best of you. Had you finished with that?"

"No." I blinked at him, surprised at how he had redirected me to our former conversation. "You had just finished detailing his parentage, which I had thought to be a secret. Where did your information come from?"

"About Uther and his lady love? It's common knowledge."

"Is it, by the Christ? I was unaware of that."

"Well, it's a common rumour, let's say. Few, if any, know the truth of it. When our men returned from Cornwall, after Uther's death, they brought word of his exploits and of his love for the woman. She had a baby son, that much was known. As to whether the brat was Lot's or Uther's, that was anybody's guess. And as for what happened to him, that was totally unknown, to most folks. But then, a few years ago, the rumours sprang up again. Some said he was in Camulod, with you, all along. Others said that you had fled from Camulod and taken the boy with you, and that you were living among the Scots, across the water. Some said the boy was dead, killed in his infant years. I knew nothing and cared less, in those days, because I was too caught up in my own miseries to care about any other's.

"I took no part in Uther's wars because I thought his wars were no concern of mine. My war was with the folk around me here, who lived in fear of me because of this face of mine. But then, nigh on eight years ago, I met my wife, Martha, and through her, I met her brother Huw, and we became good friends. Since then, I've come to see that not all I had believed was true—most of it was horseshit, born of self-pity. Now I look at life, by and large, through a different eye, you might say, and Huw respects my judgment in most things. So when he told me about you, and about the boy who is your charge, and about who he thought the boy might be, I did some thinking of my own. The lad is Uther's son. Am I right?"

"What if you are?"

"Why then, the whole world changes, and this whoreson war has found a purpose and a champion. If I am right, then Arthur Pendragon is the rightful king, born to rule in his father's stead, and all this horseshit over Carthac and that idiot Uderic is pointless."

"Pointless? How so?"

"Because the real king is with you, in Camulod. All the others are mere posturers! So what we need to do is rid ourselves of all these false claimants—the whole rat's nest of them—and recognize our king, the son of Uther Pendragon. That's why you're here in Cambria, no? To safeguard the boy's interests."

I cleared my throat. "Well, yes, and no. Arthur is yet too young." I had decided then, and only at that moment, to trust Llewellyn fully. "But there's more to it than that. As his mother's son, he holds a claim to Cornwall, as well. That, more than anything else, is why Ironhair wants him dead. And then, in addition to that, because his mother was the daughter of Athol Mac Iain, once king of the Scots people of Eire, young Arthur has blood claims to that kingship, too. And he is heir to Camulod—not king, mark you, for Camulod will never have a king. He is the great-grandson of Publius Varrus of the bow, and great-great-nephew to Caius Britannicus, the founders of Camulod."

When I had finished, Llewellyn shook his head slowly. "That is too much information, containing too much danger, Merlyn of Camulod. Why would you tell all that to me, a stranger whom you have never met until today?"

"Because Huw Strongarm trusts you, and I find I do, too, now that I've spoken with you and listened to you. You are strong in your belief in the rightness of the boy's claim to Pendragon Cambria. Would you support him?"

"Of course. I've said so, haven't I?"

"Will you support him now?"

Llewellyn frowned. "Now? How would I do that? He is not here, and you have said he is too young."

"Not too young, yet not quite old enough. He is sixteen, or will be on his next birthday. Right now he needs a teacher, and I think you could be the one to teach him what he needs to know. Would you be willing?"

He slumped back, evidently mystified. "A teacher? Me? The lad would run in fright at the sight of me. Besides, I know nothing worth teaching."

"You don't know the lad, Llewellyn. He would not flinch from the sight of you. And as for your having nothing to teach him, I take leave to doubt that. He is a Cambrian Pendragon, as you are, but he knows nothing of the land or its people. He speaks the tongue, but he does not know the folk. He'll be a warrior of note, I have no doubt of that, yet he knows only cavalry and horses, swords and spears and clubs. He is a big, strong lad, but he's no bowman yet, and he knows nothing of your mountain ways. I would like him to learn these things. No one knows Arthur in this land. That's why the Cave Man tried to kill Bedwyr. But if I bring him here, then everyone will know exactly who he is, because he is with me. Instead I would like you to ride back with me to Camulod, to meet the boy and bring him back here with you, so that he can live a year or so among your clan and learn to be the Pendragon he must become. Would you do that for me? For him?"

"For all of us." He sat silent then, for a long time, and when he spoke again it was with an emphatic nod. "Aye, I would and will. He'll be my prentice. I'll set him to the work of shaping metal, but I'll make him known among the people, too, and he'll be taught the skills he'll need to know—hunting and shooting and living quiet, off the land. When do we go?"

I laughed. "Not before we take care of Ironhair, Carthac and even Uderic. We can't walk away prematurely."

Llewellyn grunted, "Nah, that's already begun, simply thanks to your being here in Cambria. That horseshit with the ambush won't go unremarked or unrewarded. There was nothing there of honour or bravery, and it was clear proof that Uderic has begun to treat with the invaders. He has done little enough to endear him to Pendragon in the past, and any music in his song has become hard to hear, these past four months. This latest treachery will kill him—at the very least, it will kill his designs. You mark my words, Merlyn of Camulod—within the month, you'll have as many Pendragon bows at your command as you have troopers now, and that will bring an end to Carthac and the filth that follows him. With every new Pendragon in your camp you'll take a step closer to uniting all Pendragon under one head. That head won't be Pendragon, true enough, since you are nominally Outlander yourself, but we will at least follow a leader who has Pendragon's interests at heart."

"What about Huw?"

Once again, the curious stillness I had noticed before descended upon Llewellyn. Now he moved his head minutely to look at me attentively. "What about him?"

I had no answer, yet I felt a rightness in me and so pressed ahead.

"I don't know. I'm merely wondering aloud. I'm an Outlander, as you correctly said. I have no ambition to lead the Pendragon anywhere in anything. And yet, for them to coalesce, to come together as you have said, they'll need a leader. It strikes me now that Huw Strongarm might be the one. Isn't he some kind of chief among you? I know his family held the land to the south of here, along the coast. It was he who rented holdings there to Liam Twistback, for the raising of his beasts, and I remember him saying his family had held those lands since long before the Romans came."

Llewellyn sniffed, then nodded his head in a tiny gesture of acknowledgement. "That's true. Huw is a chief. One of our foremost, if you think in terms of claim to leadership. His forefathers have ranked among our best and most able chiefs since pre-Roman times, as you have said. But Huw has no desire for kingship. All he wants is peace and the chance to lead his life at ease among his family."

"But he has been at war for years. When did he last spend any length of time at home?"

"Long years ago . . ." Now Llewellyn's face twisted again in what I was coming to recognize as his favourite kind of smile, a tiny flicker of wry amusement. "What are you saying, Merlyn of Camulod? Spit it right out."

"I am saying, I suppose, that the quickest way for Huw Strongarm to win home in peace might be for him to take upon himself the burden of leadership, don't you agree? He's an honourable man—"

"Horseshit! You can't feed on honour. That's a Roman concept—we have no need of honour. But you're right if what you're saying is that Huw Strongarm is highly thought of among his people. That's a fact, and it's not an easy status to achieve."

"Well then, we should convince him that he is responsible for helping bring this conflict to an end. Would the people follow him, were he to step forward?"

"They would. I'm sure of that. But would he be willing? That's what I don't know . . ." He paused, thinking, and then continued. "Let's go back a bit, to what we were talking about earlier—young Pendragon, your Arthur."

"What about him?"

"About his father, first. Huw was Uther's closest friend among all our folk, did you know that?" I merely nodded, and he continued. "Aye, well it was more than that, too. Uther was Huw's king, you see. There was no slightest doubt of that in either of their minds. Huw was Uther's man, to the death, and had always been so. That's why he has never had the slightest wish to rule the Pendragon: when Uther fell, the kingship fell, and Huw never thought in terms of kingship for himself. He is, above all else, a king's man, not a king. If Uther ever set a task for him, that task became Huw's life till it was done." Again he paused, and I waited. "So, it seems to me that Huw Strongarm might stand up and fight to champion the boy, the son of his true king. What think you about that?"

"I think we should ask him, now, while it is fresh in our minds. Where might he be?"

"Not far from here, wherever he is." Llewellyn stood up. "I'll find him and bring him back. Stay you here."

While the enigmatic one-eyed man was gone, I sat alone, rethinking everything that had come to pass so surprisingly in the previous hour or so. It was growing dark rapidly now, so that I could barely see beyond the firelight, and I threw some new fuel on the embers that remained in the shallow pit in front of me. It had caught and been more than half consumed by the time Llewellyn returned, accompanied by Huw Strongarm.

I could see from the look on Huw's face that Llewellyn had said nothing about why he had brought him to me. It took almost an hour of talking, during which several of my men came looking for me and were all sent away again unheard, but by the end of the hour, Huw had agreed to my suggestion, backed as it was by Llewellyn's quiet, strong support. He would, he agreed, serve as a rallying point for those of his people who might come to him—his modesty was such that he had serious doubts that any would—and he would, furthermore, prepare the way, and the people of Cambria, for the coming of their true king, Uther's only son, Arthur Pendragon.

I had to bite hard on my lip, hearing those words, for memories of what my brother had told me of another, firstborn son reared up again to frighten me. I stifled the thought, nonetheless, and swore in return to Huw that, if he were as true to this as he had been to Uther, I would be no less true in supporting him, with all the strength of Camulod, in his endeavours to end this present war. And so we were agreed. By midafternoon of the following day, not a single Pendragon Celt remained in camp. Llewellyn and Huw had begun their work almost immediately, and throughout the morning the Pendragon had been assembling in groups throughout the camp, only to break up again and circulate, spreading the word and then regathering in larger groups. By noon, close to three hundred men had assembled there, vociferous in their support of Huw Strongarm. Huw had addressed them briefly then, amid a crowd of my own troopers attracted by all the activity and excitement, and shortly after that the noisy, colourful Celtic crowd had begun drifting apart and scattering to the winds, to carry the word of Uderic's perfidy and Huw Strongarm's summons to arms to every village and hamlet in the Pendragon lands.

Small in number though their group had been, their passing nevertheless left a certain quiet hanging over our encampment. To keep my men occupied and to expend the useful energies stirred up in them by the morning's events, I set them to refurbishing and refortifying the ancient walls. We would be staying in this place for two full weeks and perhaps even longer, awaiting the return of Huw and Llewellyn, and there was much to do to set aright forty years of neglect and make the place acceptable again as a defensible stronghold.

I joined in the work, stripped to my tunic and glad of the hard exercise as I sweated among a chain of men, passing heavy building blocks from the man behind me to the one ahead, towards a group of our masons working industriously to repair a fallen section of wall. I had been hard at it for well over an hour by the time Derek and Benedict found me, and so I felt no pang of conscience as I walked away from the chain with them, wiping the sweat from my shoulders, neck and face with a rough cloth. A squad of messengers had arrived, Ben said, with word from Tertius Lucca, who was holding the harbours at Caerdyff and Caerwent on the south Cambrian coast, behind us and to the east. Lucca had received word that a substantial train of supply wagons was on its way north from Camulod. It would proceed directly to him in Caerdyff, and he would redirect it to us.

In the past six weeks, Lucca's troops had found no enemy activity to report. Lucca suggested that Ironhair's shipmasters had finally accepted the loss of the south-eastern harbours and were making no effort of any kind nowadays to approach them. They had learned that lesson, Lucca stated, only after sustaining heavy damage in a succession of all-out attacks involving abortive landings, to the east and west of our positions, in the vain hope of surrounding our garrisons. Perhaps, he suggested, some of his troops would now be better employed with us, rather than languishing and growing bored, pent up in garrisons that felt no threat. He could leave a holding force in place, he reported, perhaps one-third of his current complement of three thousand, to occupy, patrol and defend the southeastern coastal harbours. The remaining two thousand could then travel the short distance to us in company with the supply train. On my approval, he said, the reinforcements would be with us in a matter of days.

I thanked and dismissed the messengers before I conferred with my own people. All of them had reservations, as I had myself. The truth was that, in our current situation, where we had had no real contact with the enemy for months, other than the ambush set by our supposed ally Uderic, we had no need of the extra troops. Until we were ready to march again, they simply represented extra mouths to feed.

Benedict, taciturn as usual, was the only one of my captains who sat silent throughout the discussion, forcing me to ask him bluntly for his thoughts. He then asked me what I had planned for Huw's return, and how many men I expected him and Llewellyn to bring back. He had, of course, laid his finger squarely on the root of our dilemma, and that now forced me to admit that I did not yet know the answer to either of his points, since the first depended almost entirely upon the second. I was reluctant to commit myself to a course of action, I pointed out, since Huw himself had grave doubts that his people would follow him.

This evoked a buzz of comment among my listeners, but it was Benedict himself who silenced them by holding up his hand. This unaccustomed gesture brought him instant attention. He looked at me, eyes squinting against the sun, then looked around at everyone.

"Not worth considering," he said, raising his voice. "Not even tenable." He jutted his jaw pugnaciously, as though expecting to be challenged. "You all know me. I don't like conjecture and I don't make predictions. But I'll make one now, and if you'll think about it, you'll admit I'm right." He turned back to me again. "Huw Strongarm will rule Cambria within the year, free of opposition. He's the natural choice and the perfect man for the task. Ironhair's here with Carthac because there's no organized will right now to drive them out. We're organized, but we can't reach his people in the high hills, let alone fight them on their terms. Besides, we're as much Outlanders as they are, and so we're suspect in the eyes of the Pendragon kinglings. Too many little kinglings, with too many little bands that think themselves armies, and every one of them out for himself, for his own good, with his own little ambitions. Strongarm's no part of that, and had he stood up before now to be counted, he'd be in overall command already. Now he is ready. The Pendragon will follow him wherever he decides to take them, and he'll take them to victory far quicker than anyone else could. So he'll be coming back, and soon, and he'll bring thousands with him. We had better be prepared to move as soon as he arrives, and to serve as a solid platform for his catapult. That's all I have to say."

Derek almost interrupted him before he could finish, with a loud, woofing grunt of approval that grew into an appreciative roar of acclamation as the others joined in the applause. Benedict looked about him almost truculently, flushing with doubt-filled pleasure.

I grasped him roughly by the shoulder. "You're absolutely right, Ben. We must be ready here when Huw returns—fully prepared, fit and ready to march." I turned to Philip. "When Lucca's squad is rested, send them back immediately with full approval of his plan. He is to delegate the harbour command to his best subordinate and then bring his two thousand here in person with the supply train, and as many extra rations and supplies as he can provide." I stood up and flexed my shoulders. "Right, then, my friends. We'll proceed as before, since there's not much we can do until the others arrive, but I want your men at their fighting best when we leave here. That might be in a week, or it might not be for several more than that, but in the meantime, I want to see our people training for real war again. We've all grown lazy, I suspect, in the past few months of inactivity. I want to see the evidence that sloth is outlawed, from this moment on. That's all."

I left them there and went looking for hot water, regretting once more the fact that the bathhouse here was irredeemable.

Tertius Lucca arrived within the week, at the head of a massive train of wagons filled with weaponry, supplies and provisions. The day of his arrival was consumed in seeing to the disposition of his force, the allocation of quarters to his two thousand men and an inventory of the wealth he had brought with him. Then, the following morning, a short time before noon, a hard-riding messenger arrived from our most northern outpost with the word that an unidentified force, numbering in excess of two thousand men, was converging on us from the north and west. In spite of my great hopes for Huw's success in rallying his people, it seemed to me it was yet too soon for such a host to have sprung up, even from Huw's most determined efforts, and so I sounded a general alarm. But hard on the heels of that first messenger, a second arrived almost before our trumpets had stopped clamouring, bearing the word that the approaching force had been identified as Pendragon.

Astounded and delighted, I took advantage of the furore stirred up by the alarm and rode out northward at the head of a hundred cavalry troopers to greet Huw Strongarm on his triumphant return. Instead I found Llewellyn striding ahead of his men, very much in command, and though my welcome to him was no less genuine, I found myself wondering what had become of Huw himself.

Llewellyn came to me directly and grasped my horse's bridle strap. Huw was still in the north, he told me, headed now into the Pendragon strongholds in the east and south-east of Cambria, gathering strength with every day. He had wanted to send these first two thousand south to me, so that I could begin a northward sweep, penetrating the central highlands, where Carthac was creating havoc at the head of a marauding mob of mercenaries. He hoped that I would be willing to use my troops as mobile walls in the valley floors of the mountain ranges, solid bulwarks to confine and demolish the detritus of Ironhair's levies as the Pendragon bowmen flushed them down from the hilltops.

I smiled to hear Huw's message endorse the exact stratagem urged by Benedict a week earlier. Already I could perceive the change that responsibility had effected in Huw Strongarm: he had left me as a subordinate and an ally; now, scarcely two weeks later, he was addressing me as an equal, and perhaps even as one subordinate to him, submitting orders thinly disguised as requests through his own subordinate commander. I was not displeased by this in any way. Huw had sent two thousand men to me in earnest of his unswerving good faith and was off gathering more. The number surprised me, and I asked Llewellyn how many men the Pendragon might field.

"In total? More than ten thousand, I would estimate, of fighting age."

"Good God! I had no idea there were so many. Five thousand fighting men, that I could see. It seems to me my cousin Uther commanded that many."

"When? In Lot's War? That was a long time ago. We are a numerous people, Caius Merlyn, and we're farmers before anything else. It's true our farms are small, nowhere near as rich or fertile as yours in the south, but they need equal tending and even harder work because of that. Five thousand was the smallest number of Pendragon men your cousin led, in the final years of the Cornwall affair, but he always left a greater number at home in Cambria, tending the land. We lost too many men down there. The last battle cost us dearly, but now we have recovered. And this war is here, on our own land, in our own fields. We'll win it quickly now, with Huw to lead us and with your help, so every man in Cambria will do his part. Huw should bring five thousand more, I'd guess, and others will come later."

I was still astonished and sat looking about me for several moments before looking back to him. "Let's head back to camp. Will you ride with me, if I offer you a horse?"

Llewellyn looked at me and grinned. "Aye, willingly, but will you un-horse one of your own for me?"

I turned to look at Bedwyr, who had been listening to all of this, and he was already dismounting. Once on the ground, he offered his reins to Llewellyn, who accepted them with a nod of thanks and swung himself easily up into the saddle as Bedwyr caught Rufio's good arm and swung himself up behind him, to ride double.

I watched Llewellyn's mount to the saddle in surprise, and he read it in my face. "Rufio taught me how to ride," he said. "I learn quickly."

"It would seem you do." I kicked Germanicus into motion and Llewellyn rode beside me on my left, knee to knee, back to our encampment. As we rode, I took up the conversation where we had left off.

"Five thousand more? How will Uderic react to that, I wonder?"

Llewellyn turned towards me but did not look at me. He kept his head down, his one eye fixed, it seemed to me, on Germanicus's ears. "Uderic? He won't react at all. He's dead." Now he glanced at my face and read my shock. His own face again wore a sardonic grin. "Uderic had difficulties with the word we spread about his conduct with the Outlander Ironhair. He didn't enjoy hearing himself being called what he was, and so he challenged Huw. Should have been a wiser man and simply left, but then, Uderic never was a wise man. They fought. It was brief."

"So now Huw is king indeed."

"Hah! I thought that was all settled between you and him! Huw Strongarm has no interest in being king. Did we not go through all that? Huw's War Chief of Pendragon and that's all he wants to be. He sees his task as settling the land for its new king, King Uther's son. Mind you, they tried to make him king, after he killed Uderic, but he laughed at them and told them all that's what their problem has been since Uther died—too many people looking to be king, and none prepared to do the heavy work. That shut them up."

We rode in silence after that, and when I broke it again it was to speak of something that had been in my mind for several days, ever since Ben had made his prediction.

"I would like to make Huw a gift of some kind, Llewellyn, a mark of my respect for the stance he has taken. What would be appropriate to give to the War Chief of Pendragon? I could offer him armour, or weapons, but I think he has no need of either—certainly not of the kind we wear and use. Can you think of anything that might please him?"

"Aye, one of those." We had arrived at our encampment, and I looked to see what it was that he had identified so quickly, but nothing obvious presented itself to me. Llewellyn read the incomprehension on my face and pointed straight ahead. "One of those. That big tent of yours."

"What, you mean my command tent?"

"Aye. Huw doesn't have one. There isn't one such tent in all of Cambria save this. What better gift could you present to a War Chief than such a visible symbol of his power? A big, wide, leather tent with a high, lofty roof, where he can assemble and meet with his own leaders in all kinds of weather, warm and dry in the foulest times. That were a kingly gift, were it within your power to bestow it. D'you have another one like it?"

I laughed aloud and slapped him on the back in my delight. "Llewellyn, you are a man of great discernment. It is, indeed, the perfect gift and Huw Strongarm should have one. Not only do I have another, I have a new-made one, never used, its leather panels still smelling of smoke and tanning and its poles and guy ropes clean and free of grime or dirt. Tertius Lucca brought it with him but yesterday, in one of his wagons—an unexpected gift from the Council of Camulod, for my use. It will be Huw's, instead, because despite the laudable concern of the Council, my own tent there is in perfect condition. Well done, Llewellyn, well done. Now, is there anything that *you* would like?"

He answered me promptly. "Aye, there is. I'd like a horse of my own, and a saddle." He was grinning widely now, the left side of his face twisted. "I find I love to ride. I would not take it with me when I'm with my own, but when I go with you, I'll go in pride and comfort."

"So be it, my friend. Visit our horse-lines and pick out the horse you want, then speak with Philip about a saddle. But you know that, once the horse is yours, you'll have to care for it yourself?"

"Aye, Merlyn, I know it. Rufio is a thorough teacher. He's the man you should have teaching young Arthur, not me."

I grinned and nodded. "I might agree, but Arthur has long since learned everything Rufio had to teach him. Now *he* teaches Rufe! That's why I need you for him: new tricks, new Cambrian skills and new techniques, to keep the lad on his toes."

We struck camp the following morning. I had dispatched written messages to Camulod, acknowledging receipt of the supplies and bidding our Council to advise Ambrose, whenever he should arrive back from Vortigern's lands, to sit there until he heard again from me, since I knew not where we might end up and we had no need of reinforcements at this time. I also sent off messengers to Huw Strongarm, bearing the gift of his new command tent—the messengers who carried it had spent hours the day before learning to erect and dismantle it—and apprising him of what we intended once we had penetrated the central highlands.

We would march north and east towards the ancient gold mines of Dolaucothi, where it seemed most likely that Ironhair and Carthac might be found, grubbing for gold in the ancient workings. I invited him to send messengers to us there, since, were we unable to find our quarry in Dolaucothi, we would then face two optional, equidistant choices of route. One, to the north and east again, was a Roman fortification with no Roman name I knew of; to Llewellyn, it was simply the Roman place at Colen, in the middle of Cambria. To the north of that, a full day's march to westward, was Mediomanum, the last of the Roman forts of central Cambria. To the south-west from Dolaucothi, on the other hand, lay the famous fort at Cicutio, a long-held stronghold of the Twentieth Legion Valeria Victrix. That would have been my natural choice, had I been free to make it, but the choice of our final destination would be based upon Huw's information regarding the enemy's whereabouts.

Once out of Moridunum that morning, we made our way quickly towards Dolaucothi, heading into the mountain glens that sank deeper and deeper into shadow as the hills surrounding them grew higher. Not a single day passed from then on without groups and bands of silent men joining us from the hills as we moved, swelling our ranks until our numbers rose to top nine thousand. So rapid and so visible was this influx that, despite our newly refurbished stores, the logistics people in our quartermasters' company grew concerned at the number of mouths we had to feed. But food came to us without our seeking it, sent in from villages and hamlets and from solitary farms along our route, few of them ever seen by us, since we kept to the valley bottoms and most of the dwellings we passed nestled in the shelter of the thick-treed hillside slopes.

As I sat on a hillside outcrop one morning, reviewing the turnout as my army swept by my perch, I noted the division that had grown apparent in my forces and paid more attention to Llewellyn's Celts than to my own troopers. Dour and silent, grim-faced and self-absorbed, these newcomers were different from the Pendragon Celts our soldiers had known before. These were hillmen, the true Pendragon people, born and bred among mountain solitudes that seldom knew the presence of Outlanders, and they held themselves apart from the rest of us with a fierce, distrustful and self-centred pride. They made it plain, without words, that they marched with us in answer to the call of their people and their land; they owed no allegiance to us, or Camulod, or any other Outlandish power. They marched in utter silence, for the most part, and they bristled with weapons of all shapes and sizes, the most prevalent among them the great weapon known as the Pendragon longbow. Every man, it seemed, now carried a bow stave as tall as himself, and at least one quiver of long arrows made from the wood of ash saplings and flighted with goose feathers.

The sheer quantity of bows perplexed me, for I knew from my own readings of the chronicles of Publius Varrus and my own grandfather, written mere decades earlier, that these weapons had then been few and precious, numbering in the mere hundreds. Ullic Pendragon, Uther's grandfather, had decreed in those days that the new longbows were the property of the people; no man could own one as his personal possession. Each man served as the custodian of a bow for a time, responsible for its upkeep and well-being, then passed it on, at the end of a year, into another's keeping. Many of the bows I was seeing now had been among those protected by that very law and were now fifty, sixty and more years old.

For decades now, Druids had walked these lands searching for yew trees in their journeying, and planting and cultivating new groves of yew wherever they found places suited to their growth. And as increasing supplies of yew staves were brought home, the number of bow-and arrow-makers had grown, too, and mastery of the skills required to make the weapons had become the greatest art of these fierce folk.

I took note then of the bows themselves and found more room for surprise. All of the longbows I had ever seen before were round in section, each carved with loving care from one dried, cured stave of yew. Some of these I was seeing now were different, apparently rectangular in section like the huge, laminated bow I owned myself, now far more than a hundred years in age and polished with a patina of untold decades of close care and maintenance. The Varrus bow, as I thought of it, was compound in make-up, with a double-arched shape—two bows, in fact, above and below the carved handhold at the centre—made in flat layers of some dark, exotic wood backed by hand-shaven plates of animal bone and braided strips of sinew, glued and dried to iron hardness, the whole crafted and bound and baked by unknown means in Africa by a long-dead Scythian master and defying duplication here in Britain.

When Llewellyn himself passed by me I asked him about these new bows, and he confirmed what I had suspected. They were, in fact, made in laminated sections, although they each possessed the single arch of the traditional Pendragon longbow. Most of them were made of ash, he said, though some were still of the rarer yew. The original round bow required a stave of specific dimensions and properties, thickness and straightness being the first two of these. Since not all saplings grow straight, it followed logically that not all were suitable for making bows. But the Pendragon bowmakers remembered that the Varrus bow, on which all their new bows were based, had been laminated in sections. In consequence, some had continued working with the lesser woods which, though they lacked the resilient strength of yew, yet had other valuable qualities: dense, narrow grain and pliability. Someone, then, had discovered that a suitable length of sawn ash, well-cured, kiln-dried and straight-edged, could be split laterally with great care and then rejoined, bonded with impermeable glue, the pieces reversed so that the grain of one piece opposed and reinforced the other. That done, the resultant stave could be hand-planed, shaved and tapered to produce a formidable weapon, lesser in strength than the long yew bow, but nonetheless efficient and deadly when it came to piercing enemy armour, even from great distances.

Absorbing that, I thanked Llewellyn courteously and then moved on alone, thinking about what had been achieved in the art of warfare, almost within my own lifetime, here in this land of Britain. The huge longbow itself had sprung from nothingness within a hundred years, inspired by the enormous bow that now rode with my own baggage. The cavalry who rode now in extended formation to my right existed only because I myself had stumbled upon the secret of the stirrups that now supported each trooper's feet. The long, cross-hilted sword that hung suspended from an iron ring between my shoulders was one of only three similar weapons in the entire world. The iron ball that hung from my saddle-bow, secured by a thong around its short, thick wooden handle and swinging on a length of chain, had first been made by my cousin Uther and was now in widespread use, a lethal, deadly flail that, whirled around his head, gave a man five times his own strength in combat. And the long and slender spears, lightweight and almost flexible yet indestructibly strong, carried by the majority of my own troopers, had sprung from our need to have a weapon that our men could use effectively from horseback, on the run. Even our cavalry, I now realized, had doubled upon itself, expanding its effectiveness, with the development of the Scouts.

As I rode, deep in thought, I realized how easy it had been to take all these weapons and developments for granted, and to assume that everyone possessed them. But of course, that was not the case. Few people, beyond Camulod and Cambria, had ever seen their like; no people were equipped to stand against them, and none had the skills, the years of training or the discipline in fabrication to duplicate them. At that precise moment, it came to me with the force of a revelation that if we used our forces and advantages properly we would truly be invincible in war.

That evening, I convened a meeting. I wanted to share my new-found revelation with my companions, my subordinates and my allies. My listeners—among them Llewellyn and several of his captains, as well as my own troop commanders—sat in silence for a long time, mulling over all that I had said. Though much of what I had told them they already knew, none of them, for all that, had seen the truth of it in its largest dimensions. The value of the exposition made itself immediately apparent the following day, implicit in the new air of confidence and good humour everywhere as the commanders communicated their own enthusiasm, mostly by attitude alone, to their troops.

Our northward thrust pressed forward effortlessly and with complete success, and the few concentrations of the enemy that we encountered were exterminated mercilessly by the swarming hillmen who ranged the hills above and ahead of us. Very few of them escaped the lethal hail of arm-long arrows, and those who did flee with their lives lost them soon afterwards, when their inevitable descent from the heights brought them into the ken of my massed formations. Within days of setting out from Moridunum, I had joined the fighting on the high ground, leaving my heavy troopers and infantry formations far below and leading my lighter Scouts up into the hill passes. Our presence there restricted the enemy's movements to the hilltops and crests, where Llewellyn's bowmen dealt with them as farmers deal with pests, trapping and destroying them.

For all my hard riding, nevertheless, I had blooded my sword only once, in a fleeting skirmish with some fleeing Cornishmen, by the time we reached the abandoned gold mines at Dolaucothi. Huw Strongarm had arrived ahead of us, I knew, because word had come back to me the previous day, from the leading party of Llewellyn's bowmen, who were ranging far in advance of our troopers in the valleys below. They had made contact with Huw's people, who were ranged among the hills to the north and east of the valley closest to the gold mines. Llewellyn's forces had occupied the southern and western slopes, keeping behind the crests and exercising great care to ensure that the mob of Cornish and mercenary levies in the valley remained unaware of their presence until the infantry and heavy cavalry had arrived to seal all the exits. Confident of Philip's ability to marshal our main forces, I kept to the higher valleys, in the hope of being able to bring my Scouts to a hillside position that would allow us to strike downward.

We were within sight of the last ridge remaining between us and the site of the anticipated battle, however, when a storm of noise erupted ahead of us, and I knew that someone had been unable to wait for the proper moment. I never discovered who or what caused the premature outbreak of fighting, but the rapidly swelling noise told me clearly that battle had been joined in earnest. Cursing with frustration, I signalled to my men and led them forward as quickly as we could go.

Unfortunately, the terrain in which we found ourselves precisely at that time made it impossible for us to build momentum, and our advance quickly lost all coherence as men and horses surged this way and that among loose boulders and deep-scored gullies that defied efficient pro-gress. I had an immediate lesson in why and how cavalry is useless in mountainous terrain. I set Germanicus at an ascending track that looked like a wide and much-used game path, but even as his massive haunches thrust us up the hillside, the men on either side of me had to fall back as the track narrowed rapidly and finally ended at the precipitous edge of a ravine. I reined him in hard and swung him left again, downhill, and had to lean far back in my saddle, braced hard in my stirrups, as he picked his way delicately downward, following the ravine's edge. I could hear someone else coming down behind me, but I did not look back to see who it was; I was too busy gauging the confusion among the other Scouts scattered along the hillsides and the valley floor below me.

I found a place where I could cross the ravine, and after that the going improved slightly, so that I was able to make better speed towards the crest of the ridge that concealed the fighting. I came to a tumbled rock pile just beneath the crest and Germanicus slowed again, before picking his way around the pile and gaining a flat surface that edged another ravine, this one small and shallow enough to leap. I stopped him at the lip and turned him around, leading him back as far as I could to give him at least a few paces before he launched himself. Then, as he surged forward again and settled himself for the leap, I saw a man come into sudden view above me, on a ledge above the spot where we would land. He held a spear, angled back for the throw; the leading fingers of his left hand were pointed at me as he balanced himself and then launched his missile. It was a long, heavy spear, and its shaft was warped, so that as it spun in flight, its butt end wavered in a circular motion. I saw the long, sharp, barbed head clearly as it arced towards me, and there was nothing I could do to avoid it as my mount leaped clear of the ground and sailed forward. As we rose in that great, uncoiling leap, the spear's angle of flight steepened rapidly and the weapon fell away in front of me. I had just begun to breathe a prayer of thanks when I heard it strike my horse. It hit with a solid, wrenching sound. I felt the great beast beneath me flinch in mid-air as his head snapped back and he grunted in agony. Then his knees hit the ground on the far side and he fell forward, throwing me over his head.

So stark, so agonizingly detailed was my vision of what was occurring that it seemed time itself had slowed down, enabling me to retain all of my faculties and react instantaneously. I landed, somehow, on my feet, sprawling forward but not falling; my sword hilt was already in my hand without my being aware of having unhooked it. I stripped away the scabbard and threw myself at the slope, bounding upward to where the spear-thrower crouched, axe now in hand, waiting for me. I knew Germanicus, my faithful friend of many years, lay dead or dying behind me, but I did not look at him. I concentrated only upon scrambing up the steep slope to the top of the knoll. His killer rushed forward as soon as I arrived, to cut me down like a tree, but I was still possessed by the same preternatural awareness that had come upon me earlier and I skipped away easily from his clumsy, flailing rush. His scything blow came nowhere close to me, and the edge of his enormous axe hit the ground where I had been, striking sparks from the stone. The force of his swing had unbalanced him and as he staggered forward, trying to right himself, the short sheepskin vest that was his only upper body covering flapped up and forward, baring his arched back. I sprang towards him then and smashed him with a full, two-handed, overarm swing that caught him clean-edged and cleaved through his waist, a cut so clean and deep that, in pulling my blade away, I sliced through the guts of him and cut him in half. It may have been the rage that fuelled me, but I have never struck any other man as hard or as savagely as I did that man, and the long, sharp tongue of the skystone sword sliced through him so easily that he screamed long after he had seen his severed lower half kicking in front of him.

I stepped back from him, unsurprised and unimpressed, and then I heard running steps approaching. I glanced over my shoulder and saw three of his companions rushing at me, one with a spear and two with short, Roman-style swords. Almost without thinking I struck the head from the thrusting spear and spun on my right heel, whipping the sword about again in a complete circle to decapitate the spearman. As his body reeled off to one side, I dropped to my right knee and drew back my sword arm so that my hand almost grazed the ground by my ankle. The first sword-bearer was coming on much too quickly and had realized his error, but before he could slow down he died from a long, stabbing thrust beneath his breastbone. I jerked my point free, sprang to my feet again and launched myself at the third man. To his credit, he hunched his shoulders and, throwing up the small round shield he carried, came straight towards me. He was helmetless, and I cleaved his skull before his short sword could begin to come anywhere close.

Then I was alone on top of the knoll, whirling again to face the sound of feet scrabbling against the stony surface of the hill's flank. But even as I began to launch myself towards the sounds, my sword arm whirling high, I saw the horsehair crest of one of my own helmets and then Donuil's face surged into view beneath it. I grounded my point immediately and reached out to pull him up to join me, and we both stood wordlessly, looking at the carnage around us. Small knots of men were fighting everywhere, but the enemy were fighting with the desperation of doomed men and they were dying quickly, in large numbers, most of them picked off by the deadly arrows being fired from the ridge above us. One massive, huge-bellied man, swinging a long, clumsy-looking blade, was thrown into a gully by the force of an arrow that struck him just above the ear, plucking him off his feet and hurling him aside as though he were weightless.

I became aware then that Donuil was shouting at me. There was noise everywhere, and apparently I had been deaf to all of it for some time. I shook my head and forced myself to listen. Donuil was asking me if I was hurt, or wounded, and that surprised me until I looked down to see myself covered in crimson; my armour, my tunic, my arms and hands and the sword I gripped were all running with blood, and I experienced a surge of fear as I thought, for a moment, that all of it was mine. But I had escaped unscathed.

I shook my head and looked about me again, this time taking better note of all that I was seeing. The fighting had died down and now only a few fierce, widely separated struggles were still being waged. Murder was being committed before my eyes, for men were throwing down their weapons, attempting to surrender, and were being killed out of hand, mainly by arrows from the ridge above. I drew a deep breath and ordered Donuil to find our trumpeter and sound the recall, and as I spoke I heard the tremor in my voice. He looked at me, wordlessly, then turned and disappeared over the edge of the knoll again.

I walked stiff-legged to the other side of the small eminence. I do not remember going down to my horse, but I found myself kneeling by his head, staring through tears at his noble face and at the milky glaze that was already forming in the one large eye that I could see. The spear had pierced him cleanly, plunging deep into his chest even before its butt lodged against the ground and the full weight of his plunging corpse fell upon it, hammering the point home to burst his great heart. For almost a score of years, this magnificent beast had borne me bravely, offering nothing but total obedience and love in return for the meagre attentions I bestowed upon him. Now the spectacle of his egregious death unmanned me completely and I sat down and wept, leaning my back against his shoulder and laying my left arm flat along his solid, silky neck. All around me, strewn among the rocks and gullies of this inhospitable place, the bodies of dead and dying men lay like discarded garments and lacked any power to move me to grieve for them. Their deaths had been a natural consequence of their lives as warriors and mercenaries. The death of my noble and unselfish friend Germanicus, on the other hand, was intensely personal, and it overwhelmed me with a sense of loss and destitution.

Some time later, I felt Donuil's hand upon my shoulder and I stood up, dry-eyed by that time, and followed him to where he had tethered another horse for me. We rode in silence to meet Huw Strongarm.

The victory, Huw told me later, had been much greater than I had realized. The invaders had been summoned to Dolaucothi in numbers far surpassing our expectations, gravitating towards the gold mines in large bands. Surprised from the north and the south simultaneously, however, they had been broken and routed, their ranks decimated and devastated by the Pendragon bowmen on the hillsides above them. The survivors, thousands of them despite their enormous losses, were now in full flight westward, back towards the sea, harried and pursued relentlessly by the terrifying hillmen who could strike men dead with their long arrows from nigh on half a mile away.

Huw was in high spirits, full of excitement and enthusiasm, and he seemed larger than I remembered him, far more regal. It took me only moments to identify the change in his appearance, and he saw me notice it and broke off what he had been saying, looking at me strangely.

"What?" he asked. "What is it? You look . . . Is something wrong, Merlyn?"

"Your helmet," I replied, shaking my head. "I recognize it, though I've never seen it. It belonged to Ullic Pendragon. I've read descriptions of it in my uncle's books. But it must be a hundred years old, and yet it looks new. How can that be?"

His eyes flared in surprise, and with both hands he removed the war helmet and held it out to me. The head of the great golden eagle that fronted it looked alive, so fierce were its eyes. The huge wings were folded on either side of the helmet's dome and the spread tail feathers fanned out and down to cover his shoulders. "Take it," he said. "Look closely. This bird was in the air, last year. Ullic's was similar, but this is mine, new-made for me." I examined the eyes, made of glass or polished stone, and the precise way the neck feathers had been arranged over the helmet's brow. "The eagle helmet is the ceremonial helmet of the War Chief of Pendragon, Merlyn, and each new War Chief receives his own. Uric and Uther were both King, as was Dergyll ap Griffyd, but only Ullic was both King and War Chief, so he had the helmet. I am the first War Chief of all Pendragon since Ullic."

I handed the helmet back to him with the reverence it deserved, and he led us then to where his huge new tent was being erected and his senior subchiefs and captains were already assembling to await his next dispositions. As I listened thereafter to the details of his planning and the way he absorbed and adjusted to every new report being brought to him, I found my excitement rekindled, and I felt myself more able to accept the aching loss of Germanicus with a resigned pragmatism.

For the following three weeks, we stormed through the mountain passes of western Cambria, leaving a trail of slaughter in our wake. We reached the western shore at the end of that time to find the remnants of Ironhair's embattled levies drawn up along the strand, facing us defiantly behind crude and hastily made fortifications. Their evacuation plans had fallen into ruin. The fleet that should have been there to carry them away to safety had failed to meet them, and there was no sign of its coming. They were vulnerable to siege, starvation and thirst, crammed into a narrow space backed with saltwater and bare of any kind of vegetation other than the wrack of seaweed cast up by each high tide. Yet still they refused to surrender, fearing, I had no doubt, the total lack of mercy shown by the Pendragon to any of their ilk.

By the end of the third morning of the "siege," the defenders were completely encircled and at the mercy of the overwhelming superiority of the Pendragon besiegers. I sought out Huw Strongarm and asked his blessing to return with my people to Camulod. Ironhair's invasion, to my eyes and his, was over. The principals, Ironhair himself and Carthac Pendragon, had escaped unscathed, as far as we knew, their bid for mastery in Cambria having failed abjectly. As surely as Ironhair's army had expected to be rescued by a waiting fleet, I, too, had expected to see signs of Connor Mac Athol's presence in the waters off the coast. As neither fleet had been seen, my conjecture was that they had met at sea and, dependent upon the outcome of the battle, either fleet could materialize at any time. Whatever developed, however, Huw now had sufficient strength surrounding the enemy bastion on the beach to handle it. He did not need our continuing presence, or the aggravation of continuing to feed us when we might be better employed at home in Camulod.

Huw believed that Ironhair and Carthac would be likely to return, but not for another year, at least. By that time, Cambria would, under his leadership, be unassailable. A spirit of unity among the Pendragon had been unknown for long enough now—since the death of Uther—that its nearly miraculous re-emergence gave it an exceptional fire and vigour. Should Ironhair invade again in days to come, Huw would request our assistance again, in return for his wholehearted support of young Arthur's claim to Cambria as Uther Pendragon's son. I told him then about my agreement with Llewellyn, which would bring the lad to Cambria the following year, and Huw immediately relieved Llewellyn of his current duties and released him to return to Camulod with us. We two then embraced as friends and equals, and shortly afterwards I turned my two half-legions around and led them home to Camulod. We had been away from our Colony for nearly half a year.

XI

AUTUMN HAD ALREADY touched the trees with its mordant breath by the time we came down from the highlands and began to approach Camulod from the north-west, having made our way without incident from Dolaucothi in the central hills. We travelled down to the southern coast of Cambria and thence eastward along the littoral, collecting our holding forces from Caerwent and Caerdyff in passing. Then we forded the river mouth to the west of Glevum at low tide—a relatively simple task at summer's end—and struck inland, south and east, to skirt Aquae Sulis and find the great road running south from there to Camulod. Pleased though we were to be going home, we were nevertheless strangely subdued; an air of dissatisfaction hung over us, born of the barely mentioned but inescapable conclusion that it had primarily been the Pendragon Celts, not the forces of Camulod, that had beaten the invaders. We knew we were the anvil against which the Celtic hammer had crashed down to smite and flatten the enemy; it was our solid, unyielding weight against which they had found themselves trapped and crushed. Llewellyn himself had constructed the analogy. But our Camulodian pride was not accustomed to accepting a secondary role, and so many of our number felt discontented and unfulfilled, believing themselves to have achieved nothing of moment.

Needless to say, the mood of our army lightened as we grew ever closer to Camulod and the comforts of home. My men were looking forward to removing their armour and taking their ease for a spell; the thought of making love to a wife or sweetheart was present in the mind of every man who rode with us, and I was no exception.

Our homecoming was both triumphant and chaotic. Never before had an army returned victorious to the Colony with so few casualties—less than a hundred men had died in the summer-long campaign, and no more than three hundred had been wounded. The chaos, meanwhile, was precipitated mainly by the arrival of thousands of hungry mouths. Notwithstanding the fact that our advent had been expected and awaited, the abrupt appearance of our swarming numbers caused immediate dismay and consternation among the Colony's quartermasters, for as Publius Tetra, my own senior campaign quartermaster, had pointed out to me days earlier, it is one thing to contemplate the existence of six thousand legionaries, knowing that they once belonged and lived in one place. It is quite another matter to overlook the fact that those six thousand have another thousand in attendance upon them, and then to see full seven thousand living men descend upon your camp, eyeing your stores and granaries.

Thanks to the foresight of Tetra and his fellow quartermasters, however, we had been at pains to annul the impact of our arrival from that viewpoint, at least; I had sent organized hunting parties out to scour the land for game in the last five days of our approach, and we brought wagons laden with fresh meat and even grain, gleaned from the granaries of those new garrisons we had passed by. Heartened by the new strength offered them in those outlying areas, and encouraged by the prospect of a new, safe and bountiful harvest within the month, the farmers in three communities had been grateful and happy to supply us with their surplus at summer's end.

Another, unforeseeable aspect of the chaos arose from the number of guests in the Colony who had been, with differing degrees of patience, awaiting our arrival. I learned immediately that Connor Mac Athol was in residence, having arrived mere days earlier to find his brother Brander already there, also awaiting me. Ambrose and Arthur had returned the previous month from Northumbria, too, expecting to find me already returned from Cambria, and Ambrose had brought several of Vortigern's senior advisers back with him. They had come, ostensibly, to meet and confer with me about the expedition I would lead north-east the following year, but in reality Ambrose's intent was to demonstrate to these powerful men—and through them to their king—that Camulod, which no one among them had ever seen, was indeed what we had said it was: a prosperous and self-sufficient colony and a source of allies far richer than the five hundred Scouts Ambrose had led forth. Finding me still from home, Ambrose had been playing host to the Northumbrian leaders ever since, and those duties had expanded to include Brander, from the moment of the Scots king's unexpected appearance with a full retinue that included his wife, Salina, her niece, Morag, and a round score of the Scots chieftains who were his counsellors. And as though that were not enough, an entire delegation of eleven bishops had then arrived under the leadership of the elderly Bishop Enos, who had ministered to my Great-aunt Luceiia. They, too, had come seeking me.

I discovered all of this from Dedalus, whom we found awaiting us at the head of a magnificent honour guard when we reached the boundary of Camulod at the great north-south road. The protocols of welcome and entry to the Colony quickly taken care of, Ded and I rode knee to knee while he warned me of how many people would try to claim my attention. When he had done, I laughed at the irony of my thoughts of Tressa and the wishes I had had so recently. I shared my thoughts with him and he laughed with me, his laughter softer than mine and rich with sympathy.

Moments later, we rounded the last bend and saw the walls of Camulod ahead of us, crowning the hill, and we were immediately caught up in a whirlwind of welcome and felicitations that swept all of us away.

A succession of images and partial memories is all that remains to me. I know I met and greeted Brander and his wife, Salina, and Bishop Enos, but I can barely recall the separate groups that escorted each of them. Those faces, all strange to me, blended into a welter of inconsequential greetings. I do remember thinking that since the Eirish Scots were recognizable by their bright colours, and the clerics by their homespun, ankle-length robes, then the others who were strange to me must be the Northumbrians who had arrived with Ambrose.

Ambrose was the first to reach me, and as I embraced him, hugging him close, I looked about me for Arthur, and I remember the keen disappointment I felt when I saw that he was not among the crowd who surged to greet me as I stepped down from my horse. Then Tressa moved forward shyly, and my heart soared with delight as I released my brother and turned to her with open arms, drinking in her beauty. She was dressed all in green, her gown a drape of some fine, soft material that moulded to her every curve and closed my throat up tight with love and longing. The noise of the surrounding crowd fell away in my ears and I lost consciousness of all who surrounded us, my entire attention focused on the glorious young woman who had come to take me to my home and to her bed. She approached me quickly, her cheeks flushed and her eyes sparkling, but then she stopped short, her hands grasping my elbows as she leaned slightly backwards, gazing up at me with eyes suddenly awash with unshed tears. I stooped to place one arm about her waist, and all at once my arms were full of her and I lifted her high, as though she were weightless, to bring her mouth to mine, and all about me I could hear the strangely distant sounds of laughter and applause. Thereafter, from the moment when I set her back upon her feet, I held her tightly by the hand, keeping her by my side as I passed among the throng of well-wishers who crowded the courtyard.

The hours that followed seemed to pass in the blink of an eye, punctuated only by entreaties from each of the people waiting for me that his need to speak with me was more urgent than anyone else's. In each instance I smiled and promised to meet with him at my first opportunity, while behind my smile I wondered how and when I could find, or make, time for any of them when my overpowering concern was focused upon my own burning need to be alone with Tressa.

At last there came a moment when the three of us were almost alone for the first time since my arrival. I took my brother aside, holding him by one elbow and keeping Tressa close to me with my other hand as I requested the few others in the room to pardon us. Then, as soon as we were alone, I released Ambrose's arm and stepped away to lean against a wall, draping my arm across Tressa's shoulders. Ambrose watched me as I did so, his eyes crinkled in a smile.

"I am at your service," he said, bowing slightly, his eyes amused. "Tell me what you want."

"I want to spend some time alone with Tress. That's what I want, first and above all else, and I'll be disappointed if you're not already aware of that. Then I want to know where Arthur is and why he is not here. And then I want your insight into the reasons why so many people want to talk to me, because I have to find some order in which to meet with them. I can't sit down with all of them at once, and each of them seems to think his need is paramount. Connor has news I want to hear, I have no doubt of that, and I'll speak to him first. But until I know what all the others want, I can make no decisions. So, what do you know?"

His smile did not waver. "In order of importance? Very well. Your first urgency should be your own. Take Tress and disappear until this evening. I will make apologies for your ... tiredness. Your second urgency is Arthur. The boy's in love, and that is the only thing that could ever seduce him into being away when you arrived. In his defence, we had no idea you would arrive so soon. The word we had was that you would arrive tomorrow, at the soonest. Then your messenger reached us yesterday with the news that you were ahead of expectations, but by then Arthur had already gone, with Shelagh and young Morag. They have gone hunting, and will be home this afternoon. Arthur will be sick with disappointment to have missed your coming. He's been talking about it for weeks now. You'll see great changes in him, don't you agree, Tress?"

Tress nodded, smiling at me. "Aye, he will that," she whispered.

Ambrose continued. "Connor you've decided to see already, and you can do that as soon as you come back up from the Villa. As for the others, Brander has been waiting longest and must leave immediately, once he has spoken to you, but his request is of no great or worrisome moment—I mean, it is to him, but should not be to you. It's not even you he wishes to speak to, really, but Huw Strongarm. He is seeking Huw's permission to move Liam Twistback and his cattle-breeders back onto Pendragon land for a time. It seems the clime in their new island home does not lend itself sufficiently to such operations. I offered to pass on his request and assured him I could see no difficulty in the granting of it, but he feared that perhaps Strongarm himself might have come to grief in the war, so he wished to speak to you in person. But you have been long in coming and now he is fretting, wishing to be gone again, back to his own duties ..." He paused then, reflecting, before he went on. "My Northumbrian guests can await your pleasure. They are in no particular hurry.

Bishop Enos, on the other hand, I cannot speak for. I have no idea what his mission consists of, or what time constraints may press upon him. You will have to be the judge of that. That's all I can tell you. My suggestion would be Connor first, then Brander, since he is a king, then Enos, and then the Northumbrians."

"So be it. That's the order I'll adopt. Now, can you get us out of here without our being seen?"

Before Ambrose could answer, Tress turned in my arm and brought one hand up to lay her fingers over my lips, pressing me to be silent. She pointed out that neither she nor I could be so rudely selfish. She had waited half a year for me to come home to her, she said, blushing to be speaking so openly in front of Ambrose; another half-day would be sufferable. I attempted to interrupt her on several occasions, but each time the insistent pressure of her fingertips against my lips kept me from speaking out, and as I listened, I reluctantly acknowledged the truth of what she was saying. Ambrose stood silent, throughout all of it, watching us intently. Finally I nodded, mute. Tress read my submission in my eyes and removed her hand. I stooped and kissed her briefly, then straightened again to look at Ambrose over her head.

"Well," I said, "such willing self-sacrifice demands respect. Where will we find Connor?"

We met with the admiral in Ambrose's day room, where we closed and locked the door behind us to ensure that we would be undisturbed. It was cool, almost cold, with that hint of winter that insinuates itself into all places unlit by the sun on short, bright autumn days. Ambrose lost no time in lighting the fire that lay ready in the brazier, and while he did so I went directly to the chest in which he kept his mead and poured a small cup for each of us, gently bidding Tress to sit and let me wait upon her. By the time I turned around with the mead for Connor and Tress, the two of them were already deep in conversation, talking about the new Scots settlement in the islands of the far north-west. I handed each of them a cup and then held one ready for Ambrose when he rose from in front of the brazier, rubbing pieces of ashy grit from his knees. I saluted each of them with my raised cup, and we drank together. After I had sat down, I looked inquisitively at Connor, who then immediately launched into what he had come to tell me, half story, half report.

As I had suspected, he had intercepted Ironhair's fleet on its way to evacuate the Cornish mercenaries. The meeting was accidental, just after daybreak on a windless morning, when the surface of the seas was obscured by drifting fog. When the fog cleared, the two fleets were in plain sight of each other, and Ironhair was disadvantaged by being between Connor's vessels and the too-close, rocky shores of a wide bay. The fleets were almost evenly matched, Ironhair with his bireme and twenty galleys and Connor with his own bireme and eighteen galleys. But Ironhair was also saddled with an enormous fleet of smaller vessels, mainly fishing boats and shallow-draft barges, destined for the shore where he had planned to meet his levies upon their withdrawal from the interior and Dolaucothi.

Ironhair surprised Connor by attacking at once. His massive bireme heeled hard over as its oarsmen put their backs into angling the huge craft out from the shore towards the Scots admiral's vessel, building up quickly to something approaching top speed almost before Connor had had time to assess what was happening. Once he saw what his enemy intended, however, Connor took immediate evasive action, swinging his bireme to the right and then angling back immediately, hard left, as the approaching ship changed course to meet his first feint. As he did so, he released the attack signal to his fleet, turning them loose against the assembled shipping that stretched in an undisciplined sprawl along the coastline, and from that moment on he gave all his attention to the task of dealing with the other bireme.

For more than an hour, he said, the two great vessels swept and cavorted in a dignified yet deadly dance, each captain seeking to outmanoeuvre and out-sail his opponent and to put his own vessel into the winning position. From the outset it was clear that Ironhair's plan was to ram Connor's ship, crushing its hull beneath the water-line with the huge, metal-clad ramming horn that projected from his bow. Connor's plan, on the other hand, was to bring his craft alongside his enemy's and capture it, and this desire forced him into a defensive, evasive role. He would await the enemy ship's forward rush and then sweep clear of its path, to one side or the other, before cutting back across its wake and positioning himself to await its next attack. In this, Connor had one massive disadvantage, for his desire to capture the enemy vessel, rather than simply destroy it, exposed him to a hazard that he could not match.

At each pass, the catapults on Ironhair's raised rear-deck hurled pots of blazing oil towards Connor's sails, and although most of these missiles fell harmlessly into the sea, the fire-fighting parties on Connor's decks were hard-pressed to smother and contain the flames from the three that did land on the fighting platforms, smashing against the dry, pitched wood and throwing streams of blazing oil in all directions to ignite timber, cordage and human beings alike. These fire-fighting duties were carried out grimly and in double jeopardy, since the danger of the flames—and there is no greater danger on a ship at sea—was enhanced by the danger from flying arrows. Bowmen on both vessels exchanged heavy volleys, every time they came within range. Connor told me that he had wished passionately for a contingent of Pendragon bowmen on his rolling, pitching decks, since he could see plainly how the the superior speed and strength of the Pendragon longbows would have sharpened the edge for him in such a conflict.

Connor's prinicpal strategy, however, involved a manoeuvre on which his crew had been working for some time, one that he carefully held in reserve until the time was right. Connor Mac Athol played a wily game that made his efforts to evade attack seem ludicrous and cowardly. At first, each sideslip away was without design, save that whichever way he avoided the enemy's charge, he cut immediately across their wake and withdrew to a safe distance. Soon, after several of these flights, his men could hear the jeers from the enemy vessel as they passed by. But that was what they had been waiting for; they had been working hard to earn the enemy's scorn. Now they began to work their master strategy, aiming each lumbering evasion to move themselves subtly closer to the shore. Finally one swift attack, as it went hissing by them, took the enemy vessel into the confines of the bay itself and directly towards the shallow coastal shoals. This time, as soon as the enemy ship had passed, Connor gave the signal and the driving drumbeat of the overseer changed immediately. The rowers on the left all shipped their oars for one long stroke, while those on the right dug deep and heaved, spinning their massive vessel so that its prow now lay towards the enemy's stern, within half a bowshot's distance. The left oars dipped, the tempo of the drumbeat escalated, and Connor's ship went leaping in pursuit of the other bireme, which found itself, for the first time, in the role of prey and in rapidly shoaling water.

The enemy ship's captain was now practically helpless. He had grown careless, convinced of his own superior shiphandling skills, and had underestimated the man against whom he was pitched; it was a fatal error. Beneath his hull the water was growing shallower with every stroke of the oars, yet he could not break to either side without exposing himself broadside to Connor's ram. Instead, showing great courage and determination, he attempted to alter the inevitable by stopping his ship dead in the water. In the space of a single oar stroke, all his sweeps started backpaddling, cutting his vessel's headway so abruptly that Connor's bireme seemed to leap forward, closing the gap between the two craft so suddenly that Connor himself was almost completely taken by surprise. It was a brilliant move, and Connor found himself admiring it even as he moved to counteract it, changing his own craft's heading so that it would sweep alongside the enemy instead of ramming it directly in the stern.

As the two vessels closed, Ironhair's oarsmen struggled to ship their oars, swinging them up and inboard, and they might have succeeded had Connor's bireme not been one oar stroke too close, moving too swiftly, and one beat ahead of them in reacting. Connor's left banks of oars swept up towards the vertical moments before the other bireme's right banks attempted to do the same, and the overtaking vessel swept along the slower one's right side, shearing the rising oars like icicles hit by a stick, smashing them to kindling and creating havoc, carnage and utter destruction among the rowers, who, chained to their sweeps, were cut down by jagged flying splinters and flailing oar stumps. Only a few benches of rowers towards the bow of the stricken vessel were able to ship their oars in time, but even they fell victims to the chaos behind them.

While the left banks of oars were high out of the water, the front right quadrant of Connor's rowers stroked again, driving their bireme sideways into their quarry. As they did so, the two vertical gangway towers fore and aft slammed down to drive their holding spikes into the other ship's decking, creating bridges to the other ship, and Connor's Scots surged forward in a screaming tide.

Ambrose, Tress and I sat spellbound as Connor described the encounter. The ensuing fight was short and decisive, he said, and he was aided by the fact that his men were not slaves and all could fight. Connor took the bireme into his possession and threw its crew, save only the slaves and leaders, overboard, to drown or swim.

Only then did he give his attention to what was happening with the remainder of his fleet. The entire shoreline was littered as far as the eye could see with the wreckage of the smaller vessels that had sailed up from the south in convoy with the fighting ships. Eventually, he would learn that his Scots had won a great victory, inflicting huge losses on the enemy, sinking nine of their twenty galleys and crippling and capturing five others. Only six managed to escape completely. The price of the victory was three Scots galleys sunk with all hands, and two set afire. There were many survivors picked up from all five of these vessels.

I was glad to hear of the victory, but I was afire to find out about Ironhair and Carthac, and Connor's news on that topic stunned me. Neither man had been aboard the bireme. The man who had captained the ship was captured and he told Connor that Ironhair had not been with the fleet, nor had he been with the armies in Cambria. He was not even in Cornwall and had not, in fact, been seen by anyone in more than two whole months. He was away, the man said, with Carthac, replenishing his armies.

Upon learning that, Connor had set out to find me immediately, first sailing north to where Huw's forces penned the hapless enemy upon their narrow strip of beach, then heading swiftly south and east to intercept me at Caerdyff. Too late to find me there, he had struck southward again, to find his brother Brander's fleet anchored at the point closest to Camulod. From there, he came inland, arriving at the Colony ahead of us.

Connor's revelation about Ironhair came as momentous and unwelcome news to me, for since the outset of his tale I had been convinced that the ending would involve the capture or death of my enemy. To learn that he was still alive and still a threat appalled me and left me speechless. I was conscious of the pressure of Tressa's fingers around my own and knew that she was squeezing my hand tightly, but whether in sympathy or in distress I could not tell. Ambrose and Connor both sat silent, watching me until I was ready to speak again, and Ambrose was frowning slightly, evidently perplexed.

"So," I said at last, "he's still alive and still plotting. That is simply wonderful—exactly what I had hoped and needed to hear. Damnation take the man!"

Now Ambrose leaned towards me, his frown deeper than before. "Brother, I don't like this, but I have to speak and to ask you something now, so please understand that my question comes from simple ignorance and curiosity. Why are you so violently concerned about this man? Your reaction seems . . . disproportionate, somehow. I know that you and he are enemies. I also know that he has successfully attempted to suborn some of your people in the past. You threw him out of Camulod, but he has never sought to return here—not really. Why does the mere mention of his name incense you so?

"Peter Ironhair has never been a direct threat to Camulod. He has never moved overtly to attack us. Certainly, he has invaded Cambria, but that was in support of Carthac Pendragon, who has, however ludicrous it might be, a blood claim to the leadership he seeks. Ironhair's support of his cause may indeed be specious. Nonetheless, Brother, what he does in Cambria should not concern you as greatly as it does, here in Camulod. If and when he ever does move against Camulod, then you will be justified in seeking his death. Until then, I must say I believe you are overreacting, and you are wrong to feel and behave as you do."

I sat staring at my brother as he spoke, making no effort to mask my astonishment and, I must admit, my displeasure. It was the first time he had ever voiced any doubts about my motivation or my beliefs. Hearing him speak so plainly in disagreement with me made my face flush, and I had to bite back the bitter words that sprang to my tongue. I forced myself to sit still and absorb what Ambrose had said, thinking it through objectively, to the best of my ability, and attempting to see my behaviour through his eyes. But that was impossible: my anger flared, overriding coherent thought. Ambrose knew he had infuriated me, but he was his own man, and he spoke his own beliefs openly and without fear.

The silence stretched and grew. Connor sat as though carved from wood; Tress, I knew, was gazing down into her lap. Finally, when I felt sure I had mastered my voice and the tone of it, I replied.

"Very well, let me see if I can satisfy your curiosity. Are you familiar with the old saying, 'The enemy of my enemy is my friend?' " He nodded. "And do you agree with the sentiment?"

He shrugged his shoulders. "I suppose I do."

"Good. What about the corollary: 'The enemy of my friend is my enemy.' Would you agree with that?" I held up my hand, palm outwards. "Don't answer, because it's not important right now. What is important is that I believe it. You and I have not talked about what happened in the final stages of the campaign in Cambria, but the turning point came when Huw Strongarm took up the leadership of all Pendragon. Huw has no ambition for himself—had he any, he would long since have declared himself a contender for the kingship. He is now War Chief of Pendragon, and he has sworn to uphold the honour and freedom of Pendragon in Cambria, maintaining it in trust for the man he believes to be his true king, the son of the king he followed all his life, Uther Pendragon. So Huw rules now, or will rule soon, in Cambria, as regent for Arthur, just as surely as Flavius Stilicho ruled in Rome as regent of the young Emperor Honorius."

Ambrose grunted. "Let's hope he fares better than Stilicho did."

I saw nothing amusing in that. "Think you that's unlikely?"

Ambrose was already waving me down, shaking his head. "No, of course not. It was a poor and ill-considered jest. Please continue. I knew nothing of Huw Strongarm's change of status. You really believe he will support Arthur's claim?"

"Completely. It is already in hand. I brought Huw's most trusted captain back with me, a man called Llewellyn, an ironsmith and a warrior. He will take Arthur back with him to Cambria, incognito, to live among his own people for a year or so, to learn their ways and live their life among them. I had been excited for the lad, imagining how well he would adapt to new ways without either you or me around to influence him. Now, however, hearing that Ironhair is out there, replenishing his armies, fills me with new concerns. Should he invade again, young Arthur will be there without our support."

Ambrose sucked air sharply through his teeth. "Should he invade again, with Arthur there and under these new circumstances, then he will indeed be contravening our peace and threatening our nephew—"

"And mine!" This from Connor.

"Aye, Connor, and yours," Ambrose continued. "That would change everything, and my concerns are already laid to rest, Cay. I did not know you had made these plans."

I nodded, mollified, but spoke on. "Thank you for that, but hear the rest of it. I have had dealings with Peter Ironhair. You have not. I know the man, and, to tell the truth, I could have liked him, had things been other than they were. He has much to like about him—a good mind, great strengths and a subtle turn of wit—and he is often generous to his close friends and allies, who value his friendship highly. People follow him instinctively, because he has the attributes of leadership. But he also has much in him to detest. There is something wrong with the man, inside him, and it's not mere ambition. I could live with that. Ironhair has shown himself, to me at least, to be fundamentally treacherous and venal, a venomous creature who will do anything to achieve his own ends. He deals in perfidy and in subornment, seducing friends to vileness and murder. In my mind, he is a serpent. I would kill him with as little thought as I would kill an adder, and feel better for the deed being done, because there would be one less threat in the world for innocent people. I detest him. But more than anything else, I distrust and fear him—not the man himself, but his capacity for evil. I would prefer to know him safely dead."

"Hmm." Ambrose wrinkled his nose, then nodded. "I think I begin to understand, now."

"No, Ambrose, you do not—not really, not yet. You never knew Hector's wife, Julia. She was Bedwyr's mother, and a gentle, lovely woman who never caused a moment's pain to anyone. Ironhair caused her death, directly, when he sent hirelings sneaking into Camulod to murder young Arthur. For that alone, I swore that he would one day die by my hand. Before that day, this Colony of ours had been like Eden. Ironhair destroyed that innocence and drove us out of Camulod into the world, in fear and distrust."

Connor spoke up, changing the topic. "You said he was replenishing his armies. How can he do that? I know he uses mercenaries, but where does his gold come from? He has to pay them. That's what mercenaries are—a walking demand for payment that you ignore at your peril."

"No, Connor. He needs no gold." My companions looked to me for an explanation. "I've discussed this several times with Huw and Llewellyn. Ironhair's mercenaries are not from Britain. Most of them are Burgundians, from Gaul, and some are Franks. The Burgundians were causing problems for the Romans long before the legions left Gaul, and the entire land across the Narrow Sea is being fought over from north to south. There are far more people over there than are to be found in all of Britain, and they are living in anarchy. There are thousands of landless men, bandits and brigands. Those are Ironhair's conscripts. He offers them the plunder they can find in Britain, and he offers them a home and food and drink and women. So they flock to fight for him, because they're fighting for themselves. It makes them fierce and bitter foes of everyone they meet over here. The only problem he will have with them is in controlling them—and since he simply turns them loose to serve his purposes, with no concern over what they do otherwise, that is no problem at all."

In the pause that followed someone knocked at the door, which we had locked on entering the room. I glanced at Ambrose, who shrugged in annoyance and shouted, asking who was there. I recognized Arthur's muffled voice at once, and I released Tressa's hand and strode to the double doors. I swung the door quickly open, my face breaking into a grin that changed immediately into wide-eyed shock as I set eyes on my ward. He stood directly outside, eye to eye with me, taller than I would ever have imagined he could have become in the short space of months since I had last seen him. He had left me as a boy, approaching manhood. Now, in height at least, he was a man.

I stepped back quickly, gazing at him, aware of the young woman who stood close behind him but ignoring her as my eyes devoured Arthur Pendragon and the changes I could see in him. He hesitated on the threshold, grinning shyly at me and nodding tentatively to Ambrose, Connor and Tressa in apology for his intrusion. A mere flick of the eyes was all he gave to them, however, and thereafter his eyes remained on me.

"Merlyn," he said, his voice uncertain. "Welcome home. I wanted to be here when you arrived, and I can hardly believe I was not. We did not expect you until tomorrow."

I stepped towards him again, spreading my arms, and he came into my embrace, clutching me fiercely. I crushed him in a hug, then pushed him away to arm's length, gazing into his face.

"You've grown up. I knew you would have, but these three here did not tell me how much." He smiled, but before he could respond I stepped aside, stretching out my hand to young Morag, who stood shyly behind him. "Come in, come in. Morag, it pleases me to see you again. Was your hunting successful? I know you know Ambrose and Tress, but have you met Arthur's Uncle Connor?" She nodded, smiling at Connor, and then moved to stand beside Arthur again, tipping her head demurely to Ambrose and Tressa. Arthur spoke for her.

"We killed a stag, a good one, but it was I who had to shoot it. Morag decided at the last she did not want to do it." As I looked at him from beneath raised brows, he shrugged. "I would have let it go, then, but Shelagh had spent the entire morning stalking it. I did not want to seem . . . ungrateful."

I nodded, smiling still. "You made the right decision. So, you are obviously well—"

"Aye, well enough. But you must forgive us. I had no thought to interrupt your gathering; I merely wanted to see you and welcome you safely home."

"I'm glad you did, so don't concern yourself with that. Have you just returned?"

"Aye, can you not smell the sweat on me? I came straight here without unsaddling."

"Then shame! I taught you better than that. Go back, then, and take care of your mounts. By the time you've finished that, we'll be done here and you may join us."

I stood by the door, holding it ajar as I watched them walk away. The lad was broad, as well as tall, his shoulders wide and clean, his back tapering to a narrow waist and hips above long, well-muscled legs. He was dressed all in greens, in a dark, quilted tunic that was belted at his waist and emphasized the breadth of his shoulders and pale green leggings tucked into high boots of soft-looking, supple leather. His dark brown hair fell to his shoulders, and as he walked through the shadows outside, the yellow streaks that shot through it seemed to be almost white. When they had gone a score of paces, he reached out his arm and placed it about young Morag's waist, directing my attention to the shape of her and the fact that she, too, had left childhood behind. I was conscious of Ambrose standing close behind me, looking over my shoulder.

"Well," he asked. "What do you think? There's no mistaking that he's one of us, is there?"

"No," I concurred. "Neither in the size of him nor in his eye for a pretty woman. Has he . . . I mean, are they . . . ?"

"Bedding each other? Not unless they're doing it by magic. That young woman is more closely guarded than your favourite sword. King Brander takes his duties very seriously in that regard, as in all others. The two are in each other's company constantly, but they are never alone for long enough to fall into mischief. When Shelagh's not there, they're with Brander himself, or with Salina, or me, or Tress. They have no time for mischief. Not of the dallying kind."

Connor had said nothing since Arthur arrived, and now he sat smiling to himself, as though he knew a secret. I caught his eye.

"What are you grinning at, Connor?"

"Nothing, nothing at all!" His face mirrored utter innocence. "I'm merely impressed by Camulod's security, for I know that were I my nephew there, and we at home in our isles, there would be no power on earth or in the heavens to keep me from between my true love's legs."

Tress answered even before I could begin to frame a response to that. "Ha, Connor Mac Athol, but you are a bull at stud, we all know that. No woman could ever resist you—isn't that what you tell yourself? But here is a love story between a sweet young man and a lovely girl who is visiting and is begirt by guardians. Mind you, some day I'll have to hear your wife's opinion on your abilities in that arena."

"Ah, you've a better tongue on you for one so young and beautiful," Connor shot back with a deep sigh.

I looked back to Ambrose. "I would never have believed he'd grow so big so quickly. He has become enormous! How was he on your journey? Were you pleased with him?"

"Aye, as pleased as I could have been, and even more than I thought to be. I had expected him to take some time adjusting to being in my charge after having spent so long in yours, but there was no sign of anything of the kind. From the outset, from the moment we rode out, he was a willing student, absorbing all I could throw at him and adapting to my ways and wishes instantly. I kept him hard at work, too, most of the time, but there were times we talked, exchanging values and ideas and coming to know each other. He is a fine and admirable young man, and even my troopers quickly came to hold him in esteem.

"On our homeward journey, once we were clear of any threat from

Horsa's holdings, I sent him out patrolling with the Scouts, as an observer on the first few occasions and under the watchful eyes of my own commanders. But I had such good reports of him that finally I sent him out at the head of one patrol, although I took the precautionary step of providing one of my senior decurions as a nursemaid, just to ensure that nothing went too far awry. The sweep went perfectly, and Arthur showed no need for supervision."

"Did he know he had a watchdog?" I was remembering how my father and my Uncle Varrus had done the same to Uther and me, when we first rode out on patrol.

"I don't think he suspected," Ambrose murmured. "Certainly, if he did, he cloaked it admirably."

"Good. How long has young Morag been here?" The young couple were now lost from my sight and I swung the door shut again.

Ambrose cocked his head towards Tressa. "How long, Tress, three weeks?"

"Almost four. They arrived the week after you and Arthur came back." She moved close to me again, slipping her arms about my waist.

We spoke for a while about the situation in Cambria, and decided that we would send spies out into Cornwall throughout the coming winter, to learn all we could about Ironhair and his plans for the future. Connor contributed little to the conversation now, and I asked him how long he would be staying. He stood up and stretched, balancing himself precariously upon his one foot and his wooden peg, and said he would leave the following morning.

'And what about your brother?"

"Brander? What about him?"

"He's been waiting to talk to me and, according to Ambrose here, what he has to say will not take long. Then he'll be leaving, too. He has affairs of his own to be about. You two might be able to travel together to the coast, if I can conclude our business tonight."

"Aye," Connor agreed. "Then if we can, we will. Now I'm going to go and sleep for a while. I think I'm growing old. If I do not appear by dinner time, send someone to wake me, will you?"

I sat with Brander and his wife at dinner that night, and as it transpired, we had no need to meet further than that. As Ambrose had said, Brander's sole concern was to arrange for Liam Twistback to renew his tenancy of Huw Strongarm's southern lands, for a mimimum of three more years and a maximum of five. They had quickly discovered that the very young bloodstock they were attempting to breed needed better pasturage and did not take kindly to the harshness of the northern winters. Huw's assent to Liam's return was scarcely in doubt, since the relationship they had formerly shared had been a mutually advantageous one and Liam had ingratiated himself with the southern Pendragon, who could be less than cordial when they chose to be. And now I was able to reassure Brander that Huw had survived the war in Cambria, and that the arrangement could be secure. The new king nodded benignly, finally convinced that he could return home and begin gathering his stock together with confidence in their future safety.

The brothers agreed that they would leave together on the day following the one ahead. As I listened to them, I began to think about how this second parting might affect Arthur, and I glanced about me, looking for him in the body of the refectory. He was sitting among his friends Bedwyr, Gwin and Ghilly, all of them listening closely to Dedalus. Ded was regaling the whole table with some tale either of war and great events, or of nonsense and dark, ironic humour, the latter being much more likely. Sure enough, no sooner had I thought the thought than the entire table exploded into raucous laughter, the boys laughing just as loud and hard as the veteran troopers whose board they shared. Leaning forward then, I peered along the table to my right, where Morag sat beside her mother, her lovely face turned towards the noisy group. That Arthur would be made unhappy by her departure was beyond dispute. His new adventure into Cambria was, I decided, the best thing I could wish for. With the resilient energy and curiosity of youth, he might be able him to bury his grief in the challenges ahead. I resolved, then and there, to pack him off quickly.

Tressa's right elbow dug into my ribs as she laid her left hand over mine. "You are staring at another woman, Caius Merlyn. Should I be jealous?"

I started and turned towards her, reaching up to touch her cheek. "Forgive me, love, I didn't think you'd notice." Then I smiled and shook my head briefly. "I was wondering about Arthur, how he'll behave when Morag leaves again."

She glanced towards Arthur. "It will be different this time," she said quietly. "That first time, they had barely met, only to lose each other immediately. This time, they have had weeks together. Although they've been inseparable, they have known from the first that they had but little time, and that your return would see them parted again. They will have made their plans to meet again. You'll see, my love. There will be no anger at this parting. Sorrow, perhaps, but no anger."

She was very close to me, and I could smell the fragrant scents of her clean hair and the aromatic herbs she carried in a tiny, sweet-smelling bag upon her breast. Filled with warmth and love for her. I dropped my hand to her thigh, beneath the table, but withdrew it hastily after a single squeeze of the soft, pliant fullness. This evening was not yet over, and if

I were to come through it successfully, I needs must keep my mind distracted from the pleasures so tantalizingly close at hand. She noticed the withdrawal and smiled at me.

"Be patient, love. How much more talk must you indulge in after dinner?"

I exhaled noisily. "Little, I hope. I may speak with Bishop Enos for a while, but the Northumbrian envoys I will meet tomorrow. So, Bishop Enos first, for a short time—and then I have affairs to bring to your attention. Grave matters of a compelling urgency, with which I hope you will help me to deal smoothly and quickly."

Her smile grew wider. "Quickly? Well, perhaps at first. Smoothly? That I can promise you. But you had best reserve some large amount of time for all, Commander Merlyn. I promise you, I intend to detain you at my pleasure . . . and at yours."

She picked up my nerveless hand and gently kissed the back of it, pressing it against her pouted lips to let me feel and know their fullness. I cleared my throat loudly and pushed back my chair, stooping to bring my mouth against her ear as I did so, my whole awareness filled with the warm, sweet smell of her.

"This is intolerable," I whispered. "More than flesh can bear. If you will give me leave, I'll speak to Bishop Enos now, in the hope that what he has to say to me might be brief enough to let me turn immediately to . . . this."

She inclined her head, smiling gently, and I made my way immediately to where the venerable bishop sat among his peers.

Enos saw me approaching and began to rise, but I waved him back to his seat. I came up behind him and laid my hand on his shoulder, conscious of the curiosity in the eyes of all the other bishops, who took stock of me before turning away to make pretence, at least, of leaving us alone to speak in private.

The old man bent his body to the side and sat gazing up at me, his face at repose in a gentle, welcoming smile as he waited for me to speak.

"Forgive me, Bishop Enos, if it seemed I was neglecting you. I know you have information for me—"

He cut me short, raising one hand to stem my words as his smile widened. "It is I, it would appear, who should be asking your forgiveness, Caius Merlyn. My tidings are for you alone, that is true, but there is no looming urgency that you should leave your table and come seeking me like this. I regret that you should have been given any impression otherwise. You are fresh home, to fresh responsibilities, and your time is precious. Believe me when I say there is no need for haste between you and me. You have kings and men of high position here, waiting upon your pleasure, and you must fit your timing to their needs. You are but one solitary man, and their requirements must be more than mine. I merely bring you greetings, but I promised him from whom they come that I would deliver them into your ears and your hands." I made to speak again, but he denied me with a single, gracious motion of his head. "I tell you nothing more than simple truth, Caius. I bring you greetings, and no more—no urgencies, catastrophes or pains."

"You have word from Germanus?"

"I do, from Gaul. We have just returned from there, charged with a new duty he has laid upon us. He looks upon you as one of the few fast friends he has in Britain. You will be happy to know that he is well, although careworn and overworked. I have a letter for you from him."

"I am delighted, but also curious. What duty could the Bishop of Auxerre have allocated to bishops in Britain? Surely what happens here is beyond his jurisdiction?"

Enos nodded. "That would be true, were we but dealing with the world of men, but when the matter at hand deals with men's immortal souls and their relationship to God, then earthly jurisdictions lose significance. Our friend is yet charged with responsibility for combating the teachings of the heresiarch Pelagius."

That startled me, and in my desire to learn more I asked the bishop on Enos's left to move along the bench a bit, so that I might sit. There was a whispered colloquy around the table and everyone squeezed closer to his neighbour to make room. I muttered thanks to all of them before turning back to focus my attention upon the old man.

"Pelagius? Again? I thought all that was settled?"

"So did we, when last we dealt with it. The debate was lengthy, as you might recall. Not all of the findings were resolved to everyone's satisfaction, but the conclusions reached were clear and the final dispositions were absolute: Pelagius was declared heretical and his teachings anathema. No spiritual cost or punishment would be applied to those who accepted the error of their ways and sought to correct their lives thereafter. Schools were established where the word was to be taught in clarity, according to the rules established by the Fathers of the Church. Bishops who defied the rule and continued in the way of Pelagius were, ipso facto, excommunicate, banished from the communion of the Church and from receiving or dispensing its Sacraments."

I made no attempt to conceal my perplexity. "I remember all of that; it was all clearly established and agreed to by the bishops in convocation. They might not have been happy with the outcome, but they all agreed, and so they bound themselves to act in accordance with the tenets of the Fathers. I was there. I may not have understood all that was going on, but I clearly recall the outcome of it all, since Germanus himself explained it to me. It was final. Whence, then, and what, this new difficulty?"

Enos looked down to the wooden platter that lay before him on the table and I followed his glance. The platter was clean and bare, save for a few small bones from the wing of some fowl and a scattering of bread-crumbs. He had eaten lightly. Now he reached out and pressed one finger on a few crumbs, transferring them into his mouth. It was a slow, con-templative gesture. Finally he sighed and looked at me again.

"Do you remember Agricola—the bishop, not the soldier?"

I frowned, searching my memory and thrusting aside all thoughts of Julius Agricola of antiquity. "Bishop Agricola? Aye, I met him, I believe, in Verulamium, in Vortigern's encampment, if my memory is not playing tricks. The two were friends, although not close. Is that the man you mean?"

"It is. He was—and remains—foremost among the teachers of the Pelagian belief. Vortigern, who sympathized with the teachings although he never openly espoused the creed or became a Pelagian himself, per-mitted Agricola to live and teach within his lands. He had a close confi-dant and colleague, Fastidius. Did you meet him?"

"No, I don't believe so. Why?"

"Both Agricola and Fastidius were students of Pelagius in their youth. Aged men now, both of them, they still cling to those beliefs they ab-sorbed from him as youths and teach his tenets in defiance of all else."

"But that is infamous. They are men of God and they swore, publicly, to accept the decree of the convocation in Verulamium. Revoking that acceptance would open them to charges of perfidiousness and hypocrisy. They would certainly suffer excommunication."

I was aware now that the other bishops about me were listening openly to what we were saying, and Enos looked across the table to one of them and sighed, shaking his head. As he did so, a fresh noise broke out towards the front of the hall, where a group of Connor's musicians had entered and were tuning their instruments, preparing to present an entertainment. Enos stretched out his hand and took my wrist, an ex-pression upon his face that I could read only as resignation. He nodded once again and indicated the musicians.

"You have brought me thus far, Caius Merlyn, so now I must accom-pany you for the remainder of the way. Will you walk outside with me? In a few more moments it will be impossible to talk in here."

I rose and followed him out into the yard, winking and smiling to Tress as I passed by and indicating with a wave of my hand that I was leaving but that she should wait for me.

Once we had left the noisy hall and entered the cool silence of the empty courtyard, Enos led me over to a long, low bench against the north-ern wall, where he seated himself and spread his robes, wrapping his outer cloak across his shoulders to ward off the slight chill of the autumn eve-ning.

"Now," he said, settling himself. "Where were we? You were speaking of the absurdity of a so-called man of God defying his beliefs and disregarding the threats of excommunication."

"Yes. It seems ridiculous."

"And so it is." He looked at me speculatively, his head cocked slightly to one side. "I hope you will forgive me if I seem to speak in ignorance, Caius Merlyn, but we do not know each other well, we two. I was your aunt Luceiia's confessor and confidant before her death, but you and I had little to do with each other. I know you met my saintly brother Germanus on the way to Verulamium, where you helped him win his impressive victory over the pagan forces who opposed him, but I suspect you know little of Pelagius or his teachings. Am I correct?"

"About Pelagius, you are. I know little of him. But I know even less about this impressive victory you describe. What are you talking about? When we first met, Germanus and his people had been trapped by raiders in an abandoned farmyard. We drove them off, fortunately without great loss to ourselves. But that was a skirmish, not a victory of any kind. After that we had no trouble anywhere, other than a minor confrontation with some would-be bandits in Verulamium itself. So what is this victory you speak of?"

"The Alleluia Victory, men call it."

"The *what?*"

Enos held up one hand. "Allow me to explain, if I may. According to Bishop Germanus, who told me the tale in protest at what had been made of it, he and his party, perceiving themselves to be in a countryside that lacked danger, had allowed themselves to become careless. The soldiers riding with them were merely an honour guard, a relic of the Roman garrison in Gaul, who rode with Germanus and his brethren by their own choice. Germanus, as a former soldier, rode in soldier's garb, fully armed, in order to be able to protect his brethren should some dire need materialize. Nevertheless, and naturally enough, they were behaving like clerics, not soldiers. They slept one night at an abandoned farm, and awoke to find themselves surrounded by a roving war-band of Picts and Saxons. The bishops thought they were about to die when out of the morning sky came a hail of deadly arrows, fired from a distant cliff above the farm. The missiles, which were accurate and lethal, wrought havoc among the enemy and forced them to abandon their attack and to charge uphill towards the new aggressors. That withdrawal, in turn, enabled Germanus to lead his men safely out of the entrapment of the farm's stone walls. Then, once his fellow bishops were safe, he led his few riders to attack the rear of his former assailants.

"You, I know, were one of the bowmen on that distant cliff, and with two others you distracted the enemy. In the meantime, you had also sent your cavalry around to enter the valley to the north and then charge back southward to give succour to the farm's defenders. The raiding force was demoralized completely, and they broke up into small groups, easily disposed of." He stopped, and gazed at me, smiling. "Is that as accurate as your recollection of what happened that day?"

"Precisely, save that I saw it from the vantage point on the cliff top and missed the origins of the conflict, the initial surprise." I stopped then, and shrugged. "I suppose it *was* a victory, of sorts. But it was not *impressive*. We chanced to be in the right place at the right time, with the right force, and the enemy was a rabble. All else was inevitable." I hesitated. "So how did it come to be called the Alleluia Victory?"

Now Enos laughed, a slight, almost frail sound. "Bishops, men of God, are nonetheless men in every other sense. You saw nothing impressive in the affair—a mere skirmish with a raiding enemy, as you have said, effectively concluded with few losses. But the bishops, Caius Merlyn, the *bishops!* What *they* saw was altogether different. Imagine it—the identical scene—from their viewpoint.

"They had travelled far, much farther and for a much longer period of time than most of them were used to. They made camp in a pleasant valley, sheltered among some ruined walls, and after praying long into the night, they took their rest, only to awake to find a savage death threatening them, with painted savages and bull-horned Saxons screaming for their lives. Their leader and their spiritual guide, Germanus, was unable to protect them. He could lead no counterattack in safety, since there was but one exit to the place and it was held by the attackers. So the men of God fell to their knees and prayed, in terror of their lives. And as they prayed, a rain of arrows fell from Heaven and began to destroy the enemy, who turned and withdrew. Mere moments later their champion and fellow bishop, Germanus, led them to safety beyond the walls that had so quickly become their prison. He left them with an escort to protect them and led his own contingent of warriors to attack the rear of their fleeing attackers. The last word that he cried aloud before leading his men to the charge was *Alleluia*—Praise be to God.

"No sooner had the badly frightened bishops fallen to their knees to give thanks than they heard the sound of yet another charge approaching. As this new contingent of rescuers miraculously appeared and swept by them, the bishops raised the self-same cry of Alleluia, which was taken up by the galloping riders who then advanced into the fray with the praises of God upon their lips . . ." His voice faded away and he continued to gaze at me for some time before concluding.

"So you see, my son, both parties witnessed precisely the same events, but they experienced them from widely divergent viewpoints. To the clerical brethren huddled there by that abandoned farm, their salvation was miraculous, a divine intervention in their lives. Their faith in that was, and is, implicit. You say you merely happened to be there at the right time, with the right force to aid you. They believe you were Heaven-sent, to be precisely where you were at their time of greatest need. Had it not been so, Bishop Germanus would have perished there and the debate at Verulamium would never have taken place. Which version of the tale is truer? As a Christian, can you doubt theirs and believe that God was unaware of your nearness that day?"

"But . . . the *scope* of it, Enos! It was a minor squabble!"

"Ah!" His utterance was terse and dismissive. "And was the outcome minor? The debate in Verulamium? Your intervention that morning saved the bishop's life and saved the Great Debate. It served the very fabric of God's Church and brought about the undoing of a creed of heresy. Those elements transform your minor squabble into a major victory in these old eyes and in the eyes of many others, Caius Merlyn, so may we leave it at that? If modesty forbids you to acknowledge what occurred in truth, then so be it! I suppose, then, that you will be pleased to hear the tale's aftermath." His smile broadened, provoking an answering smile upon my lips.

"And what is that, this aftermath?"

"Why, it had nothing in the least to do with you. Your name has never been mentioned, in any version of the tale." Now he was positively grinning, ear to ear. "The Alleluia Victory belongs to the saintly Bishop Germanus alone! That is why he is so greatly vexed. He thinks that is egregiously insulting to you and outrageously flattering to him. Shall I tell him, then, that you prefer it thus?"

"Hah!" I threw back my head and laughed aloud, exulting in the old man's pleasure. "Indeed, Bishop, do so, for nothing could please me more than knowing that such an impressive victory had nothing to do with me or Camulod." He joined in my laughter. Then he leaned forward and slapped his fingers lightly on my knee.

"But we have digressed. We were speaking of other bishops and how they can seem to vacillate. I was about to comment on your knowledge of the doctrines taught by Pelagius. I said you seem to know little of them, and you agreed, did you not?" I nodded, watching him closely now, and he continued. "Do you know anything of what he taught? He had six arguments that formed the basis of his theology—are you familiar with them?"

"No, not at all. I heard them spoken of at the Debate, but understood little of it. I have been sympathetic to his teachings although unfamiliar with the meat of them, simply because an old friend of my father's, Bishop Alaric, subscribed to them, and Alaric was all that is best and finest in true men of God."

"I knew him, when I was very young, and I agree. Very well. Six points Pelagius made, and I shall keep them brief. Each of them bore on one, or both, of two central tenets of the Christian Church: the original sin of Adam, and the divine gift of grace. Bear in mind, though, we speak of heresy here, so do not be seduced." As he began to speak, he enumerated the points he made with his fingers, starting with the little finger of his right hand.

"One, and first above all: Pelagius averred that life is inseparable from death. He taught that even if Adam had not sinned, he would have died. Two, and even more seditious: he maintained that Adam's sin was personal. It harmed only Adam himself, and not the entire human race. In case number three, which is based upon number two, he claimed that newborn children are in a state of innocence, as was Adam before his fall. Four, perhaps the most unacceptable of all his claims, he asserts that the whole human race neither dies through Adam's sin or death, nor rises again through the resurrection of our Blessed Christus. Five." He paused before stating this point, and I waited, holding my breath. "Pelagius would have us all believe that the ancient Hebrew writings, the Old Testament containing the Laws of Moses, are as sure a guide to heaven as are the Gospels . . ."

I waited for him to continue, but he seemed lost in thought, apparently upon the latter point, which, of all the five, had meant the least to me. Finally I cleared my throat. "And six?"

"What?"

"You said there were six points. You gave me only five."

"Oh, forgive me. Let me see . . . Six: Pelagius swore that even before the advent of the Christ, there were men who were without sin."

I sat back quickly, resting my shoulders against the cold wall and breathing deeply. That last point had hit home unpleasantly to me. I had heard it spoken, although differently phrased, by my father. He had been taught by Bishop Alaric that, even before the Christ and his Redemption, good and noble men had known the difference between right and wrong, between good and evil. There was much difference between the two versions of that thought, I realized, and for the first time since my journey to Verulamium so many years earlier, I found myself unwilling to peer into the metaphysical abyss that suddenly yawned in front of me. Men, and particularly clerics, I recalled again, had infinite capacity for splitting hairs of meaning. Enos, however, had noticed nothing of my reaction and continued speaking as though we had never left the point he now pursued.

"Agricola and Fastidius were the champions of Pelagius in Verulamium, as Germanus himself and Lupus of Troyes, who accompanied him, were the champions of the Church. Both men agreed to abide by the decrees established at the Great Debate, and both indeed did so, overtly at least, for several years. In recent years, however, both have recanted and returned to their heretical ways.

"Your question was couched in disbelief that they could be so wilfully intransigent, and in conscience I must inform you that, in their own minds at least, they are guilty of no sin in their reversion. Arrogance may be reprehensible, but it is not a sin, save when it is viewed as pride. They choose to disbelieve in Adam's original sin, and in the divine grace that is the Church's vehicle to Heaven and salvation. They adhere, arrogantly, be it said, to the ancient wisdom of the Stoics of Greece, which avers that the moral strength of man's will, when reinforced by asceticism, is suffi-cient force to generate salvation. Hence the simplification of their creed: men have always had the will to chose between goodness and evil; those who choose goodness, so be it they deny their baser natures, eschew sin-fulness, and aspire to God, may gain salvation on their own merits. It is a very seductive and sweet-seeming path that beckons to the unwary."

"Aye," I said, speaking for the first time in what seemed like hours. "And particularly here in Britain, where men have always felt that moral rectitude and personal probity are admirable."

"Quite so, indeed." Enos glanced at me sharply, however, as he agreed with me, and I wondered whether he had thought to detect some irony in my last words. "But that has nothing to do with the recognition that the Fathers of the Church have spent long years and written many vol-umes concerning their analyses of all Pelagius taught, and have decided in their wisdom that, doctrinally, Pelagius is unacceptable. He is declared heretical, anathema, and all his works condemned. Agricola and Fastidius have made their choice, and stand condemned, but the danger they pose to others cannot be ignored, and so Germanus will return to Britain in the coming year.

"Forgive me, I may have spoiled your delight in my friend's letter. I had not wished to tell you anything of that before you read the tidings in his letter, but Germanus himself decided I should inform of you of his intent, since that would remove the need for him to spend long hours explaining it to you in his letter."

I sat stunned, so that all I could do was question what I had already been clearly told. "Germanus is returning? To where?"

"To Verulamium."

"That is impossible, Enos! Verulamium is in Saxon hands today. The entire east is overrun with Danes, Saxons, Anglians and others. These people are utterly savage and pagan, with no concept of love or tolerance or any other thing the sweet Christ teaches. They'll devour any Christian bishop fool enough to show his face there."

I saw him shake his head and tried to discern the expression in his eyes, but it seemed to me like pity. "Caius Merlyn," he said, quietly, "what is it that you think we do, we bishops? What tasks do we perform? Do you know?"

"I—" His question left me blinking, and I began again. "You minister to others, teaching them the way of God, and the way of the Church."

"That is correct, but who are these 'others' of whom you speak?"

"Why, your Christian flock."

"And whence came this flock?" He took pity upon me then, indeed. "I work among the Anglians of the eastern shores, the Saxon Shore, as you call it. So do my brethren here, all ten of them. We minister to the souls of those poor folk whom you scorn as 'invaders.' Not all of them, of course, for some are still . . . well, 'arriving' is a kinder word, I find, and the one that I prefer to use in speaking of them. Many of the newcomers are fierce and warlike, there is no disputing that. But their belligerence is rooted deep in fear, for they are newcomers and have to win the land on which they will support and rear their families. When they are settled, secure and more content, their bellicose and hostile ways will settle into calm, and they will lend themselves to the teachings of the gentle Christus.

"Germanus will go into Verulamium in peace, and the Christian people there, Anglians all, will see to his protection. I have no fear for Germanus, nor does he. Our flocks in that region have held their land for years, some of them for generations. They are no longer pagan, and they are no longer dangerous to God's servants."

"But there are some who are." I could not bring myself to countenance what he was saying.

"Some, that is true. But in the fullness of God's time that, too, will change. God's Will will prevail over men's forever. The emperors of Rome, when Rome was at its peak, could not stifle His word, nor His love. Think you these unlettered Saxons will be stronger than imperial Rome?"

"So, are you saying that when you leave here you will go over to the Saxon Shore, to preach to these . . . pagan peoples?"

"I am, but I will also make shift to spread the word of Bishop Germanus's return next year, so that when he arrives, his coming will be awaited and his congregation gathered."

"And what about these heretics, Agricola and Fastidius? Do you expect them to attend, when all will know them as apostate?"

"I hope they will be there, but that will make little difference. Their persons are not in danger from the Church. It is their souls that should concern them more, and the matter of their teaching heresy to simple souls who take them at their word. That, above all, must be redressed. The last great meeting in Verulamium was a debate. The next one will be greatly different. It will be an exposition of doctrine, a declaration of canon law, and a condemnation of this heresy and all who cleave to it."

"But won't that be dangerous for Germanus and his people?"

"Dangerous?" The old bishop's raised eyebrow made me feel foolish, and the feeling deepened as he smiled. "We are speaking of bishops here, Master Merlyn, not of warriors. How could there be danger to Germanus, or any other?"

"Precisely because of what you just said, Bishop. This next meeting will be an exposition of doctrine and a declaration of canon law. It will be a condemnation of Pelagius and his heresy and all who cleave to it. That means it will be a loud and unequivocal condemnation of Agricola and Fastidius, and of their followers, and it occurs to me that even if the bishops themselves remain calm, not all of their followers will meekly accept condemnation. And that could involve danger for Germanus and his people. They'll be far from home."

The old bishop raised his hand and blessed me with the sign of the Cross. "Have no fears of that, Caius Merlyn, Agricola and Fastidius are men, as well as bishops, and they would take no pleasure in being publicly chastised before their followers—and make no mistake, they know that is what will happen, for they have earned public censure. If they come at all to Verulamium, they will bring few of their flock with them. The two of them will come, I believe, in the hope of finding clemency, but I could have no faith in any renewed conversion they might undergo. I believe they will come, and sue for clemency, and hope to return to their home in Vortigern's lands, where they can continue their subversive teachings. And that, of course, we cannot permit. But whether I am right or no, any followers they bring with them will be greatly outnumbered by the faithful there. Germanus will never be in any danger among so many Christian souls."

I shrugged, slightly mollified but far from being convinced of that last statement, although I could see that Enos believed it utterly. Before I could say more, however, I heard the noise as the doors of the refectory swung open behind us and the sounds of laughter and noisy people spilled out into the chilly evening air. The old man stood up.

"I have detained you far longer than I wished, my friend. I trust you will apologize for me to all who have suffered for my laxity in that. The dinner is ended, and people are returning to their homes. I will have one of my bishops bring you the letter from Germanus."

I assured him that would be unnecessary—I would send a soldier to collect it for me later, within the hour. Then I led him back into the hall and delivered him to his brethren, who were preparing to leave.

As soon as I left Enos, I went to Rufio, who was Officer of the Guard that night, and asked him to send a trooper to escort the bishops to their quarters and then to collect the letter from Enos and bring it back to me. I walked back towards where Tressa sat between Connor and Brander. Arthur stood on the dais by her side, talking intently into her ear. She noticed me approaching and said something to the boy, and he straightened up to watch me coming. Even before I reached them, I knew something was amiss, but as I arrived, Brander stood up and clapped me on the shoulder, bidding me a good night and promising to see me in the morning before he and Connor left. As he began to usher his wife and the others in his party towards the door, I turned to face Arthur, whose eyes were wide, fixed upon mine.

"What's wrong?" I asked him.

"Am I to go to Cambria with Llewellyn One-Eye?"

I glanced, surprised at Tressa, but she shrugged her shoulders eloquently, indicating that the knowledge had not come from her.

"Who told you that?"

"Is it true?"

"Yes, it is. Are you displeased?"

"You promised I would ride out with you when you returned. Now I am to go to Cambria with a man I do not know. A man who wears a mask."

Llewellyn had worn a leather mask since reaching Camulod, ostensibly to spare our women the sight of his ravaged face. Nevertheless, something in the tone of the boy's voice, conveying a wordless slur upon a man whom I had come to think of as a friend, angered me.

"Have you asked yourself why he might choose to wear a mask, Arthur?" The boy stared at me, startled by the sudden acerbity in my tone. "Perhaps to set himself apart, so that people unknown to him might find scope for their cruelty in belittling him? Or could it be that perhaps he finds the insults he endures wearing that mask more acceptable than those he might have to face without it? They call him Llewellyn One-Eye for good reason. His is not a pretty face. It was ruined by molten metal when he was a lad younger than you, and the sight of him can frighten children. You're no such child, are you?"

Arthur was gazing at me now in consternation, and I realized he had not meant to be as cruel as I had taken him to be. I was instantly contrite, although I did not allow my face to show that. Instead, I moderated my tone to one much softer.

"Llewellyn One-Eye is a fine man, Arthur, and I have quickly become proud to call him friend, as will you, once you know him. We'll discuss this further, tomorrow, but for the moment I will tell you this. You are the son of Uther Pendragon, the rightful king of all southern Cambria and the lower Pendragon lands against which we now live, and yet you know nothing of your folk, nor they of you. Llewellyn will rectify that. He is an ironsmith and a great warrior, a bowman respected among his own, who, as you know, are the greatest bowmen in Britain, and probably beyond.

"I have decided that you will live with him for one full year, to learn his ways and the ways of Pendragon. I can be no help to you in that. Being seen with me, you would be recognized for who you are, and before you are ready to take your place, that recognition could mean your death. Llewellyn knows the truth of it, and so does Huw Strongarm, and Huw Strongarm is now War Chief of Pendragon and sworn to serve you and your house. Between the two of them, these men will introduce you to their folk, their ways and customs, and their life. A better understanding of your own can only be of service to you." I could see that he still looked less than comfortable with my tidings, so I gave him the chance to speak. "One year, that's all, I promise you. What say you?"

He looked away from me, his gaze sliding slowly from my face to some distant point beyond my shoulder while he appeared to gnaw at the inside of his cheek. Then he drew a quick, deep breath and straightened up. "You are convinced this is something I should do." It was a statement, not a question.

"I am, completely. As for the matter of your riding out with me, I did not suspect you set any great store upon such a thing, so if I have disappointed you then I regret that. It is remediable. You'll go to Cambria for one short year. And despite the fact that a year seems endless at your age, it is a short time, and each new one grows shorter as you grow older. So, one year. After that, you'll return to Camulod, then we'll ride out together, if you wish. By that time, you'll be of age and will have your own command. Ambrose tells me you have surpassed all his expectations to this point, and that pleases me more than I can say. Now what I want you to do is arrange matters so that Llewellyn One-Eye will say the same of you, when next I see him." Behind his back, I saw Morag leaving with her mother and the other ladies, hanging back to glance our way in the hope of catching Arthur's eye.

I looked back at Arthur. "Tomorrow, I will introduce you to my friend Llewellyn, and I promise you, you will enjoy him, the real man beneath the mask. Now I believe there's a young woman trying to attract your attention." He turned to see what I had seen, and in mere moments he was gone, striding towards his love. I turned around, finally, to Tressa, who was sitting, smiling up at me.

"I thought you were going to be too hard on him, at first. He was upset, but mainly about losing the opportunity to be with you."

"I know. My first reaction was unjust and hasty, but thank God I saw my error in time to avoid any grievous damage." I glanced over her head to Connor, whose sleepy eyes were already half closed. "Well, Admiral, are we feeding you well enough?"

He grinned, slowly. "Aye, passing well, but I'd gladly trade some of your endless beef for a bowl of good oat porridge."

"Ach!" I shuddered. "Are you growing oats again, then, up in your heavenly isles?"

His smile grew broader, though his eyes remained half closed. "We will always grow oats. They sustain us and give us our enormous strength."

"You should have told me! We, too, grow them, but we feed them to our horses, which, I suppose, is why they have *their* enormous strength. Our stable storehouses are filled with them. That reminds me, I have to procure another horse. Did you know I lost Germanicus?"

Connor jerked up straight. "Your big black horse? No, I didn't know that. How, and when?"

I told him briefly, and then laid my hand on Tressa's shoulder. "Connor, my friend and companion-in-arms, might I induce you to retire? I have another companion here, as you have noticed, so if you will permit us to withdraw and leave you here alone, you will earn the gratitude of both of us."

Connor grinned and stretched and then yawned hugely, ignoring Tressa's little cry of outrage at my lack of discretion. He pulled himself to his feet and stood there wavering, gaining his balance. "Too much mead," he said. "I hope the same cannot be said of you, comrade-in-arms. I'll bid you a good night, then, since you clearly have no wish for me to stay with you. Sleep well, if you have time."

He turned majestically, pivoting on his wooden limb, and aimed himself towards the double doors at the end of the hall, negotiating the step down from the dais with ease before clumping unsteadily away. As he approached the doorway, I saw a trooper entering, carrying my letter from Germanus. Apart from Tress and me, there were no more than half a score of people left now in the hall, and I needed to speak with none of them. The trooper snapped to attention before me with a smart salute and handed me my letter. I thanked him and pushed the scroll inside my tunic, then extended my hand to Tressa, who took it, swinging lithely to her feet.

"What now? Must you read that? Or have you finished with talking, so that there's time for me, at last?"

"Something akin to that." I laid one hand gently on the back of her neck and we walked together to the vestibule where we had hung our cloaks on entering. Rufio had ordered a light, two-wheeled, canopied wagon to be waiting at the doors for us. The driver, another trooper, helped us to climb up into it, then covered us with warm, fleecy coverings. Tressa snuggled against me and I reached for her thighs again, this time allowing my hands to explore as they would.

I nodded to the guards who saluted us at the gates and then turned back to Tress, and mere moments later, it seemed, we entered the main portico of the Villa Britannicus. There we found Plato, the major-domo, waiting to welcome us and show us to our sleeping quarters on the second floor. The large room he led us to was brightly lit with fine, wax candles, some of them flickering in the gentle breeze that stirred the delicate hangings by the window, where the louvred shutters had been left slightly open.

I remember closing the door behind Plato as he left, and then I remember turning to look at Tress, drinking in the beauty of her, subdued yet enhanced as it was by the light from the flickering candles. I remember crossing to her and taking her in my arms, feeling the full richness of her body and the sweetness of her mouth as we kissed each other thoroughly for the first in time in long, lingering months. I remember the soaring urgency that took possession of me then, but I have no recollection of the time that passed between that moment and the moment when we both stood naked, skin against skin, by the bed. I remember the weight of her in my arms as she fell backwards beneath me, pulling me down to her. It seemed to me she looked harder, or firmer—different, somehow, but I took little note of that at the time, distracted by greater urgencies.

I have no concrete memories of what transpired between us then, but something deep within my soul recalls the delight of feeling her move beneath me, her thighs parting to welcome me, making room for me to enter her; I have a blinding, fleeting memory of outrush, from my lips and loins, as she drew the very life from me and sent me crashing into ecstasy, and after that I recall nothing.

XII

 I AWOKE THE following morning to find myself alone in bed, with no sign of Tressa other than the rumpled bedclothes that covered the spot where she had slept. I raised myself up on my elbow immediately, calling her name, but she was not in the room and I fell back down into the bed, stretching luxuriously in the warmth of it and smelling the scent of her among the bedding.

I must have fallen back to sleep again, because the next time I opened my eyes she was sitting on the bed above me, bent over and whispering my name. I came awake at once, reaching up for her and pulling her down to where I could kiss her, and my hand sought her body beneath the voluminous garment she wore. She quickly glided away from me, however, and my fingers slid down the warm slope of her thigh to land on the bedclothes as she bounded to her feet and went to fling wide the shutters, allowing bright daylight to pour into the room.

"By the Christ, Tress, what time of day is it? Why didn't you wake me before now? It must be almost noon!"

"No, it is not yet mid-morning, but your body needed sleep, and so I allowed you to sleep on when I arose." She grinned, a quick grin, filled with mischief. "I thought it necessary."

"How? What do you mean?"

"What should I mean? Once you are rested sufficiently, you'll become strong enough again to use me as I wish to be used, without falling asleep."

"Without—? Did I do that?" I knew, of course, that I had. Kissing her own hand gently, she came back to the bed and reached out to caress my cheek with it. I felt myself growing hard again and tried to catch her by the wrist, but she was too quick for me. "Come back to bed, then," I rasped.

"Tonight I will, but not now, my love. Ambrose, Arthur, Dedalus and that man with the strange mask are all downstairs, waiting for you, so you must be quick, and I must be even quicker. I don't want them thinking that we might be doing what is clearly foremost in your mind. Plato is bringing up hot water and will be here directly. Wash your face quickly and come down. I've set out a new suit of leathers for you, over there, and a new tunic that I sewed myself. Be quick."

She spoke the last words as she went out the door and I groaned and heaved myself around to sit on the side of the bed, looking at the clothes she had mentioned. Rubbing the remnants of sleep from my eyes, I went to examine them more closely and found myself whistling admiringly at the magnificent workmanship that had gone into their creation.

Plato knocked and entered, bidding me good day. Two troopers followed, one bearing a collapsible washstand with a suspended leather bucket and a large pitcher of water, the other carrying a larger, steaming pitcher. As they set up the device under Plato's watchful eyes, I turned my attention again to the strange-looking garment in my hands. It was a single undergarment of some kind, made of a very fine, light, brushed wool. I soon identified the holes for my arms and the shape of the collar, but it took me some time longer to identify the purpose of the lower appendages. Then I realized how the garment worked. The bottom end of it contained two sleeve-like openings for my thighs. Between those hung a flap that I reasoned must come up between my legs like an ordinary breech-cloth and attach, somehow, in front. Satisfied that I had some understanding of the thing, I dropped it and went to the steaming washbasin. Plato and his assistants had departed by then, and I made short work of my ablutions, drying myself with a clean towel before beginning to dress.

The undergarment went on smoothly, once I had discovered that I must insert my legs into the requisite openings before pulling the body up around my waist and attempting to shrug into the upper part. The legs were short, perhaps a handbreadth long, and clung comfortably to my upper thighs, but their very snugness emphasized the looseness of my dangling genitalia. I ignored that, for the moment, and concentrated on the upper part. The armholes were sleeveless and I shrugged into them without difficulty, then laced up the deep V at my chest, experimenting with the tension of the lacing and finally leaving it loosely tied. I bent forward then, and pulled the hanging rear flap up between my legs, cinching it so that it was both tight and comfortable. I fed the two narrow tapes I found attached to the outside corners through two loops sewn to the shirt's body and then tied them in a bow across my middle, smiling now at the clever simplicity of the design. I would be able to reach up beneath my tunic and release the flap with a single tug, then hold it aside while I answered nature's call.

Feeling light-hearted now, I pulled on the leather trousers and fastened them securely about my waist before slipping my new, white tunic over my head, feeling the softness of the stuff with which it was lined. Even on the quilted breast and short sleeves and almost knee-length skirts of this garment, which would seldom if ever be seen by anyone, Tressa had worked designs of flowers and plants in silken threads, her needlework so delicate and fine that the depictions seemed to be an integral part of the tunic's fabric.

Finally, I picked up the leather top piece and looked at it closely before putting it on. It hung open in front, and from its middle depended two lengths of leather belt, one three times the length of the other and each of them made from braided strips of differently coloured leather, yellow and blue. I pulled on this coat and flexed my shoulders, arching my back and trying to find tightness anywhere, but the soft, buttery leather hung perfectly, shaped to my size and width without constricting my shoulder-blades. The garment hung open and loose in front of me and the longer of the two belts hung from the right side. I fed that end through a vertical hole, edged with fine stitching, in the central seam of the left side and pulled it tight, flattening the front right flap across my belly. Then I brought the belt around my back, pulling the left flap into place and tying the two ends in place at my right side, allowing the ends to hang free. I could not see the finished effect, but I knew it must be fine.

The lower part of the coat, beneath my waist, was cut into wide fringes, much like armoured flaps, a thumb's-length wide. The flaps themselves were decorated handsomely, stamped in relief with a simple, Celtic scroll pattern and outlined in blue stitchwork. Similarly, the shoulders of the coat were of multiple layers, stiff as armour, and from them smaller leather flaps hung down to frame my upper arms in wide fringes of blue and gold. A pair of fleece-lined boots in the same soft, supple leather completed the array. I laced them up quickly, enjoying the solid feel of their heavy, nail-studded soles and knowing that I would have to be careful to walk upon carpets here in the upper chambers, where the floors were made of highly polished, decorative wood.

Tressa was waiting for me at the top of the broad stairs that led down to the main part of the house, and from the smile on her face I knew she was happy with the results of all her work. As we descended the stairway together, Dedalus gave an appreciative, drawn-out whistle that was sheer lechery, although it was intended sarcastically for me, not for Tressa. I decided to ignore his ill manners, but I could not resist pausing at the foot of the stairs and preening, showing off the craftsmanship that had gone into my new garments. All four of them then, Ambrose, Arthur, Ded and Llewellyn, acknowledged my sartorial splendour and complimented Tressa sincerely. She nodded her head graciously, well pleased, and left us alone.

Ambrose cut immediately to the heart of the matters we had to discuss that day. Connor and Brander's party had already left Camulod, shortly after daybreak, and had been adamant that I not be disturbed from my rest, since we had made our farewells the previous night. Now Ambrose wanted me to go with him to meet his Northumbrian guests.

In my confusion over the lateness of the hour and my delight over my new clothing, I had completely forgotten that this was the day Connor and Brander were to leave, but the reminder offered an immediate explanation for Arthur's mood, which was somewhat subdued and faintly melancholy. Morag was gone from him again, and I knew the best thing I could do was turn the boy's attention towards what lay ahead of him.

"Your Northumbrians, are they assembled yet?"

"No, but they are waiting for our summons."

"That is good, because I have not eaten yet and we have another matter to discuss before we come to them. Let's see if we can beg some scraps from Plato's pantry."

A short time later, the five of us sat around a table in one of the storerooms flanking the Villa's enormous kitchens, helping ourselves from the heaps of food Plato had piled before us. There was bread, newly baked and still warm from the oven, tiny, fresh apples, plums and pears from the gardens in the central yard and a wide variety of cold cuts of whole meat and spiced sausages. There was also a choice of fresh milk from the barns or well-watered vinum. Once satisfied that starvation was not to be my lot that day, I turned to Llewellyn.

"Someone told Arthur last night that he is to return to Cambria with you, and he was taken unawares, since he knew nothing about it and did not—does not—know you. It occurred to me then that you know equally little of him, and yet you'll be responsible for him while he is in your care, so I decided to tell you something about him while he is present to hear it. He is an adequate bowman, perhaps slightly below average at this stage. It is my hope that you will refine his shooting skills while he is in your care. He has the makings of an excellent swordsman, according to his teachers, Rufio and Dedalus, though I know he'll have little use for swordsman's skills among your folk. He's also bred to horseback and that, too, will have to change in your homeland—under your tutorial influence, he will learn to use his legs and increase his wind and stamina . . . You should also be aware that he can read and write Latin with perfect fluency, and has read widely in his great-grandfather's books." I glanced at Arthur to see his expression before continuing. The lad was narrow-eyed, listening closely.

"I've told you, I believe, that his great-grandfather, Publius Varrus, was a master ironsmith and a maker of superb weapons. He even taught me something of his craft in my boyhood, albeit very little. But little as it was, I still remember much of it, and it taught me a great respect for swords and for the iron from which they are made." Now I turned directly to Arthur. "Llewellyn, here, is also a master smith, and it is my hope that he'll consent to teach you something of his craft. It could teach you much about why the weapon you prefer, the sword, contains the greatness that

it does. It should also teach you to respect the properties of the materials—all materials—with which you must work, be they metals or men.

"You commented last night on the fact that my friend here wears a
mask, and I responded harshly and, I fear, wrongly." I paused, and Arthur
looked mortified. "As you grow older you will learn, as all of us have
learned, that all men wear masks of one kind or another, some of them
as seemingly harmless as a smile, although that smile may be the most
deceitful mask of all. All of us seek, at some time, to conceal what lies
beneath our faces. Many do so because they fear their treachery will shine
through their skin. Some, a compassionate and unfortunate few, wear
masks to spare the people who surround them from pain, or fear, or embarrassment." I turned back to Llewellyn. "Will you remove your mask,
my friend?"

He must have sensed what I was about, because he straightened
slightly and then simply pulled the narrow headband that secured it up
over his skull. The silence that greeted the sight of his ruined face was
profound, and he grinned, the good side of his face smiling while the left
side grimaced hideously, baring his eye-tooth through the hole in his
cheek.

"This is the true mask," he said, speaking directly to Arthur. Then he
held up the leather flap with its stark eyeholes. "This one is merely a
curtain. Don't feel badly about how you feel, I've had a lifetime to grow
hardened to that. Mine is a face to frighten children, I know, but I never
see it. I spent years hating myself and everyone around me, for I did not
always look like this, and I remembered how it was before I was disfigured.
But in recent years I have learned that some people, friends, can see
beyond the scars and horror. I have a wife who loves me and respects me.
I have children who have seen no other face on me, and therefore accept
me as I am, for who I am. I've learned to live with it."

Arthur's face settled into an expression of concern and sympathy,
showing no trace of the initial horror that had flared in him when the
mask first came off. Now he leaned slightly towards Llewellyn. "How did
it happen?"

"Molten metal, carelessly handled. It should have killed me, but I was
young and strong, so I survived. I was apprenticed to a smith who liked
strong drink. One day he drank too much, and stumbled, and the liquid
metal splashed. Not much, but it landed on me."

Arthur shuddered, and so, I noticed, did the others. "And you are still
a smith?"

"Not *still*. I wasn't then. I was a beginning prentice, twelve years old.
I became a smith later, once I discovered that I had more in common
with iron than I did with people. So, will you come with me to Cambria,
lad, to meet your father's people and to learn about his land?"

Arthur looked at me, and his eyes filled up with tears. Although I had no notion of what was going through his mind, I found a great relief welling up inside of me and felt a thickening in my own throat and an unaccountable prickling behind my eyes. "Aye," he whispered, nodding emphatically as though to convince some inner part of himself that doubted still. "I will."

"There's on you, boy! We'll have a time, I promise you, and Huw Strongarm will teach you even more than I, once we come by him. We'll leave as soon as may be, for I'll tell you, I find myself uncomfortable here, cooped up by walls I cannot climb. Mountains are higher, and much wilder, but a man can pass freely among them and find sustenance in any part of them. Here, you have only kitchens, filled with folk all hungrier than you, and you must live with what they leave. No freedom here, boy— no fish to catch, nor fowl to shoot nor rabbits to snare, no eggs among the heather and no deer grazing in the stone courtyards. Tomorrow and today we'll spend preparing, and the morning after that we'll be away, free with the winds and rain. You're going to love your Cambria, my lad. I'll work you hard and drive you mad, but you will thrive on it. And wait you till you see the flashing eyes and other parts on Cambrian lasses! *There's* a treat in store for you! None bonnier there are in all the world, you'll see. Do you sing?"

Arthur looked at me again, mystified, but I merely smiled. "Do I sing? No, I don't, not much. But I *can* sing."

"Aye, if you're your father's son you can. You'll sing among the mountains, won't be able to stop yourself, for there the gods dwell, boy, and they all sing."

I stood up, grinning, and spoke to Ambrose, who had uttered not a single word in all of this. "Time now to go and meet your guests. Shall we?"

The meeting with Vortigern's representatives was straightforward and un- eventful and contained only one startling piece of information. One of the Northumbrians, the senior man among them, spoke of Vortigern's hopes for a peaceful settlement of the problem that had been simmering for so long between him and Horsa's young, land-hungry warriors. Ac- cording to his report, some form of accommodation had been reached between Vortigern, or Horsa himself, and a small, well-established settle- ment of Danes in the far south-east, in that region known as the Weald but which the Danes were now calling Kent, or some such Outlandish name. This corner of Britain, the original Saxon Shore, had recently begun to attract massive incursions of Germanic tribes seeking a foothold in Britain. Although the local residents, so recently arrived themselves, had so far been able to repulse these attacks, the numbers of marauders had continued to grow consistently and frighteningly, so that defeat seemed inevitable to the land-holding defenders.

This situation, ironic though it seemed to me when I considered invaders fighting invasion, had led the leaders of the south-eastern Danes to approach Vortigern in the far north-east, knowing that he had long since sheltered and protected the Danes in his domain, and to ask for his assistance in defending their own lands. The result had been a lessening of the pressures on Vortigern, thanks to the eagerness with which Horsa's young warriors had greeted this opportunity, apparently sent to them by the Fates: a war to fight, new lands to claim, and unknown women of their own race to meet their needs in amity and commonality. Hundreds of Horsa's warriors had left already, it appeared, sailing swiftly southward, and were not expected to return to Northumbria. Horsa had gone with them, although none could say with certainty that he expected to remain long in the south.

This discussion reminded me that I had not yet read my letter from Germanus. I forced myself to listen politely, impatient now to return to my own quarters and find it. This information from Northumbria weakened Enos's arguments about Germanus's safety should he attempt to ride through south-eastern Britain. Horsa was no Christian warrior, and his army was a pagan horde, a very genuine threat to Germanus's plans for another meeting in Verulamium if the bishop thought to travel from Gaul to Verulamium via the Weald.

Engrossed in these thoughts, I missed the transition from the discussion of Horsa's Danes to the wonders these dour chieftains had found in Camulod. I snapped back to attention when one of them asked me something directly, and fortunately, I was able to answer his question without betraying my distraction. They praised the Colony's war-readiness, and I emphasized that that we stood prepared to face threat or attack from any direction, and at any time. I reassured them that I would indeed lead another expedition into Vortigern's lands within the coming year, to demonstrate our status as his willing allies. Shortly thereafter, I began searching for an acceptable reason for returning to my duties, until Ambrose himself came to my rescue, standing up and thanking me for taking the time to come and meet with his guests.

I rose and thanked all of them for coming to Camulod, and requested them to pass my greetings along to King Vortigern with my promise to meet with him in person the following summer. Then I bade them a cordial farewell and made my way back to the Villa, where Plato told me that Tressa had ridden up to the fort with the lady Shelagh, and would return late in the afternoon. I thanked him and went upstairs, where I found the leather cylinder containing Germanus's letter lying on the table by the window in our sleeping chamber. I took it back downstairs with me again, flicking my thumb idly against the wax that sealed it, and made myself comfortable in the sunshine that lit the atrium.

Caius Merlyn Britannicus
From Germanus Pontifex
Auxerre, Gaul

My Dear Friend:

Even as I write these words, I know that months will have elapsed and you will already have spoken to my old friend Bishop Enos by the time you have read them. Enos has been with me now for nigh on three months and will shortly be returning to his duties in the town once known as Venta Belgarum, in those territories of Britain which you deem lost to invaders.

By now, Enos will have told you that I intend—I am directed by my superiors—to return to Britain and conclude this affair of heretical mutiny among the bishops of your unhappy land. I fear there is enough danger there for men's bodies and souls as matters stand, without the added perils being poured upon them by misguided teachers. Accordingly, I shall arrive in Britain in midspringtime of the coming year, crossing the Narrow Sea directly to the old Roman harbour of Dubris and making my way northward from there to Verulamium.

Believe me, my friend, I clearly envision the alarm with which you will receive these tidings, since, to your eyes, that particular region of your country is swarming with Godless pagans. Such is not the truth, however; Enos and his brethren have brought many hundreds into the light of Christ in recent years, particularly among the Anglicans of the south-east, and it is to these good people that I will entrust my safety, secure in the benevolence of He whom I serve.

As you know, nonetheless, that part of me which was once a soldier refuses to allow me peace of mind when travelling through strange countrysides, and reminds me that I shall not always be in the domain of our Anglian Christian brethren. In addition to that natural and ingrained caution, there is a commonplace saying that the Lord, our God, helps those who help themselves, or words to that effect.

May I impose upon you to assist me in God's work? Your presence in my train, with a contingent such as the one you brought to Verulamium before, when first we met, would be a manifold blessing, both on the road and at the meeting place itself. I fear the gathering to which we ride on this occasion will be less cordial than that we last attended. I ask this of you with no knowledge or consideration of your own affairs, or plans, or your condition, in full cognizance of the selfishness of what I do.

Should you be unable to accede to my request, I shall be disappointed but not offended. On the other hand, should you decide to join us, I shall be happy indeed to renew our acquaintance and to thank God for His beneficence.

Enos will arrange to bring your answer back to me, and you and yours are remembered always in my prayers.

Your friend and brother in Christ
Germanus Pontifex

I was pacing my quarters by the time I finished reading, my thoughts leaping erratically like dried peas dropped on a drumhead. Since talking with Enos the night before, I had already accepted that he and his fellow bishops had been successful in converting at least some of the south-eastern Anglians to Christianity, but the thought of Germanus entrusting himself to such people nevertheless appalled me, for despite all of Enos's optimism and goodwill, to my own mind these people were, and would always remain, pagan savages, aliens and invaders whom a thin overlay of Christianity would never pacify or change. The knowledge that Horsa's horde of Danes would be present in that region when my friend arrived further underlined and emphasized my fears for his safety.

On the other hand, this invitation to accompany Germanus on his errand was less inconvenient than my old friend might have thought, and I could see it held certain incontestable advantages, were I to examine it purely from a political viewpoint. Horsa's removal of his armies to the south-east offered an immediate and obvious benefit to Vortigern in the far north-east; he would no longer be under such great pressure to find a solution to the problem their presence represented in his own territories. The greater the number of Danish warriors who poured south-eastward, the less imperative would be the demands placed upon Vortigern's people to provide additional land for these mercenaries in their own territories, land they did not possess. Ergo, I reasoned, Vortigern's pressing need for our visible support in the north-east would be proportionally lessened by the Danish exodus. I suspected he would be more than pleased were we to demonstrate our presence in the south-east, prior to riding north to join him as we had promised. That tied in well with my own desire to explore that region of the country, something that might be achieved only through the presence of Germanus and the acquiescence of his Christian Anglian converts. Certainly, as escort and honour guard to the bishop and his party, leading them northwards from the coast, my own troops would be able to move more freely through the area than they could possibly have done under any other circumstances.

Despite the strategic attractiveness of the invitation, however, the whole affair was vastly convoluted and fraught with political risk. Conflicting thoughts and notions flitted through my mind more quickly than I can define them now, all of them influenced by my own reservations over the manner in which Enos had defined Vortigern's sympathetic stance towards the heretics. It occurred to me that Vortigern might not be over-pleased with my commitment to Germanus and his orthodox views on Pelagius, despite and notwithstanding the consideration that my commitment, if indeed I made one, would be born out of loyalty to my old friend and not out of any active dedication to the premise he espoused.

In fact, the teachings of Pelagius, as I had been taught to understand them long ago, made eminent good sense to me. I accepted the basic belief that mankind was made in the image of God, born in possession of the divine spark enabling him to choose between goodness and evil. I could find no moral fault in the premise that each man and woman was therefore capable of communing directly with God and achieving his or her own salvation. The Fathers of the Church, however, had decided in their wisdom that this belief was a form of pride, one of the greatest of the Seven Deadly Sins, and that mankind was incapable of achieving anything without the intervention of divine grace, administered through God's deputies, themselves. The theological hair-splitting in the controversy that was bringing Germanus back into Britain was beyond my grasp, but I was fundamentally unswayed by the theologians' disputations. I had been taught the Pelagian way by the living example of my own dearest relatives and friends, and I could find no fault in any of them. The result was that I lived my life according to the dictates of my conscience and I sought to sway no other person to my own beliefs.

Vortigern, however, I suspected of being more politically concerned in this dispute. He called himself a Christian king, though he admitted he was no theologian and therefore unconcerned with fine theological distinctions. He had never openly taken sides at the debate on Pelagianism in Verulamium. Yet it was true, nonetheless, that the two most outspoken champions of the Pelagian way, the bishops Agricola and Fastidius, were from Vortigern's domain, and he had allowed them thus far to function as they would, spreading their teachings throughout his extensive lands, north to Hadrian's Wall and all the way westward into northern Cambria, far north of the Pendragon lands. From that viewpoint, I thought, Vortigern would surely be inclined to look upon my services to Germanus with displeasure—a displeasure much allayed by the advantages to him in having Camulodian cavalry present in Horsa's new territories.

By the time I stopped pacing and sat down to read the letter a second time, I had arrived at a number of decisions. I sat thinking for a while longer, and then took up a pen and a pot of ink and wrote down my list, simply to see how it looked. I found myself smiling as I did so, aware that my own habit of writing things down, now ingrained by years of practice, had led me to distrust, instinctively, the essential shape, outline and content of any idea that was *not* written down.

I read my list when it was done and felt some satisfaction. I would, as I had promised, lead a thousand cavalry into Vortigern's territories in the coming year. Before that, however, I would dispatch messengers to inform Vortigern that I would be delayed until midsummer, since I first must ride southward to meet and greet our old friend Bishop Germanus and bring him safely to Verulamium again. Should Vortigern come south to Verulamium for the occasion, I would lead my people back to Northumbria with him. In the meantime, I would have had a space of months in which to assess what dangers threatened Camulod from the Weald and the regions that surrounded it, and to impress the resident invaders there with the strength and power of our cavalry and our willingness and readiness to go to war against anyone who thought to abuse our peace. By the time I arrived back in Camulod from Vortigern's domain, it would be autumn again and Arthur's Cambrian sojourn would be at an end. He would then be of age to take up a full command as a captain and commander of the Forces of Camulod.

I had attempted, in drawing up my list of decisions, to define the impediments to success I could identify, but there were none of any importance. Ironhair had suffered a resounding defeat, on land and sea, and Cambria was now safely in the hands of Huw Strongarm. Huw's presence, aided by Connor's vastly increased naval strength with his two captured biremes, would, I believed, prove strong enough to deter Ironhair, and with him Carthac, from any quickly renewed attempt at conquest of the Pendragon. Similarly, Horsa's newly launched colonization of the Weald would remove the threat of war from Northumbria and the north in general.

Only in the far south-west, in Ironhair's Cornwall, could I see any threat of unrest, and there was nothing I could do about that, outside of sending my own spies into Ironhair's lands to discover what was happening there. I resolved to do that as soon as possible, after consulting with my brother and our senior strategists. In the meantime, I would write to Germanus, in care of Enos, and also to Vortigern.

Thus resolved, I set out to look for my brother, to share my thoughts with him.

XIII

I AROSE EARLIER my second day home, but dawn was already bright in the sky and Tress was absent from my bed again. I made my way downstairs, my head still full of sleep, and found my way to the bathhouse, but judging by the evidence of water splashed about, she had already been there and gone. Some time later, fully dressed and hungry, I entered the Villa's kitchen to break my fast and learned from Plato that my lady had made her way up to the fort to join Shelagh, as she had the previous day. Curious now as to what these two might be about so early in the day, I asked Plato to have my horse brought to the main entrance, and when I had eaten I went directly up to the fort to find them.

I had another mission that morning as well. I needed to go to the stables and talk to one of our masters of horse about selecting a new mount to replace my faithful Germanicus. My requirements were simple: the horse merely needed to be physically large enough to bear my weight. I would have preferred it to be a black, but I was prepared to accept anything I could find, for the time being. The loss of Germanicus was yet too fresh for me to relish the thought of having to replace him with another mount of which I might become fond.

Although the morning sun was now high in the sky, it had not yet penetrated the open doors; the stables were still dark and cool, illuminated by flickering lamps set into mortared sconces over wide bowls that would catch any falling sparks before they could ignite the straw that lay piled on the floors. I rode directly in through the large double doors, to be surrounded immediately by the thick, living smell of the place. Nothing else in the world smells like a horse barn. I breathed deeply and looked about me before dismounting, searching for the groom who ought to be on duty, since the stables were never to be left untended. On this occasion, however, I was alone in the huge building, save for the animals, more than three score of them, in their stalls.

I tied my reins around a post, intending to return and unsaddle the animal and brush him down once I had looked at the horses at the far end of the barn, where single stalls housed the aristocrats of our equine population. The stables had been swept very recently, the streaks of broom sweeps still clearly visible on the hard-packed floor, and a fresh pile of

straw had been brought in but not yet spread. Clean as the floor was, I
picked my way carefully as I walked, attempting to keep my fine new boots
dry. There were twelve single stalls, but I went no farther than the first
of them, where I found a high and noble head craning high above mine,
looking down at me. My first impression was of tremendous height, and
then of jet black ears twitching and pointing downwards, the space between them filled with a stiff, high-standing mane. And then I saw the
eyes.

Hardly daring to believe that such a horse could be here, in these
stalls, I moved forward and opened the gate. He backed up nervously,
tossing his head and whuffling through his great nostrils as I approached.
When I was face to face with him I stopped, looking up, and then
stretched out my hand. He hesitated there for a count of three heartbeats,
then gently dipped his head and stretched his neck to investigate my hand
with his soft muzzle. I felt immediate regret that I had brought no gift
for him, but I contented myself with stroking his muzzle silently and
simply looking at him, or at as much of him as I could see. He seemed
coal black, but so was the interior of the stall. He made no effort to
withdraw from me, and finally I hooked my fingers into the plain rope
halter that he wore and led him, first out into the central aisle of the barn
and then out into the full light of the morning, where I could examine
him properly.

He was magnificent, taller at the shoulder and more heavily muscled
than even Germanicus had been, and a lump swelled in my throat as I
looked at him, at the way the light made his glossy coat shimmer like
black water. His mane and tail were long and clean, and great feathery
leggings grew down over his fetlocks, almost concealing his hoofs completely. His back was straight and broad and the muscles of his chest
rippled as he moved, backing up, away from me. There was not a blemish
on his entire coat; he was black from the tips of his ears to the polished
black horn of his hooves.

"His name is Bucephalus." I swung about at the unexpected sound
of the voice so close behind me. Shelagh and Tress were watching me
from the doorway of the stables, and so astonished was I to see them
there that it did not occur to me to ask them how they came to be there.
Instead, I turned back immediately to the horse.

"Whose is he?"

I heard Tress laugh. "He's yours, of course." By the time I had
whipped my head around to look at her, all trace of laughter had faded
from her face and voice. "We did not expect Germanicus to die, any
more than you did, but Ambrose had this colt set aside for you four years
ago, before he was even a year old, and had him raised in secrecy. Germanicus was beginning to grow old, and Ambrose foresaw the day when
he would no longer be strong enough to carry you . . ."

Shelagh took up where she had left off. "Donuil told me about Germanicus as soon as he arrived, and so we had Bucephalus here brought in yesterday from the farm where he was raised."

I smiled at Shelagh, thanking her wordlessly, and then turned back to the horse. "He's been well broken, I can see that. There's no fear in him, no skittishness. Who trained him, do you know?"

"I did." Shelagh's statement, and the casual way she said it, brought me around on my heel to gape at her, but she ignored my surprise completely. "And there's coltishness in him to spare. He's a wild one, but he has a sweet disposition once he has given his trust." She smiled at me, no more than a trace of mockery in her eyes. "Much like you, in fact."

I was still gaping. "You broke him by yourself?"

"No, not by myself, not all alone. I worked with the master of horse. But I was first up on his back and I was first to ride him. He taught me all his tricks; I taught him mine."

"I see." I could tell from the colour in her cheeks that Shelagh was proud of her achievement in this, and justifiably so. I glanced at Tress. "And did you name him, too? Bucephalus?"

"Not I! Yon's a foreign name from foreign parts. I had nothing to do with it."

"I believe you, Shelagh," I told her, grinning widely. "But d'you know who Bucephalus was, the first Bucephalus?"

"Aye, the horse of some Outland king."

"Emperor, Shelagh, he was more than a mere king. He was the greatest warrior of all the ancient world, before the time of Rome. Alexander of Macedon. Men called him Alexander the Great, and his horse was Bucephalus."

"Aye, I've heard. And it threw him over a cliff, did it not, and killed him? Bad omen for a king who would ride this one. It was your brother Ambrose who named him."

"Ah, Ambrose again. Then I had best thank him soon, for he has made me a fine gift, here. The name is wrong, nevertheless, and we'll change it now. Bucephalus was white, as I recall. This fellow's name is Germanicus. The ninth Germanicus to serve Britannicus."

Tress had moved forward to stand beside me, and as I placed my arm over her shoulders I became aware for the first time of how strangely she was dressed. I had grown used to seeing Shelagh in men's riding clothes over the years, but now I realized that beneath her long, concealing cloak, Tressa was also wearing some form of armour. I brought her around in front of me and pulled apart the edges of her cloak, staring in amazement at the toughened leather cuirass she was wearing over a short, military kilt of armoured straps. Her long legs were breech-clad like a trooper's, albeit in far finer leather and far more richly worked, very much like my own.

By the time I raised my eyes from her legs to her face, she had blushed crimson. I looked from her to Shelagh.

Tress could see the confusion in my eyes, and it was then that she and Shelagh told me how they had passed their time while I was away at war. Shelagh had taught Tress to ride, and had taught her well, training her strictly and with little gentleness, ignoring the fact that Tress was female just as single-mindedly as she denied her own femininity in the performance of men's activities. For months, they told me, Tress had been up at dawn and out to the stables with Shelagh, learning first the use and care of her saddlery before graduating to groom and saddle her own horse. And then, once she had mastered the art of staying in the saddle, she had learned to ride as a man rides, sometimes spending entire days in the saddle, accustoming her muscles to the disciplines of riding and controlling horseflesh, and inuring herself to the pain of saddle sores and cramping, aching leg, thigh, back and belly muscles.

Listening to Tressa's enthusiasm, and admiring the high colour in her cheeks and the way her eyes danced with delight as she described what she had learned, I realized that here was the explanation of the fleeting thought that had occurred to me when I had bedded her, my first night home. She *was* harder, her muscles firm and full and clearly visible, her entire shape slightly less voluptuously rounded, although no less womanly or desirable.

Not only had Tress learned to ride, she had learned how to use a short-sword, our new, light cavalry spear and a bow. The latter, with a full quiver of arrows, now hung from her saddle horn, she told me, and the sword hung from her right side. She was no cavalry trooper, but Shelagh assured me Tress knew how to use both weapons and could defend herself in any situation. They now passed their free time together every day, riding the length and breadth of Camulod's holdings.

I listened in silence to all they had to tell me, and when they were finished, I reached out my hands to Tress. She had been eyeing me nervously, wondering how I would respond, and I set her mind at ease immediately by asking her to show me how she rode. Both women immediately re-entered the stables and I followed them in to find them leading their mounts, already saddled, from the stalls in which they had hidden themselves from me.

Shelagh's mount was her favourite of years, a large, well-made, dun-coloured gelding of no great physical beauty but of great stamina and willingness. Tressa's mount was chestnut coloured, and larger, too, than I would have expected. She held him confidently by the strap of his bridle as she brought him out, and then she caught the saddle horn in her right hand, raised her foot into the stirrup, hopped twice and swung herself up into the saddle effortlessly, finding the other stirrup with her right foot and standing on straight legs to arrange her cloak comfortably behind her. I laughed in delight and brought my arm across my chest in a punctilious salute to such prowess before asking them, out of mere curiosity, where they were bound that morning. They had no idea, Shelagh said. They would head out northwards, at first, towards the old Villa Varo, our closest neighbour, but then they might cut eastward towards the Colony's main horse farm, which lay along the route towards the Mendip Hills, where Publius Varrus had found his skystone.

My immediate reaction was one of concern, occasioned more than anything else by simple fear for two women riding alone. These were not two mere women, however; Shelagh was a warrior, and her word regarding Tressa's own prowess was sufficient warranty for me that Tress could look after herself should the need arise. Nevertheless, I wanted to tell them to be careful, but I mentally bit my tongue rather than offer what might be construed as a patronizing comment.

"You always ride armoured?" I asked, instead.

"Of course," Shelagh said, somewhat scornfully. "What else would you expect? It's the law. And we have helmets on our saddles. To unknown eyes out there we appear as men. I'm sure you would not tolerate our riding out otherwise."

I had to meet with Ambrose, I told them, but afterwards, were Ambrose so inclined, he and Donuil and I might ride after them, purely for pleasure, mine being the pleasure of acquainting myself with my new mount. They agreed, and left me standing there with my new horse, fighting the temptation to saddle him immediately and follow them and leave Ambrose to wonder what had befallen me. But good sense won out over wishfulness, and I led him back into his stall before unsaddling the horse that had brought me up here to find him.

That one unexpected encounter marked the beginning of a brief and idyllic period of months during which I came to see Tressa through new eyes, and the love we shared grew stronger and deeper in the warmth of the true friendship we discovered as we rode together every day. I marvelled daily, too, at the unexpected skills she possessed. She rode like a centaur, fully as well as Shelagh, whose riding skills were legendary among our troopers, and she handled the long, light spear of our Camulodian troopers as though it were an extension of her own arm, effortlessly picking up targets from the ground with her spear point at full gallop, to the mock despair of our own troopers, few of whom could match her skill. She was even more impressive with her light bow, seldom failing to place five out of six arrows in the central target ring from fifty and eighty paces. Only beyond a hundred paces did her accuracy falter, and that was due more to the fault of her light weapon than to any lack of skill in her marksmanship. Even from horseback, sitting in the saddle and turned sideways, Tress could hit the mark four times in six. I was more than impressed.

It was only with the short-sword that she showed womanly weakness. Her arm muscles lacked the hewing strength required for real sword work. I told myself that she would never need to use a sword, but nonetheless I replaced her old *gladium* with a shorter, double-edged dagger that would be easier to handle, and even more effective than her clumsy sword should she ever need to perform such deadly, close work.

Arthur left for Cambria with Llewellyn within the first week following our arrival, but before he did, he stood as witness, with Ambrose, to our marriage, presided over and sanctified by Bishop Enos before his own departure. It was a very quiet ceremony, private and dignified but filled, nonetheless, with delight and the love and admiration of our friends. Our nuptial celebrations lasted but one day, and then our guests departed and our life as man and wife began, stretching out ahead of us as life had never done before. We settled into a new dimension of happiness, aided by the fact that everything was progressing smoothly in our holdings, without grief or trauma.

With no urgent concerns pressing us into action, we fell into a habit that was pleasant and beneficial for us and for all our associates. A party of us, consisting usually of myself and Tress and Donuil and Shelagh, with various others providing the pleasure of their company from time to time, took to riding out on patrols to visit each of the ancillary garrison communities that were springing up like mushrooms outside the formal boundaries of Camulod and lining the roads to the north, south and east. The *idea* of this resurrection had spread like spring fires in dead grass, and each of the communities we visited was caught in the grip of an ever-widening excitement. Their people laboured daily to construct enough new holdings to meet the demands of the newcomers who were now flocking towards them from all around the countryside. Organized bands of brigands and would-be looters who descended on several of the new communities found themselves repulsed, savagely and with implacably ruthless determination, by a new phenomenon: a populace that had suddenly found itself blessed with the power of self-defence, the confidence of righteousness and the certain knowledge of support from outside forces. No lawless rabble could survive in the face of such determined unity; those who attempted to invade the new communities were killed in the attempt, or hanged after its failure, their bodies left to swing in the wind outside the towns and camps.

Long-disused fields were being re-broken to the plough everywhere we looked, and new land was being cleared, the trees cut down and sawn into logs to be used as building materials and the stumps uprooted to provide new crop land. Houses, most of them of raw logs, were springing up, too, and we saw potters, weavers, tanners, cobblers, smiths and coopers establishing new enterprises far and wide, their equipment temporarily housed beneath hastily raised roofs, frequently left open to the weather because there was no time to waste on building walls. No matter where we went, during those months, the smell of new-cut wood and sawdust hung in the air, like the tang of distant smoke. And in every community, there was military activity all day long, as new arrivals of fighting age trained eagerly beneath the stern gaze of veteran troopers from Camulod, temporarily residing there for that purpose.

After long decades of anarchy and fear, the people everywhere around us were coming together again, determined to protect themselves for ever more against the ravages they had experienced since the departure of the legions. There was a new and vibrant spirit of hope and resurgence every-where. It was impossible not to be aware of it as the warm autumn days turned the entire countryside into a tapestry of reds and golds, ripening the crops to perfection and permitting a bountiful harvest even from the fields that had been but recently planted. For the first time in longer than I could remember, musicians, mummers and tumblers emerged among the populace and long, golden afternoons were frequently, and always surprisingly, enlivened by the sounds of music carrying from long distances through the calm, clear air. When the word went out that there would be an entertainment, the gathering was always attended by more people than anyone could have imagined, the women and children in their bright-est, most festive clothes and the men laughing boisterously as they clus-tered around the drinking booths, exchanging small talk and growing ever more expansive as they enjoyed the almost forgotten sensations of ease and safety.

It was true, as Ambrose once remarked to me, that there seemed to be soldiers everywhere, but we rejoiced in the knowledge that these were of the finest kind: local men, family men whose soldierly demeanour was born of determination and resolve to see their families flourish and grow in peace and prosperity. Such men were seldom, if ever, undisciplined or unruly. They were prepared to fight for what they cherished, but they were equally prepared to enjoy the benefits of their regimented presence and their vigilance.

Winter announced itself that year with a sprinkling of snow late in December, then relented and withdrew again as it had the previous year, so that the greying skies did no more than scatter gentle rains from time to time. We had no winter storms that year, no gales, no howling winds at all. The bare branches of the trees were mostly still, and the grass remained green underfoot, so that we were able to continue our visits to our outlying friends without interruption. The traffic of commerce flowed smoothly all winter up and down the length of the great Roman north-south road, from Camulod north to Nero Appius's new colony of Appia close by Corinium, and south towards the new garrisons at Ilchester and the smaller outposts south of that, on the road to Isca. This road had become known as the Appian Way, after the greatest road in Italia, which led, as all roads did, to Rome. Because of the trust fostered in times past between the benevolent Appians and the leaders among the farmers around Corinium itself, the people of that area had begun to refurbish the original walls of the ancient Corinium camp, tentatively at the outset, but with growing confidence as the work progressed. With the ready assistance of the Appians, a rudimentary garrison soon moved in to occupy the newly reclaimed space. Once established, and with a council of elders appointed to maintain the common law, the population grew almost overnight, like a mushroom, and Corinium became a scheduled checkpoint on our regular patrols.

And then one morning Tress came to where I sat writing in a patch of sunlight and laid a little cup, filled with tiny white and blue and yellow flowers, on the table by my elbow. Spring had arrived; these blossoms were its first bright smile. And yet I sighed to look at them, for their mere presence marked the end of our lovely idyll. Spring, and the new year, meant I had to ride away again, this time eastwards to meet with Germanus, and I truly had no wish to go. Tressa asked me what was wrong, thinking that she might somehow have offended me, and so I told her what was in my mind. She was greatly surprised to hear that I had even considered leaving her behind in Camulod, and was so astounded at the very thought of it that she failed utterly to see my own astonishment that she might even have considered any possibility of accompanying me.

Our differing reactions created one of those dangerous moments when monstrous conflict can spring from the most innocent beginnings, and fortunately I was astute enough, for once, to recognize that. Instead of blurting out the rejection that had sprung to my lips, I bit down hard and waited, allowing Tress to speak without interruption, and forcing myself to really listen to what she had to say.

Unaware of the enormity of what she was suggesting, she informed me that she and Shelagh had decided their place was with us, no matter where we went, short only of riding into battle. Battle was for warriors, she conceded, and women had neither the training nor the strength for confronting male enemies in all-out, hand-to-hand warfare. This journey, however, could not be considered a war campaign. She was prepared to concede that we were riding out as a military force and would comport ourselves accordingly for the duration of the expedition, but she saw that, and Shelagh agreed with her, as being no impediment to their accompanying us. They dressed as men and rode as men and behaved as cavalrymen behave; they were skilled in the use of weapons and in the care of their mounts, and they expected no man to do for them what they could not do for themselves. They could contribute to the expedition in a number of ways, including hunting, foraging, standing guard and, if need be, treating minor wounds and injuries.

As she prattled on, presenting what seemed an unending succession of arguments against being barred from coming with us, I found I had to suppress a reluctant grin of admiration. All my objections melted away like snow in a warm wind, so that I had made a momentous decision even before she had finished speaking and long before I had said a single word to countervail her logic. Tress and Shelagh would come with us. Donuil, I knew, would find no fault in that. And I had no fear that others might disapprove. Shelagh and Tress were the only two female riders in the Colony whom our troopers would accept, since they did not ride as other women ride, daintily and aware at all times of their appearance.

When Tress had finished speaking and stood staring at me, wide-eyed and patently unsure of how I would react, I nodded and made a humming sound in my throat, then advised her to be packed and ready to go within the week. She gazed at me disbelievingly, then gasped aloud and kissed me hurriedly and fiercely before rushing off to share her tidings with Shelagh. As I watched her go, I wondered how she would have reacted had she but known the true reason for my accession to her wishes. The last time I had ridden off to Verulamium, and incidentally to meet Germanus of Auxerre, I had left a wife behind me, in the protective safety of my home, only to return and find her brutally murdered. This time my woman would be by my side day and night, and anyone who wished to threaten her or harm her would have to pass through me to do it.

Germanus arrived at the appointed meeting place around mid-morning on a glorious day in late spring. The three craft that bore his party made their way westward along the coast, with lookouts straining to see the signal we had agreed upon to direct them safely to where we waited. Behind me, ranged in disciplined, concentric ranks upon the sides of a small, natural amphitheatre among the rolling, shallow hills, my thousand men sat watching his advent. In truth, there were more than twelve hundred in our party, for a thousand troopers at large require much service and supply in the way of commissary wagons, quartermasters' stores, medical services and extra horses.

I cast my eyes over my assembled force one last time, then nodded to Dedalus to take command and made my way down towards the shore, where a crowd had already assembled to welcome the bishop's party. Behind me came Donuil, Philip, Falvo, Benedict and a dozen other troop commanders and, of course, Tress and Shelagh. I rode at the head, holding my own reins in my right hand and those of a riderless, pure-white gelding in my left. I did not know if Germanus still rode or not, but I hoped he would and had selected this mount especially for him.

Enos and his people had made their preparations thoroughly, for we had found that, all along the route east, following the Roman roads from Camulod to Sorviodunum and thence to Venta Belgarum, our arrival had been expected by the local people. From Venta, proceeding directly south-eastwards across country towards the coast some sixty miles away, our experience was quite remarkably similar. We were accompanied by an escort of brown-clad clerics, carrying staves and crosses, who were at pains to impress upon us that, despite our impressions to the contrary, we were moving now among God's own Christian flock, who bore us no ill will. And to our vast surprise, in apparent confirmation of that, we encountered no panic and no fear, either of our numbers or our presence, in the lands we crossed, despite the fact that most of the people we encountered were alien to us. This was the Saxon Shore we were traversing, and all its folk were Saxons.

Of course, we did encounter some hostility upon occasion as we progressed southward, but none of it was directed towards us. One particular event made a lasting impression upon me, and it was Dedalus who brought it home to me. He had been riding with the advance guard, and they had happened upon a raid in progress on a solitary farm far from any other signs of habitation. They had driven the raiders off in short order and without casualties among our men, and Ded had come straight to report to me on his return, finding me in my usual position at the head of our advance, in conversation with Benedict. Blunt as ever, Ded interrupted us.

"Here," he grunted, holding some form of weapon out to me. "What d'you make o' that?"

I examined it perfunctorily. "Looks like the poor cousin to mine," I said, hoisting the thing in my left hand and reaching with my right to lift the iron flail made by Uther Pendragon from its hook on the front of my saddle. Uther's flail, now mine, was an iron ball on a short, heavy chain, attached to a thick wooden handle. The weapon I now held in my left hand was similar, but differently made. Instead of an iron ball, its head was a heavy, almost spherical stone, wrapped in a network of hempen rope, each strand of it as thick as my little finger. The longitudinal strands, four of them, were plaited together then from the head of the thing to where they joined the handle, and the handle itself was completely encased in the plaiting, which had been cleverly and painstakingly wound back upon itself and interlaced, the ends of each strand hidden, with no sign of a knot anywhere. The entire weapon had then been steeped in some kind of hardening liquid or wax, to stiffen it and protect the fibre of the ropes. It was a deadly thing, flexible and lethal.

"That thing's no poor cousin to anything." Ded's response to my comment was scornful. "That's a work of art."

I looked at it again and could not find it in me to disagree with him.

"I suppose it is, but it's a weapon of stone and rope, Ded, whereas mine is good, solid iron."

"Precisely," he said. "That's why I brought it back. You remember the time we talked about how things had changed since the Romans left? You were bemoaning the fact that swords had become hard to find, because when the armies left, they took their armourers with them."

"Yes, I remember that."

"Well, then, here's the proof of it. Look at the work that's gone into that thing, simply to house a stone. That's a flail, Merlyn, made by someone who had seen the real thing, the iron flail, but couldn't find the means to make one for himself. That thing would smash your skull as thoroughly and quickly as an iron one would. Now look at this."

He reached into his saddle-bag and produced another weapon, this one far more crude. It was, or had been, a makeshift spear, a rusty dagger lashed with hardened rawhide to the end of a wooden pole. It had been broken off half an arm's length below the lashed dagger hilt. Once I had seen it, Ded tossed it contemptuously aside, where it disappeared among the long grass through which we were riding. "That's the kind of weaponry those whoresons had." Seeing my raised eyebrow, he hurried on. "We found a band of savages attacking a farm, about three miles ahead of where we are now. They might have been Saxons, but I doubt it. Plain bandits, is my guess. Thieves and killers. Killed four of them, drove the others off, about ten of them. But not one of them had a decent sword. Most only had knives and wooden clubs. That thing you're holding there was the best weapon in the bunch."

"Hmm. So what's your point?"

"My point? My point is that we may be the only force around today with any real weapons."

I grinned at him then, and Benedict joined in. "You could be right, Ded," I said. "But we won't throw all our swords away for a while, for fear you might, *might* be mistaken."

That scene recurred to me as I sat watching the crowd of more than a hundred waiting on the beach. They were mostly Saxons, too, though sprinkled here and there with the brown robes of clerics, and I could scarcely see a weapon of any size among them. They were Christians, of course, and recently converted, most of them, but that should not have robbed them of the will or of the capacity to defend themselves away from the safety of their homes. They had looked askance at us when we arrived the previous afternoon, but mildly, with more curiosity than hostility.

Now I looked more closely and confirmed my initial impression: I could see no weapons. I pulled my mount to a halt on the grass strip above the pebbly expanse that stretched down to the water's edge, smiling in wonder at the way these people craned their necks and strained to see, hoping to catch a glimpse of three small ships approaching, when simply by coming up to where we sat they could have seen everything with ease and then walked down to meet the incoming travellers when they stepped ashore.

There was not a single Celt among the assembly, and I noticed that simply because of their dress, which appeared drab and colourless to my eyes after years of living among the weltering colours of my volatile Celtic countrymen. All of the people there beneath me wore rough, homespun, monochrome garments, dull browns and lustreless greys. Nowhere was there a hint or a dash of colour, not even solid black or white, and I could see no pattern woven into their plain clothing.

Now, watching Germanus's little craft draw closer, I was glad I had been so insistent upon changing the place of his landing. He had planned to land at the old fort of Dubris, some fifty miles along the coast, where the high white cliffs of Britain's southern shore came closest to the mainland of Gaul across the Narrow Sea. I had demurred at that, claiming that too much danger lay in such a landfall, both for his party and for my own. He would be landing on an alien shore, trusting himself to strangers who *professed* to be Christian; I would be riding through an alien land to meet him, entrusting the safety of my men similarly to other men's assurances of goodwill. Furthermore, Dubris lay on the southern edge of the Weald, and any journeying to or from there must now entail crossing through Horsa's territories.

We agreed that his ship should veer westwards at Dubris, hugging the coastline until it reached the ruined fort at Anderita, the most westerly of the ancient forts of the Saxon Shore. He would then round the headland that thrust south-ward beyond Anderita and continue to cling to the coastline, this time heading north-westerly until the shoreline again pointed due west. Directly south of Londinium, and of Verulamium, which lay some eighty miles inland, we would be awaiting his arrival and would signal him to safety with the smoke from three large fires, two on the westerly side of his landing point and the third to the east of it.

The small fleet approached as close as it could to the shingled beach which, at low tide, appeared to stretch full half the way to Gaul. Then came a period of intense activity as tiny boats were lowered and men scrambled aboard them to be rowed ashore. Watching, it occurred to me to be grateful that the sea was calm, for the process that took half an hour might well have been impossible to attempt at all had the water been rougher. I watched the first three laden boats approach the strand and saw the people waiting there surge forward to greet the newcomers, and I held up my hand in a needless warning to my companions to wait where we were. We had travelled far to be here on this day, but we had ridden. The people there below us had all walked. Had we moved forward then, our advent would inevitably and unjustly have commandeered all attention and deprived those waiting afoot of any opportunity to greet the man they had come to welcome.

My eyes picked out Germanus immediately, but my heart surged into my throat when I saw the changes in him since we two had last met. Then, I had seen the former legate of Rome's armies, a stalwart, clean-shaven man in his fifties, strong and agile, thick in arm and leg, with cleanly muscled, vise-like thighs that could clutch a horse's wide back without effort. That Germanus of Auxerre had been a general who had chosen to become a man of God. The man I beheld now, albeit from a distance, was a man of God who bore no resemblance to a soldier. And he was an old man, with a flowing, snow-white beard. He saw me and raised a hand in greeting. I waved back, but made no move to approach, content to allow him to conclude his greetings to his friends and followers, every one of whom genuflected and kissed the hand he extended to them. Some few embraced him after that, when they had straightened up again, but most simply moved aside to make way for someone else.

Behind me, a horse whinnied and stamped noisily, apparently stung by some insect, for there was a scuffling surge of movement as several people reined their horses aside and fought to bring them back under control. I kept my eyes on Germanus, my mind racing back over the years. It had been the summer of 429 when we last met, the year Cassandra was killed. Two years later, in 431, Arthur had been born, and he was now sixteen, so eighteen years had passed. Germanus must now be close to seventy, and ruefully, I reflected that I myself, who had been under thirty then, was now forty-six.

"Will you go down to him?" Tress had moved forward to flank me on my right.

"Soon, now. He knows we're here. He'll let us know when he is ready."

As I spoke, the activity centered around Germanus died away as others in his party now bore the brunt of greetings, and for several moments the bishop stood alone. Some other cleric approached him then, wishing to speak, but Germanus waved him away and looked up to us on the crest above. His face broke into a smile as he raised a hand to wave us forward. I eased Germanicus forward down the sloping beach, but he was skittish on the pebbly surface, so quickly dismounted and left him there, ground-tethered, alongside the white gelding, as I strode down towards my old friend. I dropped to one knee, extending my hand to take and kiss his in the offering of Christian peace. He allowed me to do so, but then he pulled me to my feet and embraced me as a dear and long-unseen friend, surprising me with his strength. Briefly then I introduced him to my companions, and then to the other officers, introducing each by his rank. Germanus greeted them with gentle pleasure, finding a different word or two for each and thanking all of us for the trouble we had undertaken on his behalf.

Behind us, farther down towards the water, the orgy of greetings and salutations had died down and the entire crowd had quieted to form a silent, semicircular audience, watching what was transpiring between us and their leader. Germanus turned to face them, raising his voice and his arms at the same time to capture their attention before he realized that everyone was already staring at him, waiting for his words. He lowered his arms immediately.

"Dear friends, it heartens me to know that by these signs and portents, God is indicating His pleasure in the rightness of the scared cause that brings us here to Britain. He has sent perfect weather to accompany us on our journey across the sea and to ensure that we arrived on the appointed day to find all of you waiting here to greet us. Most of all, however, He has seen fit to reunite me with my friend here, Caius Britannicus, who saved our lives when first we came to Britain almost two decades ago, escorting us to Verulamium, and has now returned to escort us once again, although this time in vastly greater strength and at our invitation.

"You will meet him and his friends, all of you, in the time ahead, for the road to Verulamium is long and might well have been beset with perils, had our friends from Camulod not come to see us there in safety. For the time being, our escort sits above, full-armoured, in the sun, awaiting our passage. It would be uncharitable to cause them to remain there in discomfort longer than they must. So please, let us move onward for a space." He paused and glanced at me. "How far? Where will we camp tonight?"

"Close by. Less than a mile from here. It seemed to me good sense that you would wish to rest at least one day after your crossing, so we have made arrangements to set out tomorrow, and by the time we reach the encampment, our commissary should have a welcoming meal prepared for you. For everyone, including those who came to meet you. Think of it as a reward for coming so promptly. My men think of it that way, for they never receive a hot meat meal in the middle of the day, except upon the most effulgent of occasions!"

"Wonderful." He passed on this information to his people and then beckoned with his arms, inviting them all to move forward. As he did so, I looked more closely at what he was wearing and saw that his long robe was split vertically from the waist, and that beneath it he wore leather breeches and serviceable, highly polished leather boots. As he turned back to me I grinned at him and took hold of his left elbow, prompting him to walk with me.

"I'm glad to see you still garbed as a rider, Bishop. You wrote to me once that you had not ridden a horse in years."

"I did, and promptly realized that I had shown ingratitude to God, committing the sin of pride by presenting myself as too busy with His affairs to take time for His pleasures. I set out to rectify that immediately and had reconditioned myself to the saddle before you ever read that letter. I have been riding ever since. Have you a horse for me?" He was leaning into the slope of the beach as we moved upward.

I laughed. "Aye, Legate Bishop, I have. But it is saddled, with stirrups. Can you ride thus?"

He stopped walking for a moment and laughed back at me, very slightly short of breath from the effort of walking on the pebbles. "Need you ask? Bear in mind, if you will, that the first stirrups that you ever saw crossed from Gaul into Britain. You adapted them then, and once having seen your stirrups and the power they bestow, how could any Gallic rider fail to copy them? One of my brethren made drawings of your saddles before we left Verulamium, and from those the remaining details, the making of them was simple to achieve. So yes, I ride the way you do."

"Alleluia," I responded, and he looked at me sharply, his head tilting to one side.

"Ah, so you've heard of that, have you? Does it vex you?"

"The Alleluia Victory? How could it vex me, Bishop? I was there, don't you recall?" I was smiling as I spoke, and he brightened visibly. I nodded towards the white gelding.

"Will that suit your purposes?"

His eyebrows shot up as he looked at the magnificent beast. "How could it fail to? But I am a bishop, Merlyn, and this is a horse fit to bear a king. Could you not find a lesser animal for me?"

"I could indeed, but aren't you being proud again? This one came straight to meet me when I went looking for a mount for you." I hesitated for a moment, and then went on impulsively. "He even matches you in colour, mane to beard. Here, let me help you up."

Germanus laughed again, heartily, then leaned a hand on my shoulder and placed his left foot in my cupped hands. I straightened my knees and raised his foot to the level of the stirrups, where he swung his right leg across the horse's back.

"His name's Pegasus," I said. "No wings, I fear, but the correct colour, and he's swift, but gentle." I went to Germanicus and swung myself up onto his back, seeing that Tress was already mounted and moving ahead of us to where our troopers sat. When I turned to Germanus, he was sitting erect, gazing at the lines in admiration.

"Magnificent, Merlyn, quite magnificent. Rome never saw the equal of these." He paused, his very seat indicating that the military man was reincarnate in him now. "May I inspect them?"

"That would be an honour, Bishop, but one they have earned. Yes, that would please them, and me, greatly."

"So be it. Ride with me."

Thus, for the next half of an hour, the troopers of Camulod stood to be reviewed and inspected by a legate of Rome.

When it was over, and the troops had been dismissed to return to the encampment, I rode knee to knee with my visitor, explaining to him that we had brought comfortable wagons with us, fitted with padded benches so that he and his bishops could ride to Verulamium in comfort, rather than walking as they had on the previous occasion. We spoke of many things on that short ride, but we were close beset with people all around and I knew that I would have to wait some time before I might have an opportunity to discuss with him the things that were most prominent in my mind. So it was with great relief that I heard him say, just as we rode into camp, that he was looking forward to spending time alone with me, away from the duties of his bishopric and his current mission, and that he would set aside some time to speak with me the following day, once we had completed the first leg of our journey to the north.

Our camp was laid out, as it always was, in the fashion of the traditional Roman military encampments. For this occasion, however, with the feeding of close to fifteen hundred personnel, I had ordered the quartermaster cooks to set up a feeding area beyond the camp itself, and the smells of spit-roasted sheep and venison were carried on the gentle breeze to every corner of the camp. I led the way through the centre of the camp to my own quarters and those of my senior commanders. I had ordered three additional tents set up beside my own, for Germanus's use; the two tents flanking his own were commodious enough to house as many of his personal staff as he might choose to place there. I led him directly to his own tent and we dismounted, handing our reins to the troopers who were waiting there to take our mounts. As I turned to leave him, however, Germanus caught me by the wrist and held me there until the troopers had gone; then he cocked his head to look at me.

"Your officers, those whom you introduced to me. I can't recall their names, but they were tribunes, centurions and decurions. I found that strange."

"How so? Why should it be strange?"

"Those are Roman rankings."

"So? That is unimportant, Bishop. They are military titles."

"Call me Germanus when we are alone. Why Roman? You are not Roman, are you?"

"No, we're not, we're British, but our roots are Roman nonetheless."

"Hmm. What do you call your officers?"

I blinked at him. "Forgive me, but what do you mean, what do I call them? They're my officers, I call them by their names."

Germanus shook his head, smiling now. "No, you should forgive me for being so unclear. But the historian in me knows that no Roman tribune was a cavalry officer by birth and training. The same applies to the centuriate. They were infantry to a man. Decurions were cavalry, but *all* your officers are cavalry."

I was still confused. "So? What are you saying?"

Now he shrugged. "I suppose I am saying that, if you are determined to adhere to Romanness, then you should adhere strictly to that bent. The founding fathers gave their name to the Patrician order in Rome, and all others were Plebeians. Later, another order emerged, between Patricians and Plebeians, and to mark their rank, the state awarded them horses, fed from the public purse. Thus they became Equestrians, known to the world today as Knights. All of your men are equestrian, therefore your officers deserve the title of Equestrians. You should call them Knights, my friend, and find some way of distinguishing them in the eyes of other men, not merely your soldiers."

"Knights? You mean—" My mind was racing now, seeing a host of possibilities. "You mean we should found a new order of nobility? Within Camulod?"

"Why not? Perhaps not an order of nobility, per se—nobility is such an abstract word and all too frequently misleading—but certainly a new order of military excellence. From the appearance of your troops today, I would say Camulod has come of age sufficiently to honour its own in some such signal way. It was merely a thought, but it might be worth considering. It could provide incentive for your aspiring warriors."

"Aye, it could indeed. But how would we mark such an honour? We all have horses already, and the Colony looks after them."

"Who knows?" Germanus shrugged his shoulders. "No doubt something will come to you. As I say, it was a mere thought. Think on it further, my friend. God will guide you, of that I am sure. Ah, and on that thought He now guides me. Here comes Ludovic, my secretary and my personal cross to bear throughout this life. Pardon me, for I must speak with him before we take the time to eat."

I left him to the attentions of the corpulent, pink-faced cleric who came bustling over to claim him and went looking for Tress, my mind in a turmoil with the idea he had stirred up in me so quickly. I had to share it with someone, and she was first and foremost in my mind.

We talked about it while we ate, and Tress grew nearly as excited as I was, her nimble mind perceiving almost from the first the exciting possibilities that founding such an order might present, were we to approach it properly. By the end of that afternoon, when Germanus was deeply involved with his British bishops in a session that would last long into the night, I had mentioned the idea to all my closest associates. None of them, however—and I was saddened to note this—appeared to see in it the

potential that had screamed itself into my mind and Tressa's. Even Shelagh merely blinked her lovely, long-lashed eyes and said little. I covered
my disappointment and lowered the intensity of my enthusiasm, fearing
to embarrass any of them, but the idea would not lose its resonance.

That night I awoke long before dawn with a vision in my mind, a
vision that might well have been a dream. I saw Arthur, years older than
he was, holding Excalibur in front of him as he stood within a ring of
shining young men, all of them helmed and uniformly armoured and
gazing at him in love and admiration. I sat up in bed in the darkness and
concentrated upon what I had seen, drinking in the brightness and the
light that surrounded this assembly until it faded from my memory, and
then I lay back down and vainly tried to go back to sleep.

XIV

I WAS UP and abroad well before dawn the next morning, but by the time I emerged from my tent the business of breaking camp was already well in hand. Indeed, it had been the noises from the horse picket lines and the sounds of wagons being loaded that had driven me from my cot. I washed quickly in cold water at the communal ablutions area and foraged a cold breakfast for myself in the camp kitchens, then spent the next few hours touring the encampment, supervising the preparations for departure.

A strong, warm breeze sprang up out of the west soon after daylight and grew warmer as the sun climbed higher in the sky, so that by the time we set out, the small banners on our squadron leaders' spears were fluttering almost horizontally and our standard bearers were having difficulty with the great, square banners that proclaimed our identity: my own great silver bear, picked out on thick, black cloth, and the rampant dragon of Camulod, white on a field of red.

Our exodus seemed chaotic at first, since most of the throng who had gathered to welcome Germanus waited until we were ready to set forth, then fully half of them scattered to the winds to make their own ways homeward. By the time we had travelled half a mile, however, most of these travellers had disappeared from view and we were left alone, an arrow-straight, strong column moving northward at the pace of our slowest wagons, the heavy, wide-wheeled, mule-drawn vehicles that housed our commissary. Here, far from any road and travelling through a countryside of gently rolling, treeless hills, these wagons were our greatest strength, since they held our supplies, and also our greatest weakness, since they were vulnerable to every hillock and declivity they encountered. The ground was firm, however, and there were few boulders on the chalky, grass-covered terrain, so although the progress of the wagons was slow, they moved forward without difficulty, their wide, iron tyres leaving sharp-edged impressions in the shallow soil.

We carried our travelling rations in our saddle-bags and ate in our saddles at noon without pausing to rest, since our leisurely rate of travel posed no threat to our horses' stamina. Some time after that, perhaps an hour later, I smelled an elusive hint of smoke. Philip, who was riding at my side, detected it on the same gust of wind and identified it as grass smoke. I nodded, and we rode on, but the hint we had detected strengthened to an ever-present, growing stink, and soon the distances ahead of us were obscured in a drifting haze through which I saw Dedalus and Benedict cantering back towards us from their advance position with our foremost scouts.

The hills ahead, to the north and west of us, were all ablaze and burning fiercely, they reported, a blaze fanned and fed by the steady, constant western wind. They had approached the fire's leading edges, hoping to find them narrow and quickly passable, but the chalky subsoil yielded there to a deep layer of peaty roots and the fire was smouldering far beneath the surface, knee-deep in places, precluding any hope of dashing across the flames to safety. Access to the north was blocked, Dedalus said lugubriously, and we would have to swing right, towards the east, to circumvent the fires.

There was no point in complaining, and even less in growing angry. A single glance at Ded's condition—grimy, red-eyed and soot-stained—bore out the truth of his report. I issued orders to Philip to change the direction of our march and sent Ded and Benedict to pull our scouting parties back and away from the fires, matching our change of heading. Our train swung right immediately, heading directly east, and that pleased me not at all, although I kept my dissatisfaction to myself at the time. Directly ahead of us on this new course lay the Weald and Horsa's newly landed horde of Danes, and I had no wish to stir up that nest of wasps.

Our change of direction produced an immediate reaction among Germanus's retinue, and within a very short time the bishop himself came riding to join me at the head of our procession. We were expected to the north, he pointed out with some anxiety, and arrangements had been made for us to pass unmolested through the lands we would traverse, but no such measures had been put in place to the eastward. How far did I intend to deviate from our planned itinerary?

I explained that we would ride east until the wind changed and the fires to the north of us died out, and then we would skirt the edges of the burn until we could swing west again and regain our original route. He nodded his head in acceptance, but his frustration matched my own. Even were the fires to die immediately, direct access to the north would be denied us, since the blackened ground precluded any grazing for our horses. Our route lay now within the hands of God, in whom we must place our trust.

For the next four days we rode in a great, looping arc, headed generally east but tending to the north as much as possible. Armed scouting parties scoured the lands ahead of us in double strength, and every man in our main column was on the alert for trouble at all times. The winds died down during the night of the second day, and regular reports arrived from

Ded and Benedict about conditions north and west of where we were, so that by the morning of the fourth day we had descended from the uplands and were headed north-west again, through a landscape of saplings and dense brush. This route took us past surprisingly prosperous farms, carved from the bushy wilderness that formed the outer edge of a huge, forested area to the east of us. There were still no roads in this region, which had been of no use to the Romans, but there were signs of human habitation everywhere and wandering paths abounded, meandering from farm to tiny farm between the larger, impenetrable thickets.

All of the people hereabouts, Germanus informed me, were Anglians, many of whom had landed in these parts decades and even generations earlier and were now settled peacefully, working the land and providing for their numerous progeny. I sniffed and kept my wits about me, implicitly distrusting and disliking anyone who was neither Celt nor Roman-bred. I saw no signs of hostility among these folk, however, and I took note of the genuine warmth that seemed to exist between them and the bishops. I was relieved, too, when I realized that the sheer population density of these Anglians, the way they swarmed upon the land, was a form of protection for us in itself. Horsa's Danes would find no foothold here, for all the space was taken up.

On the afternoon of that fourth day, we finally intersected our original route and headed directly north again, and as the afternoon was growing late, the shadows lengthening from the setting sun, we reached a group of people who had evidently been awaiting us. As we approached them, a man and woman came forward to meet Germanus. Despite the fact that they were obviously Anglians, I was struck by the dignity and self-possessed authority that marked them. The man's name, Germanus told me, was Cuthric. I could see for myself, merely from his posture, his height and the way he comported himself, that he was some kind of leader among his people. He was a tall, upright man who held himself as though on permanent display, and he moved with an easy grace and a natural sense of dignity that set him apart from everyone around him. He was richly dressed, his clothes made of a heavy, dark-green fabric that seemed luxurious beside the plain, homespun garments of his fellow Anglians. Full-bearded, he seemed to flaunt a mane of thick, golden hair that hung down to broad shoulders that suggested their owner could hold his own against any challenge to his strength. The woman was clearly his wife, almost as tall as her consort, with the same thick, lustrous, golden tresses, and a single, draped robe of white, edged with the same dark green. She bore herself with such unconscious regality that there could be no question regarding to whom she belonged. Together, they presented a portrait of self-possession and close-knit probity.

Germanus's face was creased in an enormous, welcoming smile. "Pardon me, Merlyn," he murmured, then addressed the newcomers in their own tongue, rattling the incomprehensible gibberish off as though it were Latin. I gaped, never having heard him speak this language or suspected that he might be able to. Finally the bishop turned to me again, laying his hand on my forearm.

"Their names are Cuthric and Cayena," he began, and I took note of the woman's strange but lovely name. I bowed my head towards the two and smiled at them, murmuring something pleasant and meaningless, which Germanus translated into what sounded like an ode. He must have been eloquent indeed, because man and wife both looked at me and inclined their heads, as though in gratitude or deference.

"Cuthric has great power among the Anglian people," Germanus told me then. "He is not what we would call a king, because the Anglians themselves do not deal in kingships, but he is undoubtedly the paramount leader in these parts, revered for his wisdom and his gift of dispensing justice even-handedly. His correct title is *jarl*, but to call him a chief might be a better way of describing him, but he is also something of a . . ." He paused, searching for a word. "I was about to say a holy man, but that is inaccurate, in the context within which I was speaking. Holy man he may be, but he is a devout and exemplary Christian. The Latin term *magus* is closer to the mark."

I blinked, looking at Cuthric and then at Germanus. "A magus? You mean a magician? A sorcerer?"

"Of course not. Have I not said he is a devout Christian? He is a sage, a wise and learned man, steeped in the ancient traditions of his people, and as such they honour him greatly. Now he will accompany us northward and his presence—even more than your thousand—will ensure that we are not molested." His smile took any hint of insult from his last remark.

"Good, then, that pleases me. We need every helping hand stretched out to us until we are well clear of Horsa's threat. I'll leave you now, to tend to your new guests. I have matters enough to keep me occupied until you are ready to leave again."

I saluted Cuthric and the stately Cayena with a crisply military clenched fist raised to my left breast, and then swung my horse around and headed back towards my troops, who were looped in a long, loose formation about the farm. I stood them down and sat on the ground next to Tress, Shelagh and Donuil for the next half hour, exchanging pleasantries while Germanus conducted his affairs. When he reappeared, with the Anglian couple in tow, we found room for them in one of the passenger wagons, and shortly thereafter we were on our way again.

In the days that followed, I found myself in Cuthric's company frequently, for he was always close to Germanus, the two of them prattling away in whatever tongue it was they spoke together, although I must admit, in justice, that they never failed to abandon whatever they were discussing when I appeared, after which Germanus and I would speak in Latin while he translated for Cuthric's benefit.

I had two of the most important conversations of my life within the week that followed Cuthric's arrival, one of them carefully planned and much thought over in advance, the other purely spontaneous, and it has galled me for years that the second of them did not occur until that week was almost over. Had it occurred sooner, on the other hand, the first conversation, undoubtedly the more important of the two, would never have taken place at all.

I had expected to be able to spend some time alone with Germanus within the first few days of meeting him, but that was not to be. There was an endless traffic of clerics along our route, finding us as if by magic, no matter which way our path might wend. Those messengers, each of whom brought tidings of great or lesser gravity to the bishop's attention, demanded all of his time for the first period of days, the meetings sometimes lasting well into the night. Germanus told me that as he grew older he found less and less need for sleep, and after hearing the talk among our troopers, who often passed the time with him on the predawn watch, I believed him. Yet he was never out of sorts or sleepy looking when the new day dawned. Instead he was up and about, bright-eyed and cheerful, feeding himself and climbing into the stirrups like a much younger man.

A few days after we had settled back onto our northward route, on a late evening after the watchfires had burned past their first height, he called to me as I was passing by his tent on my way to my own, after a cursory patrol of our perimeter. I stuck my head in through the flaps and found him sitting at the folding table, talking with two of his bishops. He looked up with a smile.

"Do you think you could conjure a flask of mead tonight, my friend? We have almost finished here, and I am aware that I have spent no time with you since dragging you out here to meet with me. I know we both have much to discuss with each other."

I nodded to the other two bishops, then grinned at him. "Aye, I can find a flask or two, but what about food? Have you eaten today? No matter, I'll bring some bread and fresh-broiled meat, and we'll eat here. When should I come?"

Germanus looked at the other two and both men shrugged their shoulders and professed themselves well satisfied with what they had achieved.

"How quickly can you find the victuals?"

"Stay there, I'll be back directly."

I returned a short time later with two flasks of Shelagh's own mead, drawn from the enormous keg she had insisted on transporting with us in the commissary wagons. I crossed to the table and set the flasks down safely, then pull two horn cups from my scrip before unhooking the long sword that hung in its sheath between my shoulder-blades. I had forgotten I was wearing it. Now I placed it carefully in a corner of the tent, propping it in the angle of the leather walls.

"The food will be here shortly," I said over my shoulder.

I filled both cups and handed one to him, and we had barely raised them to our lips when three troopers came to the entrance of his tent, one carrying another folding table and the others each bearing an enormous wooden platter; one contained a mound of thick-sliced, succulent wild boar and a large jug of dark, red wine, and the other two loaves of fresh, crusty bread, a dish of boiled greens still steaming from the pot, a jar of olive oil and another of olives pickled in brine. Germanus marked my amazement and smiled, gesturing towards the delicacies and the wine jug. "I brought them for you, as a gift," he said. "I remember how much you enjoyed these olives in Verulamium, and how you said you had not seen or tasted their like in years."

"Nor have I seen them since," I said, with reverence in my voice.

His smile grew wider. "The wine is from our own vineyards in Gaul. I had my brethren deliver these things to your quartermaster, knowing he would hold them in trust for you. He evidently decided to broach the supplies tonight. We can but hope he did so in secrecy, for I brought merely enough for your own enjoyment."

We ate like kings that evening, enjoying the lack of urgency and the pleasure of renewing our friendship. We spoke of many things throughout the lengthy meal, and most of them were inconsequential, although we discussed the Cambrian campaign against Ironhair and Carthac and spoke at even greater length about the growth of the communities around Camulod and the resurgence of hope that was occurring there. By the end of the meal, when the last of the brine-pickled olives had been consumed and the few remaining drops of olive oil had been mopped up on soft, rich bread, little remained of the wild pig meat and even less of the full, rich, heavy wine.

Germanus slumped lower in his chair and belched delicately, covering his mouth with one hand. "You cannot know how good it feels, my friend, to eat to satiation for once. I seldom take the time to eat an entire meal nowadays, and when I do, it is rarely that I eat this well. Show me that sword of yours, will you?"

I rose and collected the sword from where it leaned in the corner, unsheathing it carefully before offering it to him hilt first. He held it straight-armed, horizontally in front of him, with greater ease than I would have thought possible, considering his age. He squinted along the blade to test its straightness, then tested the edge with the ball of his thumb, producing a hair-thin line of blood. "I barely touched the thing," he whispered.

"Aye, it's a sharp one."

"Miraculously so, some men might say." He was still peering closely at the weapon, now touching its broad crossguard with the fingers of his left hand. "I have never seen its match. Where did you find it? May I ask you that?"

"Aye, you may. Our master smith made it, in Camulod."

"Ah, but whence came the iron? It seems . . . different, somehow."

"It is. It's skystone metal." I saw from his face that he had no notion what I meant, and it might have been the excellent wine that prompted me, but I suddenly found myself telling him the story of Publius Varrus and his skystone. I tried to keep it brief, and I omitted any mention of Excalibur, but it is not a tale that lends itself to brevity, and by the time I had finished, it was growing dark within the tent. He sat silent, his eyes gleaming in the heavy shadows as he thought of what I had told him.

As I looked around the tent I saw the glimmer of a tiny, solitary votive candle in the farthest corner. "The light of learning," I murmured.

"What?"

"It's dark in here, quite suddenly, and I was recalling that you used to burn fine candles in profusion late at night."

"I still do, though not as profligately as I recall you did. Here, let's light some."

He pulled himself out of his chair and gave me back my sword, then crossed to where a makeshift curtain hung against one wall of the tent and pulled it back to reveal a long, low table ranked with candelabra. He then lit a taper from the single votive lamp and went about lighting the larger candles, almost a score of them, turning the tent's interior into a fantastical array of soft, yellow, dancing light. I sat and watched him, aware that the effects of his fine wine had worn off in the telling of my tale, and remembering that the mead I had poured for both of us hours earlier still sat upon the small table, virtually untouched. I rose and fetched the cups, handing his to him as he settled down again.

"So," he began immediately, "the statue that your uncle made sat unused for years before you thought of turning it into swords. What prompted you to try that?"

"Hmm?"

"What made you think, so suddenly and after such a long time, that this statue—this Lady of the Lake—might be induced to yield fine swords?" One corner of his mouth was twitching in a smile that his neatly trimmed beard did not quite conceal. "And bear in mind, if you please, that I am a bishop, consecrated to God's truth."

"I . . . Forgive me, Bishop, I don't follow you."

"Oh yes you do, you know exactly what I mean. There was another sword, wasn't there? Varrus made a sword from the statue. That is the only thing that would explain the difference in weight you spoke of at one point, and the pattern of this sword, which is unique, while you, who supposedly designed it, are no armourer. There are holes in your tale, Master Merlyn, although you do conceal them very well. I suspect you have a secret of some kind, but if it is indeed a secret, then say so and I'll ask no more questions."

I raised my horn cup to him in a wry salute. "To perspicacity," I said. "You miss but little, Bishop Germanus, and I salute you. I appreciate now why it should be you who was selected and appointed to come here and debate theological imponderables. You're right, of course. There is another sword, Excalibur, and you are the first person ever to have guessed at its existence."

He leaned forward, his eyes alive with interest. "There *is* another? Still extant? I had thought there was, once, but supposed it had been lost or stolen."

"No, it has lain hidden now for years. I am its guardian. It is the King's Sword."

"What king?"

"The High King of Britain. The *Riothamus*—Arthur Pendragon, I believe."

"Arthur? The boy who is your charge? Tell me of this, Merlyn. I smell a story here. What is so wonderful about this sword, this . . . what did you call it?"

"Excalibur. Its hilt was poured and cast in a mould, as was this one I have here. A solid mould." I saw his blank expression and a thought occurred to me, bringing me to my feet. "I've something in my tent that will show you what I mean. I'll be right back."

When I returned, I handed him the small white cube of fired clay that I used as a weight to anchor the small pile of documents and notes that my desk attracted daily. "Here. Break it apart," I told him. "It's made in two pieces." He did so, after only a moment of examination, and the brass apple it contained dropped into his hand. "It's solid brass. My Uncle Varrus made it, years ago, and I've carried it with me since his death, as a memento of his skills. Each half of the mould is a perfect replica of half the apple, as you can see now that it's open. He packed the mould with wax, then bound the halves together with strong wire, so that no air could enter. Then he poured molten metal, slowly, through that small hole at the top. The metal melted the wax, which escaped slowly through a series of tiny holes in the mould—slowly enough to ensure that the metal settled evenly and perfectly within the mould, leaving no air bubbles, since no air was present when the metal was poured. The result is a perfect, solid brass apple.

"The hilts of these swords were made the same way, but with the mould for the hilt constructed around the tang of the blade and the skeletal side bars of the guard. When the pour was complete, the molten metal had bonded perfectly to the sword's tang and guard and the entire hilt was flawless, one solid piece. That's where the name Excalibur came from: it means 'out of the mould.' "

Germanus sat silent for long moments, rubbing the surface of the apple with his thumb, then reached out again to take the sword and gaze at its hilt, fingering it in the same way. Finally he looked up at me. "I've never seen a finer sword, Merlyn, nor one so large and long. How much finer is Excalibur, that you must keep it hidden?"

I grimaced and shrugged my shoulders. "Excalibur makes this sword here look worthless, dull and lustreless. Excalibur's blade is so pure, it seems made of shining, burnished silver, dazzling to behold, and its very fabric contains lines of layered metal so fine that they form a pattern that shimmers like water, when held up to light. Its edge will cut a hair, yet is so strong that it will slice through other, lesser swords. This one will, too, but this lacks the spectacle Excalibur imparts to every swing. And where this guard is plain, Excalibur's is intricately wrought with Celtic scrollwork, and its hilt is bound in the rough belly-skin of a great shark, then tightly woven with both gold and silver wires, never to shift in the wielder's grip. Its pommel is a golden cockleshell, perfectly wrought in every detail to the size and shape of a real cockleshell found by Publius himself. The artist who created it, a priest called Andros, had a heavenly gift for artifice. Where this sword here is plainly fine, Excalibur is ornately dressed perfection."

"Hmm. And what does young Arthur think of this sword he will some day wield?"

"He doesn't know of its existence. I have not shown it to him."

I knew I had surprised him again, but he concealed it well, merely resting his right elbow on his left wrist while he raised his hand to twirl the hairs of his moustache reflectively. At length he sniffed and reached again for his cup, sipping a tiny amount of mead and rolling it around in his mouth, all the while deeply immersed in his thoughts.

"Tell me about the boy," he said, at length.

"What would you like to know?"

"Everything, but first about his right to be a king. Excalibur is the King's Sword, you said, Arthur's sword. Not *a* king's sword. Explain your thinking to me, and believe me when I say I do not ask this lightly."

I launched myself again into talk, explaining Arthur's lineage in full and relating every aspect of it to my own grandfather's vision of the future, the great dream he had shared with Publius Varrus and the other founders of our Colony. And once again Germanus listened intently, making no attempt to interrupt me.

When I finally fell silent, he leaned forward again. "So he has claims through both sides of his parentage to Cambria, to Eire, to Cornwall and to Camulod itself. That equates to all that remains of Roman Britain, save for the regions now occupied by your invaders. It is a huge territory, and if your anticipation of his destiny is accurate, it will be a terrifying responsibility. I know him, from his letters to me—and from the correspondence you and I have had concerning him—to be a serious young man, and dedicated to the tasks you have defined for him, but he is yet very young. So young, in fact, that I have to ask you again, face to face, is he capable of shouldering such a weight of responsibility? And do you think him worthy of such enormous trust?"

I nodded. "I believe he is, completely capable and completely worthy. He is an amazing young man. His entire way of life, his thinking and his behaviour, all reflect the integrity of his beliefs. Besides, he has been much exposed to Ambrose, and greatly influenced thereby. And Ambrose, as you know, does not flaunt his piety, he merely lives it . . . to such an extent that I believe he might have become one of your own bishops by now, had his destiny not brought him to Camulod and me. Enos certainly thinks that is so."

The old bishop nodded. "I know, he has told me so himself. And the boy thinks highly of Ambrose?"

"As of a god. Mind you, he thinks the same of me, and God knows I am neither devout nor pious. But his morality—his Christianity and his living of it—owes far more to the example set by Ambrose than to any tuition of mine."

I spoke for a time then about the boy's education and training, and the role that each of us in Camulod had played therein. Germanus listened attentively, even though little of what I said was new to him. But then I went on to speak of Arthur's own emerging philosophy—as if any boy of his young age could be said to have a philosophy. I talked about the lad's ideas on justice and on human dignity, citing his anger by the side of Lucanus's grave when he considered that the grave might be defiled by strangers in the years to come, with no one there to speak for Luke or to defend his resting place. This time, when I had finished speaking, Germanus stood up.

"Walk with me," he said. "We still have much to say on this, and it is late. Some cool night air will blow the cobwebs from our minds."

We made a circuit of the encampment together, and he did all the talking as we walked. He was greatly concerned, he told me, by the escalating ravages of the invading Saxons. The Anglians were becoming Christians at a pleasing rate and were, for the most part, willing settlers and strong providers for their families. The Saxons, on the other hand, were a different matter altogether, and they had declared war on God's Church and its missionaries. Increasingly frequent reports were reaching him, through his fellow bishops, of appalling and inhuman atrocities committed against Christian clerics: decapitations, mutilations and fiendish torture, prolonging agony for as long as possible before death intervened. Bishops and priests were being flayed alive, he said, the skin ripped and peeled from their bleeding flesh to expose their entire body's living muscle to the air. Some were then left that way, hanging by the wrists to die in excruciating torment, while others had been roasted alive over slow-burning fires. The people who could do such things were not God's children, he maintained, but animated creatures of evil, sent from the Pit by Lucifer himself to torment mankind. Even the apostate bishop Agricola, the man whom he had come to Britain to denounce, had written to warn him of the dangers of travelling by Britain's eastern coast.

As we walked the perimeter of the camp, acknowledging each guard in passing, I found myself becoming more and more depressed and despondent at the litany of unsuspected ills my friend was pouring into my ears. I had known that Britain was being ravaged, but I had not suspected half the evils that he had described, and I found myself wondering if we in Camulod were blessed or cursed by our isolation in the west. By the time we returned to the central area of dimly lighted tents, we were both walking in silence.

Inside the tent again, Germanus shrugged off his cloak, and I sat in my chair observing him.

"You paint a bleak picture, my old friend," I said.

He pursed his lips, looking me in the eye, then nodded, sharply. "Aye, it's bleak, but I have begun to think it is not entirely hopeless. This lad of yours, young Arthur Pendragon, might well be the salvation of us all."

At first I thought he was being facetious, but then I saw immediately that he was not. "You believe Arthur might be the salvation of us all *today*? That is ridiculous. How could you even think a thing like that? He's but a boy, barely sixteen!"

"He is a king, you said. *The* King. You named him as the possible *Riothamus*."

"Some day, perhaps, but not for years to come."

"No, next year. He'll be seventeen. Flavius Stilicho was seventeen when Theodosius sent him on embassies to foreign kings. At twenty-one, he ruled the armies of the whole Empire. He was my Imperator and your father's."

"But that was Stilicho, the greatest military mind since Alexander— greater than Gaius Marius, greater even than Julius Caesar! And he was favourite of the emperor, with all the patronage a man could ever want. Arthur Pendragon is a boy, unknown, and no one's favourite save mine. He'll be of age next year, and he will have his own command in Camulod, but he must learn to *exercise* command. Until he does, no warrior of note would follow him, a stripling boy. The very thought is ludicrous."

"Is it? And would it still be ludicrous if he were crowned by me, or by the highest bishops in this land, and named Protector of our Holy Mother Church? I swear to you, my friend, such patronage is worth more than an emperor's favour nowadays, when Rome's own emperors have vanished from the earth." I sat gaping at him, robbed of the ability to speak, and he smiled down at me. "I mean it, Merlyn. I am not speaking lightly."

"But how . . . why, in God's name, would you suggest such a thing?"

"Precisely for that reason: in God's Holy Name. You have answered your own question. God needs a champion today, Merlyn, to defend His people and His faith right here in Britain, and you have described that champion to me this night, in Arthur Pendragon. He will lead Camulod, by your own admission, and you could, if you so wished, arrange it so that he comes into power sooner, rather than later. Wait you! Hold your rejections. Think about all I have said tonight before you refuse to hear me.

"Britain is falling into darkness rapidly, in danger of being overrun by devils. The bishops who present the word of God to all His faithful are being slaughtered wherever they are found by these marauders. They know safety only in the north-east, where Vortigern holds power, in the south-east, where people such as Cuthric still rule, and in the west, in Camulod. Vortigern has problems with his Danish friends, but between them, they hold the Saxons to the south. And recently, you say, the Danes have moved into the Weald. If it is God's wish, they may combine with Cuthric to have the same effect. But in the west, where Camulod holds sway, there is no danger for our people or our Faith. And Camulod—Camulod's armies—are invincible. Nothing like them exists in Britain or elsewhere. Who rules those armies could, and should, rule Britain, providing that he be a man of simple faith and Godliness, of dignity and in-born nobility. Arthur Pendragon will be that man, I believe, for we will place him high upon a throne that all the land will see, and under his leadership and guidance all the folk of Britain will combine to throw these Saxons out and make this land once more a place where Christian folk may worship without fear."

Still I sat shaking my head, wordless and incapable of framing any of my thoughts. He turned away from me, crossing again to where my sword leaned against the wall. He came back and sat again across from me, holding it by its sheath.

"Do you recall my mention of a new order?"

"Aye," I responded, blinking. "Knights, an order of horsemen. I've been thinking about that."

"And what have you decided?"

"Nothing." I shook my head, wondering at this sudden change of topic. "It would need something . . . some means of achieving status, and

I have no idea what that might be. Simple possession of a horse is not enough. Every one of our troopers has a horse."

Germanus whipped the sword out of its sheath with a rasping sound and jammed the point of it hard into the ground, leaving it to sway gently back and forth. "There's your status!"

"How? What do you mean?"

"Look at it, man! Look at its shadow there, on the wall." He picked up a candelabrum so that its light threw the shadow of the sword onto the wall of the tent. "It's a cross! The symbol of our faith. We talked of symbolism once before, do you remember?"

"Aye, I do." The shadow of the sword, with its straight cross-guard, did look like a cross. "You said that every great popular movement required a recognizable symbol to stir the people."

"Good man, you do remember! Well, every order requires a symbol, too, and what could be a better symbol for a Christian fellowship than the Christ's own Cross? Let it be known that Arthur's most deserving followers may become Knights *once they have earned the right to enter the new order.* That earning must involve commitment, and a sacred oath to safeguard Mother Church and all her flock, from the most exalted to the humblest. Your Knights must become defenders of the Christian Faith itself, and when they do, they will have the blessing of the Church and the sworn right to wear the symbol of the Cross upon their armour. Can you see that now? Can you visualize it?"

"Aye, I can," I whispered, feeling my heart begin to hammer in my chest and recalling clearly my dream of several nights before. "The Cross, in red, upon their breasts."

"In red? Why not? The symbol of the Redeemer and the colour of the sacred blood He shed. On a field of white, for purity of soul and spiritual humility." Germanus seemed to have grown taller as he spoke, and his eyes were glowing with a huge excitement. "Do you think that concept might appeal to your young King?"

I nodded, feeling a slow grin widen on my face. "It would, it would indeed. It is an idea made for his beliefs . . . I need a drink."

I rose and filled my cup, looking at Germanus to see if he wished me to pour for him, too, but he was deep in thought. He was tossing the apple mould from hand to hand, relishing the weight of it each time it thumped solidly into his grasp. Then, as I sat down again, he looked across at me.

"A coronation," he whispered, almost to himself. "We must have a coronation." Again he fell silent, and I wondered what was going on within his mind. Moments later he was on his feet, pacing about the tent briskly enough to set the candle flames flickering.

"That would be perfect, Merlyn, think of it. A coronation, just as in the days of ancient Rome, when the greatest champions were honoured with the placing of a crown upon their brows, an honour that set them high above all other warriors. Arthur will be our crowned warrior, the Church's champion, Defender of the Holy Christian Faith, and all his men—his Knights—will be God's warriors, protecting Arthur's people and his lands. But the appointment must be public, and widely heralded, presented with great ceremony and high import in some distinguished place . . . in Verulamium, in the great theatre there! It holds full seven thousand people, seated.

"Visualize the scene, Merlyn. All the bishops of Britain will be assembled, to concelebrate a great, triumphal Mass. Arthur will enter there, escorted by his Knights, while his armies are spread around the town, protecting the proceedings. And after the consecration of the sacred Host, before the congregation is dismissed, I, or some other senior bishop, will place a golden circlet on his brows, the champion's corona, and proclaim him King, in the name of the Church. Think of the effect, Merlyn! None could dispute his kingship."

I grunted. "Vortigern might, for one."

Germanus threw me a look of pure disdain. "Vortigern has no cavalry, and no long swords like these. Besides, he has been less than zealous in his work on our behalf. Agricola and his heretical fellows thrive under his patronage. No, I believe Vortigern will accept the Pope's decree, if he has hopes of his immortal soul's salvation."

"The *Pope*'s decree?" I grinned at him, feeling better by the moment. "You know, my friend, you should have been an impresario. The world of public spectacles and entertainments would have been improved by your presence."

He did not react to my humour as I had expected, but spoke with gravity. "You mock me, but you should not. Appearances matter greatly in such things as these we are discussing. In order to create a great impression—and that is exactly what I intend to achieve—you must make it memorable. Spectacular proceedings foster awe, and reverence, and therefore memories. Colour we will use, and music and spectacle, and massive ceremony carried out with dignity and due solemnity. Remember Rome, and the imperial persecutions of our faith. Thousands of the faithful died in dreadful purges, but those most readily remembered died in the arena, torn apart by lions and wild tigers, trampled and gored by angry elephants for the enchantment of the Roman mobs. We will have spectacle at this, the coronation of our King, and people will remember it and talk of it forever. Mark my words."

He glanced down at the mould that lay on the table beside him, and reached to pick it up. "May I keep this, for now? I will return it." I nodded, and he tossed it in his hand, then broke it open once again and stared at the perfection of the half-apple that he could see. "When will you show Excalibur to Arthur?"

I shrugged, shaking my head. "I don't know. When he is ready, I suppose."

"And how will you know that?"

I scowled at him. "I have no idea, but I suspect you have. Am I correct?"

"Perhaps." He removed the apple from its mould and then replaced it carefully. "There is only one way to put this apple back . . ." I said nothing, and he pursed his lips thoughtfully. "I have an idea—yet unformed and incomplete, but fundamentally sound, I think. But it will entail keeping the boy in ignorance about the sword until the moment of his coronation. Is that feasible?"

"Of course it is feasible, but why must we keep him in ignorance?"

"Because I believe he must be as overawed as everyone else when we unveil it to the eyes of the world. If we are to present what will appear to be a miracle, then everyone involved—*everyone*—must see and *experience* the miracle."

I shook my head, suddenly feeling tired. "Now you have lost me. A miracle, you say? I know you are a man of God, Bishop, and I also know the power of your mind, but tell me, please, how you intend to pre-arrange a miracle."

He told me, and I could find no sleep for the remainder of that night.

XV

IT IS ALMOST impossibly difficult for me to write about the period that followed that discussion. I have spoken of the fact that I had two momentous conversations in the course of that one week, and I have written fluently about the first of those, recalling every word, every inflection of Germanus's voice with clarity and exactitude. But the memories that haunt me of the ensuing time are harsh and bitter; fragmentary, pain-filled images of grief and terror and despair and disbelief; images that withstand recall and defy description.

My old friend Dedalus, who had some training in the art of engineering, once told me a fundamental truth he said was known to every engineer. The occasion, I believe, was a discussion we were having about the way in which the army engineers had drained the mountain lake in which Publius Varrus had hoped to find his skystone. The lake had lain at the end of a mountain glen, formed by a dam of rock blasted from the mountainside itself in a cataclysm; they had examined the exposed side of the dam and then undermined it, cracking it open like a broken bowl. Using the example of the keystone found in every bridge's arch, Ded told me then that every construction, natural or man made, contained a central, focal point on which all its energies depended. Remove that point—that beam, or rock, or log—destroy it or dislodge it, and the entire construction would come crashing down in chaos and ruin.

The construction that I thought of as my life came crashing down after that second conversation, splintering in ruin and chaos on the hard floor of reality, and the disruptive force that brought it down was a human voice, speaking an alien tongue.

Briefly, we encountered a large force of Outlanders the day after I had talked so long with Germanus. Benedict brought the news of their arrival. He had been scouting with his forward force on our right flank, and one of his foremost outriders, riding beyond the limits of his own appointed sweep, had seen the enemy approaching. Had he been obedient to his orders and performing as commanded, he would have been elsewhere and would have missed them. As it was, he reported back to Benedict immediately.

From his concealed position, two miles ahead of us. Benedict watched and counted more than a thousand men, all of them afoot, moving in five divisions each perhaps two hundred strong. They had emerged from the forest in the east and crossed the valley bottom, headed directly towards us, moving steadily and in good order. Benedict waited to see no more, convinced that they knew where we were and were moving directly against us. He withdrew his scouts and rode back at full speed to report his findings. Between the enemy and us lay two wide valleys. The hillsides of the farther of these two were thick with trees; those of the nearer valley, atop which we now sat, were grass-covered, with not a tree in sight.

I made my dispositions quickly, I recall, thinking clearly and logically. A thousand-strong force must have been organized long since, and the odds were great that they had marched to intercept Germanus and his party and were unaware of our cavalry. A plan came fully formed into my mind, drawn from my memories of my grandfather's notes on the tactics of Alexander of Macedon. I quickly ordered a hundred of my men to dismount and present themselves as infantry, and sent the remainder of our forces out of sight on the far side of the hill. I then briefed Germanus quickly on how he should proceed.

He would descend into the valley at the head of a small, mounted party, riding towards the enemy in company with three wagons filled with another twenty of my men, all of them dressed as clerics. When confronted, my hundred would form a line and hold their position, waiting until the enemy attacked. The wagons and the riders would turn and flee, my "clerics" leaping out of their slow-moving vehicles, abandoning both them and their defending foot soldiers and tempting the enemy to attack. Then, at the first sign of an enemy advance, my hundred would fall back uphill, in formation, to break and run only when the hostile force was committed to a charge across the valley bottom and up the opposing hillside. At that point, with the enemy charging uphill, I would loose my cavalry to sweep around and down on either side.

Germanus listened as I outlined my strategy, and then smilingly asked if his men might shout Alleluia! I smiled in return, and then withdrew beyond the hilltop, where I made my final arrangements for the disposition of my cavalry in the coming fight, and assigned a strong escort to the safekeeping of Tress and Shelagh, here behind the brow of the intervening hill. I did not want either of them to witness the events that lay ahead and to my gratified surprise they acceded to my wishes without protest.

The clash was quickly over, and hardly worth the mention, save for the carnage that took place. The enemy fought bravely and showed more discipline than I had seen in any of our recent enemies in Cambria, holding their individual formations well, and even constructing defensive walls with their shields to stave off our attacks. The sheer weight and numbers of our horses were too much for them, however, and the shield walls buckled, then disintegrated. From that point on, they were in defeat and few of them escaped alive.

I moved among the banks and rows of their dead and wounded, and I noted that they were, as Dedalus had said they might be, very poorly armed. Few possessed swords: their most common weapon was the battle axe, and some of them had heavy spears. Most of them, however, were armed only with thick staves and daggers, and many had no more than heavy, crudely craved wooden clubs.

Many of the wounded might survive, I thought, could they but gain some medical attention, but that was not my concern. I had neither the time nor the desire to care for aliens. Germanus, however, refused to abandon them to death and set his bishops to go in among them, offering aid. Shamed by the sight, some of my own troopers, especially the medical personnel, began to lend assistance, too, and thus we passed the remainder of that fruitless day catering to our foes and spent the night uncomfortably in a makeshift camp high in the hills.

Two days later, close to Londinium, which Enos told me had lain abandoned now for nigh upon ten years, and less than two days' travel from our destination in Verulamium, the talk about the evening campfires was still of the cavalry charge and how we had mown down the Outlanders, whom someone had identified as Jutes. I was distempered and out of sorts, for I had slept but little for the previous two nights, disturbed by terrifying but ill-remembered dreams that startled me awake, time and again, drenched in clammy sweat and gasping in horror. My inability to recall what it was that had brought me screaming into wakefulness infuriated me because it frightened me deeply. I had spent a lifetime dreading dreams that eluded my recall, but I had dared to hope myself all done with that in recent years.

It was frustration born of those fears that made me impatient with such silly talk of victory that night, and I said something snappish about how fortunate we were that these had been mere Jutes and not Horsa's Danes. We had consumed our evening meal by then and were grouped around a fire. I was sitting beside Germanus with Tress on my left. Cuthric sat on the bishop's right, and on his right sat Cayena. Then came Dedalus, and Benedict, and I knew not who else, for the fire was high and fierce and concealed those people sitting across the circle from us.

I saw Cuthric raise his eyebrows at my words and then lean close to talk to Germanus, who answered him, listened again, then shrugged and turned to me.

"Cuthric heard you speak of Horsa and his Danes, and wondered how you know of him."

"I know he's there, and that's enough to know. Only now am I beginning to breathe freely, knowing that he and his horde lie far behind us. For the first few days, and in particular when we were headed directly east, I thought we might penetrate their new territory and encounter them at any time. We have women with us, and that thought did not appeal to me."

Germanus translated this for Cuthric and the big Anglian grunted in surprise and spoke again, looking this time at me. I waited for Germanus's translation.

"He says he is surprised that you should know of Horsa's presence in the Weald, but that the Danes are no longer there and your concerns were groundless. They remained there for a time, many boatloads of them, settling temporarily in several of the ancient Roman forts along the shore while they explored the land, looking for holdings they could seize. But then they left again, all of them, in a great fleet, nigh on a month ago."

"What? They went back to the north?" I was incredulous.

Again Germanus questioned Cuthric, but this time as the big man answered him I saw the bishop stiffen, and the blood drained from his face. "Dear God," he said, turning back to me, his voice gone slack with shock. "Cuthric says that Vortigern is dead." He swung back to face the Anglian and the conversation between the two became fast and filled with tension. I could hardly bear to listen without interrupting, but eventually the elderly bishop slumped and spoke to me again.

"It's true. He's dead, slain in battle by Horsa himself. The report was brought to Cuthric by one of his own elders, whose daughter fell enamoured of a Dane of Horsa's party, and the fellow boasted of his prowess in the fighting, and of how he had struck off the hand of the Northumbrian king, the hand that had dared to threaten Horsa. Cuthric has no idea who Vortigern is, or was, nor did he suspect that you or I could know of him. To Cuthric, he was but an unknown, faceless name who happened to be a king, far in the north. God rest his soul."

"Amen," I whispered. "Do you know, I heard my father say it would come to this, when I was just a boy. He knew, even then, that naught but harm could come from bringing Outlanders into this land to live." I heaved a sigh. "So Vortigern is gone. And so is Horsa, back to the north. He will be king in Northumbria now, I suppose."

"A Danish king, in Britain? I hope not."

"How does your Cuthric come to know so much about Horsa?"

The bishop shrugged his shoulders. "He shares a common interest with you, I suspect. Horsa and his Danes are a threat to the settled Anglians close by, to the north of them." He hesitated. "I wonder, though, how much he truly knows. He says the sky was black with Horsa's banners."

I frowned. "Why should that trouble you?"

"It rings false, somehow. The Saxons don't use banners, nor do the Anglians or Jutes. None of these people do."

"Horsa's a Dane, not a Saxon, Bishop, and he has lived his life observing Vortigern. Now *there* is a man who uses banners. His emblem is—damnation, was—the wolf's head. I can't believe he's dead. Anyway, Vortigern used his banners all the time, for spectacle's sake. You understand that, do you not?" He ignored my jibe, which was ill-timed, and I continued. "So you see, it's more than possible that Horsa has taken his example. Ask Cuthric what Horsa's banner was."

That took but a moment. "He says it's a bear, not unlike yours, save that Horsa's bear is black, while yours is silver. Every one of his ships' crews has a black bear banner, but the markings on the individual banners vary."

He turned back to talk to Cuthric again, and I watched the expressions on the faces grouped around the fire as the word spread of Vortigern's death. I was talking to Tress about it when I felt the bishop's hand on my arm. He was still deep in conversation with Cuthric, but I knew he had something he wanted me to hear. Finally he turned back to face me, his eyes troubled.

"Horsa returned to the Weald, nigh on a month ago, as Cuthric said earlier. He summoned his warriors, spent a week collecting them, then sailed away again. But less than one third of the total fleet sailed north again, with Horsa. The major portion sailed south, commanded by a senior captain."

I felt an instant chill of premonition. "South? There's nothing to the south except the Narrow Sea. You think they crossed to Gaul, without Horsa?"

"I doubt it." Again he swung away, towards Cuthric, and I leaned towards them, listening closely to the rattle of the alien language that sounded guttural and hoarse to my ears. They seemed to speak for hours, this time, but among the gibberish I suddenly heard the first word I had ever recognized upon the Anglian's lips, and it was Ironhair.

By the time Germanus had swung around to look at me I was already on my feet, the blood roaring in my ears and my body reeling from the crashing understanding that had flooded me. Ironhair! I had no need to hear another word than that accursed name to understand what had happened. Ironhair, the great collector of allies, pirates and mercenaries, had not been in Cambria when we went searching for him. He had been away, no one knew where, while in the meantime his armies had searched for Dolaucothi and its gold mines! I cursed myself because I knew at that moment what I should have known long before, because the information had been given to me by the man himself. His emissary, the man called Retorix, had suggested that I might choose to make peace with Ironhair, in order to have the time to assist my ally Vortigern in dealing with the Saxon problem in the far north-east. He had *told* me he knew about Horsa's Danes! How blind a fool could a man be? I should have known instantly which way the devious mind of Ironhair would lean!

I might have fallen headlong into the fire had not Donuil sprung up at Tressa's cry and grasped me by the arm, pulling me to his chest. I saw Philip and Benedict looming behind him, all amazed, because they could not know what had occurred, what had been said. Not even I knew all, and yet I knew too much from the utterance of that one name alone. I dragged in a deep breath and mastered myself. Donuil leaned over me, refusing to release my arm until I was seated, and I could see the concern and confusion in his face. Benedict and Philip had moved to stand behind me, and now Dedalus was there on my left, his fist clenched upon the hilt of the dagger at his side.

Tressa's fingers were digging painfully into my upper arm, and I reached up to take her wrist, nodding my head to reassure her that I was well. Then I turned immediately to face Germanus once again. My friend had aged visibly, within a matter of moments, the lines in his cheeks suddenly graven deeper before.

"What did he say?" I asked him.

He had to moisten his mouth and swallow before he could reply. "I am afraid I may have undone all your work, with this request to join me here, my friend—"

I cut him short, dismissing his apology with something approaching gruffness. "You're a bishop, not a seer," I growled. "Whatever has happened is no fault of yours. Tell me what Cuthric said."

The others were all listening now; the only sound to be heard was the guttering of the fire in its pit. Germanus cleared his throat, then spoke quickly.

"The first wave of Danes came into the Weald last autumn, and spent the winter in the empty forts along the Saxon Shore. I told you that. Then, less than a month ago, Horsa returned with another, larger fleet and summoned all of them to rejoin him. He had made alliance, he said, with a king from the far west, a man called Ironhair, who required assistance in pacifying his domain. In return for that assistance, he was willing to provide land holdings in the territories to his north and west, and to provide the Danes with open access to the gold mines of Dolaucothi in the land of Cambria, in addition to the riches they could all win for themselves in the process of conquering the king's enemies. Ironhair was there, with Horsa, aboard his ship, and made his promise personally to the Danish warriors. They left within the week."

"How big was Horsa's fleet?"

Germanus relayed the question, and Cuthric listened closely, then shook his head in answering. Germanus nodded. "He does not know with certainty, but he was told there were in excess of two hundred ships."

"Two hundred! God curse the man to Hades, he is determined to become a king. The lands to the north-west of Cornwall are ours. He plots against Camulod, as well as Cambria. I must return, now, Germanus. Tonight." They dissuaded me from that foolishness quickly.

Germanus thought our entire force should head homeward at first light, but I rejected that. The bulk of them would move too slowly, tied as they were to the speed of the wagons. Instead, I would ride home ahead of them with a small escort—small enough to travel at maximum speed and large enough to discourage interference. Our main force would follow at its own best speed.

There was some discussion of who would accompany me and who would remain, but I made short work of that, having no patience with the democratic process in time of extremity. Donuil would ride with me, as would Tressa and Shelagh; Ded would come, too, and Benedict, and Bedwyr, together with a score of our best troopers, selected by Dedalus. Philip would remain behind, in overall command, with Falvo and Rufio. Their orders were to bring our thousand home to Camulod as quickly as they could. Germanus and his party were close enough now to Verulamium to make it safely on their own. A mere twenty miles separated them from their destination, and they were secure in their numbers, thanks to the multitudes of well-armed Anglians who had flocked to welcome the bishop. We had seen no signs of local unrest—the roving war party we had encountered earlier had travelled from far afield—and I shared Germanus's confidence that his plans would now unfold without disruption.

I dismissed everyone then, and sought my bed, determined, if not to sleep, at least to seek some rest for my aching bones and body while I wrestled with my fears.

In spite of all my anxiety and the turmoil in my soul, I slept heavily, awakening with a cry of fear from some dark dream only when Dedalus came into my tent and shook me by the shoulder in the darkness before dawn. He had had people working through the night, preparing marching rations for our journey—enough to last us for ten days, at least, should we be forced to rely on them alone for sustenance—and our horses were saddled and ready, an extra mount for each of us. The score of troopers who would ride with us were waiting in the darkness, highlighted intermittently by flames from the high-piled fires. I was fully dressed and tying the long, dark shaft of the Varrus bow securely beneath my saddle flaps when Germanus found me. He embraced me in silence, then held me by the shoulders, gazing into my eyes.

"Go with God, my friend," he said. "And I hope you will find it in your heart not to think badly of me for removing you from Camulod at this of all times. My prayers for your swift and safe homecoming will assail the ears of God Himself, beseeching Him to set His heavenly hosts to watch over you on the road. When you have dealt with this threat and come home safe, remember what we spoke of in my tent. Enos will stay in constant touch with you and will bring word from each of us to the other with no needless loss of time. I'll pray we meet again next year, at Eastertide, to share the celebration of our heavenly and earthly kings. Farewell, and journey safely."

I sighed, and clasped his arms above the elbow. "Pray hard, old friend, and often, for I fear we'll all need prayers. Arthur is in Cambria, alone with Llewellyn, and none know who he is, so he may yet be safe. If we emerge alive from this travail, we'll see him crowned just as you described, and Christian Britain will have a Christian King."

He turned away and kissed Tressa and Shelagh on either cheek, then blessed our party and stepped back.

I looked about me from my saddle. A throng of our men had gathered to see us leave, but they were silent, shrouded still in the dark of night, black among the blackness. I saw Philip standing close by, flanked by Falvo and Rufio, and I raised my right hand to my helmet, acknowledging their presence. All three snapped to attention and saluted me, and I heard the metallic clatter of armguards against cuirasses as the throng about us did the same. I swallowed hard and nodded once again, abruptly, afraid to trust my voice to speak without betraying me, then swung my horse around and led the way out from the firelight in search of the road home to Camulod.

Despite the Bishop's promised prayers for succour on our journey, it quickly became evident that God and His heavenly host had other matters on their minds while we were travelling, for our progress was a nightmare from the outset. More than a hundred miles of unknown territory lay between us and our destination, with dangers at every step of the way. We were beset with conflicting urgencies that kept us angry and frustrated: my overriding temptation, and my prime imperative, was to move with the utmost speed, but the paradox therein was that the utmost speed involved far too much slowness. *Festina lente* was the ancient watchword of the Romans, *hurry slowly*, and we were constrained to recognize the truth in the old warning. We could not put the spurs into our mounts and ride flat out; we had to conserve their strength and nurture their endurance lest we kill them on the road, leaving ourselves on foot. And so we chafed against the discipline of travel but endured it, changing gait each quarter-hour, from walk to trot to canter, then galloping and reining in to canter, then to trot, and then to walk again.

We seldom took time to rest in daylight, and then we always stopped beside a running stream, tending to our ablutions hastily, splashing ourselves with water and shocking ourselves back to reality with its cold kiss. We were filthy, and we soon began to stink of sweat, human and equine, and of other, less pleasant things. The women suffered far more than the men, as it transpired, for I discovered that both were going through their menses, and the discomfort and inconvenience that entailed must have been almost more than they could bear, atop the agonies of all else. We rode long into the night when the skies were clear and the moon bright enough to light our way, and therein we were fortunate; the first three nights were clear and cloudless and the moon was almost full. Only when the moon went down and darkness thickened sufficiently to hamper us did we unsaddle our horses and fall down to sleep for a few hours, rolled in our blankets on the open ground.

Twice in the first two days we encountered bands of alien looters and marauders, but we were fortunate enough to see them before they could see us and so avoided detection. But the knowledge that such bands were abroad along our route took its toll on us, so that by the end of the fourth day, somewhere amid gentle, rolling hills long miles from anywhere, yet still three hard days' riding away from Camulod, we were all reeling from exhaustion and I realized that this was folly. *Festina lente*, I reminded myself, *more haste, less speed*! We found a dense copse of low trees and made a camp that night, pitching our leather, one-man legionary tents and posting guards on two-hour watches, and although we did not dare to ignite a fire, we all slept soundly for the first time since leaving our companions.

Some time in the middle of that night, I awoke to the sound of rain striking my tent, and as I listened, it grew quickly to a solid downpour. All the world was wet when we broke camp, cursing the slimy wetness of our tents as we sought to roll and secure them, and we rode that day in a huddle of misery, eating from our rations of roast grains and nuts in the saddle as we went and wishing our woollen travelling cloaks were denser, warmer and more heavily waxed. Early in the afternoon, one horse slipped heavily in the mud of an incline and went down, breaking a foreleg. Fortunately, its rider was unhurt, merely winded by his fall, but we had to kill the screaming horse quickly, for fear that unfriendly ears might hear its agony. The trooper changed to his spare horse after distributing its load among his mates, and we moved on, beginning now to penetrate a heavily forested region of low hills where an occasional bare cliff face reared above the trees.

I remember my face being chilled from the rain that streamed down from my helmet to spill sideways from the hinges of its face-protecting cheek flaps and flow down my jaws on either side, and I remember comparing our current journey to the progress we had made on our outward expedition. Then, we had ridden slowly, the air about us filled with the sound of laughing voices and the squeaks, groans, clinks and rattles of saddle harness, wagon springs and turning wheels. Now we pressed forward grimly, silently, each rider struggling with his or her own discomfort and worst fears, the world about us blocked by the sound of hurrying horses' hooves and the steady, constant hiss of driving rain. From time to time in the early stages Tress or one of the others would try to speak to me, hoping to comfort me or to take my mind off the troubles that beset me, but eventually all conversation ceased and we drove forward in bleak, miserable silence.

Then, around mid-afternoon, the rain stopped falling and the clouds began to break apart, allowing beams of sunlight to illuminate the landscape around us and lifting our spirits for a brief time. Too brief, alas, because even though we felt no breeze, the skies were soon fouled again by enormous banks of fast-moving storm clouds that changed shape visibly as they were torn by high, turbulent winds. As they swept overhead they seemed to distort the light until it took on a yellowish, threatening colour, and thunder rolled ominously in the far distance.

It was shortly after this last change began that I saw horsemen flanking us, galloping swiftly away along the upper reaches of a hillside on our right. I had been deep in thought, watching the scudding clouds and paying little attention to where I was, and I had only a fleeting glimpse of these riders among the trees before they vanished. My first thought was that they had been our own, ours being the only horsemen I had seen since leaving Camulod, but a swift glance about me verified that all our party rode together. I felt alarm flaring in me. I called to Dedalus then, pointing to where the riders had disappeared, but there was nothing there for him to see, and I could tell that he was sceptical. Angry at being doubted, yet at the same time doubting my own eyes, I sank my spurs into my horse's sides and bounded away, uphill, to where I thought I had seen the phantom riders, and I could plainly hear Ded following me.

Sure enough, there on the soil of the hillside was a double set of tracks, made by unshod hooves. Dedalus cursed and led the way as we rejoined the others, and from then on we rode with straining vigilance, drawing together into the wedge formation we used for both attack and defence. We had no idea who these people might be, but the fact that they were horsed had shaken us. I rode at the point, flanked by Ded on my left and Tress on my right. I removed my heavy cloak and rolled it up, securing it behind my saddle with my sleeping roll, and unsheathed my sword, lodging the point of it securely in the wooden stirrup with my right foot and gripping the hilt as though it were the shaft of a spear. Tress, on my right, rode with her spear held in the same fashion.

The depression through which we were riding was almost too shallow to be called a valley. We were riding upward along its length, and the crest of it lay half a mile ahead of us. Then, when we were less than a hundred paces from that point, a sudden shout from one of our troopers brought my head around and I could see that the bushy hillside on our right was alive with running men, bounding towards us. A second warning cry, from my left, announced the same message: we were under simultaneous attack from both sides. I rose in my stirrups, swinging my sword around my head, and led my people in a charge towards the top of the rise, the only exit open to us. We were trapped in a funnel, and I cursed myself uselessly for not having sent outriders ahead of us.

The terrain changed abruptly on the far side of the gentle crest. We came thundering to the top to find the surface falling in a chute away from us between thick banks of tall, thin evergreens. The narrow aisle we had been following was blocked a short way beneath us by a rearing crag of stone around which men were clustered, with long, sharpened spikes, cut from those same straight evergreens, stretching to meet us, their butts pressed against the base of the crag. I saw the entire entrapment at a glance, as did Dedalus, who was already turning towards me, waving me away to his right as he pulled his horse's head hard to the left. We split apart, and as we did, I saw that Tress had understood and was already veering outwards to my right. Behind us, the others followed at the full gallop, wrenching their mounts away from the certain death ahead of them, to follow right or left depending on their position in the wedge. And then I was among the densely packed, tall, narrow trees, my full attention concentrated upon staying in the saddle and preventing my mount from killing himself or me by colliding with some obstacle.

In mere moments, we were reduced almost to a standstill, faced with the impossibility of moving quickly through such dense growth. The ground underfoot sloped steeply downward and was littered with dead and fallen trees, many of them caught between the boles of their living neighbours. All of these fallen obstacles were small, but any of them was capable of piercing a horse's gut. I heard much crashing and cursing behind me, and the occasional clang of iron, but I had no time or opportunity to look back. Tressa was safe, that I knew, for I could see her just ahead of me. And then the trees began to thin slightly, and I kicked my horse forward faster. Soon we were able to gain momentum, and I broke free again to find myself in the treeless central aisle we had followed to the crest above. I swung my horse around then to look behind me, and the pathway above me was thick with men, leaping down towards me. More of my own men were beginning to emerge from the trees on the hillside now, but the enemy was closing quickly. I saw little point in approaching them up the steep path, so I decided to stand my ground and fight where I was.

The long sword felt almost weightless in my hand, and I used it efficiently, killing the first three men who came within my range before any of them had a chance to aim his weapon at me. The fourth thrust upward at me with a long, heavy spear, but my arcing blade cut it as though it were a hollow reed, and my next swing, backhanded, caught my attacker clean across the eyes with the blade's tip. An arrow clanged against my cuirass and knocked me backward, reeling, and while I was unbalanced someone grasped my leg and tried to pull me down. I clutched my saddle horn with my left hand and stabbed downward, but my assailant had already released me, staggering back and scrabbling to reach between his shoulder blades where Tressa's spear had pierced him. Another fell beside him, transfixed by a thrown spear, and a third man fell on top of him, spewing blood from his throat. I felt a hand tugging at my bridle and heard Ded's voice shouting in my ear, yelling at me to fall back. I did, swinging my mount around, and moments later we were descending again, our horses' hooves slithering on the steep, rain-slick surface.

We were close to the bottom by then, and soon there was level earth beneath our hooves. I looked back yet again, attempting to count our numbers, and was surprised to see that almost all of us had survived the trap. Shelagh was close beside me, Donuil at her side. Benedict was bleeding from a shallow cut across his nose but seemed strong otherwise. Our pursuers had fallen behind, outdistanced by our horses' longer gait. I lost count of our people at nigh on a score, confused by the moving bodies, but I felt my heart lighten within me. I would not have been surprised to discover we had lost half our number. I heard someone ask how many men had attacked us, and another answer that it must have been more than a hundred, since he had seen at least two score of them on our right before the left attacked.

I heard Dedalus yell again and looked ahead to see a group of mounted men in the distance, watching us. They were making no attempt to come towards us, it appeared, merely waiting for us to arrive. I estimated the distance separating us at somewhere near two hundred paces.

"Eight," Donuil shouted, and Ded answered, "Aye, eight that we can see . . . The good Christ only knows how many more there are in hiding. But we've little else to do and nowhere else to do it! We can't go back, so let's keep moving forward. To me!" He stood upright in his stirrups, brandishing his sword, and then sat back and spurred his animal forward.

We had neither the time nor the space to form a wedge for this attack, so we had to rely on individual speed and impetus, and we were clawing for both when disaster struck. Dedalus was ahead of all of us, closely followed by three troopers riding hard on his heels and four others more widely spread. Then came Tressa, Shelagh and Donuil in a row, barely ahead of where I rode half a length behind them. I checked over my shoulder, and seeing that all our men were still with us, I set myself to catching up with the others, crouching forward over Germanicus's ears and slapping him with the flat of my blade. And then I saw Dedalus hurled backward from the saddle as though he had hit a wall. His feet flew up, high above his head and completely over, so that he spun in a backward somersault and crashed to the earth face first. Immediately, the three men riding close behind him were hurled from their horses in the same manner, snapping backwards from their saddles and crashing to the ground. So violently were they unseated that I thought they had been hit by Pendragon longbow fire, and I was looking for the arrows in their chests when two more men went down. It was then I saw the rope that killed them, stretched taut between two trees, at the shoulder height of a mounted man. One more man threw himself sideways in his saddle, vainly trying to avoid the deadly thing, but it caught the crest of his helmet and I heard the snap of his spine clearly, above the thumping of our horses' hooves.

Donuil and Shelagh and Tressa were almost upon it, headed for certain death and completely unaware. I screamed, I believe, and spurred my big black savagely, sending him leaping forward with a scream of his own, trying to overtake my companions as I stood in the stirrups and swung my sword high above my head. I leaned far out over my horse's ears and brought the long blade whistling down, afraid I had misjudged the distance and my stroke would miss, yet knowing that I might already be too late to save my friends.

I barely felt the contact as the tip of the sword's razor-sharp edge cut through the rigid rope, but I heard the thrumming twang as the strands parted and the ends flicked away. Then I heard another, double scream. The rope's end, recoiling with the sudden release of tension, had struck Tressa's horse full in the muzzle, and the animal had thrown itself violently backward, rearing erect, forelegs flailing. I had a glimpse of Tress herself, her feet free of the stirrups, pushing away from the animal, and then I was beyond her, my chest filling up with murderous rage as I saw the eight observers, the architects of this slaughter, preparing to scatter.

They were much too slow. I was among them before they could recover from their shock at seeing me cut through their rope. Two of them died on my first charge, one on my left, the other to my right as I swung my blade with the strength of dementia. I pulled my horse around hard, veering to my left, and swung directly back to attack again, cleaving one fleeing craven from behind so that his right arm fell away, severed cleanly by the blow. Then another, more brave than his fellows, came charging towards me, his arm bent backwards to hurl a short, heavy spear from a close distance. He threw, and I swung and caught the heavy missile just behind the head with the centre of my blade, smashing it from the air. The sudden, jarring weight of the spear caught my sword's edge and pulled me sharply and uncontrollably to my left, out of balance. My right foot slipped out of my stirrup and I felt myself falling.

I did not lose consciousness, but every bit of wind was driven from my body as I hit the ground. I was incapable of moving for some time, my chest and throat a mass of agony. There was noise everywhere, all around me, and then I felt hands pulling at me, raising me up, and I gasped for breath. Donuil hauled me to my feet, his fingers hooked inside the armholes of my cuirass, and I saw his eyes peering, wide and anxious, into my own. He shouted at me, asking if I could move, and I nodded and pushed him weakly away, but he hung on to me and half dragged me to where my horse stood, snorting and rolling his eyes, held firmly by one of our young troopers. Donuil cupped his hands and hoisted me back up into my saddle. As I hung there, still fighting for breath, I saw Tressa and Shelagh, both mounted, sitting their horses tensely, staring at me and obviously waiting to move again. I looked down at Donuil, who was pulling himself back into his own saddle.

"Where's Ded?" I thought this was a shout, but it emerged as no more than a pain-filled, choking wheeze.

"He's dead, Cay," Donuil shouted back. "They're all dead, all of them who rode into the rope. Now move, or we'll be joining them!"

He pulled his horse in, close to my right side, while Benedict flanked me equally closely on the left, and we began to move again, gathering speed quickly until we were riding at full gallop. As we went, my breathing became easier, and soon I nodded and shouted to my two escorts, letting them know that I could now control myself and my big horse. They nodded and edged away from me, and after a short time I was able to look around me again. Our party had shrunk by half, perhaps more.

Donuil knew what I was thinking. He leaned closer to me and shouted again, his voice interrupted by the wind roaring through the ear-flaps of my helmet: ". . . don't know who those people . . . too many of them to fight . . . lucky to break through them . . . lucky to stay ahead of them. Most of them were afoot, but . . . horses . . . don't know how many . . . won't be far behind us, though, if they're coming at all . . . best keep moving . . . outrun them."

Some time after that, the ground began to rise more and more steeply beneath us and our horses started to flag. Germanicus was foaming at the mouth, and I knew he was close to foundering. Then we came to a spot where the steep pathway levelled out for a stretch, and on an impulse I drew rein, calling to the others to halt, and turned to look back the way we had come. This spot would be defensible, I thought, for the crest of the rise was almost a straight edge and beneath it was a fringe of low, thick bushes. Anyone coming up towards us would be totally exposed, while we might remain concealed.

I jumped down immediately and untied the bindings that held Publius Varrus's great bow in place beneath the flaps of my saddle, calling to one of the troopers to unlash the quiver from the other side and bring it to me. As he did so, I fumbled in my scrip for a bowstring and made the weapon ready, shouting to Donuil to organize the others and change the saddles from the horses we had been riding to the spare animals. Somehow, we had come through that running fight with almost all our spare mounts. They had been roped together in four groups, and we still had three of those with us. As that work progressed, I stood on guard, an arrow nocked and ready to draw at the first sign of movement on the slope beneath. Behind me, Tress finished transferring her saddle to her spare mount, then set about tending to Germanicus, but Donuil relieved her of that task and finished it.

For half an hour I stood there on guard, while my people and their horses caught their breath and regained their strength. Towards the end of it I started looking at the skies again, where the heavy, sullen, strangely coloured clouds were still boiling. Someone behind me cursed, briefly and viciously, but when I spun to ask what was wrong he merely held out his hand, palm upwards. It was starting to rain again.

Below me, on the flank of the hill, I heard a dull, scrabbling sound and a muffled curse. I jerked my arm up, warning the others, and then scanned the trees below. As I did so, four running men emerged, one of them limping, running like a crab and scrubbing at the fresh mud that caked his right knee. They were all peering upwards towards where I stood, but there was no focus to their attention, and I realized they had not seen me. I was still concealed from them by the brow of the slope and the low screen of bushes just below it, and from the way they ran, dogged and silent but showing no sign of caution, it was evident that they did not expect to find us there so close. Five more men followed them, and now I could hear the sounds of others farther back among the trees.

I had twenty-three arrows in my quiver and one nocked to my bow-string. I pulled and loosed almost without aiming, bringing the leading man down in mid-stride, the force of the arrow knocking him over back-wards. I immediately loosed another missile, then a third, and two more men went down. A chorus of howls and shouts broke out momentarily, and then all sound and movement ceased, except for the writhings of the third man I had shot. I ignored him, putting aside the temptation to waste another arrow, and scanned the greenery below. The fourth man had thrown himself down behind a hummock of grass, and I could see one of his legs projecting into the open.

It was raining heavily again, and the noise of the rain hammering on leaves drowned all other sounds from below. Behind me, however, I could hear the sounds of my people mounting and preparing to leave. I was taking careful aim at the exposed leg when Donuil appeared at the edge of my vision. I turned my head slightly to look at him and as I did so, all the world exploded in a blinding flash of blue-white light and sizzling heat that sent both of us reeling backwards, away from the lip of the crest. As quickly as it had come, the light vanished, and I was blind, blinking my eyes uselessly in panic with the stink of something alien in my nostrils. I heard people and horses screaming in the blackness all around me, and then my vision started to come back to me, imperfectly, marred by glaring spots of brightness that shut much from my sight. Staggering with nausea, I ran back to the edge of the path and looked down again, still blinking wildly, and saw movement beneath me on the slope. Nothing at which I looked directly was visible to me, but I could see men rushing on both sides, as though around a hole in my sight. My mind told me that a lightning bolt had struck beside us, and it told me in the same flash that the men below, further away from it, had not been affected as I had, and that they were now swarming up the hillside.

I nocked another arrow, made out a target on my left, then swung towards the running shape and fired, but as soon as I did so, I lost sight of both target and arrow and had no idea of whether I had hit or not. Undeterred, and feeling a snake of fear biting at my entrails, I repeated the manoeuvre, this time spinning to my right and loosing at a half-seen shape; this one went down, spinning to fall among long grass. More than half blind I might be, but the attackers had no way of knowing that, and once again they dropped to the ground. Still, I saw movement among the growth, far on my right, too far away and too indistinct to offer a target. I knew what the movement represented, though: people moving uphill to outflank us. I shot two more arrows into the area directly ahead of me, pulling the bowstring back to my ear each time. The blind spot before my eyes was diminishing.

It was then I saw a most amazing, overwhelming thing. The very surface of the trees below me seemed to bend and flex, as though pressed flat by some enormous, unseen hand. Everything in my sight faded almost instantly to an impenetrable greyness and was lost in a swelling roar of deafening sound. I barely had time to marvel, for almost instantly that alien force came beating down on me. It was a hailstorm, massive and elemental, and the sheer fury of the onslaught hammered me to my hands and knees. The noise against my metal helmet was appalling and the weight of hailstones beating at me was insupportable. I allowed myself to fall face down, abandoning my weapons and rolling my body up into a ball. Every exposed portion of my skin was a mass of sharp, stinging pains and I wondered if I might die there, battered to death by ancient forest gods. But then the force of the storm abated slightly, and I opened my eyes.

Donuil was riding towards me, bent forward from his saddle, his right arm outstretched to seize me. I uncurled my body and pushed myself erect, grasping my long bow in my left hand and reaching upward with my right, aware as I did so that I clutched a single hailstone the size of a horse turd. I dropped it and bent my arm, locking elbows with Donuil as he galloped by and leaping upwards as he swung me across his horse's rump. It was a trick we had practiced a hundred times. I clung to the back of his saddle as he turned, just short of the path's lip, and headed back towards the others. I leaped down and pulled myself up into my own saddle, fighting my horse as it struggled and reared away from me, maddened by the pulverizing hail. I managed to mount, eventually, and to bring my horse under a degree of control, and then we were moving again, seeking shelter that was nowhere to be found. Even among the trees there was no respite, for the hailstorm had stripped the leaves from the thick canopy above. And then, as suddenly as it had begun, the deluge of ice ended and a profound silence settled everywhere.

None of us moved in that silence, not even our horses, as though all of us were afraid to stir lest the gods of the storm detect our movement and unleash the ice again. But the silence held, and grew, and we began to accept that it was over. I twisted in my saddle and looked about me, gratefully conscious that my sight had fully returned. All the land about us was carpeted with solid ice and slush. I pulled myself together and kicked my horse into motion again, beginning to feel the smarting ache of the pounding my body had taken, and the others moved with me, gathering themselves and moving slowly towards the path again. Only twelve of us remained: Benedict was there, and young Bedwyr, who looked exhausted and far older than his years, Shelagh and Tress and Donuil, and six troopers. Germanicus, my black, was still with us, though he had lost his saddle-bags, and beyond him I could see the other spare horses, more than half a score.

An arrow shot close by my face and glanced harmlessly off the cuirass of the man ahead of me, startling us all and reminding us abruptly and frighteningly that we had enemies in close pursuit. I raised my bow and reached behind my shoulder for an arrow, only to discover that I had none. I had lost the entire quiver somewhere below, most probably when Donuil had snatched me from the ground. I waved everyone forward and we rode again, spurring our mounts and cursing loudly as we tackled the steep slope above us, all of us painfully aware of the ice beneath our animals' hooves. Mere moments later, the rain came back, lancing down heavily through the fading light of the late afternoon and cutting visibility to where we could barely see the rider ahead of us. The cursing grew louder, but we took some comfort in knowing the enemy were all afoot and must be suffering even more than we were.

The pathway grew rapidly steeper and narrower, slippery and treacherous underfoot. It swung around to the left, where we found ourselves on an exposed slope, with a steep cliff above us and a yawning chasm falling away on our right. Far out, above the mist-shrouded valley below, a jagged fork of lightning flashed and was mirrored instantaneously by a much closer one. Shelagh rode directly ahead of me now, and in front of her several of the spare horses followed three troopers, who rode directly behind Donuil. Beyond Donuil I could see Benedict's red-crested helmet and in front of him rode Tress, with another trooper on her left. Another arrow fell in front of me, wobbling spent and harmless. I turned in my saddle to look back, but there was nothing there to see. I felt sure that this was a parting shot, a last, defiant arrow. We had beaten our pursuers.

It was then that my horse reared, whinnying in panic. Ahead, I saw one of our horses, its legs kicking wildly as it fell from the pathway into the void beneath. The scene ahead of me was terror and madness, a mass of rearing, plunging animals and milling arms. A second horse went over the edge, a rider clinging to its back, and I saw another flailing human form plummeting down.

Directly in front of me, Shelagh's horse slipped and fell, sliding backwards into my mount and kicking the legs from beneath him. As he went down, I threw myself from the saddle, sideways, to my left. Shelagh landed flat on her back in front of me. I heard a splintering crack as I fell sprawling and felt something give, sickeningly, beneath me. Stunned, I waited for the pain that must surely accompany such a sound, but I felt nothing other than the solidness of the ice-covered earth. I looked down then, and saw that the noise had been the splintering of my bow, the mighty and ancient Varrus longbow, which now lay broken and useless beneath me. In a curious condition of mindlessness, I stared at it, thinking that this weapon had been more than a hundred years old, cared for by generations of proud owners, and now it was shattered and dead.

I snapped back to awareness. People had fallen! I scrambled to my feet and saw that Shelagh had not moved; she lay with her arms and legs sprawled wide. In that same glance, I saw someone else, on the far side of the path—a helmet and shoulders, hands clutching at the icy edge of the pathway and huge eyes peering terror-stricken into mine. I threw myself forward in a dive, reaching for those arms, but they fell away before I could grasp them. I landed face down on the ice and slid forward on my metal cuirass, head first, over the edge. I twisted violently, reaching frantically for a handhold, and fell, only to find myself arrested and dangling by one leg, upside down over the abyss.

I have no knowledge of how long I hung there, but I remember some of the thoughts that went through my head. I knew that I was hanging suspended by one of the metal greaves I wore on my legs. It had evidently snagged on some protrusion, perhaps a sapling or a root. Only two thin leather straps secured that greave against my leg. If either of them broke, the other would snap, too, and I would fall head first. I knew that my sword was still safely at my back, for as I fell it had slipped freely through the metal ring between my shoulders, and its cross-guard had lodged beneath the neck flap of my helmet. I could feel the weight of it, pressing against my helmet and pushing it forward onto my brow, forcing my chin-strap hard against my jaws to choke me. Someone far below me was moaning in agony, and lightning still flickered in the darkening sky, setting thunder rolling in great, crashing, concussive waves. And the rain still poured.

It was Benedict who found me. I heard his voice above my head, calling my name and warning me not to try to move. I tried to answer him, but my helmet's strap had jammed my mouth tightly shut. Some time passed, and then I heard sounds of movement, and two men came down to where I hung, lowering themselves on lengths of rope, Benedict and a trooper called Marco. Marco held an additional length of rope, and once he had anchored himself securely he passed it carefully around my shoulders to Benedict on my other side. I felt them cinch it tightly, securing my sheathed sword against my back in the process, and then Benedict held on to me while Marco reached above and cut the straps that held my greave in place. I fell free, safe in Benedict's grasp, and found myself facing the cliff face, solidly supported by the rope. Benedict told me to hang on, then both of them swarmed back up to the path and began to raise me to safety. I was grateful and unsurprised as I arrived at the top to see Donuil standing there above me, his giant body braced on thick-muscled legs as he hauled me upward, hand over hand, while the other two stood watching anxiously.

My legs would not support me when I reached the path above, and Benedict had to untie the rope about my chest. Donuil had returned to kneel over Shelagh, who was propped against the wall of the cliff face, her eyes open but staring vacantly. I asked if she was well, and he nodded, his eyes huge and wide. I looked about me then. Benedict and Marco were close by and I could see two other men working with the horses some distance above.

"Where's Tress?" Even as I asked, I knew the answer, and Benedict lowered his head.

"She's gone, Cay. Her horse took her over the edge."

I felt nothing, except an enormous lassitude that settled over me like a cloud of fog.

"What happened, Ben?"

He drew a long, deep breath. "It was a wildcat."

"What?"

"A wildcat, or some such animal. It must have been crazed by the storm. I saw it leaping from the cliff face above us, and then it landed on a horse's neck and all the world went mad. I saw it happen and there was nothing I could do. The animal it landed on spun around screaming, rearing and kicking the horse behind it, which tried to do the same but fell and slid back down the hill into the animals behind. Once that had begun, it was chaos. I saw Tressa's mount rearing and circling on its hind legs while she stood in the stirrups trying to pull it down, and then one of its hooves slipped off the edge and they went over. My own horse fell sideways, the other way, pinning me against the wall, and I was stuck there until it got to its feet again. Donuil leaped off his horse and managed to avoid being crushed. Marco and Rufus went down, too, but they were fortunate and landed between horses. Bello, who's working with Rufus, fared similarly. Shelagh was thrown safely, though she took a hard, hard fall, and you went over the edge. I didn't see you go. I thought you were dead with the others. Thank God we looked for you."

I remembered the moans I had heard coming from beneath me. "Someone's alive down there," I said.

"Aye, we know. We heard him, but we can't see where he is."

"It might be her—it might be Tress, Ben."

He grimaced. "I doubt it, Cay. Tress went over with her horse, much farther up the track, and the sounds I heard were made by a man, I think."

I struggled to rise to my feet and fell back. "We have to look. We have ropes. We'll climb down."

"Merlyn, we can't. It's too dark now, too dangerous. There are only seven of us left, and we're all frozen and exhausted. If we go clambering down there in the darkness, we could all be killed. We'll have to wait till morning."

"By morning they might all be dead."

"I know. But there's no other possibility."

Again I gathered myself and attempted to rise, and this time I made it to my feet, but when I took my first step my right leg, the one from which I had hung for so long, folded uselessly beneath me and Benedict barely managed to catch me as I fell headlong. My face hit his cuirass, then all the world went black.

XVI

MADNESS CAN TAKE many forms. Mine took the form of Peter Ironhair, and because of it, a year was to elapse before I would truly mourn my Tressa. My first great love, Cassandra, had been two years dead before I mourned for her, but then I had been ill, incapable of understanding my loss, since my wits were scattered and my past life hidden from my mind. Tressa, the only other woman who could claim my soul, having mastered my heart, had to wait a conscious year while I, with all my faculties apparently intact, went through the madness of vengeance. I was aware of loss, through all that time—aware that grief boiled, unspilt, filling me totally; aware of yawning emptiness in all my world; aware that all the joys I had ever known were gone from me—and yet I wilfully refused to think of those things or countenance what ailed me. I had been set one task to complete before I died, a task forged and hammered into being in the emptiness of my soul: the personal destruction of an enemy and the excision of his living heart.

In sleeping and in waking dreams Ironhair's face was never absent from my mind for longer than it took me to complete one minor task and turn towards another. I would discuss some strategy or other with my officers—for I had no friends at that time, and dealt with people strictly on the dictates and requirements of the moment—and then would turn to walk or ride away, and there would be Ironhair, the creator of my despair, grinning at me in my mind. I saw him always as he had been in Camulod, before we threw him out: an open-faced, attractive, smiling man with the suggestion of goodwill and fellowship ever about him. His face, clearly recalled in every detail, came to be more familiar to me than my own, which I saw but seldom in those days. Even in sleep he was with me, and he was everyone I dreamed of. Each solitary night I was startled awake as his face appeared on Tressa's, Ded's and even Arthur's shoulders. Lucanus came to me in dreams, to talk, but even he never failed to become Ironhair, mocking me with his smile.

I have said that in those days I had no friends; that is both true and false. My friends stood by me—Donuil and Shelagh, Benedict and Falvo, Philip and faithful Rufio—but I abjured them and avoided them, cutting them cruelly with coldness and indifference whenever they sought my company and treating them as mere subordinates when I had to deal with them in government or war. They bore it stoically, knowing whence it came, but nowadays, when I think back to how I was, I sense their pain and loss, which must have seemed to them as bitter and unwelcome as my own.

It passed, in time, that dreadful misery, but I was never able to recapture the easy intimacy I had known with all of them; I had progressed by then from being simple Merlyn, trusted companion, brother-in-arms and laughing friend, to being Merlyn the predator, the avenger and the sorcerer.

A year, lost to me save for minor, insubstantial memories, as surely as the two years when I lived as someone else; and a lifetime, forfeited in payment for a dream of vengeance.

It began on that steep path above the gulf that swallowed Tress.

The morning sun rose in a cloudless sky that revealed no trace of the killing storm and found us huddled still in sleep, seven chilled and agued bodies shuddering in soaked clothes and huddled together for warmth in a single mass like nested spoons in a field-kitchen case. Someone, I guessed Benedict, since he lay on the outside, had covered the sleeping mass of us with cloaks and bedroll blankets and layered leather tents in an attempt to conserve our body heat. Shelagh lay pressed against my back when I awoke, her arms about my waist hugging me tightly, and I, in turn, was clutching the trooper Rufus. When the first of us awoke, the others followed, and I remember feeling every ache and pain of all my forty-plus years as I rolled free of our makeshift bedding, shivering from the chill of the morning and the dragging dankness of my cold, wet clothing.

We broke our fast briefly and in silence, eating without awareness from the rations left in one of the remaining saddle-bags, and then we began searching for our friends.

The abyss that had seemed so deep and dark in the storm the previous night turned out to be nothing so enormous. At its deepest point, it was less than a score of paces, vertically, from the path above. Its bottom, however, was littered with loose boulders that had long since fallen from the cliff face and were now hidden by scrub and bushes. The sapling from which I had hung—my greave was still in place, lodged in the dirt at its base—had suspended me no more than my own height again above the ground, sufficient to have killed me, had I fallen down head first, but nothing resembling the depth I had imagined to be under me as I swung there. There, too, below and to the left, his lower body twisted in a shallow pit and his torso partially hidden by a tree trunk, we found Bedwyr, unconscious but alive, his left leg broken beneath him, a splintered length of bone protruding from his thigh. We left Rufus and Marco, the medical orderly attached to our troop, to straighten and splint the broken limb while Bedwyr was still unconscious and then to extract him from the pit in which he lay. The rest of us went looking for the others who had fallen.

Tressa had died beneath the weight of a falling horse—not her own, which lay several paces away, but mine, the beautiful big black gelding that she had called Bucephalus. Tress lay seemingly asleep on her back, her face at peace though tinged with the faintest shade of blue. Her helmet was still in place, covering her lustrous hair so that she looked more like a sleeping boy than a woman. Her lower body, however, from the rib cage downward, lay entirely concealed by the enormous bulk of the black horse's massive hindquarters, which were covered in blood and offal from its ruptured abdomen.

She had been right, I thought as I stood gazing down at her. The creature had been aptly named. I remembered how she had teased me in bed, on the evening of the day I changed his name. She had preferred Bucephalus to old, mundane Germanicus, she said; Bucephalus had *dignitas*, the rolling majesty of a magnificent, historic name. My response had been to gather her into my arms and mount her, laughingly telling her that Bucephalus had killed the most wondrous man in all the world of his day, throwing him from a cliff, and I had challenged her to throw me from her saddle with such ease. But she had had no wish to unhorse me that night, and Bucephalus had been forgotten as we rode together, repetitively seeking the temporary little death to which we both knew she could always throw me. And now another Bucephalus had killed the most wondrous woman in my world.

It took us half a day to bring down the horses and haul the big black's hulk away from Tressa, and then to bury her. I found a sheltered spot for her, between two spines of rock some way below the place where she had died, and by myself I dug the shallow pit that would hold her, loosening the earth with my sword and scraping it away with my remaining greave. When I could dig no deeper, I laid her gently in the stony grave and packed her body carefully in the earth I had removed, leaving her beautiful face free of dirt. That done, I placed two slanting slabs of stone over her head, angling them so that they would form a roof above her face, and then I placed a multitude of rocks over the mound that marked her resting place, piling them with great care so that they fit together and would yield to no marauding wolf or bear. For hours I toiled at that, travelling farther each time in my search for stones till all the grass and earth around was trampled flat and her funeral place was covered by a chest-high pyramid. Only then did I stop, feeling the laboured ache within my chest threaten to overcome me.

While I had been employed in that, the others had been similarly busy, above me, piling rocks over the three troopers who had met their deaths beside my Tress on that treacherous chute. Gunnar, Casso and

Secundus, their names had been. I had known them all as casually as any leader knows his men, but I had not loved them.

As I climbed back up the steep slope beside the path, Donuil came forward to greet me, holding out his hand to help me clamber up the last short distance. But as I took his hand, his face changed into Ironhair's, and I leaned back and pulled him, hard, attempting to throw him out and over, above my head. Thank God he had already braced himself to take my weight, but even so, I almost succeeded in dislodging him, so great was his surprise. He grunted, frowned and then heaved, pulling me up onto the path and then pushing me aside. I know I was demented, and he told me afterwards that he had seen it in my eyes. The moment passed and I stood there, shaking my head as he asked me what was wrong.

We came to Camulod days later, bearing Bedwyr on a litter made out of leather tents slung between two long poles cut from tall, straight saplings and carried between two horses, front and rear. I have no recollection of the journey, or of our arrival.

My first awareness of being home again came when I opened my eyes in the *sudarium*, the steam room of the fort's bathhouse. I was sitting up, and had been talking, apparently, to Benedict, who sat across from me. I was instantly assailed by a kind of vertigo, with images springing to my mind of similar awakenings, years before when I had lost my memories of myself. Benedict leaned towards me quickly, his face creased with concern, asking if I was well. I nodded that I was and decided then and there to say nothing of my loss of awareness. He continued to eye me uneasily, nevertheless, but the moment passed without further comment.

My clothes, when I located them, were clean, and different from the clothing I had worn out on the road, so I knew I had been home long enough, at least, to have changed them. I went in search of Dedalus, hoping to pick his brains without betraying myself, and had gone half the way across the yard before I remembered seeing him fly from his horse and crash to the ground. Dedalus was dead. Again the vertigo swept over me, and I moved slowly to the nearest wall to lean against the stones, feeling the nausea churning in my gut. I vomited, explosively, but felt no better for it, and then all at once I was down on my knees and falling forward.

I awoke again with Ludmilla and Shelagh hovering over me. When they saw my open eyes, Ludmilla bent and placed a cool, soft hand across my brow.

"You have had a fever, Caius, and have made us all afraid for you, these past few days. Now lie still until I bring Mucius. Shelagh will stay with you."

When Ludmilla had gone, I tried to turn to Shelagh, but I could not move my head, and panic flared in me. My thoughts leaped back to the time of my earlier injury, when Lucanus had had to drill a hole in my skull to relieve the pressure there. He had strapped my head to a retaining device to do so. Shelagh, however, had been watching my eyes and now she bent over me, slipping her arm beneath my neck and raising me slightly, setting my fears to rest. I had simply become too weak to move my head. I tried to speak to her, but my lips were stuck together. She quickly moistened a scrap of cloth and wiped my mouth, and I recalled the pleasure I had felt long years before when Aunt Luceiia had done the same thing for me. I licked my lips and spoke, but what emerged was a mere whisper.

"What's happening, Shelagh? Where's Ambrose?"

She frowned. "What do you mean, where's Ambrose?" The door at the foot of my bed swung open and Mucius Quinto swept into the room, crossing directly to my side and placing his hand on my brow. His eyes seemed to be on Shelagh, however, and he did not glance down to where I lay watching him.

"What's wrong?" he asked, speaking to Shelagh.

She shook her head, frowning still. "He doesn't remember anything."

Quinto looked down at me, then, and raised his hand a little from my brow. "Hmm," he grunted. "Better. I'm not afraid of losing my hand this time." He smiled. "I've seldom felt, or seen, a fever such as you have had, my friend. You were afire, for almost a week. Absolutely burning up. Is Shelagh right? How much do you recall?"

I blinked at him. "Of what?" I asked, again in a whisper.

"Of anything. What is the last thing you remember?"

Tressa's high-piled grave flashed through my mind, choking me suddenly. I forced my thoughts on, past that, and saw Donuil above me, reaching down to me. "Ironhair," I said.

"Hmm," Quinto murmured, seemingly unsurprised. "Do you remember coming back to Camulod?" I shook my head. "Hmm!" he said again, more emphatically this time. "Donuil was right, then." He turned away and stepped out of my sight but returned mere moments later holding a horn cup. "Here, drink this." He reached his hand behind me to support my head.

"Donuil was right?" I rasped. "Don't you mean Shelagh?"

"She, too. Come now, drink."

I kept my mouth closed, however, refusing the cup. "Am I losing my mind again, Quinto?"

"Losing—? Oh, you mean your memory!" He laughed, throwing his head back, and I felt relief touching me. "No, of course not! Not the way you did before, at least. You know us all here, don't you? And you know who you are, so your memory is fine. You have been ill, that's all, Caius. A raging fever and a rabid cough. Pneumonia, and not surprisingly. Benedict had it, too, though to a lesser degree, and this skin ailment that you show did not appear on him. Your memory is fine, I assure you. You may have lost some recent details, here and there, but that was the fever's fault, not your mind's. Now drink, and sleep."

"Why can't I move?"

"Because you're as weak as a baby, famished and dehydrated. Be grateful you're alive, because now you'll start to regain your strength. Drink, man!"

The potion had a chalky, bitter taste, but I drank all of it, and when I had, Quinto lowered my head back to the pillow and moved beyond my sight. Shelagh leaned over me again and wiped the corners of my mouth before stooping closer and kissing me gently on the forehead. I felt her lips, cool and soft, then felt her move away.

"What skin ailment?" I asked, but no one answered me.

I knew I was dreaming from the moment I opened my eyes, for the room was dark and yet I could see perfectly. Ironhair sat beside my bed, slouched in a padded armchair, leaning his chin upon his bent left arm and gazing at me through narrowed eyes. He wore the *toga praetexta*, the purple-bordered toga of a Roman senator. When he saw that I had come awake, he smiled and straightened up.

"Caius Merlyn Britannicus," he drawled. "My people tell me you've been seeking me. How may I serve you?"

"Serve me by staying alive until I come for you," I answered, and he laughed, his voice filled with what sounded like genuine amusement.

"I will! You may rest assured I have no plans to die. But why would you come for me?"

I simply lay and looked at him, seeing the misleading attractiveness I had always seen in him, the apparent lack of malice. "Why?" I asked him then. "Why did you set out to destroy my life?"

"Destroy—?" He laughed again, but when his laughter died away, there was perplexity stamped between his brows.

"Why would you think that I would waste my time destroying *you*? Are you that arrogant in your conceit?" His voice grew colder, angry now. "You're but one man, Britannicus, and though it may offend your ears to hear it, I have worthier, more important matters to occupy me. I have a kingdom yet to win for my prime client, Carthac Pendragon, and until I have done that I can have little time for squandering upon my own past grievances."

He paused, and I interjected, "Your *client*? Are you then become a senator, in truth, that you have clients?"

He ignored my interruption completely, continuing as though I had not spoken at all. "Oh, it's true enough, I'll grant you, that you and I had different viewpoints once, and that you used your power to thwart me.

But that was long years since, and life has moved along since then—new challenges, new lands and different hills to climb! I've seldom thought of you in years, except for one or two occasions when your name came up in casual discussions. Merlyn of Camulod, you call yourself today. A far cry from Caius Merlyn Britannicus, Legate Commander of the Forces of Camulod, as you once named yourself to me."

"That stuck in your craw, didn't it?"

"Stuck in my craw? Come now, Merlyn! We have both grown up since then. That long and overblown self-entitlement was the posturing pride of a self-important little man who feared his spurious powers might be challenged. Admit it."

"No, it was a statement of fact, made with authority, and it sufficed to put you down and quell your plans for usurpation of this Colony."

"Only temporarily," he drawled, almost inaudibly.

"What did you say?"

He smiled, a long, slow smile. "I said it set my plans back temporarily. I will have Camulod, you know, once Carthac has claimed his place in Cambria."

"Never," I murmured. "Not while I am alive to stop you."

"You? Ah, Merlyn, you are already half-way dead. Fully alive, perhaps, in mental terms, but physically? No." He shook his head. "Your leprosy will write an end to you in Camulod."

"It might," I said, totally undismayed to hear him name my deepest fear. "But not before I chop the living heart out of your breast."

"Hah!" He rose swiftly to his feet and moved behind the chair, then slowed to settle the folds of his snowy toga to drape perfectly before he placed his hands on the chair's back and leaned over it, towards me. "Merlyn," he said, his voice betraying a hint of impatience, "you are not a stupid man, I know. Tiresome, indeed, but not stupid. So if you hear no other word from me but this, hear this clearly: I will die, as all men must, but I will not die by your hand. Believe that. You and I will never come together, chin to chin, as warriors do to test each other's mettle. Believe that, and let me do what I must do. Live out your silly, miserable life however you will but please—if I must implore, I will—do not delude yourself that I would stoop to notice any detail of your life. Now let me go, I am required elsewhere."

"Carthac," I said.

"What of Carthac?"

"Why do you aid him?"

"Carthac is a means to my own ends. He is insane, an animal, un-worthy to be called a human man, but he is necessary, for the time being, at least. He is impervious to pain, you know, and utterly fearless. I think he may be truly invulnerable. He bleeds like any man, so I suppose that is not quite true, but I seriously doubt he can be killed like any ordinary man. I once watched as a surgeon butcher carved his thigh and dug a long, barbed arrow from the wound. Carthac bore it all without a grunt, without a flicker of annoyance. Mind you, he killed the surgeon afterwards, but that was merely as an afterthought. As I said, he is insane."

"And when he turns to rend you limb from limb, what then, Ironhair?"

"He never will. He loves me, in his own demented way. I am the only friend that he has ever known, and he trusts me completely. And now I must go. Release me, if you will."

"Presently I will, but you have much to answer for. The assault on our children, years ago, and the murder during that assault of Hector's wife, Julia, a blameless woman if there ever was one. The recent death of my own wife, Tressa. The death of my good friend Dedalus, and much, much more, the tally of which has barely begun—"

He made a tutting noise, cutting me short. "These charges are nonsense, Britannicus. I know nothing of this woman Julia, although I'll take your word that she was killed. That was unfortunate and incidental to the main concern, which was to stifle the Pendragon brat. In that, I struck at you, once and no more. I was displeased with you. Mind you, had I known then what I know now, I might have tried the harder, but that was before dear Carthac came into my life.

"As for your wife and friends, what fault lies there of mine? Yours was the choice to come thus howling home, abandoning the simplest steps that might have saved their lives. You were the one who rode though unknown land with no protective scouts ahead of you. And why? I have yet brought no threat to bear on Camulod, nor will I, till I'm done in Cambria. Really, you must admit I am blameless, there."

"What about Horsa?"

"What about him? I required mercenaries, and he provided them."

"He is a Dane, an Outlander!"

"He is a mercenary, Merlyn! He fights for payment."

"Aye, and for land and plunder and rapine. He slaughtered Vortigern, who was more than good to him and his kind. You'd turn his people loose among your own?"

His lip curled in a sneer. "What's this about my *own*? I have no people of my own, other than those I own by right of purchase. Spare me these minatory mouthings and let me go."

I nodded to him and lay back. "Go then, but be prepared for me. I'm coming for you, Ironhair, and I will find you."

He smiled again and began to fade from my sight, the light that revealed him to me dimming slowly. "I have told you, Merlyn, you will not find me. Look to yourself, and to your charge, Arthur Pendragon. There is the one you should be grieving for and fretting over . . . He is accursed . . . much like you . . ."

When the room was completely dark and he was gone, I tried to shift myself upright but could not move. I raised my voice, instead, and was answered by another, coming from beyond the door. Then the door swung open and a young woman came in, bearing a lamp with a brazen reflector.

"Master Merlyn? Can I do aught for you?"

"No," I replied, pleased to hear that my voice was as strong as it had ever been. "What is your name?"

I cannot recall her name, but she told me she had heard me talking in my sleep, and I smiled and told her that I had been dreaming. She left me alone again, and I lay staring up at the darkened ceiling in wonder, stroking my fingers up and down the roughened surface of my scaly, dry-skinned chest. Her lamp had been bright, amplified by the polished brass reflector. It should have dazzled me, after hours in a darkened room, but it had not. My eyes had grown accustomed to bright light before she entered.

I have never since been able to explain it, but I believe that Ironhair was in my room that night, and I have often wondered if he knew of it.

I was fully recovered and up and about a week later, little the worse for my strange illness, save that my skin was still rough and reddened. I checked myself and found nothing in the least resembling lesions; rough, scaly skin was all I had to show for my exposure on the night of the storm. Rough, scaly skin externally, and an equally rough, scaly texture to what lay inside me.

I reviewed everything that had happened prior to our arrival, and by the time Philip and Rufio and Falvo brought the remainder of my thousand back to Camulod, I had everything in hand, functioning efficiently.

Connor had seen the Danish fleet on its arrival, after it came around the tip of Cornwall's peninsula. He had spied it sailing downwind from afar and fled ahead of it with his two biremes and his fifteen escorting galleys. Vastly outnumbered—his estimate of the enemy's fleet was two hundred sails—he made no attempt to linger and fight but struck north-ward instantly, intent on gathering his own fleet. In passing, nonetheless, he dispatched two groups of messengers to bring warning to us and to Huw Strongarm, who lay encamped at Caerdyff. He would return, he said, when he could fight effectively against such numbers.

When the word arrived in Camulod, Ambrose was left with little choice but to ride to Huw's assistance. A fleet so large would land four thousand warriors, at the minimum of twenty men to a craft, and he knew the Danes used crews of at least thirty, and would be over-crewed with warriors seeking spoil. He reckoned on six thousand warriors, and would not have been surprised to learn that they were eight or even ten thousand.

Huw's armies, Ambrose knew, had been disbanded in the aftermath of their victory on the coast by Dolaucothi. No one had expected Ironhair to raid again until the following year, and no one had expected to be confronted by another, vastly different army. Ambrose had not yet learned that these were Ironhair's new allies. It would take an entire month, at least, he reasoned, to rally Huw's Pendragon host again, for they were busy with their farms, ploughing the land in preparation for seeding. An army thousands strong, landed as unexpectedly as this one, would spread across the land like wildfire, gaining enormous impetus before it could be challenged or brought to fight. Only a mounted force from Camulod had any chance of stopping them, for fearsome as they were aboard their swooping ships, once they were on the land they were mere infantry, immensely vulnerable to our massed horsemen.

Within the week, Ambrose had taken two full legions of our total force—two thousand heavy horse, a thousand scouts, and three thousand foot—and entered Cambria, headed directly to the southern coast, to Caerdyff, where he hoped to find Huw Strongarm. Derek of Ravenglass had ridden with him. Behind him, in full charge of Camulod, Ambrose left Tertius Lucca with a holding force of two thousand, fully three-fourths of those garrison foot soldiers. He had also left word for me, should I return before he did, that I should remain in place, looking to the defence of Camulod and all the lands about it—from the Appian Colony in the north all the way south to Ilchester and beyond—but that I should send on my thousand horse to him as reinforcements, under Tertius Lucca himself, should we remain unthreatened here at home.

No word had come from Cambria of Arthur, and Ambrose had been gone for nigh on a month when we came home.

On the day following the return of Philip and the others, two troopers came to my quarters in the fort, carrying a large, wooden chest. It was from Plato, major-domo of the Villa Britannicus, and there was a single sheet of paper affixed to the lid. In it, Plato expressed his condolences on the loss of my beloved lady and informed me that Derek had left it at the Villa for me before riding off with Ambrose. I sat staring at it for some time, knowing what it contained, before I took my knife and cut the cords that bound it shut, throwing back the lid to look inside.

Beneath the carefully folded mass of his great red-dyed war cloak, my cousin Uther's armour was intact, no single piece of it missing. It bore a few deep scores, but it was in fine condition. The helmet was more splendid than I remembered, crested with a fine display of stiff horsehair, dyed a deep scarlet; the visor band above the brows had been embossed with Uther's fiery dragon, enamelled in red. The same device, much larger, was engraved into the cuirass, the cuts of the engraving similarly packed with fired enamel, so that the device stood out sharp and clear against the dull matte of the bronze breastplate: a broad-winged dragon, standing erect upon its strong rear legs and breathing curls of fire. I saw my cousin wearing it, and laughing at me, showing his strong, white, even teeth. He had told me once that I was too judgmental, and his opinion had wounded me deeply, before I realized that it was the simple truth.

Suddenly I missed him, grievously. I picked up his enormous, heavy cloak and spread it carefully out on the floor. Covering all the back of it in heavy layers of colourfully worked, rich needlecraft, that same great dragon reared its head and spread its wings over the wide-stretched shoulders, this time done all in threads of pure, finely wrought gold. Arthur would look magnificent in this, I thought, and turned my head to where I had imagined Uther watching me. He stood there still, laughing with his head thrown back, and I heard him speak in my mind. "The boy's accursed . . ." he said in Ironhair's voice. I turned away again and slammed the lid on the great box, then sat there looking at it while my mind recalled the other two great chests I possessed, those that contained the tools of death of two Egyptian warlocks called Caspar and Memnon. Murderously evil creatures of an equally evil master, Lot of Cornwall, they had been sent to wreak destruction and havoc in Camulod, and they had slain my father with their black sorcery. After their death, and guided by Donuil, I had gained possession of the two, iron-bound chests that contained all the lethal paraphernalia of their ungodly craft. Therein, all painstakingly arranged and individually packaged with the greatest care, I had found layer after layer of terrifying and potent preparations: pastes and powders; unguents and salves; liquids and crystals; leaves, berries and dried grasses, whole, crushed, and ground; and a multitude of other indefinable things contained in boxes, vials, silken wrappings and ceramic jars. Treating them all with great caution, since I was acutely aware of who had owned them, I had discovered all of them to be connected by one common element: they all dealt death, in varying, virulent forms. For months I had laboured over them at every opportunity, seeking to find their individual secrets, and I had largely been successful, although there yet remained a number, fully one third of the total, whose secrets I had so far been unable to unlock. Among the two-thirds identified, however, I had an entire cornucopia of violent, terrifying death in multitudinous forms. But now, as I sat there, the outlines of a plan began to form rapidly in my mind, and I straightened my shoulders and drew a deep, shuddering breath.

"Ironhair," I whispered, "I have a gift for you."

I attended a meeting of the Council of Camulod the day after that, and left before the business was concluded. I knew few of the Councillors after my absence of so many years, and I found I had no patience now with the minutiae of government. On leaving, I sought out Tertius Lucca and asked him to walk with me, and as we strolled outside the gates of the fort I informed him that I intended to ignore my brother's request to

send him personally with the extra thousand horse. His place, I said, was
here in Camulod, where he was particularly suited, both by nature and
by training, to oversee the conduct of the collective garrisons of the surrounding outposts and to work with the Council. I would send Philip with
the cavalry reinforcements, I told him, and would hand over full command
again to Lucca, until such time as Ambrose returned.

He listened, keeping his eyes cast down, and when I had completed
what I had to say, he nodded, then saluted me, accepting my decree. I
left him standing there beneath the walls and made my way to the bathhouse, feeling a grim excitement welling in my breast.

A short time later, I sat alone again in my own chambers, bare to the
waist, repeating something I had once seen Lucanus do. I held one of
Tressa's longest needles in my hand and I was sticking it gently, but
judiciously, into my chest, moving it from place to place and taking note
of what I felt. In most places, I felt the pain of a piercing needle. In many
others, however, at least half a score of them, the metal needle slipped
into my flesh without producing any sensation at all. Eventually I stopped
what I was doing and sat there, staring into nothingness, empty and un-
moved by the discovery. I had noticed the discoloured patches while lying
in the steam room earlier: areas of whitish, dead-looking skin, roughly
circular in shape, the body hair within their boundaries already turning
grey. Not lesions, yet, but growing. Mucius Quinto's "minor ailment of
the skin." Leprosy.

After a time, I rose and dressed again, wearing my finest leathers, and
then sent for Philip, Falvo and Rufio. When they arrived, I told them to
prepare to leave for Cambria in two days' time. I spent the remainder of
the day poring through the warlocks' chests.

That night, I sought out Donuil and Shelagh to tell them I would be
leaving Camulod for a time, and that they should not worry about me.
Donuil I charged with looking after things while I was gone; Shelagh I
charged with looking after Donuil. When Donuil sought to embrace me,
I thrust him away and he fell back, abashed. Shelagh merely kissed her
own palm and then laid it gently on my cheek. I heaved a deep, shaking
breath, swallowed hard and left them.

Hours later, when the only people stirring were the night guards, I
visited the stables, where I found a light, two-wheeled cart and a plain,
sturdy horse to pull it. I harnessed the animal and took it to my quarters,
where I loaded four cases onto the cart. One of them contained Uther's
armour. Two more were the warlocks' chests. The last held a variety of
things I thought I might need—clothing, and twine, a small hand axe,
some coils of iron wire of varied thickness, some knives of varying sizes,
fish hooks and lines, a matched set of short-sword and dagger, made by
Publius Varrus, a polished mirror that had been my Aunt Luceiia's, my
own long sword and Excalibur in its long, wooden case. I also took food-

stuffs, scavenged from the kitchens: some bread, slabs of both salted and smoked meat, a bag of flour, a smaller bag of salt, a clutch of onions and some corms of garlic, and the remainder of the olive oil, olives and wine brought to me by Germanus and carried safely home to me by the chief quartermaster. When I had loaded everything, I swathed myself in an ankle-length, black, threadbare garment which resembled a cloak, save that it had long, deep sleeves and a peaked, capacious hood that obscured my face. Then I hauled myself up to the cart's bench and set the horses moving, pulling the hood's deep cowl forward, over my face. I had appropriated the garment that afternoon, from a peg outside the refectory where it had been left hanging while its owner went in search of food. In return I had left a heavy, woollen cloak of my own, sleeveless but far finer than the one I took and much too fine for my intended purposes. As I expected, when I steered my cart out through the gates, shortly before dawn, the guards paid no attention to my passing.

I reached my little, hidden valley of Avalon as the sun climbed high enough to throw long shadows from the surrounding trees down onto the waters of the tiny lake concealed within its depths, and I was keenly aware that seven whole years and more had passed since I had last been here, and that my Tress had lived her life and died without knowing of its existence. Cassandra's grave was barely noticeable now, its mound sunken to the level of the surrounding ground, and the door to the stone hut was still securely closed. This was my sanctuary; the world held no dominion over me here. The ropes that formed the cradle of my old bed were still strong enough to bear my weight, and I soon fell asleep, only to awaken within the hour, well rested and filled with a profound sense of calm as I listened to the song of birds in the woodlands around the tiny lake.

I spent some time thereafter gathering firewood, then lit a fire in the old firepit just beyond the door of the hut. I made a meal of cold, smoked meat and some of the bread that I had carried from the fort, and then I sat by the fire and opened up the warlocks' chests, retrieving my own copious notes and studying them closely. I must have been lost in them for many hours, because when I looked about again the sun had vanished and my fire was almost out, though I had fed it several times throughout the day. I coaxed it back to life again, noticing that the hoard of fuel I had amassed that morning now was almost gone, and thereafter I sat staring into the flames, lost in my thoughts as the light about me faded into dark.

Carthac was fearless, utterly so; Ironhair had said so in my dream. Strongarm had said the same: invincible, invulnerable, fearless, afraid of neither man nor beast. Horsa's Danes were fearless, too, according to all reports that I had heard. Savage, they were; invincible in their ferocity; implacable in their fierce hatred of any that withstood them or sought to thwart them; afraid, in all their godless pride and arrogance, of neither man nor beast.

My men were fearless, too, in war: invincible in their sure strength and confident that no mere human force could withstand them. And yet I knew my men, in Camulod, had once known fear of me when I was young—not of my human strength, but of the mere suggestion that I, Merlyn, possessed powers that were more than human. Their fears had been unfounded, for the deeds that awed them had all been achieved by trickery and mere suggestions fed by me into their willing minds. The most notorious of those had concerned the disappearance of Cassandra from a guarded room in the dead of night, and that had been no mere mischief. I had feared for the girl's life at the hands of some unknown assailant and had smuggled her away unseen before the guards were set to protect an empty room. The mystery came later, when I claimed to have been wakened by a dream that she was gone, and a subsequent search had proved this to be true. For years thereafter, soldiers walked in awe of me and watched me surreptitiously, awaiting further marvels. Those fearless soldiers, scorning man and beast, had nonetheless feared me and what I whispered to their minds of darkness where their swords could not save them.

Now I had ranged before me, in the flickering firelight, an entire armoury of dark and fearsome tools, all of which could bring death and other terrifying effects, all of them garnered by two men whose evil minds possessed no other wish than to bring terror to the minds of ordinary men by causing death through awesome, mystifying and unnatural means. I had small, black, envenomed thorns that would bring instant, painful death to anyone they pricked, and I possessed a green and noxious paste that carried fiery poison that would burn a man to death from within, from the merest scratch. I had tray upon tray of unguents and oils and powders and salts and crystals, dried, withered berries, seeds and nuts, and crushed admixtures of all kinds; grasses and twigs and unknown, fibrous substances that burned with noxious, stultifying smoke; and all of these things brought death, in one form or another.

I would teach Carthac fear, I had resolved, and Ironhair, and all his swarming men. They would know fear the like of which they never could have dreamed: the fear of living death and magical enchantment; the fear of darkness and the stinking, evil things that crawled therein; the fear of being naked in the path of ravening beasts whose shapes could neither be imagined nor endured, grim, unseen creations from the human mind's darkest recesses. I, Merlyn, would teach them how to fear.

But before I could achieve any part of what I planned, I also had practical considerations to resolve, all of them dealing with the bulk of what lay spread about me. How much of it could I take with me, and how would I carry it? I would be journeying alone, a solitary man, so I would be a fool to carry anything that might appear worth stealing. I would be walking, too, once I reached Cambria, since a horse would attract attention where I wanted none. And I would be unarmoured to the point of appearing weaponless, although I would have both short-sword and dagger concealed beneath my cloak. It was my hope to travel by night, most of the time, and then I would be aided by the dark and by my long, black robe. But how much of this portable mass of death could I take with me?

Then I remembered Lucanus, and I smiled. Luke had been a gatherer of all things medicinal—leaves and herbs and roots and pods and berries—and he had devised a means of garnering and saving them that left his hands free of the need to carry them. He had had several robes made to his precise design, and had thereafter worn one every time he ventured out on any errand of collection. They were long and black and sleeveless, made of strong, homespun cloth in double thickness. Belted at the waist, they were open from neckline to ankle, and completely festooned with pouches and pockets, each strongly sewn in place and all overlapping one upon the other as they hung. I recalled the pride and enjoyment with which he had demonstrated it, when it was new. I had made some comment on its appearance, and he had brushed that aside, entreating me to think of its function rather than its look; the capacity to carry large quantities of different plants, berries and leaves, without the fear of losing them or mixing them together. Luke was long dead, but one of those garments hung in my own quarters in Camulod, where he had left it and forgotten it years earlier, before we went to Ravenglass. I had noticed it mere days before, hanging still in place, but had thought nothing of it at the time. Now I knew that I had to return to Camulod to collect it.

Pleased that I now knew how I would proceed, I set about the selection of my deadly tools. I set aside one ceramic, lidded box of the green poisoned paste first. That was my *sine qua non*, my most essential element: the death I had selected for both Ironhair and Carthac. They would both die consumed by inner fires, as had the warlock Caspar. After that, I laid apart the rolled ribbons of cloth that held the fingerjoint-long poisoned thorns, each placed beside its neighbour with great care, the deadly points thrust through the cloth for safety and for ease of carrying. As I progressed, the choices became more difficult. Vials of liquid of varying colours, each of them deadly enough to empoison an entire army, if added to the water that they drank. Boxes of powders that, mixed into food or drink, could produce frothing, convulsive, agonizing death within mere moments. Clusters of fibrous stuff that, thrown into a fire, produced a sweetish, sickening smoke that stupefied all who breathed it.

One substance gave me no concern at all, and that was the large box of combustible powder that I thought of as fire-powder. I would not have considered leaving that behind. Another substance, this one a reddish, crystalline compound evidently crushed with mortar and pestle, affected me similarly, and my sole regret was for the paucity I had of it. This substance, when ingested, brought paralysis. Years before, I had dissolved a tiny pinch of it in water and then fed it to a rabbit, which had quickly died in a spasm, board stiff. I had set the poor dead thing aside, holding it by its rigid legs and meaning to burn it later, after I had completed my notations on the day's activities. But when I looked again, perhaps an hour later, the "dead" rabbit had revived completely and went bounding from the table when it saw me move. Astonished more than I can say, I had repeated the procedure with another rabbit, with the same results. The paralysis was total, but reversed itself within the hour. The second time I carried out the test, I watched far more closely, and observed that the little creature's eyes did not glaze over as they would in death. In fact, they seemed alert, though motionless. I brought a taper close, and the pupils contracted, indicating an awareness of the light. I could not, of course, be certain, but I believed the animal had not lost consciousness but merely the ability to move. If that were true, it might apply to men, as well. I set the reddish crystals aside, checking with care to see that the lid still fitted snugly on the small box that contained them.

My final selection was no selection at all, but rather the careful removal from its packaging of the amazing, hair-crowned human mask that fitted me as though shaped to my face. Then I repacked both large chests and locked them, dragged them deep into the trees, covering them first with a leather sleeping tent, and then laying branches over them. It was almost completely dark by then, and I carried my selected treasures into the hut, where I piled them carefully in a corner before lighting the fire in the iron basket against the wall at the foot of the bed.

The following morning, I returned briefly to Camulod, avoiding everyone and merely visiting my quarters to collect the long robe that Lucanus had left there. I was back in my valley long before nightfall, and in the course of the evening I repeated the entire procedure I had rehearsed the previous day, having discovered that Luke's pocket-rich garment would hold far more than I had suspected. It was heavy, when I picked it up to put it on, but it hung easily, once donned, and when I had distributed the contents to remove the chinking sound of vials knocking on each other, I found that I could walk silently while wearing it. I then spent another entire day teaching myself which substances lay hidden in which pocket, so that soon I could reach for each package without thought.

I was prepared.

PART THREE

VERULAMIUM

XVII

THE SENTRY STIFFENED as I lunged, but before he could begin to shout or move I had clamped my fingers over his mouth and nostrils and jerked him back against me, my dagger point pressed against his exposed neck. I hissed into his ear.

"You should be dead, my friend, but friend I am. I am Merlyn Britannicus. Nod your head if you believe me and can hold your peace." I felt his head move in my grasp, and I released him and stepped back. He turned to face me slowly, his eyes wide with fear. I did not know him, but I saw the recognition come into his face.

"Comm—" he began, but I silenced him with a chop of my hand.

"Who commands the guard tonight? And keep your voice down."

"Commander Falvo, sir."

"Good. Bring me to him."

Benedict was with Falvo in the command tent, and their jaws fell open when they saw me step in. They both leaped to their feet with cries of welcome, but stopped short as their eyes took in my whole appearance. I knew I was a sight well worth beholding, but I had no time to waste on niceties. This was a large encampment, filled with men and horses, and I had penetrated it without difficulty, making my way through the outer guards simply by walking in the shadows, cloaked in my black robes.

"Benedict, Falvo," I greeted them, nodding to each in turn. "Your security is weak. Your guards are useless. None of them saw me walk in here. No one challenged me and I made no attempt to hide. Is Ambrose here?"

Benedict answered me. "No, Ambrose rode off late this afternoon with Derek and a hundred Scouts. We fought a battle here, today."

"And now your guards have earned the right to sleep on duty? I know you fought today. I watched it from the mountain top to the north. But you fought inconclusively. Their shield walls thwarted you. They gulled you into following them on to their chosen ground, and then they outfought you with Roman tactics. You achieved nothing. Will you offer me a cup of wine?"

There was an awkward silence as they absorbed my rebuke, but then Falvo said, "No, but we have mead, will that suffice?" I nodded. Falvo looked unhappy, but he said nothing more and moved at once to pour me a cup of mead.

I knew I had been harsh, and that after a separation of long months he might perhaps have expected me to be more friendly, but everything I had said was true. The Danes had held the higher ground that day, and they had used the tortoise formations of the ancient legions to frustrate our cavalry, holding their big, round shields in overlapping rows that formed a solid front against our horsemen, who were thus forced to charge uphill to reach them and might as well have been attacking the towering sides of floating ships. The battle had been broken off after a useless spell of wasted hours, without victory going to either side. I had watched it from afar, discovering it by merest chance, and had been angered by the confusion I had witnessed, as much as by the fact that there was nothing I could do to influence any of it.

Falvo offered me my mead and I took it from him with a nod of thanks and drank the half of it, feeling the fiery, honey-sweet bite of it exploding in my mouth, throat and chest.

"My thanks, Falvo. When is Ambrose due back? Or do you, too, call him Merlyn nowadays? Everyone else does, it appears." I knew I was being unpleasant, but it was as though someone else had control of my tongue.

Falvo gazed at me, opening his mouth as though to answer me, then turned to Benedict, who had been sitting watching me with a peculiar expression on his face. Benedict turned his head slightly to catch Falvo's eye, then shrugged.

"What is it? Why do you look at me like that, Falvo?"

Benedict grunted. "He thought you dead. We all did."

"Well, it's not so, as you can see. Why did you think that?"

Falvo spoke up. "Word reached us from the south that your body had been found burned and mutilated."

I shook my head. "That sounds to me like someone's wishful prayer. Its author will be disappointed."

Benedict evidently found no humour in my comment. "Aye, well, that was months ago, and no one has seen or heard from you since then. We have mourned you."

"And Ambrose has taken my name. Why so? The word is everywhere that Merlyn of Camulod leads this army."

Again they exchanged glances, and this time it was Falvo who shrugged his shoulders. "It was his wish and his decision. He says that Merlyn is a name to conjure fear. Merlyn is known, and Merlyn has the respect of Cambrian warriors, so Ambrose fought and campaigned as Merlyn right from the start of this campaign. No one remarked the difference. Then, when the word arrived that you were dead, he swore that while he lived, you would never die." He paused, and stuck out his jaw. "Your brother thinks highly of you," he said then, his tone implying that not all men did.

I heaved a short, sharp sigh and sat down in one of the chairs before his desk. "Aye, well, I dropped from people's sight, but not from life. I have been occupied as much as any of you, here in Cambria. Have you heard tell of Merlyn's Vengeance?"

Benedict's head jerked up. "Aye, everyone has, though we know not what we should make of it. We hear tales of rampant death and sorcery, of slaughter without bloodshed and of nightly terrors without end. It seems the Danes, and all their other allies, now live in fear of nightfall and the creatures that prowl there, among the shadows."

"That's true, and so they should. They live in terror of the night, and I have worked to make it so."

"*You* have worked to make it so?" Falvo's eyes showed a spark of curiosity. "Are you responsible for all of this, this *sorcery?*"

"Aye, and for the fear of it. I am. I've been moving openly among them for almost three months now, spreading terror by night."

He hesitated. "Why are you dressed like . . . that?" He nodded at my clothing.

"Because it helps conceal me, when I move through the dark. In daylight, I wear different clothing."

Benedict's voice was calm. "What can you tell us of this star thing, then? Is that your doing?"

"Aye. They call it the star of Merlyn's Vengeance. I work among them, posing as an idiot and doing menial tasks. I carry water to the cooks and do those things that warriors will not stoop to do, yet cannot live without. And in doing them I poison drinking water, and I poison food, and often wipe out whole encampments. Each time I do that, and can arrange my message without fear of interruption, I leave a grouping of eight corpses round a fire, their heads in the ashes so that they burn, their feet all pointing outwards to form an eight-pointed star.

"At other times, I murder guards, or drunken men I meet among the woods at night. Those, though, I kill with poisoned thorns, leaving the unmarked corpses to be found by whomsoever might next chance that way. My purpose is, and has been, to spread terror. And to that end I have sometimes appeared in bursts of smoke and fire, frightening drunken men who have already frightened themselves by talking of my deeds. Then, at those times, I tell them who I am, that I am Death, bearer of Merlyn's Vengeance."

Benedict laughed aloud, but the sound was strained and nervous. "By the Christ, Merlyn, you almost had me believing you, there . . ."

"Wait you."

I rose and walked away into the shadows of a dark corner, passing a small fire that burned in an iron basket upon the bare earth as I went. There, standing with my back to them, I reached into my robes and withdrew the warlock's mask. I placed it over my face, throwing the tangled locks of its wig over my head, and pulled my cowled hood up and forward to throw my face into shadow. That done, I reached again into my clothes to find a pinch of fire-powder, then turned around and walked towards the fire, head down. I threw the powder in the fire. When the blinding flash of flame and sparks had died and all the space within the tent was filled with roiling smoke, I stepped forward again and let them see my face.

Both men were rigid, straining away from me, petrified with shock and gazing at me in utter horror, seeing only the hideous visage of the mask. I stood silent for a moment, then intoned "I am Death, bearer of Merlyn's Vengeance!" in sepulchral tones. Finally I threw back my hood, pulled off the mask and opened the tent flaps to their widest, allowing the acrid, sulphurous smoke to dissipate. Neither man had moved when I returned and their eyes were still staring in shock.

"Of course," I said, "you know me well, both of you, so you would not be fooled. But these Danes are pagans, terrified of insubstantial things and beings they cannot hew with axes. They believe in demons and in creatures that dwell in awful darkness. And so I feed their fears and sap their confidence in their invincibility. It is mummery, but it is effective."

Benedict appeared to have relaxed slightly, but when he spoke his voice was tight. "Aye," he muttered. "Mummery, perhaps, but it reeks of sorcery, and murder, too. What was that . . . that flash and all that smoke?"

"It was produced by throwing a certain powder upon a flame. No more than that."

Falvo released his pent-up breath in a long hiss. "Well," he said, "you've made believers out of us, with that display . . . And you've been doing this now for three months, you say?" He snorted, almost managing to sound amused. "The Danes are either braver or more foolish than I thought. I would have fled long since, pursued by such demons. But did you come here merely to tell us this?"

"No, I came because I have had no news of Camulod for three months now. Is all well at home?"

"Aye, it is. No problems there," Benedict said, his voice sounding stronger. "Everything's peaceful, according to the last report we had, two days ago, and life is as it should be."

"Good. And what of Germanus and the debate at Verulamium? Have we heard aught of that?"

"Not a word," Falvo said, shaking his head. "It will be over now, long since. Germanus should be back in Gaul by now."

"Bishop Enos. Has he passed this way, or sent word of any kind?" I saw their heads shake in unison. "And Arthur. What of him?" I had to fight to keep my face expressionless as I asked this, greatly fearing the answer I might receive.

"Arthur is here," Benedict said. "Or he was, until today. He rode out with Ambrose."

My heart leaped with relief. "How is the boy, is he well?"

"Better than well," Falvo laughed. "And he's a boy no longer. He is a full Commander of Cavalry now, as big as you are, easily. Huge, he is, grown like a big, strong thistle, and beloved of his men. You will be proud of him, when next you see him."

"Thank you for that," I said, slumping in my seat from the intensity of my relief. "Those are the finest tidings I could hear tonight. I have been terrified that something might have gone amiss with him. He was with Llewellyn, you know, when Horsa's Danes landed."

Benedict nodded. "Aye, but they came straight to us when we arrived, and Arthur has been with us ever since. He is a sweet fighter, that lad."

"What happened to Llewellyn? Is he not here with Arthur?"

"He was, but he went back to be with Huw Strongarm. Will you have some more mead?"

I shook my head and rose to my feet. "No, I must leave now. I want to be far from here by morning, exacting Merlyn's Vengeance as usual. But before I go, I need more information. Where is Ironhair quartered, do we know? And where is Carthac? They seem to have no means of communication between their armies, save at the highest levels. Certainly none of the fools I meet have information on the whereabouts of their commanders."

Falvo stood and moved to the open flaps of the tent, his hands on his hips as he stared out into the darkness of the camp. "Ironhair is everywhere, according to reports. He never seems to stay in one place long enough for us to find out where he is. Rufio calls him the Man of Wind, since he passes like wind, and in the passing makes much noise and leaves a lingering unpleasantness . . ." He leaned forward and closed the flaps, shaking them loose from their ties, then turned back to me and moved to sit at the guard commander's table, where he tilted his chair back and crossed his feet on the table top.

"Carthac, on the other hand, is close by now. He has a well-established camp, in a mountain valley eight miles from where we sit now, to the west. It's a natural fortress and we can't approach it—not with our horses. We have to wait until his animals come down to us. They have seven or eight ways in and out, but they all feed into three narrow approaches, higher up, and those are heavily manned and guarded at all times.

"His men think he is immortal and he has become a demigod of sorts, albeit a malign and twisted one. Every excess, every atrocity that you may name is his indulgence, and the creatures that he leads revere him for his lusts. They throng around him in hundreds, fanatical in their adulation of the imbecile. We cannot come near him—" He paused, abstracted, then continued. "And even if we could, I seriously wonder if we could kill him. He is . . . elemental. A terrifying, overwhelming presence."

"Horse turds. He's a man, Falvo, and he must die. I intend to kill him, painfully and slowly. That is why I am here, doing what I do alone. But in order to kill him I must find him, and when I've found him I must come close by him. Once he is dead, your task will become much simpler." I moved to leave, adjusting my hood about my face. "Please pass on my greetings to my brother . . . Merlyn . . . and tell him that. Tell him that Carthac's death is my prime task." I smiled very slightly. "Tell him I will do nothing to contradict his identity. Tell him, too, if you will, that I think of him daily, with love, as I do Arthur, and that I hope to meet them both again some day soon, when this is over. Farewell."

Then the darkness swallowed me, and no one saw me leaving the encampment.

Six days later, in the first hour after dawn on a bright morning, I sat with my back pressed against the top of a high ridge, scanning another encampment, this one in the valley below me. I was enjoying the distant singing of a skylark as I listened to the sounds of the man who was clambering up behind me on the opposite side, towards the self-same notch in the skyline that had attracted me the day before. Thinking himself alone, the newcomer made no attempt to cover his own noise; I had heard him long before, slipping and clattering as he climbed up a steep, dry stream bed. I had been on the top of the ridge since the previous evening, arriving there too late to run the risk of trying to descend in the darkness that was gathering by the time I had completed my examination of the site below.

Behind me, the newcomer reached the top and stopped, and I could hear his heavy breathing. He was a big man, heavy set and grey-bearded. I waited, out of his sight, and suddenly saw the dipping flight of the skylark for the first time since it had started singing. Below me, a large and loose-knit group of men entered the valley at its northern end and began to make their way to the encampment. Then I heard metal clink and a soft grunt as the man behind me raised himself cautiously to bring his head into the V-shaped notch in the ridge, where he could peer unseen into the valley below. He was less than an arm's length from where I sat.

"I had a dream about you last night," I said softly.

There came a grunt of startled fear and then a breathless moment of tense, motionless terror, followed by a great "whoosh" of breath and the sound of a body sagging against the ground.

"Merlyn, you demented whoreson! Is that you? Are you trying to kill me? What kind of sorcery is this?"

I bent sideways and offered Derek of Ravenglass my hand, then leaned backwards and heaved him into sight, pulling him belly downward through the narrow opening where he had crouched.

"Careful!" I warned. "It's steep, up here, but no one can see us. We're below the crest. There!"

He sat up, breathing heavily and digging in his heels to brace himself against the slope, then set about brushing the dust and tiny pebbles from his front. That done, he removed his helmet and wiped the sweat from his brow before scrubbing the helmet's leather rim with his sleeve. Only when he had replaced the helmet and mastered his breathing somewhat did he turn to me, blowing out a short, sharp breath through pursed lips.

"Falvo and Ben told us you had been into camp, but what in the name of Lud are you doing here?"

"I've been up here all night." I nodded towards the camp below. "Carthac's down there and I'm on my way to visit him, to end his miserable life. Didn't they tell you that, too? That's the reason I am here in Cambria. What are you doing here? You must have spent the night on the mountain, too."

"I did, at the bottom of the last slope, there." His eyes swept the valley from one end to the other. "I'm here to see what's down there. What's your fancy word for it? Reconnaissance?" I said nothing, and he was silent for a few moments. "Did you really dream of me last night?" he finally asked. I smiled and shook my head, and he relaxed visibly. "Thank the gods for that, then. It terrifies me to think you might dream of me, the way you dream. What happened to your hand?"

"What?" I had been unconsciously kneading my left hand with my right thumb, and now I glanced down to where the web between the thumb and the index finger had grown dead and grey. I stifled the instantaneous urge to snatch it away and hide it from his sight, and forced myself instead to flex the hand several times. "Oh, that," I said. "I scalded it, last week. It's healing, but it still feels stiff and sore."

Derek turned his eyes away, back to the valley. "It's not much of a camp, is it?"

"No, but it's effective enough for their purposes. It's sheltered, and it's safe. Nearly impregnable, in fact."

He grunted. "What's that building?"

There was only one, a long, low construction probably built from the stones that lay everywhere down there, fallen from the cliffs above. "It's some kind of cattle shelter. Nothing else it could be, up here, is there? There's grass for grazing, but there can't be any soil down there to speak of. So it wouldn't be a house. Must be a byre."

"Well, they're using it as a house now. How many people are there down there, do you know?"

I looked again, carefully, before I answered him. Apart from the one building, there were a few ramshackle huts that I could see, but they seemed to be mere piles of stones, thrown together. And against the base of the cliff on the opposite side from us there was a line of green and brown and multicoloured patches that I had guessed, after long observation the previous day, to be a row of the roughest kind of shelters, branches and saplings propped against the wall of the cliff, then covered haphazardly with blanket coverings.

"Last night, I guessed there must be three score of them, of thereabouts. Three score in camp, I mean. I've no idea how many others are outside, defending the incoming passes. Probably as many again."

Derek sucked air through his teeth, impatiently. "There has to be a way for us to get in there."

"There is, but not with horses—not easily, at any rate, and not without a bitter fight. There are three ways in, and two of them might just be passable for cavalry, but not before the heights above each route have been swept clean, and that will be wicked work."

I had spent the previous five days examining the adits to the place. The valley was high in the mountains; not prohibitively so, but it was hemmed about with steep, unscalable mountainsides that were as flat as walls. Three entrances led into it through narrow approaches flanked by high cliffs. I had discovered that fact by doing more climbing than I had thought to do, scaling the heights overlooking the passes on both sides and lying belly down for hours while I attempted to decipher the patterns of their defences. While one careful, solitary man could penetrate the places I had reached, it would have been impossible for a number of men to have achieved the same without being discovered. Pendragon mountaineers might have had a better chance, but Camulodian lowlanders would have no chance at all.

Derek listened with a long face, chewing on his lips. I cocked my head.

"What's wrong, Derek? Why are you up here? You're growing long in the tooth to be leaping about on mountains on your own. I am too, God knows, but I've a reason to be here alone. I have a one-man task."

"And so do I, almost." He waved to indicate another hillside, to the south of us. "Ambrose is over there, with Arthur, on that hill. There are times when second-hand reports are not enough. We came up here to see things for ourselves. But there's not much to see, is there?"

"That depends what you're looking for, my friend. How high above them do you think we are? How far from here to there?"

He made a face, reckoning. "Two hundred paces? Not much more than that, I'd guess."

"In fact it's closer to four hundred. But even four hundred paces, downhill like this, would put the enemy in range of Pendragon bows." He jerked his head around to look at me as I continued speaking. "It's a difficult climb, as you know, but it's far from impossible. We two came up it, each of us alone. Where two may go, in this kind of terrain, two hundred more can follow, and with two hundred Pendragon up here, that camp would be a death-trap.

"Now I'm going down there, later in the day, timing my arrival so that I'll be there by nightfall, when there's little chance of my being seen descending from above. I'll spend tonight there, seeing how things work, and then tomorrow, or tomorrow night, I'll find or make an opportunity to put myself close to Carthac. Once I'm there, he's a dead man."

"How can you say that, Merlyn? The man's not human! They say he's enchanted, has a charmed life, protected by the very gods themselves, and he can't be killed by human weapons."

I looked at him, one eyebrow raised high. "That's superstitious nonsense. Surely you don't believe that, Derek?"

He shrugged and dipped his head, looking ill at ease. "I don't know, Merlyn. But I do believe he fights like no man I have ever seen. He won't be killed with ease."

"I don't want him to die with ease, but die he will, if I win close to him. Now, when are you to meet again with Ambrose?"

"Mid-afternoon, at the base of the mountain."

"Well, when you meet him, tell him I am here and warn him what I intend to do. Then go and fetch Huw Strongarm and his bowmen—are they close by?"

"Not Huw himself, but aye, they're here, nigh on a thousand of them, under Llewellyn."

"Then lead them back this way, and bid them bring as many arrows as they can carry, sufficient for a days-long siege. And have Ambrose move his men up and position them outside each of the three adits to this place. Once Carthac is dead, the men below will be mere cattle. The death of their Immortal will destroy their will to fight. Tell Llewellyn that when his Pendragon have wiped out this camp, he must then send them outward, to sweep clean the cliffs above the entranceways. They'll have but little opposition, I suspect. Did you bring food?" He blinked at me, then nodded. "Then let's eat," I said, bending to take my own food from the heavy pack that lay by my feet, which contained the remainder of my much-depleted supplies from the warlocks' chests as well as my long black night-clothes.

Derek stared at the pack. "Do you intend to take that with you? Down there?"

"Of course. It's mine," I answered, smiling, but his face remained stern.

"What's in it?"

I shrugged my shoulders. "Things, mainly extra clothing."

"Horse turds, I saw the weight of it when you pulled it over. There's more in there than clothing. Probably enough to get you killed, should anyone look inside it."

"But no one will. No one has, in the past three months."

"No, but then you were alone. It's too big, an invitation to thieves. Or do you intend to carry it while you're killing Carthac?"

I could see he was right. I had intended to hide the knapsack, once safely down the hill, but the valley was small and crowded with people. He saw my indecision and spoke again.

"Look, you're determined to go down there, I know that. If you fail to kill your man, you'll die, and there's an end of you. If you succeed, again you'll probably die, for his creatures there won't let you simply walk away. So, armed with the knowledge of the odds against you already, why would you add to all your risks by dragging this great thing behind you? I'd hate to think of you being killed solely because of your pack, before you even get the chance to kill yourself apurpose . . ." He paused, and I said nothing. "Let me take it with me, Merlyn, back to our camp. It will be safe enough with me. I won't open it or let anyone else open it. Then, if your god is as merciful as you Christians say he is, and you come safely out of that place down there, I'll have it waiting for you."

I tore a piece of bread from the half loaf I had been holding and chewed it thoughtfully for some time before I nodded my head. "So be it," I said then. "Take it, and with it my thanks. But don't dare open it, Derek, and guard it as you would your wife or your life. Remember Merlyn's Vengeance. I swear to you that there is enough venom and poison within that pack to wipe out all of Camulod. Eat up!"

I should not have eaten that morning. Something poisoned me—something among my rations, I guessed, most probably the dried meat. I was surprised that I had not been alerted by its smell, and blamed myself for carelessness. It was only much later that I came to suspect some inattention on my own part that might have left a minute residue of poison on my own fingers after handling the vials I carried everywhere.

The first cramps, no more than mildly uncomfortable, hit me a few hours later, before I set off down the steep slope and while Derek was still with me. I foolishly ignored them, anticipating that they would soon fade away. Instead, they increased, both in intensity and in frequency, so that by the time I was half-way down towards the camp below I was in agony and violently sick. I could barely control my descent on the almost precipitous hillside and only narrowly escaped falling to my death when my foot slipped while I was bent over, trying not to retch. I fell forward, head over heels, unable to react in any way to stop myself. A projecting spur of rock arrested me less than two paces from a vertical drop, and I lay there clutching at the stone for a long time before I had sufficient strength to raise my head and look about me. My vision was swimming; everything slid away from me sideways when I tried to focus. And then I dragged myself to a depression between two clumps of long, rank grass, where I lay gasping until my vision settled.

There was not much cover available; the hillside was open and exposed to anyone who glanced up from below. Even had I been unimpaired, the progress I had planned on making would have been slow, much of it achieved by lying flat on my belly and slinking from clump to clump of grass and stones like an adder. Now, with the excruciating pains in my stomach and ribs, the roaring in my ears and the blurred vision, along with the constant retching, progress became impossible and I had no choice but to remain where I was, in the relative security of the hollow. I could see a thick clump of bushes not far below me, but to reach them, I would have to negotiate the small cliff I had almost fallen over, and I knew I could not even contemplate such a move until I had regained some control of my spasming muscles. I began to feel light-headed, and shortly after that I broke out in a clammy sweat that soon soaked my clothing. Then it seemed to me I drifted in and out of awareness for a time.

In the infrequent intervals of clarity I had, I would giggle inanely, knowing that I, the great poisoner, had somehow poisoned myself. And now here I lay, on an open hillside above a crew of men who would skin me alive if they found me and knew who I was. I knew my mind was disordered by what was happening to me, and a large, sane part of me was appalled by my own mindless laughter. Then I was overtaken by a surge of nausea that left me exhausted and panting for breath, and in its aftermath, I passed out.

I awoke some time later to the feeling of rain on my face, and I felt slightly better; well enough, in fact, to move on down the hill. But I was extremely weak and still light-headed, and I could hear myself making too much noise as I staggered and reeled downwards. They say the ancient gods protected fools, children and drunkards; someone protected me that afternoon on all three of those grounds, for I had been a fool, I was as weak as a child, and I fell and reeled like a drunkard.

The rain grew heavier, falling from low, heavy-bellied clouds that clung as fog to the steep slopes; it was a gift to me, obscuring my movements, and I made my way down to the bottom without further mishap and without attracting attention. Once there, however, I collapsed again, my body racked by painful, heaving spasms that produced nothing from my stomach but agony and bitter-tasting bile. I could feel the sweat pouring from me and I knew I was running a fever.

When next I became aware, it was dark, the rain had stopped, and I could hear voices not far from where I lay. I had no knowledge of where I actually was, in relationship to the point where I had intended to arrive, and I thought the voices were Celtic, but in my intermittent moments of clear-headedness I thought I might merely have dreamed of understanding them. I had visions of huge, blond-haired, axe-carrying Danes with bull-horns on their helmets, conversing fluently with me in my own tongue, and I knew I was raving. I also knew that I was cold, and as though detached from my own body, I pictured myself emerging from the bushes that screened me, to crawl forward on all fours towards the beckoning light of the fires that I knew must be burning close by, where I would beg, in suicidal Latin, to be allowed to warm myself and sleep. Instead, I hugged myself more tightly, shivering and shuddering, and eventually I must have fallen asleep.

I knew nothing more until someone prodded me with an ungentle toe. My eyes snapped open to daylight and I was face down in a clump of long, rough grass, fully aware and knowing I had been discovered. I cursed and tried to scramble to my feet, but snatching fingers grasped my hair, pulling my head back and baring my neck. I felt a knee against my side, and I was heaved backwards and flipped over to land on a sharp-pointed stone that smashed between my shoulders. I saw an unkempt form leaning above me with a dagger poised to strike, and I closed my eyes, knowing there was nothing I could do to save myself. And then I heard my name, uttered in a gasp of stunned surprise. Moments later I felt myself grasped beneath the shoulders, and then I was being dragged. When the movement stopped, I felt myself being raised to a sitting po-sition, my back against a tree or a stone, and soon I became aware of someone crouching close to me.

I opened my eyes and recognized Turoc the ploughman, a Christian Celt from Cornwall who had come to Camulod the year I brought Cas-sandra home. He was one of the eight spies I had dispatched personally, months earlier, to penetrate Cornwall and discover what was happening with Ironhair. Now he kneeled in front of me, peering anxiously into my face. I managed to say his name and his eyes widened with relief.

"Merlyn, in God's name what are you doing here? I almost killed you. My dagger was on its way down when I recognized you. What's wrong with you, and why are you here? You're a dead man if anyone else sees you."

"Sick," I whispered. "Poisoned. Ate something bad, yesterday."

"Shit! Can you walk?"

I shook my head. "Don't know, Turoc. I don't think so. I'm fevered."

He sat up straighter and looked all around, barking a short, sharp grunt that was almost a cough. "Well, there's nobody around." He glanced back down at me. "You're frozen and your clothes are soaked. I'd better get something for you to wear and see if I can find something hot for you to eat. That'll be a miracle, but there might be something left of last night's stew, even if it's no more than a cup of broth. Wait you here and don't move. No one will see you if you stay just where you are. If I can find some food, I'll have to heat it over a fire, so I may be gone for a while. Meanwhile, let's get you out of those wet clothes and wrap you in this."

He loosened the voluminous cloak he wore over his shoulders, then moved quickly to strip off my clothes before wrapping me in the cloak.

"At least it's dry," he grunted. "Nothing I can do about the smell of it." It smelled wonderful: dry and warm and filled with the tang of wood-smoke. He was wrapping my own clothing in a bundle, using my tunic as a bag. "I'll spread these by the fire in my own spot. I've been here for more than a month, so that gives me a certain privilege. I've managed to clear a space of my own. Now wait here and be still. I'll be back as soon as I can."

I watched him as he moved away, walking openly into the morning light with my clothes bundled beneath his arm, and then I closed my eyes and luxuriated in the dry, rough warmth of his cloak. Turoc had stripped me naked without remarking on the marks and lesions on my skin, but then I thought of how my sick, fevered body must have looked to him; the dead, whitening areas would have seemed like an effect of the icy chill that had sapped my strength and vitality.

He returned in less time than I had expected, and he brought a thick, heavy clay mug filled to the brim with heated, salty meat broth in which chunks of meat and vegetables floated. I sipped it with great care, ex-pecting my stomach to rebel against the intrusion, but nothing untoward occurred. After the first scent of it, the first clean bite of it against my tongue, I was ravenous, and Turoc had to pull the mug away from me to prevent me from taking too much too soon and making myself sick again. Thereafter, I proceeded with more decorum, sipping the delicious broth slowly and savouring every drop of it, feeling my strength return with every mouthful. At least I felt that I would live again.

Turoc had been watching me closely, and now he indicated the bun-dle he had brought back with him. "Dry clothes," he grunted. "Not clean, but dry. Better get them on you now. No telling when we might have company. You still haven't told me why you're here or how you got here."

I waved a hand towards the slope I had descended. "Came down from up there, and I'm here to find Carthac. Where is he?"

His eyebrows rose, but he answered me straightforwardly, with no more than a grunt of surprise. "He's not here. He went out with a raiding party yesterday, before noon, and hasn't come back."

This was bitter news, and I had to bite down on my anger and dis-appointment. "Where did he go, do you know? And how many men did he take with him?"

Turoc made a face and dipped his head to one side. "Took about half a hundred with him, but I don't know where they went. I wasn't in camp at the time. I was up on the cliffs above the northern entrance. What do you want with Carthac? He'll kill you as soon as he sets eyes on you. He's raving mad, the most frightening man I've ever seen. No man's life is safe around him—no one's. Even his closest captains live in fear of him."

"I know, Turoc." I sat straighter, grunting as I felt pain rippling up and down my ribs. "But I'm here to kill him, not to be killed. All I want to do is to get close enough to reach him."

He squatted back on his heels and stared at me, shaking his head, and then his eyes scanned me from head to foot. "You can't even walk. How are you going to kill a man who can't be killed? I've seen him lost among a swarm of twenty men, all of them trying to kill him, and he's come out with barely a scratch on him."

"Aye, but he has been scratched, has he not?"

"Well of course he has!" I could see him doubt my sanity. "But never badly. The worst injury he's had was a spearhead in the right thigh."

"Aye. He killed the surgeon who dug it out of him, did he not?"

Now his eyes flew wide. "How did you know that?"

"No matter." I shook my head. "I merely need to scratch him, that's all. Once scratched, he'll die, I swear to you."

Turoc shook his head and looked away immediately, trying to hide his confusion and trepidation. There could be no logic, to his mind, in what I was telling him, and I knew that. I reached out, surprised at how difficult it was to make my arm and hand obey me, and gripped him by the forearm.

"Turoc," I said, fighting to put conviction into my weakened voice. "Trust me in this. I know what I am doing, and I can kill him. Once he is dead, his warriors will melt away like snow in spring. They feed on this . . . this legend he has spawned, this thing about his immortality. Once he is dead, they'll quickly sicken of his memory. They'll recall the cannibal, not the demigod; the torturer, not the warrior. Get me to a place where I'll be able to see him and reach him, then leave me to do the rest."

He shook his head again, more vehemently now. "You'll be recognized the moment you go in there, and you'll be killed. What use is there in that?"

"No, you're wrong, man. Look at me! Do I look like Merlyn of Camulod? Look at my beard, my clothes. You almost killed me yourself, not recognizing me, and you've known me for nigh on a score of years. None of these people know me at all, and if they think of Merlyn of Camulod, they think of my brother, Ambrose, who is now become the man that once I was. Get me inside there, Turoc. That's all I require. Take me inside, and then leave me."

"But they'll know you're not one of them! They are uncouth and wild,

Merlyn, but they're not stupid enough to fail to recognize a stranger in their camp!"

"Then I shall be a messenger. Where's Ironhair?"

"Ironhair? God knows! They say he's with the Danes, fighting to the north of here. We haven't seen his face in months."

"Does he send messages to Carthac?"

"Aye, once in a while."

"Then I shall be a messenger—a sick messenger, poisoned by Merlyn's Vengeance in a camp that I came through on the way here. My name will be . . ." I paused, thinking quickly, searching for an ordinary name that would be memorable to us both. "Mod," I said then, remembering my young Druid friend, whom Carthac had murdered. "Mod is perfect. You'll say you met me as I came up through the southern entrance, and that I was raving with fever. You knew me long ago, and recognized me. I am a . . . a fisherman, but also a warrior. No explanation of how I avoided the guards above the pass; I was but a man alone and the gods were watching over me. I have messages for Carthac from Ironhair, and while I wait for his return, I'll need to lie beside a fire somewhere, where I can be warm and recover from my sickness, which is internal—poisoned, remember—and not contagious. Can you arrange that?"

His face was still troubled, but he nodded once, and then again, more emphatically. "I can do it, but I don't like it. Besides, you've no weapons. How will you kill Carthac with no weapons? I don't like this at all, Merlyn."

"You don't have to like it, Turoc, you merely have to put me into place. Besides, I *have* a weapon. My knife there, by my scrip."

"What, this?" His voice dripped scorn as he held up the Varrus dagger in its sheath. "This is your killing weapon?"

Thinking that he was about to draw the blade, and knowing that I had smeared it thickly with the deadly, venomous green paste, I cut him short, stretching out my hand for the knife.

"It's all I need. Now belt it about my waist, and my scrip, too. And if the thought of what I am about to do frightens you, then think upon this instead: think about who I am, and about the strange tales you have heard of me, down through the years. And ask yourself this: why should the death that stalks the Danes and Carthac's other mercenaries out there in Cambria be known as Merlyn's Vengeance? And why, if you find yourself believing in the immortality of such a thing as Carthac, would you doubt the sorcery of Merlyn?"

He straightened up at that and I saw his hand thrust down behind his back, no doubt making the ancient sign against the evil eye. I waited till he breathed again, then said, "Are we agreed? Because if we are, we should move soon. I'm beginning to feel dizzy in my head again."

He grunted and stood up, leaning forward to take my hand. With his help I struggled to my feet and stood there swaying until he threw one arm about my waist and brought my left arm over his shoulder, gripping me firmly by the wrist.

"Don't be afraid to lean on me," he told me. "But try to walk, if you can. I've got you firmly, so you won't fall. We're less than a hundred paces from the longhouse, but it might seem like a long way. If anyone stops us, don't try to talk. Just leave it to me."

We set out then, and my legs felt as though they had no muscle in them at all. The light-headedness had come back and my vision was doing strange things again. I saw several men approach us, then move on after casting strange looks at us. On one occasion, directly challenged as to what was wrong with me, Turoc recited the story I had concocted, and it was accepted, with a muttered curse and a warning to keep the whoreson away.

Some time later, we entered the open doorway of the longhouse. I can remember looking up and seeing that the walls were higher than I had judged from above, and that two tall wooden doors hung limply and drunkenly from sagging rope hinges. We passed into the dim interior, and I saw open patches high above, where great holes in the thatch admitted beams of daylight. I smelled thick wood-smoke, and then I felt myself being lowered to the ground, and the heat of flames radiating against my face.

I opened my eyes again and found myself close by a large fire that had been built beneath a roofless section of the longhouse. Turoc was wrapping the folds of his big cloak tightly about me, and I heard voices all around me, and Turoc's voice repeating yet again the tale of my misfortune. He had known me for years, he swore, and had stumbled upon me this morning by accident and good fortune, since had he not found me, I might have died, and I bore messages for Carthac from Ironhair. I had survived a camp blasted by Merlyn's Vengeance, down on the plain, he told his listeners, and I had purged myself of most of the poison on the way up here from below. Now all I needed was to regain my strength, and since Carthac had not yet returned to camp, the best thing for me to do was sleep until he came. There came a chorus of mutterings, and, wonder of wonders, I slept, lulled by the sounds and the warmth of the fire.

"Carthac! Carthac! Carthac! Carthac! Carthac!"

At first it was the fabric of my dream, but as the volume swelled and grew into a roar of voices chanting in unison, I opened my eyes to find myself surrounded by a forest of legs. The demigod had returned to his worshippers.

Slowly, cautiously, I rose to my feet, pulling my cloak about me and tugging its hood down over my face. I was caught up in the pandemonium, but my mind was clear enough to know, immediately, that here might be the best chance I would ever have of coming close to my quarry. In the midst of this capering throng of wild, enthusiastic men, I should easily be able to win close enough to him to strike. I knew that I would die immediately thereafter, but I had long since come to terms with that. I had no wish to live on as a leper, and I considered that my life would be well spent in ridding the world of this particular pestilence called Carthac at the same time as I rid it of my own.

Although I had not yet seen him, I knew from the chaos of shouts that he was here, in the longhouse, and as I stood there swaying, looking about me for an avenue to go to him, I saw the fire in front of me, separated from me only by several bodies. There lay the answer to the question of how I might reach him without arousing suspicion by a head-long approach. As soon as I located him, I would throw some of my fire-powder into the fire, creating a distraction and, I hoped, some panic. Then, while everyone was disoriented by the noise and smoke, I would strike.

I moved slightly to my right, then, and saw him. He was a gargoyle, hideous and immense, a leering Cyclops, bald on one side of his head above the awful disfigurement that marred him and marked him as in-human. He had no left eye, and the place where it should have been was a ruined, indented mass of twisted flesh. His head was misshapen, flattened and distorted at his birth, and it bulged enormously at the top on the right side. Then, when he was a boy, a kick from a horse had added diabolical refinements to his lifelong ugliness. The one eye that remained to him, however, was large and bright blue, offering a tragic but fleeting suggestion of how he might have looked had Nature not decided to make sport of him. That single, flashing, bright-blue eye was the first thing I saw, before the ruin of the rest of his awful head eclipsed it.

And then I truly saw the size of him. He towered over everyone about him, hulking and huge, his shoulders leviathan and his great, deep, hairless chest unarmoured. He wore only a sleeveless vest, of some kind of animal pelt, long-haired and shaggy, and a pair of breeches made from the same skins. Heavy boots covered his feet and lower legs and a broad belt with a golden buckle circled his waist. His arms, as big as many a man's thighs, shone as though oiled, and the biceps were wound in what looked like copper bracelets.

My hands were busy beneath my cloak, opening the drawstring of the leather bag that held the last remnants of my fire-powder, perhaps two large handfuls. I reached inside and scooped a generous pinch into my right hand, and then I saw the sword he held in his. He gave a wild laugh and swung it around his head, sending his followers leaping back in fear for their lives, one of them gouting blood from a slash across the chest. Three times he swung the sword, and then he stood alone in the space he had cleared, laughing in a high, thin, chilling voice as though defying anyone to come against him.

The noise in the longhouse died almost completely away as the re-alization sank slowly home to me that somehow, impossibly, he had come into possession of my sword. I knew it was impossible, because I had left my sword at home, in my little valley, since it would have been too os-tentatious for the task I had at hand. Yet there it was, in Carthac's enor-mous fist.

As I stared at it, incredulous, his insane laugh turned into a defiant, triumphant scream. He raised his left arm and brandished something above his head. I looked at it; I saw it; and my mind refused to accept what I was seeing. He screamed again, this time my name, "Merlyyyn!" and threw the thing. My brother's head. Ambrose's head.

It flew through the air towards me, and I watched it turning as though time had slowed to almost nothing. The fine, blue eyes were wide, staring and glazed in death; the thick, yellow locks were stained with blood. I even saw that he had grown a beard on this campaign, a grizzled beard, just like my own. And then it landed in the fire, thumping heavily among the coals, and I forgot everything in the urge to save my brother from the flames. I lunged forward, a strangled scream knotting in my throat, and my shoulder struck the man in front of me as my foot came down on the inside hem of my cloak, tripping me. As I fell, my outstretched hands released the open bag I had been holding and the firepowder fell into the heart of the fire.

A gigantic ball of flame roared from the pit with a concussive, deaf-ening sound that sucked all the air in the room, it seemed, into its heart, then belched it out again in a terrifying rain of sparks and embers and great, whirling clouds of choking smoke. I had squeezed my eyes tight shut, but the brightness of the fireball seared right through my closed lids as I ripped away my cloak, casting it aside. Keening now with rage, I fumbled to pull my dagger from its sheath and clutched the hilt so hard that it pained my hand. Then, oblivious to the chaos swirling around me, I pushed myself up and ran through the smoke and the fire towards Carthac.

I found him rooted to the spot where I had last seen him, gaping open-mouthed at me as I approached, making no effort to avoid me, and before he could my dagger found his breast and plunged between his ribs. He made a strange, mewling sound and his only defence was to thrust me away from him, with both hands, one of which still gripped the sword I now knew was my brother's. Demented with grief and disbelief and hatred, I tore my blade free again and raked it towards his one, blue eye, but he turned his head away before I could plunge the point into his brain and I succeeded only in blinding him, the knife's blade striking against the bone of his eye socket. Then he picked me up easily with one huge hand, and threw me back into the firepit.

I was burning—my left hand, which had plunged elbow deep into a bed of embers, my arms, my feet, my legs—and I scrambled, screaming in agony, until I was free of the pit. I threw myself against the wall and cowered there, striking off the glowing coals that stuck to my cringing flesh and tearing off the smouldering remnants of the tunic that was my only garment. When I was naked and all the coals were off me, I lay there, shuddering in pain, incapable of coherent thought.

After a time, above my own whimpers and cries, I heard Carthac moan, a quavering, disembodied sound of torment that soon swelled into a scream. Once he had begun, he could not stop. Thrusting aside my own pain in the urgency of my need to see him, I pushed myself up with difficulty, pressing my back against the wall, and peered towards the awful sounds. The smoke had begun to clear, and he came into view through its drifting skeins, staggering about at the far end of the long, empty building, close by the open doors, his hands clutched over his head as he bumped into walls and every obstacle that lay about him. He fell down and struggled to his feet again, screaming and screaming. We were alone in the longhouse, two crippled men, and no one came back to see what was afflicting him.

Slowly, and painfully, but gathering strength and resolve with every movement, I made my way forward, shambling in my nakedness, not taking my eyes from him for a moment. He fell to his knees again, and I saw Ambrose's skystone sword lying on the ground before him. Renewed resolve flared up in me and, barely aware of my burns now, or of any weakness, I walked forward and picked it up with my right hand. Then, cradling my wrist in my burned left hand, I swung the long blade high and struck off his deformed head with one blow that took all of my strength and left me sprawled across his corpse.

I found my brother's head later. It lay lodged in a corner of the building's walls, barely damaged by the fire. I picked it up and sat with it in my arms as I wept for him, remembering all I had loved in him. I felt as though my heart would burst apart with the pain of it, a deep, anguished, all-consuming torment that eclipsed all other pains. And presently I found I was weeping for Tressa, too, and for Dedalus and all the friends and loved ones I had ever lost. And as I wept and mourned my loves in the abandoned darkness of that ruined place, a hailstorm of Pendragon arrows swept down from the hillside above and killed every remaining thing that moved in the valley beyond the stone walls that surrounded me.

Not everyone who was in the longhouse that day died. Many fled before the Pendragon attack began, in terror of Merlyn the Sorcerer, whose wicked and unholy infamy as a practitioner of the blackest arts soon spread throughout the entire land of Britain. For even though Carthac had killed Merlyn, beheaded him, and borne the severed head back to his camp, when the head was cast into the fire, flames had erupted thunderously amidst a welter of sparks and breath-killing smoke, and from the heart of the inferno Merlyn had emerged, springing whole and alive to slay their champion.

The following day, when the armies of Camulod rode into Carthac's valley, they took prisoners away with them, and those prisoners told everyone who would listen, long afterwards when they had overcome their initial fear: they had been witnesses to all of it; they had been present when Merlyn the Sorcerer came back to life.

XVIII

"MERLYN? IS THAT you?"

I smiled and turned to see a tall form step between me and one of the flickering torches ringing the interior of the great amphitheatre. The distant shape moved back, then started to approach again, now carrying the torch that had been guttering against the wall. I remained where I was unmoving, as the ring of his footsteps echoed in the emptiness of the high-walled space. Then the voice called out again.

"It must be you, I know, because no one else would ever dare to be here in the very dead of night, at the mercy of my ever-vigilant guards. And besides, whenever I see darkness moving inside darkness, I know it can only be my cousin Cay."

Arthur Pendragon looked magnificent, striding forward across the marbled floor. The high crest of his helmet made him appear even taller and more impressive than he was, and his long, heavy cloak swirled behind him. He looked, I thought, almost as magnificent as he had on that morning, nigh on two full years earlier, when he had led his troopers into Carthac's valley and found me, huddling, naked in the longhouse. When last I had seen him, prior to that day, he had been still a boy, large and strong-limbed and greatly admirable, aglow with the kind of fairness of face and form that turned women's heads, and men's too, but yet a boy in truth. That morning, when he rode into my life again, the metamorphosis had been achieved, and he approached me as a man—a hardened veteran and a seasoned warrior, Legate Commander, though he came unaware of it, of the Forces of Camulod.

On this night, he bore himself with the easy self-assurance of a successful and victorious army commander. It thrilled me to see him wearing the armour of lustrous, shaped and layered, highly polished black bull's hide that had once been mine and before that had been my father's. All three of us were large men, tall and broad-shouldered. The armour, made expressly for my father when he was at the peak of his powers, was studded with solid, beaten-silver rosettes; it was the ceremonial armour of a Roman commander of horse from the days of Flavius Stilicho who, as regent of Rome's Empire in the west, had brought the methods and cavalry techniques of Alexander the Great back into use. Arthur filled it to perfection.

Now, as my young cousin drew close to me, he reached up with his free hand and pulled off the heavy helmet of glazed and toughened leather surmounted by a finger-length–high crest of stiff horsehair, in alternating tufts of black and white, packed into a beaten silver basket. His face was shining as he flashed his white-toothed smile, and he came directly to me, embracing me with the arm that held his helmet while holding the flaming torch well clear. I hugged him briefly, my heart swelling with pride, then pushed him gently away. He cocked his head sideways, humour dancing in his great, yellow, gold-flecked eyes.

"What?" he demanded, his voice bantering. "What is it? You look as though you've been caught doing something of which the good Bishop Enos might not approve." He looked about him then, holding the torch at arm's length above his head, his eyes flicking over and away from the altar that stood close by. "What are you doing here in the sanctuary? I thought that, once the consecration had been made and the altar set in place, only God's servants could come into this area."

I shook my head, forming my features into an expression of rueful regret. "Are you suggesting that I am not one of God's servants, Arthur?"

He was unabashed. "Well, my cousin Cay is, I know that. On the other hand, Merlyn the Sorcerer? That, some might doubt."

I grinned, feeling a scar tug at the left side of my mouth, twisting my smile into a grimace. "Then they would be in error. I am here on Bishop Enos's own business, doing what he would do himself, were he not conferring with his pious brethren. Why are *you* here?"

"I've been inspecting the guard, keeping them on their toes. It inspires them with joy, and something akin to awe, to know that their Commander never seems to sleep. I learned that from you, you may recall. Have you finished here? Then come and walk with me a while. It's a glorious night."

We walked together back down the way he had come. He replaced the flaming torch in its sconce, then placed his helmet back on his head and nodded to the guard who stood nearby, as rigid as a column of rock. I sensed, rather than saw, the way the man flinched from me without betraying any sign of movement. "I would have expected clouds, had anyone asked me," Arthur suggested. "At least until the day after tomorrow."

Today had been the first of the three days of Eastertide, the day all Christian folk had come to think of as Good Friday, and we had been present at the ceremonies for the remembrance of the Crucifixion of the Christ. Two days hence would see the coming of Easter, and the Resurrection of the Flesh. Belief in that Mystery, I reflected with a rueful, private smile, explained the guard's religious fear of me a moment earlier.

As we emerged through the portals of the large theatre, wending our way through throngs of military personnel, all of whom saluted Arthur, he gestured towards the distant town, where lights illuminated what would, at any other time, have been a black and motionless emptiness.

"Who would have thought that Verulamium would stir to life again, in times like these, eh, Merlyn? What has it been, eighteen years since first you came here and met your friend Germanus?"

"Closer to twenty," I replied. "The years of your own life. My one regret remains that Germanus himself could not be here this Easter." My friend of years had died in his own bishopric in Gaul the previous year, in the summer following his return from Verulamium in 447, and I had not spoken to him or written to him since that night I took my leave of him so suddenly on the road. I had heard that his venture in Verulamium had been successful, and had received vague and unconfirmed reports that the bishops Agricola and Fastidius had been censured and declared apostate and excommunicate, and steps had been initiated to undo the damage they had instigated among the unsuspecting people in their charge. Since then, however, everything had changed in the north-east, after the deaths of Hengist and Vortigern. No word of any kind had come down to us from Northumbria in months, and had any come, I would have been astonished to hear mention of religious matters, either Orthodox or Pelagian. Indeed, for all I knew, Christianity itself might well have been wiped out in the entire north-east. True until death, however, Germanus had set in motion the plans we had prepared for Arthur, and for the survival of the Christian faith in Britain, and had passed on the responsibility for making them come true to Enos, Bishop of Venta Belgarum in the south-eastern country now being called Anglia.

"I believe that," Arthur murmured. "I wish I had met him. He must have been a fascinating man. Warrior and bishop. That's a strange blending."

"Aye, it was, and he was formidable in both aspects. You would have gained from knowing him. He would have liked you."

"How are your feet and legs nowadays?" We had been progressing slowly, Arthur mindful of the limp that prevented me nowadays from keeping pace with him.

I shrugged. "They function. Sometimes they pain me, but less and less frequently. One of these days, I'll have no pain at all." Carthac had maimed me at the moment of his death, when he thrust me away from him, into the firepit. The burns I had sustained had been severe and, when they healed, had left me with shortened tendons in my left knee and heel. My left hand had burned, too, and now its fingers were forever clawed and useless; the leprous area on the web of my left thumb had disappeared at the same time, burned into a knotted mass of hardened scar tissue. Further burns, to my face, had left me sufficiently disfigured for my friend Llewellyn to take great delight in telling me that when he was with me, he knew which of us was the better looking.

Arthur was still staring at me, so I stopped walking and faced him.

"What? What is it? I know that look of yours. You have something in your mind you wish either to tell me or to ask me. Which is it?"

As I asked the question, I heard the clattering of approaching hooves, and then a rider drew his horse to a halt and leaped from the saddle to land rigidly at attention in front of his Commander, presenting a tightly rolled dispatch in his extended hand. I shook my head in silent wonder at the concentration that could produce this evidence of superhuman discipline. I had spent half my life upon a horse, but I had never been called upon to perform the prodigious feats of horsemanship and personal performance that these young men of Arthur's did without thought.

Arthur walked away to read the dispatch by the light of a nearby torch, and then nodded to the messenger, muttering something that I made no attempt to overhear. It was apparent from his stance that the missive contained no urgent summons, and the man who had brought it was dismissed.

"How do they do that, Arthur? How do they learn to leap down from a horse and land rigid on their feet like that, at attention? I've never seen anything like it in my life, and I've only seen it since you returned last time from Cambria. Is it necessary?"

He laughed. "No, Merlyn, it is not, and I'll grant you it seems . . . overzealous, but it's a harmless enough thing—a mark of the fever for excellence and distinction that seems to burn in all my men. It's a display of unit pride, no more. It began in the final stages of the Cornwall campaign, when we were cleaning up the detritus of Ironhair's levies. One of my officers, in a great hurry, leaped from his horse like that, to speak to me, and landed upright and rigid. It was sheer luck and completely unintentional, I'm quite sure, but he carried it off and pretended to have done it on purpose. Other young officers were watching, and all were impressed. Within the month, it had become the thing to do, and now it's standard. Elite troops develop elitist idiosyncrasies."

"Aye," I said, making no attempt to hide the irony in my tone. "I know what you mean. The Praetorians developed some, too. They killed and elected emperors, in their day . . ." When he did not react to my humour, I began to wonder if the thoughts he was guarding were blacker than I had suspected. "From the lack of concern you showed, I presumed that message you received held no great urgency. Was I wrong?"

He blinked his eyes, then focused them on me more keenly. "Oh, it did. Urgency enough, but there was nothing unexpected in it and there is nothing I can do about it now. It was from Bedwyr. His scouts report that Horsa's Danes are massing again, in the north-east, around Lindum. Bedwyr anticipates that they'll head directly south this time, into our most outlying territories. We've been anticipating something of the kind. Horsa needs to expand his holdings. We threw him out of Cambria and denied him any bases in Cornwall, and there's no room for his people elsewhere along the Saxon Shore, so he has to create new space along its boundaries. That involves intrusion upon us, although he doesn't know yet on whose toes he will be treading. By the time he does, I hope to have my forces well enough bestowed to smash him. He will be far from the sea, this time, with no fleet waiting offshore to spirit him and his defeated Danes away. But that's in the future. It makes no difference to the status quo."

"Hmm. And you are sure of that? I distrust any analysis of the status quo when great distances are involved."

"I do, too. But what more am I to do? I can't be everywhere at once, so I must simply wait and be prepared to move, instantly."

"Very well." I could not argue with his logic. "Now, what was it you wanted to ask or tell me?"

He laid his right hand on my shoulder. "Come, I'll walk with you to your quarters and ask you as we go."

When we swung right and headed towards the distant lights of the town, I saw the silent, unobtrusive shadows of the squad of Pendragon bowmen who accompanied Arthur everywhere, as they fanned out and formed a ring about us. He saw me look at them and grinned again.

"My bodyguard. I've tried dismissing them and sending them away, but they are under Big Huw's orders, and it would be more than their lives are worth to obey me and thereby displease him. I'm merely their king; Huw Strongarm is their god."

I made no comment on that. Arthur had become the king of the Pendragon clans a year before, under the protection and sponsorship of Huw Strongarm, who was now as much Arthur's loyal man as he had ever been Uther's.

"I'm concerned about this matter of the sword, Cay," Arthur continued, and I immediately put every other thought out of my mind. He seldom called me Cay, and when he did, I knew that he had been thinking long and hard about some problem. I glanced at him, keeping my expression neutral.

"Why should you be concerned? Everything is arranged."

"I know, but it still worries me. I can't see the sense of it, can't see any advantage to what is so openly a ruse."

"It's not a ruse, Arthur. It is a symbol, and one of great import. The deed will be symbolic of your cause, Britain's cause. People need symbols to direct their beliefs. We've discussed this before now, several times."

"We have, but . . . Merlyn, I'm still not satisfied that the idea will hold water. Look—" He sucked air through his teeth and then let out a pent-up sigh. "It's not the symbol that concerns me—not the need for one, at least. I can see that clearly . . . I suppose it's the physical thing itself that worries me, the sword. I'm to produce my sword out of a stone. But it's *my* sword, Merlyn, *Ambrose's* sword! I've been using it for two years now, ever since you gave it to me that day in Cambria. People have seen it. They know it. They know I carry it with me every day, slung at my back, between my shoulders. Why are you so convinced that they will all be so impressed when they see me pull it from a stone? To my mind, they'll be more inclined to laugh. I know I would, were I to see such foolery."

I had been holding up my hand to silence him for some time, but only now did he pause and look at me. When I was sure that he would say no more, I smiled and nodded.

"I have a question for you, now, and it's one I have never asked you before. Do you trust me, Arthur?"

"What kind of foolish question is that? Whom else could I trust in all the world if not you? Why would you even trouble to ask me?"

"I ask because I want you to engage that trust and bear with me in this." His face fell, and I continued. "But if you have a single, tiny suspicion in your mind that I might ever do anything that could endanger or belittle you or what I believe to be your God-sent cause, then tell me now, and I'll accept it and say no more about the sword." He shrugged his big shoulders, mute. "Good, then two things more I'll say: I swear to you that no man watching the event will laugh, or will feel aught but awe and wonder. On my oath, I swear that to be true, Arthur. No man, or woman, will think less of you for what you will have done, and none will recognize the sword. You may doubt that, within yourself, but you have my oath on all of it."

"Hmm." He was grinning again, his endearing sense of mischief back. "Was that one thing or two you just told me?"

"It was one. The other is . . . something different in its meaning and structure." He had caught my hesitation, but held his peace, waiting for me to find the words I sought. Finally I nodded. "Think of this as a personal wish-granting, from you to me. When you have pulled the sword and know that what we did is right and proper and appropriate in every way to what we intend, then I would like you to do something else, for me alone. You may think it strange, but it will cost you nothing."

"Name it, and it's done."

I drew a deep breath and released it in a sigh. "When once you hold the sword, Arthur, before the assembled crowd, and are convinced you hold it thus by right, I would like you to strike the blade against the stone—hard—and then reverse it, holding it straight upright in one hand only, with the pommel's end pressed against the stone. As you know, I won't be there, in public view, but I will see you do that and accept it as a signal that your trust in me has been vindicated. Will you do that?"

"Aye, I will, of course I will." His face was troubled. I knew that he had difficulty with my desire to keep myself away from people's eyes and idle stares, but we had talked of that long before, he and I, and he had accepted my wishes, albeit with reluctance.

"My thanks for that, then, and for not asking why. Now I must find my bed, and you should, too."

I felt relief, although it was tinged with guilt, for I had extracted his promise fully conscious of a small deceit in this discussion. Arthur thought the sword he was to draw out of the stone on Easter Day would be his own, and so it would, but it would be Excalibur. And so long as he remained in ignorance of its existence until that moment, he would be as stunned by the sight of its magnificence as every other person present that day. In consequence, I had continued to conceal my secret as guardian of the sword for far, far longer than I had dreamed I might.

We walked in silence, then, until the crumbling walls of the town drew near. As we entered the gates and passed the first of the dilapidated buildings, I saw guards in unfamiliar colours standing before its door.

"Who are those people?"

"Cheric's, I think. He's one of the kings from the far north, the district to the east of Derek's lands. But I may be wrong. The kings are gathering, and not all of them have made their presence known to me yet. A full score have arrived since yesterday, each with his own retinue, and there may be more to come. Not all the bishops have arrived, and many of those are travelling with their local kings."

I grunted. "We have a mighty flourishing of kings in Britain nowadays. In my father's time, you would scarce have found a single king in all of Britain—not by that name, at least—save for Uric Pendragon. Has Brander come yet?"

"Aye, he arrived today and is quartered with Connor, Donuil and Shelagh, and her father, Liam Twistback."

I glanced at him sidelong. "Did he bring Morag with him?"

"No, not this time. He came directly form his Isles at Donuil's summons." He smiled. "Brander, at least, is one king I can trust to stand at my back without growing envious."

"He's not from Britain and he is your uncle," I said. "Does it disturb you, then, to have so many kings so close about you?"

Arthur laughed. "So close? No, I prefer them close. That way, I know what they are doing. They are all men, with men's weaknesses. But there are some I enjoy more than others. We have leaders here, too, from among the Christian Anglians. You knew Cuthric is here, didn't you?" When I nodded, he continued. "And there's one more king whose presence might amuse you: Retorix, the new king of Cornwall."

That startled me sufficiently to bring me to a halt. Retorix, Arthur told me, had finally grown tired of Ironhair's excesses, his posturing and his fundamental cowardice, and had abandoned him and his designs. Since then, Retorix had emerged as the most able independent leader in all of the far south-west, and had assumed the leadership of all the clans of that much brutalized territory. I listened, then shook my head, accepting what he told me with no more than a disbelieving grunt.

"Well," Arthur said, a few paces later. "Here we are. It's not palatial, is it?"

I gazed at the darkened, decrepit house I shared with Enos and some of his bishops. "No, it's not the Villa Britannicus, but it has almost half a roof intact, the walls shut out the wind, and it is warmed by the hot air of argumentative bishops." I faced him again. "What will you do now, when you leave me here?"

He glanced at his shadowy escort. "Sleep, I suppose. There's not much else to do." I smiled, remembering the roistering times I had enjoyed here twenty years before, in the makeshift tavern we had called the *Carpe Diem*.

"Well, it is Lent," I murmured. "A sombre time of year. The bishops would look disapprovingly on open taverns on the very night the Christ hung bleeding for our sins. Sleep well, lad. Tomorrow night, you must stand vigil by the altar all night long, and the next day, you will be crowned High King. So have a deep, sound, restful sleep tonight."

He stepped close and I felt the warmth and love of his embrace, in spite of his unyielding armour. I stood by the door until he disappeared from view, flanked by his Pendragon shadows.

There was no one in the large room adjacent to the entranceway when I looked in, but a fire burned brightly in the brazier and the air was bright with the radiance of at least a score of the fine, waxen candles that were the prerogative, it seemed to me, of clerics. In one corner, the sleeping pallet used by Bishop Enos lay neatly, its pristine condition indicating that he, at least, had not yet returned that night. The entire house was silent, and so I entered and crossed directly to the fire, where I stretched out my chilled fingers to the flames, feeling the phantom tingling they produced in my burned left hand, and looked about me.

The furnishings were Spartan, purely temporary and all portable, for this house had lain abandoned for decades, occupied only by rodents and insects. There was a scattering of folding chairs and tables, all of them brought to Verulamium on the pack mules of various bishops, and a number of sawed logs that served as seats whenever Enos held a meeting here. Other than that, the room was empty and bare. Its upper walls were constantly veiled in darkness, since the skylight opening that once admitted light had been sealed up and boarded over sometime in the distant past. The lower walls, which now glowed in the candlelight, were of a honeyed, earthen colour that had faded unevenly; they were stained now with creeping dampness in places, but they must once have been quite beautiful. The floor had been swept since we arrived, and perhaps even washed; its mosaic tiles were clearly visible in spots, but the ingrained dirt and dust of years had obscured its colours.

One of the tables not far from the fire held a jug of water, which was all that Enos drank, and another that I knew was full of mead, for I had filled it earlier that day. Beside the jugs lay a sharp knife, a thick, hard wedge of cheese covered with coarse cloth, and a loaf of rough, wheaten bread that had come fresh from the oven that morning and lay concealed under a covering of white, clerical cloth. I moved one of the chairs and the smallest table close to the fire and sat down, throwing back my hood and shaking out my hair, then combing it between my spread fingers— one of the few activities for which my clawed left fingers were quite adequate. I was tired and it felt good to sit and stretch out my legs. This had been a long, tense day, its proceedings and the manner of their presentation crucial to the plan that we had crafted with such painstaking care over the past few years.

Mere moments later, feeling the stirrings of an unfed appetite, I rose again and cut myself a portion of bread and cheese, poured a cup of mead and carried them back to my chair. Thereafter, enjoying the the almost silent flickering of flames in the stillness and peace of the room, I sat staring into the fire, but looking into the past.

I had not swung a sword nor mounted upon a horse since the day my brother died. My burned flesh and twisted sinews would permit neither activity. Arthur had sent me home to Camulod attended by a physician and borne in a commissary wagon specially adapted to my needs, and I had swung for long days in a cradle suspended from a frame his carpenters had bolted to the wagon's bed for that purpose, inspired by the similar device built by Connor Mac Athol's craftsmen to support their one-legged captain while he was at sea. Then, for months thereafter, at home in Camulod, I recuperated under the loving care of Ludmilla, whose loss of her husband Ambrose resulted, once her initial bereavement, pain and grief had passed, in the transferral of some portion of her love for him to me. She grew determined that I would survive my wounds and overcome them, as had both Connor and Publius Varrus in their time. She hectored me constantly to exercise my damaged limbs to exhaustion and beyond, driving me to more and greater exertions, stretching my maimed and fire-scarred muscles until they would perform for me again and finally enable me to walk erect. I limped, at some times more than others, and my left arm and hand were practically useless, but the rest of me was whole and strong.

It was Ludmilla, too, who eventually recognized my leprosy. But she had been trained in the medical arts by Lucanus, who had had no fear of the disease and had been filled with admiration and great sympathy for his friend Mordechai Emancipatus, who had worked for decades among those afflicted, eventually contracting it himself. Luke had taught Ludmilla that the disease was not readily contagious, and that it was not fatal, but brought death solely from lack and want and the tragic inability of lepers to find food, shunned and proscribed and dreaded as they were by everyone. She had seen my lesions and known them for what they were, and she and I had talked for hours about the consequences that must lie in store for me, if ever my affliction became known.

And it was Ludmilla, finally, who showed me my salvation in the fact that people now lived in fear of me and shunned me for my sorcery. She brought out my night-clothes, the long, black, hooded cloak and the ankle-length, pocket-hung underrobe that had concealed me in my nocturnal campaign against my enemies in Cambria and which Derek of Ravenglass had carried back to Camulod for me. Ludmilla pointed out that they were equally suited, if not more so, for concealing me and my disfigurement from prying eyes in the light of day. The large, capacious hood would completely mask my face within its shadows, and the long-sleeved arms would hang below my finger ends when I required them to. I could benefit from men's fear of me and my sorcery by using it to elude their far, far greater fear of leprosy. Seeing me dressed, as they thought, for sorcery, people would flee from me in terror, and that same terror would completely protect me against their curiosity.

While I had been recuperating from my wounds, Arthur had been at war in Cambria. Thrust into leadership by the death of Ambrose and my own removal, he overcame what some might have been tempted to regard as a premature elevation with the unstinting and committed support of Huw Strongarm. War Chief of the Pendragon, Huw immediately proclaimed the untried young leader to be the son of Uther Pendragon and the natural, incontestable king of all his people. That championship, coupled with the instantaneous commitment and loyalty of his own senior Camulodian commanders, whose trust in Ambrose and myself transferred itself with ease to our young ward and cousin, quickly enabled Arthur to display the true genius that belied his youth.

My killing of Carthac had indeed destroyed the ties that held his rabble together, but it had also destroyed the illusion of legitimacy that supported Peter Ironhair in his campaigns in Cambria. With Carthac dead, Ironhair's Cambrian cause was lost, leaving him only naked aggression to explain his continuing presence. His mercenary levies soon disintegrated, fleeing in all directions from the wrath of Arthur's infantry. Some of them sought to join with Horsa's Danes, who were a separate force, but the Danes would have none of them and turned them away to take their chances against our forces.

Arthur, acting alone in the planning stage but immediately thereafter delegating responsibility to Ambrose's former infantry commanders, de-

signed and laid out a brilliant campaign plan for mopping up the remnants of Carthac's old host. Dividing his forces into maniples and cohorts
in the Roman fashion, and employing the tactics used by Gaius Marius
four hundred years earlier—tactics that I myself had explained to him
when he was but a boy—he had sent his fighting units out to work in
close co-ordination, quartering the territories assigned to them and working with mounted Scouts who served as liaisons between the units. As
soon as the elements of his campaign were in place, he prosecuted it
ruthlessly, offering no quarter to an enemy who had forfeited all right to
clemency by their own atrocities against the common people of the land
they had pillaged.

Then, when that effort had been launched, Arthur had turned his
mind, and his cavalry, to deal with the Danes, who were the major threat.

Horsa's fierce warriors were of a different order from the rabble that
the infantry pursued, and Horsa's own military abilities came into sudden
prominence when Arthur brought the might of Camulod to bear on him.
The inconclusive battle I had witnessed on the day when I slipped into
Ambrose's camp had taught Horsa much: he had learned that when he
held the high ground and used his shield walls, he was as safe from our
cavalry as he would have been behind the walls of a fortified town. From
that day forth, therefore, he fought with an eye to the high ground and
the integrity of his defences. My own one-man campaign of nightly poi-
sonings and murder aided him in this, for I had succeeded all too well.
After three months of nocturnal terrors, the Danes had suspended their
practice of roving the land and fighting in small, independent bands.
Through fear of Merlyn's Vengeance, they had coalesced into a tight,
cohesive group, a real army, three thousand to five thousand strong, moving as one potent force, and they were formidable.

Arthur's cavalry was lethal to the Danes whenever they were caught
in the open and unsuspecting of attack, but such occasions were few and
happened only at the outset of that new stage of the war. Horsa soon
learned that attack was always imminent, and he held his men in tight
restraint, ready at any time to throw up their shield walls and hold Arthur's
cavalry at bay. That strength, however, quickly became his biggest weakness, since his powerful axemen could not deploy their weapons while the
shields were in place, interlocked. Furthermore, to frustrate the cavalry,
these shield walls had to be raised on sloping ground, above the horses,
since on flat ground the weight of surging horseflesh could simply batter
them down. This upward slanting of the enemy's forces made them excellent targets for the long Pendragon arrows.

And so the war became a struggle between a hedgehog and a tortoise,
with neither side able to win a conclusive battle and Horsa's army losing
steadily by attrition. Arthur's cavalry denied the Danes access to the low
ground and, stranded among the hills, the enemy could achieve nothing

of value. To his credit, Horsa saw the truth of this very quickly and began to lead his army back towards the coast, fighting fiercely all the way and losing heavily among the hills to the deadly Pendragon bowmen. Arthur kept pressing fiercely at their heels the whole way, throwing his mounted weight time and again to storm the shield walls. He pressed the fight to the very edges of the beach that offered Horsa access to the anchored fleet that awaited him and his men, to ferry them home again. There, Arthur halted his advance and set his cavalry to form a solid wall about the crescent of sand that he could easily have set awash in Danish blood. His clemency was easily explained, he told me later, by the fact that Horsa had been a brave and clever enemy who had learned that he could never conquer Cambria and hence would not return. Should he and Horsa meet again, elsewhere, each would respect the other and renew their battles on new ground. So Arthur Pendragon sat and watched his enemy's fleet sail off to safety.

Connor Mac Athol, Arthur discovered later, had been ravaging that fleet relentlessly since shortly after its arrival, and had caused great damage. His biremes and his galleys skirted the edges of its anchorage like hungry wolves, avoiding the counterattacking vessels sent to fight them and raiding at random and at all hours, burning and sinking ships by night and day. In consequence, the vessels that bore the Danes away from Cambria were far fewer, and far more heavily laden, than their captains had expected they would be.

In the meantime, one of my own deep-held wishes had been denied me. Peter Ironhair was dead, and the knowledge was like bitter ashes on my tongue. Ambrose had told me many times that I spent too much time thinking of Ironhair and the vengeance I would take on him when finally we two came face to face, and now that all my hopes of that revenge were gone, I was curiously relieved, no longer burdened by the hatred that had driven me for so long. He had somehow fallen foul of his own ally, Horsa, and had died for it; none of us would ever know the how or why of what occurred. I was intrigued, though, that his promise in my vision had been fulfilled. I had never set eyes on him again, nor had anyone else from Camulod except Philip, who commanded the patrol that found him hanging from a tree in an abandoned Danish camp. The irony of that was not lost on me, for his predecessor in Cornwall, Gulrhys Lot himself, had suffered the same fate, hanged from a tree by hands unknown.

All of this had taken place before the end of summer, mere months after my departure from Cambria, and with campaigning time to spare, Arthur quickly moved to consolidate his victories. He dispatched a strong force of horse and foot, conveyed in three swift journeys by Connor's massive biremes, into Cornwall, under Philip, to clean out the nests that had sheltered Ironhair and his verminous followers. The remainder of his force he led himself in a lightning-swift sweep up the length of Britain, following the western slopes of the mountain chain that bisects the land. He was spreading a message of his own as he progressed: a message that the time was ripe for the folk of Britain to unite and throw out the foreign invaders who swarmed everywhere. Camulod stood for freedom from invasion, he proclaimed, and offered strength and support to those who would join it in the fight to drive the aliens from Britain's shores.

He did encounter opposition as he swept northward, but very little. The mere sight of the thousands of heavily armed horsemen ranked behind him had a pacifying and reassuring effect, even for those kings who might have felt threatened by his coming. By the time he turned eastward, following the line of Hadrian's Wall towards the sea that divided Britain from its would-be conquerors, his name and fame were spreading ahead of him. Following the road south from the wall to where it crossed the wide river at the old Roman fort of Longovicum, he found a garrison of sorts in residence, under siege from a large army of Saxons who had sailed upriver from the coast, some twenty miles away. Taking advantage of the Saxons' surprise, Arthur split his forces and attacked immediately, destroying many of their beached longboats with burning arrows and smashing the clumps of men who ringed the old fort's walls. The king of that region was a man called Viticus, who was now in Verulamium for the great ceremony.

Within a year of coming to command, Arthur Pendragon had proclaimed himself the length and breadth of Britain, rallying the people and their separate kings to join his cause and form a united front against the Outlanders, and in the doing of it, he had discovered that our Camulod was not the only Roman settlement of its kind in Britain. There were several such, apparently, but none were so well established and maintained, and none had cavalry.

It was on Arthur's return to Camulod that I presented him with my own parade-dress armour, telling him that I had no more need of it, and with the even more splendid armour that his own father had worn. He was greatly moved, and his eyes filled with sudden tears, but from that moment on, he chose to wear my armour, claiming it to be the armour of Camulod. His father's armour, he maintained, he would reserve for dignified and ceremonial occasions, when he would wear it in proud tribute to Uther.

"Merlyn? Forgive me, my friend, I had no thought to startle you."

I had not even heard the door open behind me, and I leaped to my feet, spilling some of my mead. But then, swiftly recovered, I waved away Enos's concern. He smiled and crossed directly to his pallet, removing his long travelling cloak as he went. As he folded his cloak carefully, I poured a cup of water and cut a small portion of cheese and bread for him, knowing he would eat little of it. He accepted it with a word of thanks.

"You had no difficulties?" he asked.

"No, but Arthur almost caught me in the act."

He laughed quietly as I told him what had happened, then went on to talk about the proceedings planned for the following day. As he talked I thought about the difference between his gentle, speaking voice and what I thought of as his command voice. No longer young, he was gaunt and stooped from the hardships of his pastoral life, which involved constant travel in all weathers as he carried the Word to his far-scattered flock. Yet he was vibrant in everything he did, radiating a calm and massive conviction, and he had been indefatigable in his efforts to ensure that this unprecedented gathering would take place as planned, and would present a spectacle the likes of which this land had never seen. That much of it must be arranged in secrecy seemed only to fuel his enthusiasm, and he had handled his far-flung congregation of bishops as deftly as a successful legate must handle his legions.

Throughout the ceremonies early that afternoon, he had spoken strongly and clearly, instructing the assembled throng on the Roman history of the great theatre, and on the ceremony about to take place, and I had been as fascinated as anyone, listening to him speak with such authority and certainty. Then he had led us through the steps necessary to make the conversion from theatre to ecclesia, from house of entertainments to House of God, beginning with the sanctification of the place of worship. Upon his signal, a long procession had advanced from the grounds outside the doors and made its way down through the watching, spellbound crowd. More than a hundred bishops, led by thurifers spreading clouds of sweet incense, came forward slowly, chanting the Creed in unison. The majestic prayer, the formal declaration of the Christian tenets devised and perfected and inscribed at the Great Council of Nicaea more than a hundred years earlier, had raised the hairs on my neck as I listened to it sung by the chorus of voices.

Behind the bishops, who gathered in to form a semicircle on the rostrum behind Enos, came lesser clerics bearing a plain wooden table, a folded, pure white cloth and a block of polished, green stone, beautifully worked by a master stonemason. The table was set in place, and the cloth was laid upon it and draped about it, forming a solid block of whiteness that became the focus of all eyes. And then, with Enos describing every step of the process, the altar stone itself was laid upon the draped table and blessed with Holy Water. The stone, Enos explained, had come that day from Camulod, but its origins were in Verulamium; it had been made there some threescore years before by a Verulamian mason, at the request and under the supervision of the venerable Bishop Alaric. It was fitting, Enos said, that Camulod should provide the altar stone for this occasion, and that it should have been sanctified by Verulamium's own bishop. The stone contained the relics of a saint, one of the Britons martyred for the

Faith in earlier, Roman times, and its consecrated presence here transformed the theatre into a place of worship. So saying, he drew from his
sash a large, plain pectoral cross of gold and slotted it into the hole carved
in the stone to hold it, thereby completing the ceremony of consecration.

From that point, he had gone on to tell the story of the Saviour's
Last Supper, and of His consecration of the sacred bread and wine, and
every man and woman in the throng of thousands came forward to share
the Eucharist distributed by all the bishops from the endless baskets and
ewers brought forward for the Blessing and Consecration. When the Sacrament had been concluded, Enos went on to describe the Saviour's Passion and His Crucifixion at the third hour of the afternoon, bringing his
oration to a close at very close to that third hour, when he led the congregation in reciting the Creed again, and then observing a long moment
of silence.

Now, he intoned, the world was all in spiritual darkness, and would
so remain until the dawning of the third day. Then, with the Resurrection
of the Flesh, all the world would rejoice, and mankind would know salvation and the rebirth of hope. As he spoke, a group of bishops moved
about the sanctuary, draping and covering all the symbols of the
Church—the candelabra, sacred vessels, monstrances and crosses—with
purple mourning cloths, after which the gathering was blessed and dismissed.

I had never been caught up in the rituals of religion, but what Enos
showed me, in that simple yet convoluted ceremony, moved me deeply,
stirring fresh regret that Tress could not have been there to share it.

I realized suddenly that Enos had stopped talking, and I had no idea
what he had been saying. I felt my face flush guiltily.

"Enos," I said. "It's now my turn to beg your pardon. I was miles
away, thinking about that magnificent ceremony today. But that's no excuse for ill manners. I've been dreaming all night, since I came in, so I
know I'm tired and should be abed. Will you excuse me?"

"Happily," he said, his eyes crinkled in a smile. "I might even sleep
myself. God bless you, Caius Merlyn, and sleep well."

The day that followed was a quiet one. Rather than subject myself to the
curious stares and even fears of the throngs who now packed the town to
an unheard-of capacity, I spent the day in the confines of my quarters,
observing the activities from a second-storey window.

There were soldiers everywhere, of course, and not all of them had
come from Camulod. Even so, there was no disorder or rowdiness in any
quarter. Many of the visiting kings and chiefs had brought their own
escorts and bodyguards, their wives and families and servitors, and the
streets were bright with their colours, giving the entire gathering an air of
motley gaiety and happiness, despite the religious solemnity of the season

and the occasion. This sense of festivity was greatly enhanced by the street vendors who had emerged from nowhere, as such people always do, to profit from the gathering through the provision of food and drink, trinkets and jewellery, and any other thing for which they could find a purchaser. Overall, however, there was yet a muted quality to all the joy, for this truly was a day for quiet contemplation of the evils of a world that could condemn and crucify the Son of its own God, a day for prayer, between the darkness of the soul and the light of Resurrection that would shine the following day.

Towards evening, I was disturbed by an urgent summons from Arthur, who asked that I join him in his command headquarters as soon as I might.

I made my way with no difficulty through the crowded streets and all the way to his encampment, the crowds parting before me like the Red Sea parting before Moses. It seemed, I thought grimly, laughing at myself, that there must be something repellent in the way I walked or dressed. That self-consciousness faded quickly, however, when I saw Arthur. His face was lined with concern and he was in the final stages of issuing a rapid series of terse, no-nonsense orders to his assembled troop leaders, some hundred or more of them, when I arrived. He saw me come in and signalled that he would be with me presently. I moved into a corner and waited, feeling the awe, and sometimes the hostility, in the surreptitious glances that came my way and slid away again before I could engage them. Finally Arthur dismissed everyone else and came to me. He was dressed as he had been the previous night, save that he wore neither his cloak nor his helmet.

"What's wrong, Arthur?"

"Everything, Merlyn. Evil tidings coming as closely packed as hail, in the past three hours. I'm worried."

"I can see that. But why?"

He pursed his lips and exhaled noisily. "Last night I told you Horsa's Danes were massing outside Lindum. You recall?" I nodded, and he twisted up his face. "Aye, well now they're on the move. The word came in from Bedwyr shortly after noon. But that's not all. A messenger arrived from Gwin, not two hours after that. He and Ghilly are to the south of Bedwyr and farther east, in Anglian territory—Cuthric's country. There's trouble there, too. Saxon incursions from the existing settlements to the south, heavy incursions, and the hordes are moving west, Gwin says. That will set them on a collision course with Horsa's Danes as they come south."

"Then they'll collide, and do good work for you, killing each other."

"The Danes in the Weald are moving westward, too, Merlyn. Benedict's people there are falling back ahead of them, according to my own strict orders to observe but not engage. That word arrived less than an hour ago. Ben wants permission to attack. He doesn't like the way they're moving—thinks they're too numerous, too disciplined and too well organized to be on a mere raid."

"What about the others, Bedwyr and your other advance scouting groups? Are they falling back, too?"

"Aye, all of them are. Those were my orders: to observe, and to retreat ahead of any developing threats without engaging, keeping me informed at all times. Now I've heard from almost everyone, and something inside me is making more than is plainly there out of what I hear. That's what has forced me to take these steps."

"What steps? I'm not sure what you're saying, Arthur."

"What if the Danes and Saxons have assigned a meeting place, and are not just driving blindly towards each other? What if they've made alliance? It's a frightening thought, and it gains weight from this report of Ben's. My gut is telling me we have no time to waste, and so I've ordered my armies to assemble at dawn, all of them, in the fields about the theatre. I'm to be crowned at noon. By mid-afternoon, I want to be fully deployed outside the confines of the town, at a safe distance for the town's welfare, holding high ground but prepared to move out in any direction. I think they're coming here, Merlyn, to Verulamium."

While I knew he had no real, logical grounds for the conclusions he had drawn, I myself had taught and encouraged him to put much credence in his own, unformed convictions at times like this. "If they are, then how long will it take for them to arrive?"

He shrugged. "From Lindum to here is more than a hundred miles, closer to a hundred and thirty. That's seven days, more or less, but they set out four days ago. Bedwyr's messenger killed a horse under him in getting here to warn us. By now they'll have joined up with the Saxons, if what I suspect is true. They could be here tomorrow, if they make good time, although I think the following day is closer to the mark and perhaps, if God truly is on our side, they'll be later yet. But the same travelling speed applies to those coming up from the Weald, and they're much closer. So I've passed the word to break camp and assemble early tomorrow. We can't afford to take the risk of not being ready, Cay."

"I know that, Arthur, but my concerns are more immediate. If news of this leaks out, it could cause panic in the town and ruin everything we've planned."

"It won't get out. I've seen to that. Only my own people know, and all my troops will be recalled and confined to barracks for the remainder of the day."

I nodded my approval. "For what it's worth, now that it's done, I think you took appropriate action. Now, about tomorrow's ceremonies. I think it would be excellent for everyone were your troops able to be present for your crowning. That way, even if rumours do break out—and when

did rumours ever fail to do just that?—the sight of your troopers in tran-
quil attendance at the ceremonies will have a pacifying effect."

He stared at me for a long moment. "That's not possible, is it? There's
no room for them, for one thing."

"Yes, Arthur, there is. The theatre holds seven thousand people,
seated. Enos's clerics counted less than five thousand there yesterday.
Some have arrived late, so there may be fully five thousand there tomorrow. That leaves two thousand empty seats and ample room for another
thousand standing around the walls."

"Aye, but I have more than six thousand men."

"Have them draw lots. Make it a privilege to attend. I guarantee
they'll squabble among themselves to make sure the lots are drawn fairly.
Your troop leaders should all be there, but that's not feasible. Again, have
them draw lots. One officer in four to stand on duty. For your sub-officers
and troopers, one in every two. That will fill up three thousand places,
and I'm sure we could accommodate four thousand, if the numbers work
that way. Apart from the reassurance of their presence serving to disarm
rumours, I'd like to see them there, Arthur, and you can only gain by
having them attend. That way, they'll see you crowned by bishops, with
the blessing of the Church. They'll know they have a High King as Commander."

He sighed and nodded. "I'll think on it. About the other thing . . .
you do approve of what I've done? I've no real reason, other than my
instinct."

I smiled at him, at the earnestness in his troubled young face. "What
does it matter what I think? It was your decision and it's made, right or
wrong. But personally, I believe, wholeheartedly, that it's right."

For the first time since I had walked into his presence, he smiled back
at me.

XIX

As the result of a surprising and considerate suggestion from Enos, I travelled to the theatre on Easter morning disguised as one of his bishops, having exchanged my long, black-cowled garments for one of their equally long if less voluminous white-cowled robes. It was a chilly morning, beneath overcast skies, and as the wind bit through my ceremonial, clerical garb, I regretted the loss of my own cloak of thick black wool. But the substitution was indisputably to my advantage, for along the entire route, more than half a mile in length, no one in the watching crowds recognized me or took any notice of me, other than to gaze at the small chest I carried and wonder, perhaps, what it contained. A score more than a hundred of us walked in that silent, solemn procession, and I was the only sorcerer among the quadruple ranks. As we passed, the crowds fell into place behind us, following us towards the high outline of the great building that sat alone beyond the walls among treeless fields.

I heard some murmuring, even among the bishops, as it became plain that Arthur's entire army had been assembled on those meadows, drawn up behind its standards in regimented ranks and sitting stiffly in diligent readiness. Close by the theatre itself, the road passed through their formations and we walked forward between the masses of them ranked on either side. As the head of the procession passed, however, marked by a junior acolyte bearing a long staff surmounted by a purple-shrouded cross, squad leaders shouted commands and each unit came to the salute, greeting the bishops and adding to the air of great solemnity.

I hitched the wooden chest I carried higher, tightening my grip on it. Inside, resting on a magnificent cushion that had been embroidered years before by Tressa as a gift for me, lay a crown of gold made to fit Arthur's head precisely. It was a simple coronet, no wider than my thumb—a plain, flat, golden ribbon—bearing no workings other than a small, plain cross at the front, in the centre of the forehead, and an artfully depicted knotted bow at the back, the trailing ends of which bore golden acorns. I had no notion of what the ancient Roman military crowns had looked like, but I had seen and admired the simplicity of Athol Maclain's golden coronet in Eire and I had copied that simplicity with confidence, setting our Colony's finest craftsmen to create it from my description.

Then, just as we were about to enter the theatre, I saw Arthur. My eyes were drawn to the scarlet and gold splendour of the cloak he wore, a cloak so distinctive and uniquely visible from afar that I had once pursued its wearer far along the coasts of Cornwall. He stood with his back to me, wide-legged and elbows spread, so that the great golden dragon of his father's standard stretched its widespread wings across his shoulders. He was bareheaded, and I assumed that he cradled his helmet on his hip, beneath the cloak. Only then did I see that he was conferring with Benedict and several others, all of them travel-weary and radiating tension as they listened avidly to their young leader. I recognized, too, from Arthur's posture, that something grave was afoot. I passed my burden to my closest neighbour immediately, asking him to take it to Enos, and stepped out of the procession.

Arthur caught sight of my white robe from the corner of his eye as I approached, and frowned in annoyance, his expression stating clearly that he had neither time nor willingness to concern himself with clerics at that moment. I stepped closer, and he was about to turn on me in anger when I laid my hand on his arm.

"Arthur, it's me. I changed my colours."

"Merlyn!" He swung his head to pierce me with his glare, ignoring my lame attempt at levity. "Thank the Christ you're here! We must cancel this—this affair today." He waved a dismissive hand towards the procession streaming into the building. "You'll have to postpone it, put it off, save it for a more appropriate time. I must be gone from here, right now. I was just about to issue orders to set out."

His eyes swept me from head to foot, taking in my unusual garb, but I saw no glimmer of curiosity or interest cross his face. I glanced beyond his shoulder and saw several people, including his own front ranks, staring at us with open curiosity, and I knew that some of them, particularly those among the common throng who might have been soldiers at one time or another, would think nothing of approaching us. Arthur's obviously simmering wrath might easily spill over upon such innocent provocation, I knew, and I had no desire to see such an incident occur, today of all days. I looked at Benedict, who nodded gravely to me, and then I eyed each of the others.

"Come," I said. "There are ears hungering here for single words." I led them farther off, to where no one could hear or approach us without being warned away. "Now, Arthur, what is it?"

"Invasion, Merlyn. Massive, immense invasion on a scale never before seen in Britain, not even when the Romans first arrived. Thousands of galleys—Ben's people could not keep count of them."

"Good God! Ben, you were in the Weald?"

"Aye, I was, at first. But we fell back, according to orders, keeping well ahead of the enemy and unseen. They started out by marching north,

then angled to the north-west, towards Londinium. That's where we almost lost everything, including our lives. Our eyes were on the enemy
following us, an army of them. But they were a mere squad compared to
what we found awaiting them behind us. It's more than an invasion fleet,
Merlyn. We've all seen those before. This is a fleet of fleets, from what
we could see. The whole Tamis River is thick with shipping, from Londinium to the sea, full forty miles and more of it, with scarcely a bare
patch left on either side to beach a boat."

"Wait! How can you know all this? Did you patrol the river banks?"

He shook his head. "No, but we met with Anglians fleeing from those
parts, who told us what was happening. It was their flight that warned us
just in time to avoid riding right in among the Saxons. Londinium's completely overrun and is serving as the rallying point for whoever these people are. According to the Anglians, they're Saxons, not Anglians or Danes,
but that's all I know. As Arthur says, we crept close enough to look, but
we lost count of their ships, so God alone can tell the numbers of their
men. It's only by God's grace we escaped and won back here, but we were
forced to hide and slide to do it, so we moved but slowly for a long, long
time. I swear, Merlyn, none of us had ever seen the like of it. The land's
crawling with Saxons, and they'll soon be here in Verulamium."

I was biting my lip, appalled by the scope of what Benedict was describing. No wonder Arthur had been set to cancel this day's activities, I
thought. It would be suicidal to do otherwise. But then my reason returned and I began to think more clearly.

"How far are the nearest pursuers behind you, Ben? Think!"

He frowned in concentration. "Perhaps several hours. We covered
ground quickly, once we could do so without being seen. They could be
here by tonight."

"What about opposition? Are they likely to encounter any at all?"

Ben shook his head. "Not in Londinium. It's gone, already. They
might have stopped there, though, if what Arthur says is true. They might
be waiting there for Horsa, although I wouldn't care to hazard my life on
that. There's a thin ring of our own troops out there, between them and
us, but they'll be of little use if those whoresons come through at us in
strength."

I stared now at Arthur, pausing lengthily before I dipped my head
and spoke again. "Well, you have a decision to make, Commander, but
if you have ever valued my advice, you'll let me say what's in my mind
before you commit yourself or any of your troops to action."

It was evident that he was not pleased, but he bit down hard, bringing
the muscles of his jaws into prominence, clearly resisting the urge to tell
me bluntly that the responsibility of command was his and his alone. He
turned his head stiffly away to gaze back towards his motionless, waiting
troops, and I could tell that he was holding his breath, willing himself to

be calm. Finally he relaxed and his shoulders slumped slightly as he turned
back to face me, nodding his head.

"Very well then," he said calmly. "Tell me what is in your mind. You
have never failed me in the past, and I need counsel now more than I
ever have."

"My words may be for your ears alone, Arthur," I warned, giving him
the choice.

"No. Benedict, at least, should hear it, as my senior commander here
in the east. Tertius Lucca, Rufio, Falvo and Philip should know what's
afoot, too." He turned to the others whom he had not named. "Could I
ask you gentlemen, if you would, to find those four and direct them here
to me immediately?" The men saluted smartly and spun about to leave,
but he detained them. "One more thing, if you please. I know I need not
ask it of any of you, but the information you possess is . . . dangerous. So
I will ask you, please, not to speak of it, even among yourselves. Its effects,
emerging unexpectedly, could be disastrous." The men saluted him again
and left quickly.

When they were gone, Arthur looked at me. "Well? What's in your
mind, Cay?" He looked simultaneously very young and prematurely aged.

"You don't want to wait for the others?"

"No, that might take too long. We'll tell them what they need to
know when they arrive."

"Very well." I drew a deep breath. "Your first instinct was to postpone
today's ceremony. I can understand that, for it was mine, too, when I
heard Ben's tidings. But then my common sense intervened. You heard
Ben. Despite all our fears and worst imaginings, the most sensible answer
is that the enemy won't come here before tonight, and that means before
tomorrow, pragmatically, since no one in his right mind would fight a
night battle.

"Think of this, Arthur: it would be madness to cancel these proceedings now they're all in place. This ceremony today is more than it appears
to be. It cannot be postponed or simply put off until a better day. There
may be no better day, ever again. This meeting in this place is the cul-
mination of years of planning—"

"Aye, but there are more important urgencies! We—"

"No, Arthur, there is *nothing* more important! I thought you were
going to hear me out?"

He nodded, apologetic but implacable. "Forgive me. Please continue."

"There is no greater urgency, Arthur, no greater cause than will be
served right here, this day. All of the bishops in this land are here today
to celebrate Easter, and the new Arising of the Saviour. *You* are a saviour,
in their eyes, Arthur! The saviour of Britain and of the Christian faith.

That's why we are all in Verulamium and not in Camulod! There's no place big enough in Camulod to hold a gathering of this significance. It had to take place here, in the ancient heart of Britain, where thousands of people could assemble in comfort, in this very theatre, the only building of its kind in all the land that is still usable, where you will be decreed and proclaimed High King of Britain by the representatives of the Christ Himself. The *Church* summoned you here today, and summoned all the lesser kings of all the land to see these bishops crown you, anoint you and bless you with their full support. You command, in Camulod's cavalry, the only realistic hope that Britain has of repulsing these invasions and protecting our own way of life throughout this land." I stopped, waiting, then asked, in a quieter voice, "Arthur? Do you hear what I am telling you?"

He licked his lips, his face now noticeably paler. "Yes." It was almost a whisper.

"Good. Now, the pragmatic view. If I go straight to Enos and explain what has occurred, he can curtail the service, beginning ahead of the planned time and proceeding directly with the consecration of the Eucharist. Once that is done, he can move straight into the ceremony, crowning you with the champion's crown as the Church's representative in Britain and requiring of you that you commit your forces, and the entirety of your resources, to the preservation of the faith in Britain and the conquest of the enemies of God. It can be over in two hours, Arthur, leaving you half the day to make your preparations to confront the enemy before night approaches.

"You'll lose but little in the interval, since we're forewarned of what is coming, but think what you will have gained: God's own blessing and the championship of His entire Church, all solemnly witnessed by an assembly of the kings and people of Britain and your own army. What greater encouragement to go to war with confidence could you imagine for your troops and troopers?"

Arthur's face was now set in deep-graven lines that made him look far older than his years. He nodded, once. "So be it. I'm convinced. Let's do it, quickly."

"We will, now. But while I talk to Enos, which may take some time, have your troops start filing into the theatre as planned. You did have them draw lots, I hope?"

"Aye, they're prepared." He looked at Benedict. "Ben, pass the order, if you will. Tertius Lucca is expecting it." Again his eyes returned to me. "Well, Caius Merlyn, I am in your hands for the next hour or so, and I shall try to be attentive to what happens. Do you still want me to strike my sword against the stone when it's all done?"

I flashed a grin at him. "Aye, Arthur. Do that for me."

*   *   *

I watched the proceedings from high above, concealed beneath the curv-
ing arches of the colonnade that circled the huge building at its highest
level. The space below was filled to capacity, and Arthur's troopers lined
the outer walls three deep in places. The broad central aisle, sloping gently
from the entranceway down to the steps directly before the altar, was the
only clear space in the entire assembly; all of the lesser aisles, radiating
upwards from that central, focal point, were crowded with people. The
consecration of the bread and wine had been completed, and the throngs
should now have started forward to receive the Eucharist, but that was
plainly impossible, with such a massive gathering in so confined a space.
The bishops would distribute the Eucharist later, in the meadows outside
the walls.

At the front of all, in the seats of honour reserved for the highest
guests at each performance, now directly in front of the sanctuary, sat the
civilian contingent from Camulod. Shelagh was there, sitting beside Ludmilla, and on her other side, her face now lined with age, sat Turga,
Arthur's childhood nurse. On either side of these three sat Luceiia and
Octavia, the eldest children of Ambrose and Ludmilla and the newest
generation of Britannici, and beyond them several of the senior Councillors of Camulod.

Behind and about this group were ranked the gathered kings of Britain, representing every region of the land that had not fallen beneath
foreign invasion and domination. There were some thirty of these, and I
knew few of them. Derek of Ravenglass was there, as was Brander Mac
Athol, with his brothers Connor and Donuil, but these three were set
slightly apart from the others, in consideration of their status as visiting
guests and allies from beyond Britain. Among the British kings I could
see, even from my lofty vantage point, that there was much distrust and
tension; they managed, somehow, to remain stiffly apart, despite their
propinquity, divided by tiny barriers of empty space which all were careful
not to cross over.

Slowly, almost unnoticeably, the utter stillness of the crowd gave way
to a swelling murmur as people leaned towards each other restlessly to
comment on the strangeness of the proceedings. I looked to where Enos
stood with his back towards the crowd, conferring with six of his senior
bishops while the other clerics held their places in the semicircle that
ringed the space at the back of the sanctuary, the sacred precinct of the
consecrated Sacrament. The crowd had murmured earlier, when Arthur's
soldiers had begun to file into the assembly, filling all the empty seats
and taking up the space around the perimeter, but Enos had quickly
quelled that, raising his hands high and explaining that the soldiers had
but come to witness the Easter rituals and join in the Communion. This
time, however, the muttering was going on too long, growing in volume

with each passing moment. Enos turned about and stepped forward again, raising his hands to shoulder height, while the small group of bishops with whom he had been conferring descended from the sanctuary with dignity and evident purpose and made their way, side by side in pairs, out of the theatre.

Before they had reached the external portals, silence had settled again within the assembly. A gust of errant wind swirled about me and I looked up at the skies above restraining a shiver, whether of cold or nervousness I did not know, although if it rained now, I thought, the effect on what went on below in the open-roofed theatre would be disastrous.

As I looked down at Enos I realized I had been foolish to perch myself so high upon the outer wall. I was unable to see his face with ease and peered down, indeed, almost upon the top of his head. Enos began to speak, in a voice much quieter than that which he had used so tellingly before, and I could barely make out his words.

I turned and went back to the stairwell and the steep, dangerous stairs I had climbed to reach this place. As I began to make my way back down, one step at a time, I discovered to my fury that I had to do so with great care, clinging to the iron handrail set into the wall like an old, bent man. It was a matter of balance—my shortened, stiff left leg dragged at every step, catching the lip of each stair and threatening to throw me sideways, so I had to proceed bad leg first, lowering my weaker foot deliberately at each step before entrusting it with my full weight. The vertiginous depths of the well on my right had seemed like nothing at all as I climbed with my strong right leg, raising the other one effortlessly behind it. Now, on my weakened left, those self-same depths seemed to beckon me.

I thought about what I would do when I arrived at the bottom. Where would I go, that I might not be seen and recognized? Then, forgetting completely that I wore a bishop's robe, I resolved to go boldly into the throng and make room for myself on the steps of one the lesser aisles.

At regular intervals on the way down, I passed narrow windows looking into the main body of the theatre, and I paused at each of them, listening to what Enos was saying. He had begun by talking of the God of the Israelites, and how He always protected and preserved His faithful servants. At the next window, I heard him speak of the Maccabees, the fierce and warlike rebels who had fought the Roman overlords of Israel so well and for so long, and of how they had faced death gladly for the preservation and protection of their religious beliefs. I wondered what the Israelite Maccabees had to do with Britain as I moved on to the next flight of stairs. By the time I arrived at the window below that one, he had brought the Romans into Britain and was talking of Queen Boudicca and how she had fought against invasion. Then an understanding of the tenor of his speech began to take shape in me, so that I was unsurprised to reach the last and lowest window and hear him talking about Camulod and the Saxon hordes who threatened Britain. I had missed the greater part of what he said but I could see the Camulodian troopers, standing around the walls, looking pleased and nudging each other with enjoyment.

I moved away again, to make the final stages of my descent, but I was less than half-way down the next flight when I was stopped short by a most surprising and unexpected sound. A single, brazen horn began to blow, and I recognized the sound before the first three notes had ended. It was the ceremonial trumpet call of Camulod, played upon all our horns on special and great occasions but never before heard beyond Camulod. It began with the solo notes of the deepest cornua, the long, circular horns of the legions that were borne wrapped round the bodies of the trumpeters. I turned immediately and made my way back to the window as another, higher horn, the second of the four that would complete the call, joined in, and I stood there enthralled by the effect the sounds were having on the throng below. As the music swelled and the number of participating instruments increased, a ripple of pure wonder passed over the crowd.

Then, as the volume rose to a crescendo, Arthur Pendragon entered the assembly from the main portals at the head of the central aisle, escorted by the six bishops. He made his way slowly down through the throng to the altar steps. I could not see Enos from where I stood now; all I could see was his hand outstretched to receive Arthur. The young man walked bareheaded and erect, his eyes fixed on the white block of the altar ahead of him, his long scarlet cloak with its great, golden dragon making a brilliant contrast against the plain white robes of his escort. As he reached the top of the steps to the altar and stepped beyond, out of my line of sight, the notes of the trumpet call faded away, leaving a hushed, vibrating silence.

Cursing myself for my stupidity in being stuck out there, I turned away again and made my way as quickly as I could down to the lowest level, where I found myself out in the open fields beyond the outer walls and obliged to make my way completely around one quadrant of the massive building on my right.

I hurried to the best of my impaired abilities, hugging close to the wall and throwing my lame left leg in front of me to achieve the greatest reach with every step, knowing that on the other side of the high walls beside me, the greatest moments of my life might be unfolding. I ignored the serried ranks of troops that stood and sat out there, the footsoldiers double spaced and every mounted trooper holding the reins of a riderless horse, all of them no doubt wondering who and what I was. My mind was filled with conflicting and chaotic images, among them visions of my Uncle Varrus and the large, parchment-filled books in which he had written his recollections of Grandfather Caius and his dream of unity and freedom and greatness in this land; a dream in which the people of Britain would survive the chaotic fall of Rome's corrupt Empire to emerge victorious and strong at the end of all. And then abruptly, unexpectedly, I reached the entryway into the theatre and stopped there, abashed and suddenly afraid to enter.

As I stood hesitating, a raindrop hit my face and I looked up fearfully at the sky. But there were no storm clouds that I could see, and off in the distance, a solitary patch of blue held out the promise of a weather change. I walked into the covered entranceway and stopped again, listening, unable to believe the stillness of the thousands within. Then, faint and indistinct in the distance, I heard Enos's voice. I moved forward slowly until the voice was clearer, and soon I was standing at the top of the long, central aisle. In the distance, within the sanctuary itself, the bishops began to chant the Creed again, their united voices sonorous and majestic as they intoned the magnificent words: *Credo in unum Deum* . . .

Some ten paces ahead of me, blocking my view, a solitary acolyte stood alone in the middle of the aisle, holding a long pole surmounted by a cloth-wrapped cross, symbolically proclaiming the presence of the Christ to any who might seek to enter at his back. As I saw him, I remembered who I was supposed to be this day, a Christian bishop, and with an unexpected resolve, I knew what I must do. I pulled my cowl well forward over my head and approached the acolyte, tapping him on the shoulder and gently taking the long pole with its cross out of his hands. He saw only a bishop and relinquished it without demur, stepping aside to let me take his place. Then, holding the staff before me as I had seen him do in our procession, I walked slowly down the long, wide aisle towards the altar, the majestic voices growing clearer as I progressed. I came to a halt only when I had approached within thirty paces of the sanctuary. In all that progress, no one had paid me the slightest attention. They simply took me for what I appeared to be.

Behind the altar, facing the assembled throng, Arthur was seated in a *curia*, a backless chair with curved sides and legs; his arms were stretched along its arms, his hands gripping the ends loosely. His voluminous cloak was spread behind him so that he sat completely within it, its front lower edges gathered and draped over his knees to hang down to his booted feet. Within the opening of his cloak, the enamelled metal of his cuirass gleamed dully. He appeared at ease. I could see that his forehead was discoloured where he had been anointed with chrism and the ashes of burnt palms, so the ceremony had been largely completed, hence the singing of the Creed. As the massed voices of the bishops faded into silence, Enos turned once more to face the crowd and stepped forward, glancing at me as he did so.

"In the earliest days of Rome." he began, using his command voice, "in the time of the great Republic and long before the excesses of the Empire, it was the custom for the exploits of the very bravest of the brave to be rewarded by the granting of a military crown, a corona. There were five such crowns, each one awarded for a different, specific deed of valour, but each and all of them acknowledging and marking championship and heroism. The men who won and wore those crowns were champions and heroes, and none who saw them doubted them. All people knew them, publicly."

He paused and looked around the enormous gathering, his eyes singling out faces in the throng, then moving on again. No one moved, and he continued, lowering his voice.

"None of those crowns was awarded for horsemanship or cavalry exploits, for Romans had no cavalry in ancient times. And none, we know, were awarded in those ancient times before mankind's Redemption, for the guarding of God's Holy Faith." He paused again. "Today, we have no Romanness in us; we are Britons. Yet it seems appropriate to us, your bishops, that a champion and defender of our faith should bear some signal mark of honour. And so we have adopted this one gift from ancient Rome, we have reinstituted the corona."

As he spoke these words, Silvanus, the Bishop of Lindum, accompanied by Bishop Junius of Arboricum and Declan, the Bishop of Isca, stepped forward. Silvanus bore Tressa's embroidered cushion with the gold crown lying on top of it, and each of the flanking bishops swung thuribles that billowed clouds of heavy, aromatic incense from the glowing coals they contained. They stopped behind Arthur's chair, and Enos walked back to join them, taking the crown and standing directly behind Arthur, holding it poised high above the young man's head so that everyone could see it.

"This is the corona of God's Church in Britain. Mark well the Holy Cross upon its upper brim: *in hoc signo vinces*; in this sign shall you conquer." He glanced down at the young man's head, then raised his voice strongly. "Arthur Pendragon, scion of kings, chieftains and other noble men, will you accept this crown and all its burdens, humbly and as befitting God's anointed choice?"

Arthur sat straighter. "Yes, my Lord Bishop, I will," he answered in a deep, strong, vibrant voice. Enos lowered the crown closer to his head.

"And will you undertake the lifelong task of serving God in strict commitment to His Holy Will, attending the protection of His Church and all the followers of His Divine Son, Jesus, the Christ?"

"I will."

Enos lowered the crown onto Arthur's brow and removed his hands.

"*In hoc signo vinces*," he said again. "In the name of the Eternal and Almighty God, and of His Only Begotten Son, Jesus the Christ, and of the Holy Spirit, we pronounce you *Riothamus*, High Chief and Spiritual King of all Britain; Defender of the Faith; *Rex Britanniorum*, King of all Britons. Stand."

As Arthur rose to his feet, the silence was palpable; one mighty, hard-held breath. I felt my throat swell up with pride and love, and tears came to my eyes. But this was not yet over. There were people here, among this crowd, who would have loved to protest this that had been done, yet dared not, at this time and in this place. Even without looking, I could sense that there were kings about me who were finding little joy in these proceedings.

Enos stepped back and nodded to two of his bishops who had been awaiting his signal. They moved forward immediately to flank the new *Riothamus*, each of them taking one of Arthur's forearms in both hands and leading him forward, one on either side, with great solemnity until the young king stood directly behind the altar, facing the congregation. There they left him, each taking two paces backward as Enos moved forward again, amid clouds of precious incense, to stand beside Arthur. He grasped the young king gently by the elbow, then guided his arm, extending it until Arthur's hand rested on one arm of the purple-covered cross. Enos nodded and indicated to Arthur that he should place his other hand on the opposite arm. Arthur did so; this had been rehearsed. Enos stepped slightly aside and raised his voice again.

"It is done. Here, on the sacred stone of God's own altar, before the eyes of God Himself and all of you as witnesses, this man, Arthur Pendragon, *Rex Britanniorum*, has undertaken, on the brightest day of all God's Christian year, to bring a new beginning to all our lives so that we may live in openness and brotherhood, unafraid of persecution or invasion. It is a mighty task he faces—"

Arthur, amazingly, interrupted him. "Sir Bishop, may I speak?" The Bishop bowed his head graciously, and the new King faced the crowd, frowning slightly before drawing a deep breath and beginning in a voice that quavered very slightly on the first few words but strengthened rapidly as he progressed. His fingers flexed visibly on the arms of the cross, and I had the clear impression that he was leaning on it, drawing strength from it.

"Bishop Enos has said I face a mighty task, and I believe I do. But I also believe the task is achievable, given that I have the support and the goodwill of all of you, here today and throughout this land." He paused, and allowed the silence to grow and stretch. "I know that some of you think me far too young to take on this responsibility, both sacred and temporal. I know, too, that some of you resent and fear my seeming elevation at this time. I hope to change all that in time, convincing you that none of you—no king, no chief, no warrior, need fear for his possessions or his territories while I rule in this land. You heard the Bishop name me *Riothamus*: *spiritual* King—God's Champion, Defender of the Faith. That is what I wish to be, and that is how I intend to govern. I have been taught, my whole life long, by all my teachers, many of whom are here today, to be morally aware, and I shall strive to continue thus. This one more, extra oath, however, I will give you willingly, here on God's altar. I solemnly swear that while I live and rule, no person—woman, man or child, regardless of wealth, rank or station—shall suffer wrongly at the hands of others without redress by me. My rule will be the rule of law, with God's help and with yours."

I found myself smiling and blinking away tears, my throat choked with pride and love of this magnificent young man, whose integrity permitted him to say such things spontaneously, with sincerity and utter conviction. Enos stepped forward again.

"So be it! Alleluia! It is done and all praises be to God. Jesus is risen and the world rejoices. Now might we pray to Heaven for some sign, some symbol of God's Blessing and His Light." And as he spoke, the clouds above parted and a single beam of golden, shimmering light struck through the darkened air to illuminate the sanctuary. The crowd drew in its breath with a collective gasp of religious awe and somewhere behind me a woman began to weep, her sobs loud and racking.

Arthur, meanwhile, standing by the altar, was peering about him, seemingly unaware of the significance of this truly Heavenly sign. It took me several moments to realize what he was doing. He had had the signal from Enos, with his closing words, "God's Blessing and His Light," and now he was casting his eyes about the sanctuary, looking for the stone that should contain his sword. Enos leaned towards him and murmured in his ear and Arthur looked at him, amazed and obviously confused. The old man nodded, and Arthur reached out once more, tentatively this time, towards the cross upon which he had sworn his oath. About to grasp it, he hesitated again and looked to Enos for another affirmative nod before he closed his fist around its upright. Then, as his fingers felt the rounded hilt beneath the covering purple cloth, he relaxed and began to draw the sword slowly up from the recess beneath the altar, and yet again a hush fell over the assembly as they saw what he was doing.

Months earlier, I had personally chiselled out the slotted hole that held the cross, widening it until it would accept Excalibur's broad blade. When Arthur had found me on Good Friday night beside the altar, I had just completed the substitution of the sword for the cross that Enos had placed there earlier that day in the sight of everyone, before draping it in the purple cloth. I had used my dagger blade to punch out the wooden plug that had been glued into the table, directly beneath the wide slot in the stone so carefully aligned that day by Enos in preparing the altar, and then I had tucked the golden cross into my scrip and slipped Excalibur's long blade down through the stone and through the wood beneath it, to rest upon the floor, concealed from view completely by the long, white altar cloth. When it was there, securely and secretly in place, I had rearranged the drapery of purple cloth so that none could tell it had ever been disturbed. I had been on my knees, finding and pocketing the tell-tale plug of wood, when Arthur had called my name that night.

Now Arthur was withdrawing it, the focus of all eyes, including mine. Higher he drew the blade, and higher still until his arm was straight before his eyes, but only then did he look down at the blade itself. And as he saw the shining silver blade emerging where he had thought to see his own plain, iron blade, his whole face, illuminated by the sunbeam's light, was transformed with reverent but overwhelming awe, and he quickly lowered the sword back into its recess and released it. The cloth draped itself again about the cruciform hilt.

Enos reached out and placed his hand between Arthur's shoulders, pushing him forward again, and once again the new-crowned King reached out and grasped the hilt. Then, steadily and steadfastly, he drew the gleaming blade completely free and raised it above his head, its flawless beauty glittering in the light of the sunbeam.

Someone at the back of the gathering began to cheer, and the noise swiftly spread to become pandemonium. Quickly then, Arthur reached up with his other hand and pulled away the cloth that had concealed the hilt, and then he held the sword aloft, brandishing it and gazing up at its perfection with a glowing smile of joy upon his face while people leaped to their feet and the whole place went mad with joy and wonder. I stood gazing up at him, tears pouring down my cheeks. Moments later, he looked down and saw me and his face split into a great, white-toothed, laughing grin as he whipped the sword downward, whacking the blade against the altar stone and reversing it to press the pommel against the stone itself.

The song of the sword leaped out like a living thing, swelling from nothingness to ringing, deafening purity in an instant. People flinched away from the stunning, vibrant sound of it. Arthur, startled anew to feel the thing vibrating in his hand, lowered it quickly and the blade touched the altar cloth, killing the sound at once. Brief, however, as the ringing tone had been, it had penetrated every space in the theatre, producing instant, shocked stillness. Arthur straightened up, his wide eyes locked upon the weapon in his hand. I moved closer to him, uncaring where I was or who saw me.

"Do it again, Arthur, and this time, hold it there and let it sing."

Slowly, he raised the blade again, then, with every eye in the place fixed on him, he brought it sweeping down and struck the flat of it against the altar stone. This time, when the thrilling note sprang forth, none flinched, but merely gaped in awe. For ages, then, it seemed, Arthur held the hilt in place until the ringing tone died slowly into silence, and just before it faded completely, he raised his eyes and held his arms spread wide, the glowing, gleaming blade extended so that all could see it. Then, in a gesture that not even Germanus could have conceived of, for all his genius at such things, Arthur replaced the sword securely in the altar stone and left it there, now an obvious sword hilt, magnificent and ornate, black and gold and silver, crowned with a perfect, golden cockleshell, and with a broad, silver-white blade that sank into the stone itself.

For long moments he stood there gazing at it, and then he raised his head towards the crowd again and asked them to be seated. When they were, listening intently for what he would say, he told them, without artifice or plaint, what we had learned that morning: that an invasion had begun, and might be massive, and that he must ride to deal with it immediately, today. He asked them to remain in place while all his troopers left, then asked the kings to reassemble here within the hour, at which time he would tell them of his plans and answer as many of their questions as he could. Then he nodded to Tertius Lucca, who gave the signal to dismiss the Camulodian troopers.

The new King's men, however, were not to be dismissed until they had made their contribution to the day's events. Someone, far at the back, began to chant Arthur's name, and it spread like fire in summer grass, sweeping the whole assembly until the very walls shook with the sound of the King's name. In the face of their acclaim, Arthur drew Excalibur from the altar stone again and brandished the shining blade three more times above his head, at which their voices rose to a thunderous roar. Then he turned about and walked away, carrying the sword, to the rear of the sanctuary, where he disappeared behind a screen. The troopers were still chanting his name as they left, and it took some time for all the others to file out behind them.

I found him later, when the crowds had dispersed, gazing at the sword, its shining blade a handbreadth from his eyes.

"It's called Excalibur," I said. "Your great-grandfather made it, sixty years ago, and it has been waiting in concealment ever since then, until you came of age to claim it. Now it's yours, and there is not another like it in existence. Here's a sheath to hold it, made by me, and very recently." I handed him the leather scabbard I had prepared, and he nodded in acknowledgement but made no move to sheathe the blade. "There's a tale behind the name, of course," I said, smiling at his reverent admiration of the weapon's magnificence. "Behind the making of it, too—several stories, in truth. I'll tell them all to you as soon as we have opportunity to speak."

He was still rapt. "Excalibur," he whispered. "It sings on the tongue . . . What does it mean? Do you know?"

"Oh, aye, I know. It means, for one thing, that Britain has a King like none other before him. And it means the King of Britain has a sword all men will recognize and covet, given as it was in light and majesty from God's own altar stone before the eyes of a multitude of people. That much it means, and more. It was your great-grandfather's gift to you, unseen, unknown, but dreamed of in a dream he shared with my grandfather . . ."

"Excalibur." He slid the long blade reverently into the leather scabbard. "You knew it could sing, of course. Did you not?"

I grinned at the question. "Of course I did. Why would you even ask? Or did you suspect me of sorcery at God's own altar?"

He grinned back at me, and as his eyes fell again to the beauty of the weapon's hilt, I cleared my throat.

"Have you spoken with your aunts today?"

"No, I have not had time, but I saw them out there, in the crowd. I'll go and see them now, I think."

"You're a real king now, lad. *Riothamus. Rex Britanniorum*. High King of all Britons."

He grinned at me, somewhat ruefully, I thought, and shook his head. "I think not, Merlyn. Not yet. I have the name, and the responsibility, and I have all the duties of a king, but I still have to earn the support of those whose king I'm supposed to be. The kings who saw me crowned today, for example. I have to meet with them now. Within the hour, I told them. That meeting could be . . . difficult. And right now, I have to face all my men and tell them that we have a war to fight and win. I wish you could still ride and fight, Merlyn. I'm going to need your counsel."

"That will be yours in perpetuity, lad. I have not lost the ability to think, scheme and advise. You do the fighting, I'll do some of the thinking, you handle the deciding, I'll look after the advising, and together, we'll change this country so that you may do the ruling the way it should be done. Shall we agree to that?"

"By God's love, we will!" He smiled and threw wide his arms to embrace me. We stood close for a long moment, until he spoke into my ear. "Walk out to greet my army with me now, will you Merlyn? They are still yours, you know. Not all men fear or distrust you."

I thrust him to arm's length, gazing into his eyes.

"I'll come out with you, gladly, but not for acclaim. It suits me now to live the life I live, to be the man I am today. It is my choice. This time is yours, and all of the acclaim is due to you."

He nodded. "Very well. But will you wait, outside, till we are set to leave, and see me on my way?"

I smiled without answering and laid my right arm over his shoulder, starting him towards the door. *Aye, that I will, and willingly, lad,* I thought, but did not say, as I walked beside him in my borrowed bishop's robes. *I'll see you on your way to glory.*

And there, hours later, in the fields outside the great theatre, that is precisely what I did. Standing beside Shelagh and Ludmilla and Turga, and surrounded by his relatives and friends, I watched Arthur Pendragon, High King of Britain, pull himself easily up into the saddle of his huge bay and spread his wide, red and gold cloak over its rump before he stood up in his stirrups and unsheathed Excalibur. The great silver blade flashed in the sun's brilliance as he waved it above his head, so that I became light-headed from looking up at it and had to close my eyes and breathe deeply, standing blind among the uproar of his joyous army as they cheered themselves hoarse shouting his name.

23.95

FIC   Whyte, Jack.
Whyte
           The sorcerer.

DATE